BUCCANEERS

JAMIE McFARLANE

Cover Artwork: Sviatoslav Gerasymchuk

ACKNOWLEDGMENTS

To Diane Greenwood Muir for excellence in editing and fine word-smithery. My wife, Janet, for carefully and kindly pointing out my poor grammatical habits. I cannot imagine working through these projects without you both.

To my beta readers: Carol Greenwood, Kelli Whyte, Robert Long, Jeff Rothermel and Nancy Higgins Quist for wonderful and thoughtful suggestions. It is a joy to work with this wonderful group of people.

CONTENTS

SUCKER PUNCH

I held my gloves high, trying to cover up, but Tabby drove into my body, her fists battering me. I struggled to slip her jabs, avoiding most, but those that made it through caused my head to swim. I pushed back and danced away. Her long hair was pulled into a ponytail and sweat dripped from her face. Provocatively, she dropped her arms and tipped her head to the side. She knew it was a cardinal sin for a boxer to drop their guard. I couldn't help but smile at her well-earned confidence.

"That all you got?" she taunted, tipping her head back and forth, lips pursed.

Over the last six months Tabby had grown stronger and faster. Her legs and right arm had been regrown in a medical tank after she'd been damn near killed in a naval battle. Right out of the tank, she'd been like a new fawn, unable to control her limbs and barely able to walk. That had changed and now Tabby was in complete control. We'd been told to expect it - that she would just keep getting stronger and faster for up to a year.

My body ached, having taken the brunt of her brutal attacks time and time again over the last few months. While my own skill had grown considerably, I still struggled to keep up. But if she was going to give me an opening, I was happy to oblige.

I hunched forward, protecting my face with gloves held high, and moved in. Tabby raised up onto her toes and backed away, swinging her hips mockingly, arms still down. She was drawing me in. I knew it and she knew I knew it. From my perspective, there was only one thing to be done. I would punish her. It was a moral imperative.

My plan was two quick left jabs to be followed up with a right hook. Her left arm hadn't been regrown and it was her only weakness. She raised her gloves when I got closer but held them loosely. She was begging me to make my move, but something was off. I had a sense about these things and my instincts were telling me to get out of there. Of course, I wasn't about to obey, so I made my move: quick jab to the stomach, contact, quick jab to the stomach, contact. Tabby just took the hits.

It was then that I saw my mistake. Tabby had been waiting for me to drop my left so she could use her fist of doom (her name for it, not mine). Quicker than I could respond, but unfortunately not faster than I could track, her right glove streaked toward the side of my face. I was wearing a protective helmet, but that didn't stop all the force. The impact felt like someone had detonated a grenade next to my head. I crumpled to the mat, barely maintaining consciousness.

"Oh frak, Liam." Tabby slid to the ground and pulled my head onto her lap. "I'm so sorry." Her warrior persona was gone, replaced with the caring girlfriend.

She stroked my hair and looked into my eyes with concern. I'd only been stunned, so I quickly snaked my arms around the back of her neck, pulling her down and into a kiss. We were both wearing head gear which wasn't conducive to necking, but we managed.

"Cap. We're coming out of hard burn in ten minutes," Marny announced over my comm.

"Roger that," I replied and looked at Tabby. "Shower?"

"You need a med-patch?" she asked, still concerned.

"I'd guess so. You'll going to need to do full-contact training with Marny from now on."

"She still kicks my ass. But I'm closing on her," Tabby said.

Tabby popped up off the mat and offered me a hand. I was still woozy, so I accepted the help. Walking through the hold, we passed our single piece of cargo, a stationary gun we'd abandoned several months back when pirates invaded Colony 40. It cost ten thousand credits in fuel to make the trip back to the asteroid, but the gun was easily worth half a million. We'd taken the chance that while we'd been gone, someone else hadn't claimed it.

Once inside our quarters, I pulled off my suit liner, dropped it in the cleaner and climbed into the shower with Tabby. I marveled at how medical science had put her body back together so perfectly. I traced a line across her perfectly shaped rear with my finger, following a nearly invisible junction where synthetic skin joined her own.

Tabby looked over her shoulder and smiled. "If you start on that, you'll miss atmospheric entry."

"I was just thinking…" I said.

Tabby turned to face me. The bridge head was close quarters and her move hadn't done much for my ability to form coherent sentences.

"About what?"

"Academy starts in a few weeks," I said.

"I see," she said, her voice growing sultry. "Is there something you want to say about that?"

"No." It wasn't true. There were a million things I wanted to say about it. Mostly that I didn't want her to go back. She'd left me for the Naval Academy once and I'd almost lost her. I strongly believed, however, that she needed to chase her dreams. I couldn't take that from her.

"Don't shut down on me, Liam."

"I don't want to say anything. It has to be your decision," I said.

"I need to hear it." She looked me in the face, not letting me avoid this any longer. "Tell me what you're thinking."

I ran my hand down her arm, finally resting it on her wrist. The steam from the shower billowed around us. We stood completely naked in front of each other and I knew she was right. This was the moment of truth we'd been avoiding for months.

"I don't want you to go. I want to build my life with you out here in the stars. I don't want to share you with the Navy or anyone else." I'd been bottling up these feelings and it felt good to finally let them out.

Tabby's response was immediate. "Marry me."

The words took me off guard. I looked back at her to make sure she was serious. Her return stare was unwavering.

"Anytime. Anywhere," I said.

"Is that a yes?" she asked.

"Yes. Of course it's yes. Heck, yeah!" I said. It seemed too good to be true but I pulled her into a hug and kissed her as the water from the shower cascaded over us.

We finally separated.

Tabby gave me a mischievous grin. "We'll have time to celebrate later, but I think Marny would appreciate your help in the cockpit."

I sighed. I'd liked to have stayed in the shower with her, but she was right. Marny and Nick would be uncomfortable landing *Hotspur* on Mars. We toweled off.

"Wait. What's all this have to do with the Academy?" I asked, pulling on a fresh suit liner.

"I'm not going back, Liam," she said.

"You have to. It's your dream."

"No. It *was* my dream. Life has a way of changing people, Liam. I want to be with you. You were the one who came for me when I was lost in space. You stayed with me when I had no chance to walk again. I want to rebuild my life with you. I just had to know you still felt the same way."

We finished dressing in silence. My head was throbbing again. We'd taken longer than I'd planned, so we needed to get up to the cockpit.

"Cap. She really laid you out good. For what it's worth, I thought your combo was a good idea," Marny said as we passed through the bridge. She'd been watching our match.

Tabby couldn't resist the brag. "He telegraphed his intentions light-seconds ahead."

"You're fast, Tabby. You might give the old-girl a run for her money," Marny replied. She'd taken to calling our ex-special forces friend, Tali, the 'old-girl.' I didn't think it was even remotely possible that the nickname would stick, since we were all afraid of what retaliation would look like. Any comparison to Tali, however, was the highest praise I could imagine from Marny.

I jumped into the pilot's chair next to Nick in the elevated cockpit. "Anything to report?" I started our shift change protocol.

"All systems are reporting green. We've entered congested space above Puskar Stellar and are currently sailing under auto-pilot," he replied.

"I relieve you," I said.

"I stand relieved," he finished.

"You need a med-patch?" Tabby whispered in my ear. She'd climbed up onto the back of my chair from behind and was invading my personal space in the best possible way.

"Do they make one I can dunk my head in?"

Tabby applied a five square centimeter medical patch to the side of my neck allowing for the fastest possible transfer of anti-inflammatories to my blood stream. I imagined the little nano-bots rushing around my brain, repairing the damage she'd wrought.

"You give any thought to Big Pete's idea?" Nick asked.

My dad, who even *I* called Big Pete, had forwarded both Nick and me an advertisement from the Belirand Corporation. Belirand had been contracted by a coalition of countries known as NaGEK (North American, Germany, England and Unified Korea) to manage mining claims in the Descartes asteroid belt.

"Yeah. I'm not even remotely interested in being an asteroid miner again," I said.

Nick didn't let me get away with that. "Did you even listen to his message?"

"You gotta understand, Dad's too much the wild dreamer for me. I don't mind hard work. I just want it to pay off. Mining never pays off."

"No, I get that," he said. "But I've been checking the system. Grünholz has a cloud city that's giving away commercial warehouse bays - twelve thousand cubic meters. They even come with an apartment."

"How can they do that? What's the hitch?"

"Léger Nuage was built by the French government. They overbuilt, so now they're trying to incentivize traders. But you're right. There's a catch. We'd have to make inter-system deliveries at least once a year. If we miss a year, they could seize everything in the warehouse and bill us for storage. Until the return leg of the TransLoc gate is finished, they're about as far from civilization as you can get."

He was starting to get my attention. I'd grown up on a mining colony and Mars was more populated than I cared for.

"So, what? We haul ore for Mom and Dad and make trade runs when we're not doing that?"

"Think bigger. That return gate will be up and running in a few years. Instead of being the end of the run, we'd be the last stop before jumping back to Sol. Manufacturing, building, everything is about to go crazy in Tipperary and we have a chance to get in at the beginning. With our ships, hab-domes and defensive system, we could set up our own mining colony."

Tabby had left her arms slung over my shoulders for the conversation, listening amicably.

"What do you think about all that?" I looked back at her.

"Sounds exciting. Dad always said that vertical integration was the way to make credits. Middlemen get fat off everyone else without having to work for it and the only thing to do was get rid of them," Tabby said.

"Wasn't your grandpa one of those middlemen?"

"Dad hated it. He felt like we were taking advantage of good people. He wouldn't let me get involved in the family business," she said.

"I didn't know that about him. That's kind of cool. So, Nick, are you and Marny in? It sounds like you have a business plan in mind."

Nick gave me that look I knew meant I was missing something. "You won't last running short-haul work like we've done for the last six months. You're bored to death and I do think Big Pete is onto something. I also think this is one of those 'once in a lifetime opportunities' that we'd kick ourselves for missing."

"You've got a plan, don't you?" I asked.

"Of course, but what about you and Tabby? It's a long way to Tipperary, after all, and long distance relationships don't always work out."

Tabby hopped on that and answered, "Don't make this about me. I've already let them know I'm not going back to the academy."

"Are you ready to claim your share of *Loose Nuts*?" Nick asked.

Tabby and I both looked at Nick in confusion.

"You're a third owner of *Sterra's Gift*. I've been putting aside an owner's share for you since the beginning. As a result, you currently own eight percent of *Loose Nuts* Corporation."

"I told you I wanted you and Liam to have that," she said.

"You might want to get buckled in, Tabs, because we're about to enter atmo," I said.

Tabby swatted the side of my head lightly and retreated to the bridge couch. "We're not done with that conversation," she said.

We'd been gone for almost twenty days. I'd worked the schedule so *Hotspur* would arrive back on Mars at the same time Mom and Ada returned from one of their shorter trips.

Our lives had settled down in the last six months and this was the fifth trip I'd taken where we hadn't been fired upon, had someone attempted to board us, or had our destination been overrun by pirates. Nick was right, I was bored.

Financially, *Loose Nuts* was doing well. We'd sold off all the pirate loot from the outpost and were running a positive cash flow on deliveries. With a surplus of credits, we'd decided not to sell the two dozen missiles we'd liberated from the last of the Red Houzi.

Inform Tali Liszt that we're on approach, I requested as we got closer to the home she had built fifty kilometers from the outskirts of one of Mars largest cities, Puskar Stellar. Tali didn't like surprises or unannounced visitors and had the ability to make our landing on her property quite difficult. We had permission to be here, since we were still renting her field for our family compound. We had, however, promised to leave a couple of months ago and I felt we were wearing out our welcome.

Jack, Nick's younger brother, met us as we exited the ship. He was holding a pod-ball under his arm and, upon seeing this, Tabby leapt into action, sprinting up the grassy hill in the opposite direction. Jack waited for her to get far enough away before zipping the ball, perfectly calculating where she'd be when the ball arrived. She turned, caught it and threw it back to me. It'd been a long time since I'd played pod-ball. Jack, Tabby and I had been an extremely effective team back in high school. I returned the ball to Jack with an under-handed toss.

"Hey, is Big Pete home?" I asked.

Jack wasn't much for talking, but was plenty bright. He smiled and nodded his head, letting me know that Dad was in one of the habitation domes. Jack took off at a run, loping across the side of the hill, throwing the ball back to Tabby.

"Everything go all right?" Dad asked when I entered the dome. He handed me a cup of coffee.

"It's a lot easier when people aren't shooting at you," I said.

"Who's shooting at you?" Mom entered from an attached dome.

"The only fireworks were between Tabby and your boy," Marny said as she and Nick joined us.

I hugged Mom and scowled at Marny. "What happened to loyalty?"

With pleasantries out of the way, Big Pete couldn't hold it in any longer - he'd clearly been waiting for our return. "Did you all talk about my idea?" he asked.

I looked at Nick, who gave me the nod, and then back to Dad. "I think we're in," I said.

REUNITED

I called a meeting of the entire company and invited Tali, our special-forces friend, and Celina, a pirate-turned-friend who was living with Tali, to join us. We left Celina's sister Jenny and Jack at home to look after themselves, figuring they'd hate the long conversation we were in for.

We had a favorite pizza place back in the University Hills district of Puskar Stellar called Meglianos. Nick rented a room and we all gathered at 1800 the next evening. After we'd eaten and no small amount of alcohol had been consumed, I rapped a fork against the side of my beer bottle. It didn't have quite the same sound Commander Sterra produced when doing the same with a crystal goblet, but it had the desired effect of quieting the table.

Around the table were Jake Berandor, Tabby, Nick, Marny, Ada, Mom, Dad, Tali, and Celina. They all turned their attention to me.

"You're probably wondering why we asked you to dinner tonight," I started.

Jake broke in, holding up his beer bottle, "I'm going to need another beer if we're getting serious." Everyone laughed as the mood around the table was light.

Nick glanced at him. "You might want a clear head for this, Jake."

"Now you've got my attention," he replied in his deep baritone voice.

"Good. Big Pete and Nick have been looking at an opportunity that we'd like to share with you," I said.

Looking around the table at my friends and family, I thought for a moment about how far we'd all traveled to get here. The decisions we made tonight would change our lives forever.

"The Belirand Corporation is issuing mining claims for the Descartes Asteroid Belt in the Tipperary system. Big Pete and Silver would like to stake one of these claims."

Ada was first to pipe up. "You'd go back to mining?" Ada and I had spent endless hours sitting together in the cockpit of the *Adela Chen* talking about our childhoods. She knew my aversion to mining.

"I don't think that's in the cards for me," I responded. "Maybe this is just selfish thinking, but I've always wanted to see the rest of the known galaxy. *Loose Nuts* is more interested in setting up a trade route. I don't know how much attention you've been paying to the solar system gates, but Belirand is issuing mining claims to get material to build a new TransLoc gate from Tipperary back to Sol. Once that's done, there will be a round trip through the four systems. We believe this will turn Tipperary from its current, backwater existence into a major trading hub."

I set a small projector on the table showing the four systems and their gates.

Gates between Solar Systems

"That's three jumps. How are you going to do that? Are you leaving the tug behind?" Ada asked.

It was a fair question as she and Mom had taken over the responsibility of running our tug, the *Adela Chen*, for the last several months.

"Not decided and honestly it depends on your interest. Belirand is offering a free one-way trip through the gates. Without them, it would cost in excess of half a million credits to put the tug and a barge through all three gates, much less get them back. A return trip isn't impossible, but it's expensive."

"What about *Hotspur*?" Tali asked.

"*Hotspur* has TransLoc engines. We've never operated them, but they'll work. The fuel isn't the big expense. Most of the cost is in the engines and the fees charged by Belirand."

Nick stepped in. "There's another piece of this that a couple of you might be interested in. Léger Nuage, one of eighteen cities above the planet Grünholz, is giving away commercial warehouse bays. *Loose Nuts* is considering setting up a trading hub in one of their large bays."

"Isn't that a cloud city?" Lena asked, sitting forward. "Why would they give space away?"

Nick replied, "It is. Léger Nuage literally means light cloud. And, it's a simple matter of the city having been overbuilt. The government planners are trying to attract new settlers and businesses."

Jake's large hands moved quickly as he focused, gesturing and punching his fingers on a virtual keyboard. He grabbed a piece of information and tossed it out at the group. My HUD displayed Léger Nuage's advertisement for free commercial spaces. It showed sweeping views of verandas that overlooked a field of fluffy white clouds with well-dressed citizens out for an afternoon stroll.

"How romantic," Ada said.

"What's the population of the city?" Lena asked.

Jake answered. "Twelve thousand. It's the smallest of Nuage nation's cities."

"Sounds perfect for a fresh start," she said wistfully. When I'd first met Lena, she had been something between a slave and a pirate, angry, untrusting, and beaten down. So much had changed since we'd shown her compassion and decency, handing over control of a captured pirate ship so she could escape. It was an unusual twist of fate in which we'd found each other again and become friends.

"One of the reasons we asked you here was because, at a minimum, we'll have room to provide transport to anyone who might be interested in going through the gates. I can't promise that we'd have work for you, Lena, or even you, Jake, but we'd do our best to look out for you."

"What about Ada?" Mom asked. I knew she'd become as fond of Ada as I was and I appreciated the opening.

Ada raised her eyebrows in anticipation.

"You're part of the company, Ada, and the captain of the *Adela Chen*. Nick and I have talked about it and that ship goes where you say. If you would like to stay in Sol and run a business here, we're behind you. That said, if you're willing, we'd love to have you come along."

"Do you think you can keep a tug busy?" she asked.

Nick turned to her. "It's a risk. The Hoffen claim can't possibly keep a barge busy, but something we learned on Colony 40 was that miners lose a lot of money to middlemen. I think we might be able to make deals with other miners - even set up a co-op of our own. On the other hand, there's no question that you'd make more money managing the ship in local space around Mars."

"Isn't that true for *Hotspur*?" she asked.

He nodded in agreement. "It's hard to know how we'll do. We have enough cash reserves that even if we totally blow it, we can come back and restart. It's a big risk, but one we're interested in taking."

"When do you take off?" Jake asked.

Big Pete, who'd been quiet to this point, answered. "Silver and I submitted our application to Belirand for a claim. We have nine months to get in-system or our claim will be null and void and our five thousand credit deposit will be surrendered. I'd recommend that anyone who is coming along stake a claim if you have funds for the deposit. Once you get there, you need to work the claim for two months in each twelve month period for the first two years. After that, you own the claim outright."

"Pete. Are you trying to turn us all into miners?" Marny asked, smiling.

"No ma'am. As much as I think it'd be the best thing for you, I know better. Thing is, if Silver and I rotate claims every two months, we could keep six claims active long enough that five of you could have something of real value in the end," Pete said.

Pete's offer caused excited tittering around the table. Even I didn't know he was willing to work everyone's claims. The value of a permanent claim in the Sol system was normally in the millions of credits. The number of millions depended, of course on the minerals found. Dad's offer could turn out to be quite a gift, although if he didn't think I saw through his ploy to get me back to mining, he was nuts.

"Would you take on a greenhorn?" Ada asked, barely audible over the din. Mom and I both caught it but Big Pete hadn't.

Mom laid her hand on Ada's arm. "You want to learn how to mine asteroids?" Mom's voice was low, not wanting to embarrass Ada if she'd misspoken.

"Maybe not full time. But I wouldn't mind having a place to call my own. It'd give me something to do if we were slow on hauling," Ada replied.

Mom elbowed Dad. "Pete, you catching this?"

He looked at Ada thoughtfully and finally answered. "Can't see why it wouldn't work. I gotta be honest, you don't see too many ladies out there, but there's nothing that'd get in your way, especially if you can fly a pod-jumper anywhere near as good as you can a tug."

Mom must have stepped on the top of his foot because he yipped in pain.

"Are you saying I'm not a lady?" she asked in mock anger.

"I misspoke. I might have better said, 'attractive single ladies as opposed to attractive married ladies.'"

Mom was mollified and Ada gave Pete her peta-watt smile. Somehow he'd escaped a dangerous conversational pitfall and complimented Ada all at the same time. In a similar situation I would have, no doubt, failed miserably.

"How much time before you need to hear from us?" Jake asked.

"Let's get together for breakfast next Sunday at Ada's favorite restaurant - The Southern Gardens. Big Pete can bring a model of the Descartes Asteroid belt showing his claim and the open claims nearby."

"Are there many open?" Ada asked, still interested.

"Sure are," Big Pete said. "They've opened a section of the belt that can support at least two thousand claims. In the last two months, only forty have been reserved. I'm not sure why there's not more interest."

"See you all Sunday." Tali stood. "I need to get going."

We'd been talking for a couple of hours and her departure was all the rest of the group needed to break up. On the way out, Jake caught up with Nick and me.

"You have time for a detour?" he asked.

Nick looked at me and then asked, "What's up?"

"I've got something to show you."

He definitely had my attention. When we'd last talked to Jake he'd separated from our corporation to pursue rebuilding ships using our company's license to manufacture parts for CA-12 cutters. We'd invested two hundred thousand credits in his company and had yet to see a return.

"Sure, why not?" Nick said.

Tabby had leaned into my back with her hand on my waist and was blowing in my ear suggestively. It felt like she'd had enough social time and would prefer to call it a night.

"Hey Tabs, you mind? Jake's never boring," I said.

She purred back at me under her breath. "Your loss." I mentally kicked myself.

"It won't take too long," Jake said looking at Tabby and me with a knowing grin. I wondered if he had better than average hearing. "We can hoof it. It's only a twenty minute walk."

"Lead on," I said, though my heart definitely wasn't in it.

Meglianos was in the heart of the University Hills district of Puskar Stellar. Wide sidewalks were common and for a short time we melded into the walking traffic.

Tabby turned more than a few heads in her skin-tight, bright red leather slacks. Ever since coming out of the tank, she'd been proud of her new parts. From my perspective they looked nearly identical to her old parts, but having lost them for a period of time made her just that much more determined to flaunt 'em.

Once we finally turned off onto a less traveled path Marny observed, "Probably good you never decided to go to school here, Tabby. I don't think the male students would get much done with you around."

Tabby giggled and pulled in closer to me. I wondered when it would get old for her. I'd never say anything. I'd seen her deal with loss of limbs and hardly complain. She could strut around whenever she wanted. She'd earned it.

"Here we are," Jake said.

As far as I could tell we were still in University Hills. Dorms, condos and shopping areas had given way to more industrial buildings.

"Lots of labs out here. I rented this warehouse as part of an entrepreneurial incubator offering from the school," Jake said as he placed his palm on a security panel of an entry door.

"A what, whatty?" Marny asked.

"Cheap rent to help businesses get off the ground. Since I'm still a grad student, I got a really good deal."

We walked into a small vestibule with a desk and a soft chair.

"Is this where you're working on the ships?" Nick asked. As usual he was a couple of steps ahead of me.

Jake didn't answer but pushed through a swinging door to a huge warehouse filled with three nearly identical CA-12 cutters. My eyes searched the bow of each of them, trying to determine if any were *Sterra's Gift*. I wouldn't have thought I'd have had problems identifying her, but sitting next to her identical sisters I honestly couldn't pick her out.

"Is she here?" I asked. My heart was actually racing from anticipation.

"No, just part of the buildup. She's out back. These are my current works in progress," he said.

Nick was astonished. "You're working on three at a time?"

"Better than that. These are the last three of ten."

Nick whistled, clearly impressed. "You really got after it. Are there any more CA-12s in the area that need working on?"

"No. I'd have to go to the Near Earth area to pick up any more."

I couldn't help myself. "How'd you get all this done?"

"One of the advantages to being Professor Coffman's grad student is access to cheap labor from students trying to get into her classes. I hired out some of the harder work to pros, but only about ten percent of it. Having access to the intellectual property to manufacture the parts was really what made this all work."

"You're killing me here," I said.

Jake chuckled and walked us past the three cutters. The smell of fresh paint pervaded the warehouse as a small bot scurried across the surface of the last ship, laying down a coat of gloss. Through the glass of the bridge on that same ship I could see that the lights were on and a head bobbed in and out of my visual range. Someone was working on the bulkheads in front of the pilot chairs. I couldn't imagine how he'd successfully rebuilt ten ships in the period of six months, with or without cheap labor.

When he opened the door at the rear of the warehouse, I didn't need anyone to tell me what I was looking at. A gloss black paint job had added a dramatic flair, but it was absolutely *Sterra's Gift*. Like a mother who would recognize her own baby, I knew mine.

I pushed past Jake and Nick and ran into the graveled back lot and stood in front of her, tears welling in my eyes. I know it's ridiculous to feel so much for an inanimate object, but I felt it regardless. Tabby slid in next to me and placed her hand into my own. I squeezed it excitedly and pulled her around to the airlock, slamming my free hand on the security panel.

"Sorry, Liam, I had to replace the security core. It was riddled with Mars Protectorate security viruses," Jake said, catching up. He palmed the panel and the stairs extended down from the hatch. I ran up the stairs and pulled open the airlock door. I soon found myself in the all too familiar hallway.

Like a kid in a candy store I ran down the hall, poking my head through doors along the way to the bridge. Everything was spotless. Once on the bridge, I vaulted over the back of the pilot's chair. Tabby slid into the chair next to me. She held her fist across the aisle between us. I bumped it with my own, triumphantly.

Jake, Nick and Marny finally caught up with us.

"What do you think?" Jake was clearly pleased by my reaction.

I jumped up and surprised the larger man with a bear hug, lifting him off the ground. "She's perfect. Is it all like this?"

I set Jake down, mostly because I was having a difficult time holding him up.

"If by 'all like this' you mean, perfectly restored, then yes. Not her original engines, but given recent conversations, they're an upgrade you might appreciate."

"TransLoc?"

"Yup. They're not new, but they'll work. I pulled them off one of the wrecks I brought in," he said.

"Whoa. How much is that going to cost us?"

Jake looked at Nick with a raised eyebrow.

Nick answered, "We traded Jake a single run of the stealth armor pattern we got from the Brits and unlimited future access to the CA-12 part patterns. For that we have a brand new *Sterra's Gift*, complete with TransLoc engines. We also forgave his initial debt and he agreed to let us keep five percent of his company."

No price was too much, it was like I'd gotten a friend back. It was the best gift I could have ever received.

Nick saw it coming but didn't resist when I picked him up in a bear hug. I think he might have even enjoyed it a little.

TRADITIONS

"Are you done with her?" I asked, looking at Jake.

He wore a wide smile. I didn't trust Jake like Nick did, but he was growing on me.

"We are. There are a couple of things to know. We had to switch back to a slug throwing turret. Your blaster turret was completely ruined, not to mention the spyware in the batteries, compliments of the Navy.

"Back to sitting in the crow's nest?" I asked. The new blaster turret had eliminated the need for someone to sit behind the guns in the armory turret and I found it handy to have the gunner sitting on the bridge instead. However, we could manage quite well with the old setup.

"It will fire remotely, but it's not ideal. We had to work with the original ship layout. However, as a weapons designer, I should point out that the crow's nest, while a little slower, has a higher kill rate. Something about lining up with and actually seeing the target makes people more effective."

I looked at Marny for confirmation.

She replied, "We're really splitting hairs, Cap. Difference is in the three to six percent range and it changes based on the size of craft you're fighting. Against darts, I prefer the automated turrets and energy blasters. Anything bigger and the slug throwers are better. Too many factors to make a big statement one way or the other. Point is, it's not a downgrade."

"What about cost for ammo. Surely that factors into it," I said.

"Slug throwers are more expensive to operate. On the positive side, however, a full load of ammunition is fifty percent the weight of those batteries. You'll be faster and more nimble," Marny answered.

She had me there. I'd pay money to have agility in combat.

"You said you put new engines on?"

Jake continued, "That's right. I found a trio of rebuilt Chrysler engines. You'll get a small increase in acceleration and ten percent better fuel economy. She still can't outrun *Hotspur* over any distance, but then most ships can't."

"Anything we need to get?" I asked.

"Galley-Pro, suit fresheners, that sort of thing. All of the flight, comm, navigation and O2 systems have been repaired or replaced."

"What about the septic field?" I had a bad feeling about this. Somehow, things always came down to me slogging around in the slop. Fatalistically, I felt it was only a matter of time.

"Completely replaced. Something big must have hit it," he said.

"Always does."

Jake leaned down and opened a bulkhead door in the starboard bridge station. He pulled out a dark glass wine bottle and handed it to me.

"What's this for?"

"It's an ancient tradition to christen a ship when it is recommissioned," he said. "Originally, the captain would break a bottle of bubbly on the bow of the ship. Anymore, it's common to just open the bottle and share a drink."

Jake deftly removed the stopper, which shot up and ricocheted off the ceiling. Nick had grabbed cups from the same cabinet, holding them for Jake to pour.

Jake continued. "To long life and prosperous trade." He held his cup out, clinking it with everyone else's, in turn. The rest of us mimicked his actions, tipping back the contents of our cups.

"When do I get to take it out?" I asked.

"Yours is the last signature. Mr. James has already approved the deal. Sign off and the ship will be yours."

Jake held out a reading pad. I glanced at Nick, who nodded affirmatively. I didn't need any more convincing and signed the agreement.

"*Command of Sterra's Gift has been transferred to Liam Hoffen.*" I didn't recognize the ship's AI's voice, something I'd have to rectify.

We stood around and talked a little more. Jake was understandably proud of the work he'd put into the ship and I was genuinely interested in the details.

"You guys want to get a room?" Tabby finally asked, not quite as enamored with the conversation.

The look on Jake's face was priceless. I was used to Tabby's abrupt manner, but he laughed nervously and raised his hands in mock surrender. "You know how we get. It's exciting stuff, but I've got to get going anyway. See you on Sunday for breakfast."

I shook his outstretched hand and he nodded to Nick and Marny before excusing himself.

"Anyone up for a test run?" I asked.

"Aye Cap, as long as you don't plan on getting into any trouble. We've no missiles or ammunition of any sort," Marny said.

"Should be fine as long as we avoid Deivid," Tabby said.

"Funny you should mention Deivid," Nick interjected. "I'd like to head out there tomorrow to pick up a load of mining equipment."

"I'd say take *Hotspur*, what with the reception we got last time," I said. "What do you want to do tonight?"

"We could load the ammo I bought last week," Nick said. "It's in our space-side warehouse."

"Man, I underestimated your ability to keep a secret. What else haven't you told me?"

"Guess you'll just have to wonder," he replied. It was good to see him so relaxed.

I jumped back into the port side pilot's chair and pulled up our preflight checklist. Once all items had been verified I asked. "All stations, report status for departure."

Marny and Nick replied, "Green." Tabby looked at me questioningly.

"As co-pilot, you only need to reply if you see a problem."

She looked at me as if I was telling her something she already knew. I was missing something. I punched in a navigation path to our warehouse that was in orbit above Puskar Stellar and then it dawned on me. "Tabs, you want to take us out of here?"

"I thought you'd never ask," she said with a satisfied grin.

Tabby had a light touch on the flight stick. I was comfortable lifting *Sterra's Gift* out of the tight space behind Jake's temporary shipyard, but that was because of the number of hours I'd logged in the pilot's chair. Tabby didn't have anywhere near the same hours, but she deftly lifted us up anyway, slowly rotating so that we got a nice view of the surrounding area. A low sun glinted off the red clay tiled roofs of the buildings of University Hills.

Without access to the stick, it was difficult for me to get a feel for how much thrust Tabby was putting into our takeoff. From the co-pilot's chair it seemed effortless, which I knew to be more of a statement of our gravity and inertial systems than our power. Regardless, a few minutes later we left the atmosphere behind and fell into the heavy traffic of Puskar controlled space, arriving at our warehouse fifteen minutes later.

Upon approach, Nick sent a command to our bay, requesting the door be opened horizontally. The door doubled as a thin ledge for *Sterra's Gift* to perch on. "Let's lock everything down and do a zero-pressure load," I said.

"Aye, Cap," Marny replied.

Twenty minutes later I looked up to Nick as he closed the airlock behind him. "We get it all?"

"That's it, Cap," Marny answered. "Why don't you all come out and we'll get a load of missiles."

Sterra's Gift had the capacity for six missiles, although we'd never had enough money for more than four. The two pallets we'd liberated from Red Houzi changed all of that.

Moving missiles was something you wanted to do deliberately and without mistakes. We certainly didn't want to find out what two dozen might do. Once again, Marny showed her professionalism by walking us through safety protocols. We paid attention. It seemed like common sense as she explained it, but that's the nature of experience. It also wasn't the sort of thing you wanted to take two shots at.

An hour later, *Sterra's Gift* was loaded for bear. We had a full complement of missiles and nearly a full load of ammo.

Bring it on.

"What now?" I asked.

"You know it's 2300 local, right?" Nick asked. He knew darn well I had no idea of the time.

"Why not sleep up here?" I asked.

"Works for me," Nick said. "But *our* bunk room was the only one that didn't get trashed. I'm not sure you have linens in the captain's quarters. And I bet we don't have any soap for the head. Want to rough it?" He looked to Tabby and Marny.

"I know we have blankets in storage, I'll check inventory," Marny said. "Yup. Right where I thought they were." She pinched at her vision and flicked directions to a crate. "We can run over and get beer from the space-side terminal and I have a deck of cards if you guys just want to hang out."

"I'll put in an order while Liam is fetching pillows and blankets," Nick said.

"Bring the whole crate with you, Cap. That's all stuff we salvaged from our last voyage."

I left the three of them to talk through the evening's snacks while I went into the warehouse to retrieve the crate Marny had specified. It was bigger than I'd expected, so I instructed my AI to lower the port cargo-hold's floor while I pulled the crate over. I recalled having rescued Ada by dragging her life-pod into that very hold. It seemed like such a long time ago.

After closing the warehouse bay, we sailed to the space terminal where Nick and Marny disembarked to get snacks. I didn't think we'd be up too late, but since we were getting started at 2330, who knew? It didn't take them long to return.

"Ready to get out of here?" I asked. We'd all made it back to the bridge. Tabby was seated behind my chair on the floor, clearly ready for cards.

"Where are we going?" Tabby asked.

"We always sail to a random point in space so we're not easy to find," I said.

22

"No shite? I thought you just made that up so we'd have a place to neck," she said.

That caused everyone on the bridge to erupt with laughter. She sounded so sincere in her disbelief. I pulled out of the terminal and set a course for ten thousand kilometers away. It'd take us twenty minutes to get there, but we'd be out of the way of normal traffic.

We played cards, drank beer and ate chips and salsa until well into the morning, finally retiring at 0300.

I woke up to Tabby's mostly naked body draped over my own. I loved how she now lived life with such abandon. She knew what she wanted and wasn't at all afraid to ask for it. Just like she'd known that she was finished with the Navy and wanted to go adventuring with Nick, Marny, Ada and me. She'd always been confident, but since her recovery, she'd taken that to the next level.

I couldn't imagine anyone I'd rather spend the rest of my life with. I ran my hands over her, tickling her ribs. She swatted my hand, which hurt, because she didn't know her own strength. I jumped on her and held her down, kissing her naked back. She had a hard time complaining and finally rolled over beneath me.

"We should go shopping today," she said. I was holding her down, but we both knew she could easily throw me off.

"Nick gave me a list – Galley Pro, Brew Master, Honda Class 2 Replicator."

She punched me and I looked at her in confusion.

"Rings, dumb-ass," she said.

Frak. She was right. I'd totally forgotten that it was a tradition to get rings when you got engaged. In my defense, I hadn't seen it happen too often. "Right. Sorry. What do you have in mind?"

"I want us to have identical rings. It's probably easier to show you. Can we go to the Open Air District? Kathryne gave me the name of a jeweler." Tabby wasn't a shopper, she was a buyer. I bet she'd talked to Tali, who'd made a call to her mom, Kathryne.

"Not that I don't like the idea, but I think you should probably put some clothing on," I said.

"I've seen Marny naked tons of times," she said. This got my attention. Marny and Tabby were two entirely different body types. Tabby was lithe with small tight muscles and a ripped stomach, but Marny was well muscled and more rounded in places. Tabby knew I was enamored with Marny and liked to set traps for me. I gave her my best disapproving school-marm look. She patted my head patronizingly, acknowledging my growth in this area.

"I think they bought coffee last night. Want some?" I asked. I vaulted off the bed platform and landed softly on the floor. I'd learned to hold on to the edge of the bed on the way over to help line up my landing so I didn't hit my prosthetic foot awkwardly.

"Wait. I'll come with." She gracefully rolled off the bed and landed on her feet. We both pulled on our suit liners and vac-suits.

Once we opened the door I heard voices on the bridge. Nick and Marny were looking at an asteroid map at Nick's engineering station. I didn't recognize any of the larger asteroids. I nodded my head when my AI offered to overlay the map with additional information using my HUD. The asteroid field suddenly filled with rectangular boxes, which I recognized as claim markers.

"Coffee? Tabby, Cap?" Marny acknowledged our entrance by handing us each a cup.

I accepted it gratefully. "Whatcha have here?"

Nick touched a corner of one of the claim boxes. "This is Big Pete and Silver's claim."

I looked at the claim and recognized a number of features we often talked about. Someone had done a very detailed scan of the belt and as I zoomed in I saw that Dad had done his own homework. At a minimum, his claim was heavily loaded with iron. The way a few of the asteroids looked, I'd have been willing to bet there was a chance of concentrations of precious metals too.

Show open claims next to Big Pete's. I said.

I was surprised. A few claims were taken, but at least a dozen near Dad's looked to be almost as rich as his. He'd made a good choice, at least by Hoffen standards.

"We were trying to figure out if we wanted to make a claim. I think we probably will," Nick said. "Like Ada said, if we run into downtime, we can do a little mining. At least enough to make the claim permanent."

"Big Pete'll make a miner out of you one way or another," I said.

"Are you going to make a claim?" Marny asked.

"Yeah," I said. "Dad would be upset if I didn't. Besides it will give him twice as many asteroids to pick from. He'd pick yours too, if you asked him."

Nick nodded. "Good idea."

"Tabby and I were going shopping this morning. You have anything going on?" I asked.

"We were thinking Deivid later this afternoon," Marny said.

It was only 1000 local. "That's about two hours for *Hotspur*. We have a quick trip into town, what if we were back by 1400?"

"Aye, Cap, should work fine," she answered.

"Last time we were out there, they didn't like that we showed up unannounced. Might be worth a comm," I said.

"I'll set it up," Nick said.

Tabby was content to let me sail, so I took the controls. After an abbreviated checklist we made for the compound on Tali's land, where we dropped Nick and Marny and then turned back for Puskar Stellar.

"Soman Emporium," Tabby said, sending the location of a shipyard where we could temporarily park *Sterra's Gift*.

We joined a stream of traffic and flew into town, landing on the designated parking spot in the Open Air Market. I extended the stairs and before we could get down, a short chubby man, wearing a stained, white sleeveless t-shirt stood at the bottom, blocking our way.

"Two hundred a day," he said.

"We'll be here two hours. We've prepaid," Tabby said.

"I'm Benny. This is my yard and it's two hundred a day. I've already extended the locking clamps."

"Sorry. We already paid and if you mess with the ship, you'll be eating through a straw for the rest of your life." Tabby glowered at the little man.

"We'll see," he said.

Secure ship. Maintain security perimeter, I said to my AI. The top turret popped up from beneath its armored cowl. It wasn't a great threat since it couldn't actually hit someone standing this close to the ship. I doubted this guy would want to stay within the perimeter, however.

I pushed around Tabby and addressed him. "We're not looking for any trouble. If everything's good when we get back there'll be a tip in it for you."

"Maybe you're not getting it. I'm not intimidated by your little ray gun up there. This is my lot. Pay the fee."

"Get out of my way," Tabby attempted to push her way around him and the rest happened pretty quickly. Initially he seemed to allow her to get around, but then he spun and leveled a nasty looking blaster at her.

"Don't get pushy, sister ..." He got that much out before Tabby's right arm snaked out at light speed and punched his wrist.

Whatever she hit caused his hand to relax and drop the gun, which she neatly grabbed out of the air.

"Frak," he said in surprise.

Tabby field-stripped the gun, pulling the energy cell and then reassembled it. "Look. Benny, was it? When we come back, I'll give you *your* little ray gun. If you mess with anything we'll send our security footage off to Puskar Stellar defense. I doubt they like their citizens getting the shakedown. Savvy?"

"Fine. Whatever." Benny moved away from the bottom of our ramp and allowed us to pass.

"What a jerk," Tabby muttered as we walked away.

"I heard that," he said to our backs.

Once we exited the shipyard we found ourselves in the heart of the Open Air District. It was always fun to visit in the midday, when all the vendors had their colorful awnings and umbrellas extended. It took only a few minutes to locate Soman Emporium.

A middle aged man wearing off-white robes with a wide, colorful belt met us after we'd looked at the displays for a few minutes.

"Miss Masters. It's good to see you again. I take it this is your young man?" When he talked his deeply tanned face lit up with a warm smile. He held his hand out to be shaken.

"Yes, Mr. Soman. This is Liam," she answered politely. I shook his hand and returned his smile.

"If you'll follow me, I think you'll be surprised at how well they turned out." He gestured toward the back of his small shop.

I leaned into Tabby and whispered in her ear. "I thought we were going shopping."

"Hmm…" she said thoughtfully.

Mr. Soman moved behind the counter and laid out a small black cloth that held two rings. He picked one up and handed it to Tabby. She slipped it onto her ring finger and held it for me to see. To my miner's eye it looked like platinum with a small sliver of light blue stone embedded in the ring. The stone had been shaped to follow the curve of the ring and was flush with the platinum.

"It's beautiful," I said.

"You have good taste, Mr. Liam," Soman said.

"Platinum?" I asked.

"Very close. How well do you know your metals?"

I pulled the ring closer. I doubted that it would be white-gold, because that would be … "Rhodium," I said.

"Nicely done." He held the other ring up. It was slightly wider but otherwise identical. I noticed the gem had been shaped to follow the curve on the outside as well as the inside and I could see light through the gem.

"I didn't know you could shape a gem like that," I said.

"It is not a gem, but a blue parallax crystal, a crystal only found in a remote region on the planet of Curie."

"In the Tipperary system?"

"The same." He looked at me expectantly so I slipped the ring on my finger. It slid on comfortably. "A perfect fit. There is something to know about the parallax crystals of Curie," he continued. Tabby smiled like a Cheshire cat. "We get cast offs from a laboratory where they make secret communication devices. The scraps aren't large enough for their purposes but fulfill ours beautifully. Miss Masters, would you demonstrate?"

She looked at me still smiling. She spun her own ring around so the crystal was facing down. When she touched the crystal with her thumb, my ring lightly pulsed. I looked up in surprise.

"How far will it reach?" I asked still looking at Tabby.

"If you know enough to ask the question. You no doubt already know the answer," Soman said.

He was right. I did. They were the same crystals used in the Navy's comm devices. As far as I knew the crystals were not limited in distance.

I nodded. "They're perfect."

A LONG EXPECTED PARTY

The little troll who had tried to shake us down was nowhere to be seen when we returned to *Sterra's Gift*. With rings in hand, literally, we purchased and arranged delivery for the parts that would make *Sterra's Gift* fully operational. I'd sure enjoyed sailing her again, but I knew we'd outgrown her. Having sailed *Hotspur* into combat, I'd never want to give up the sheer versatility and power of the larger ship.

Open comm, Nick James. "Nick, we're on our way back." We were going to be a little late.

"Sounds good, we'll be here. Big Pete is going to ride along," he said.

"Roger that," I said.

Ten minutes later I set *Sterra's Gift* down next to her larger sister, *Hotspur*. It's hard to express just how proud I was of my two girls (well three, if you counted Tabby).

As we disembarked *Sterra's Gift*, Big Pete, Marny and Nick exited the habitation dome on their way to *Hotspur*.

"Big Pete's coming?" Tabby asked.

"Yes. A good portion of the load in Deivid is his."

"Oh?"

"It's Wellington Corporation," I said.

Growing up on a mining colony, that name gave Tabby all the context she needed. To a miner, Wellington was known for their equipment. Decades of mining had convinced Big Pete there was no equal to the brand. He'd been like a kid in a candy shop when he'd ordered the equipment and I wasn't surprised that he wanted to ride along to pick it up. I wondered if he would actually make it back home before he popped a crate to get a look.

"Hope you don't mind me tagging along," Pete said as we

approached.

"Sounds like you're itching to get back to pounding rocks," I said.

He gave me a sardonic grin. "It's true. I guess it's just in my blood."

"As long as it's not contagious," I said, waggling my eyebrows at him. I was glad we'd finally gotten to a place where we weren't arguing about the fact that I'd chosen a different life.

He shook his head in mock dismay. "I hope I got everything. I had to draw down our savings to make up the amount the insurance company didn't pay out."

"You won't be on your own out there," I said placing my hand on his back as we both moved through the open airlock of *Hotspur*.

"Just don't get us shot down over Deivid," Nick said.

"Well, that could be a problem. Marny, any thoughts?" I asked as we took the lift up to the bridge deck.

"Aye, Cap," she said. "I talked to Deivid Air Defense about your last visit. This time they're providing a protected corridor. They also said that if you'd asked, they would have warned you about the bandits."

"Ugh. Live and learn, I guess." I started working on the system checklist. I felt an unfamiliar tug on my ring finger. It took me a second, but I remembered the function of the ring and I looked over to Tabby. She smiled back and we shared a private moment in the midst of all the departure activity. I earned a return wink by finding the crystal in my own ring and giving it tap.

"All stations, report status for departure," I said, to which Marny and Nick reported clear. "You want the helm?" I asked Tabby.

"All yours, Captain," she said.

I pushed forward on the throttle and pulled up on the flight stick. For such a big girl, *Hotspur* lifted off the ground like a ballerina. I loved the feel of the ship slicing through the atmosphere and the sensation of lift caused by the stubby wings. A few minutes later we entered a high orbit and I accepted the course Nick had laid in. It would take a couple of hours to traverse our way to the other side of the planet.

"Take the helm?" I asked Tabby.

"Aye," she replied.

I hopped out of my pilot's chair and sat on the floor between Nick and Marny's workstations. I'd been reviewing Nick's proposed purchases for our move to Tipperary and had a few items I wanted to discuss. On my HUD, I pulled up the planning worksheet we'd been working on.

"What's up?" he asked.

"I've been researching Grünholz. Their biological products are off the charts for the materials we need for meal bars and med-packs. If we brought along a Class-F medical grade replicator, we'd be able to generate trade goods that most miners need regularly." I was proud of myself for having done the research.

Nick looked at me appraisingly. I knew the look, he was trying to assess how much effort I'd put into it. "Class-F replicators are expensive," he said.

"Right. Best price I can find is three hundred thousand. We'd have to be aggressive to get a payback in three years, but that's not my focus. We're going to be in a foreign system and if we can't get access to food and medical supplies, it will end our trip."

"What are we trading for on Grünholz?" Nick asked.

"It's perfect - a heavy gravity planet, ninety-five percent covered by water. The cities are carved out of the plant growth on top of bogs. The water isn't more than ten or fifteen meters deep for the majority of the planet."

"What's that got to do with trade?" Marny asked.

"Limited access to minerals," Nick said.

"That's right," I agreed. "They're basically in the stone-age. The expense of getting into the crust of the planet is so high that refined minerals hold a high value. The problem is they don't have much to trade."

"Except biological materials," Nick added. "That's a good find, Liam. Any thoughts on where we come up with three hundred thousand?"

So far, selling the items from the pirate outpost had topped us out at just over one-point-one million. The list of what we needed was long and included items like a Class-D Industrial replicator, an old barge for the *Adela Chen*, and mining equipment to use as trade goods. We'd already spent or spoken for all but seventy-five thousand.

Once we were in the Tipperary solar system we wouldn't have much use for Mars Credits. Moving goods from Sol to Tipperary was outrageously expensive. The only thing we'd be able to use our Mars Credits for would be to purchase replicator patterns. Seventy-five thousand was the number we'd agreed upon leaving untouched.

Nick was right, we didn't have enough funds to purchase the medical grade replicator.

"I think we need to let go of a few of the missiles we got from the Red Houzi," I said. After fully loading out *Sterra's Gift* and *Hotspur*, we had fourteen left.

"Yup." It was Nick's standard reply for when he'd already thought about the problem and was waiting for me to come around. "I'm glad you're thinking about that. Maybe we should sell the mech suits."

"Will M-Pro have a problem with that?" I asked.

He had thought this through. "If we sold six missiles and the suits, we could raise almost three million credits. With that we could set up a small co-op refining station and lay out a sensor net. Imagine what we could do with refined ingots, a Class-D Industrial replicator, a renno-bot and a construction bot."

Big Pete joined us while we were talking. Nick had clearly grabbed his attention with talk of the refinery. "You'll need a few more pieces to make that work, but I wouldn't accuse you of thinking small, Mr. James," he said.

"Like what?" Nick asked.

"To start with, a rolling mill would give you sheet products," he said. "Your industrial replicator will do that, but a roller would speed you up by two orders of magnitude."

"A hundred times faster?" Nick looked at dad skeptically.

"At peak, absolutely. Also, there are patterns for buckets, carts, rail and a few items that you could manufacture on-site to really amp up your production. Once you can produce basic sheet, you have a product that should sell. The only problem I see is that it turns into a full time job if you want to make consistent income. Give me a minute, I'll send you a list," Dad said. He returned to the couch and started gesturing, obviously doing research on his HUD.

"You really want to get into this?" I asked Nick. For the first time I wondered if we might be interested in different things.

"It's a perfect use of our capital. There's a lot of demand for refined material in the system," he said.

He wasn't understanding my concern. For once, I was thinking further down the road than he was. By investing so heavily in a colony start-up we'd be seriously tied down.

"Won't someone need to stay behind and run that operation?" I asked.

"To start with, that's true," he said. "But check out these projections based on actual demand I can find in the system. My conversion back to Mars Credits isn't perfect, but if anything I'm too conservative."

He tossed a graph to my HUD showing that we'd be able to return the value of our capital in less than five years.

He continued, "And that's assuming we hire two people in the first year. We'll be busy, but it's a heck of an opportunity."

Nick continued to explain the ins and outs of his plan. I understood most of it, but having gotten him started, there was no stopping him. I hadn't seen him so excited in a long time. If this was his thing, then I would support it.

"Here you go," Dad said, seizing on the quiet that finally settled between us. He flicked a list of items. He'd separated it into what we needed patterns for and what we needed to purchase right away. It was a long list, with a healthy price tag of just under three million credits. He had included all of the refinery equipment that I was familiar with from working on Colony 40, as well as the robots and replicators Nick had already mentioned.

"I thought I'd heard you say you had about three million. That's how I'd use it. You could pick some of it up from Wellington, today even," Dad explained.

I sat back and waited for Nick who was busy moving items around on an invisible worksheet. He finished up and spun his chair around to include Pete in the conversation. "That's a good list. I made some changes, what do you think?" He flicked a sheet back at Pete.

I stood up. As much as I enjoyed a good conversation about inventory, I was getting bored. I put a hand on Nick's shoulder so he wouldn't think I was annoyed. "I'll let you guys work that out. I'm in either way. I don't mind selling off the suits and missiles. Just leave me a full load of ammo on both ships. "

"Your idea about the medical replicator is solid. It would give us independence as well as a good introduction to Grünholz. We might be able to find more items to trade with them," Nick said.

I rejoined Tabby in the cockpit. We were clear of the busy space over Puskar Stellar and speeding toward Deivid.

"What was all that?" Tabby asked.

"Nick's got it in his mind to start a colony when we get there," I said.

"Seriously?"

"Roger that. Refinery, sheet production, sensor net, the whole shebang."

"Sounds like my grandpa. Always building toward the next bigger thing."

"I didn't think you liked your grandpa," I said.

"I don't. But you gotta respect how he gets things done. Fortunately Nick's not an asshat," she said.

"Hey, I heard that," Nick's voice filtered up from the bridge.

An hour later I took the helm and lowered us into the atmosphere, following the path given to us by Deivid. It called for our approach to the white walled city to be executed at three thousand meters, giving us an excellent view of the landscape. We could see small clumps of homes and green circles of irrigated crops.

"See that?" Tabby asked, highlighting a heavy gun emplacement ten degrees off our starboard.

"That's a big gun," I observed.

"Aye, Cap," Marny joined in. "They must've had a pretty tough run of it down here. I've seen at least half a dozen of 'em so far. And you can bet there are some we haven't seen. It should be a nice quiet ride in."

"Do you think that's why they have us flying so close to the ground?"

"I believe they're looking to restore their reputation with us," she answered.

Hotspur's AI had been negotiating our approach with the city since we'd shown up in their airspace and we'd received instructions to proceed directly to the Wellington factory. A few minutes later I landed in an open bay.

Tabby and I joined Marny in the armory and we pulled on our armored suits.

Landing on the deck, as opposed to using the block-and-tackle lifts, allowed us to load considerably faster. We filled three hundred of the available six hundred cubic meters. Nick had added the refinery equipment we needed. With the short notice, we had to settle for re-manufactured pieces but Wellington insisted they were every bit as good as the original.

The trip back from Deivid was as uneventful as it had been on the way out. Dad and Nick spent the entire time discussing where and how to set up the refinery, co-op main building and ore grav-pads – basically an incredibly long, drawn out conversation with infinite detail that they seemed to both relish.

We spent the rest of the week delivering supplies to our warehouse. When we ran out of space, Nick rented another temporary area to handle the overflow. We weren't interested in placing anything onto the barge until the last minute.

Finally, Sunday morning came. The Southern Gardens restaurant was as beautiful as ever. The all-white wood décor was covered with green vines and brilliantly colored flowers. I was disappointed, but not surprised to hear that Tali Liszt and her

entire crew had turned us down. On the other hand, I was thrilled
to find that in addition to my crew and parents, we'd been joined
by Celina Dontal (Lena), her sister Jenny, and Jake Berandor. Even
more surprising was how chummy Jake and Lena seemed.

I looked around nervously, not seeing Ada. "Has anyone heard
from Ada?"

"You don't think I'd let you off this planet without me?" Ada
asked from behind me. I stood up. As usual I was struck by her
brilliant smile. I gave her a hug and she sat on the other side of
me. I felt a tug on my ring finger from Tabby, so I pinged her
back. I wasn't sure if she was warning or reminding me.

I let the group talk for a few minutes - it was impossible not to.
Mom and Ada had become best buds, having sailed the *Adela
Chen* on dozens of missions together and apparently they needed
to catch up. Nick and Dad still hadn't finished their conversation
about the refinery and Jake and Lena were intently discussing
something I couldn't hear.

Once we were halfway through breakfast, I stood and rapped
an orange juice glass with my knife. Satisfyingly, it actually made
a clear ringing tone and quieted the table.

I addressed the group, "I'm glad you all could make it this
morning and I know you've been thinking about our next
adventure. At the end of this week, we plan to get underway. Our
first stop will be the Bethe Peierls TransLoc gate where we'll join
the Belirand expedition to Tipperary.

"We've more than enough room for everyone and have
sufficient supplies for several months. Ultimately, we'd like to
know your interest and how you'd like to participate. I was
thinking I'd start by just going around the table, if that's okay?

"But before we do that, I'd like to make an announcement," I
said. I looked around the table at my friends and family who were
smiling back at me. I had no doubt that most of them knew what
was coming. I reached over to Tabby and held my hand out to her.
She grasped it and stood up.

"Tabby are I engaged to be married," I said.

If I thought we were going to get much done in the next few

minutes, I'd have been dead wrong. Ada bolted from her chair, pulled me into a hug, kissed me on the cheek and then pushed me to the side, grabbing a startled Tabby.

"I can't believe he finally worked up the nerve. Show me the ring," she said after she stopped hugging long enough to let go. "I know he wanted to, but you know how men can be."

"Well, I guess, technically, he didn't," Tabby said.

Ada looked at me and then back to Tabby and guffawed. "Of course you did. So, what is that stone? It's so gorgeous," she continued, nonplussed.

To be honest, the conversation continued after that but I tuned it out. I loved Ada as much as I could love another woman other than Tabby, but when she got fired up about this type of thing I lost interest. After a few minutes of congratulations and well-wishing, everyone finally returned to their chairs.

"So about our trip," I said, squeezing out a polite laugh from the group. "Ada, would you mind going first?"

"Are you kidding? You pledge your undying love to another woman and *then* you ask if I want to run off to another solar system with you?" She looked at me and then to Tabby. My heart fell. I'd seriously underestimated the situation.

The table grew quiet as all eyes turned to me. Blood rushed in my ears and I started to feel dizzy.

"Oh frak, that's too good. Sorry, just messing with you," Ada said, winking at Tabby. It was hard to ever be mad at Ada for long.

"I'm in," she said. "I've already applied for a claim with Big Pete's help and I'm hoping that I can both set up a mining operation and run loads with Silver."

I nodded at her, still shell shocked from her earlier joke.

"We're in," Marny said looking at Nick. It came as no surprise.

Big Pete was next, but looked to Mom who answered for the both of them. "Same here."

Jack had taken a position between Mom and Jenny. I wondered what direction his relationship with Jenny was going. They seemed to be no more than good friends. Given the trauma they'd both endured, I wasn't surprised they'd found each other.

Lena was next and piped up, "Jenny and I are hoping for a ride to Léger Nuage."

"That will be our first stop in the system, so no problem. Do you mind if I ask what you're planning?"

"Not at all. Jenny and I both have a lot of experience running diners. We've made an offer for one on level twenty-four. We need to talk about how much cargo room you'll have available," she said.

I looked at Nick, who answered, "How much do you need?"

"Thirty meters," she said. I was surprised at the volume but also knew we had lots of room.

"That's not a problem. We've a hundred meters open beyond that. Even more if it could be put on a barge," Nick said.

"No. That should do it," Lena said.

"Jake?" I asked.

"I'm in. I've a lease on a bar around the corner from Lena. It even has a pass-through to her kitchen, assuming she leaves it unlocked."

"You never struck me as a bartender," I said.

"I hope to just manage it. Lena said she'll show me the ropes. I'm really looking to create my own trade-hub. The bar thing is mostly because the price of alcohol in system is disproportionate to other goods. With Belirand paying for fuel and TransLoc passage, I figured it was a good time to carry high mass, high value goods."

"Sounds about right," I said. "Without being too specific about our departure time, we'd like to be loaded and ready to go before Saturday. Does anyone have an issue with that?" I looked around the table. We'd already communicated the schedule so it shouldn't have been a surprise. "Great. We'll be talking to you all a lot this week as we get ready to go."

Over the next week, we shifted from buying to packing. We'd moved the barge into position next to our warehouses and carefully executed Nick's load plan. With our entire family's net worth on the three ships, we'd taken to sleeping on *Hotspur* and running round-the-clock watches. It was overkill with the warehouse's already heavy security, but the risk was too high.

Finally, late Friday night, we were all loaded – Mom and Dad on the *Adela Chen*, Ada, Jake and Lena on *Sterra's Gift* and the rest of us on *Hotspur*.

Open comm, Loose Nuts Fleet. All ships' announcement.

"What's up, Captain?" Ada's cheery voice greeted me.

"*Adela Chen* here," Mom said over the comm.

Cue Willie Nelson.

I heard groans from all around me but they were soon replaced with the dulcet tones of an ancient singer.

"On the road again"

"Just can't wait to get on the road again ..."

IRON GATES

Gates between Solar Systems

I glanced over my shoulder and caught a glimpse of Mars receding behind us. It brought back memories of our arrival a year before and I wondered when I'd once again see the red planet. While it was beautiful, it was too crowded for a space rat like me. I'd miss the friends we were leaving behind, but in front of us lay an adventure of our own making.

The Belirand Corporation expected us at the Bethe Peierls Trans Location Terminal in two weeks. Belirand must have pretty deep pockets as they were not only paying to jump us all through three gates but would top off our fuel tanks after each jump.

I wondered what it would feel like to travel under the effect of the folded space of the TransLoc engines, but we'd find out soon enough. The technology behind a TransLoc jump was mostly beyond me. To the best of my understanding, the idea had been theorized for longer than humans had been in space. Like most things, a theoretical understanding and the ability to practically implement were two different things. The first TransLoc jumps were performed about eight centuries ago. Unfortunately, each jump was so expensive, not to mention unpredictable, that the entire field of study was dropped for decades.

It hadn't been hard to convince adventurous crews to take blind leaps into the dark corners of our galaxy. Ultimately, what caused these missions to fail was the communication technology.

It was actually too good. It's one thing to send ships off, never to be heard from again. It was another thing to watch crews starve to death or asphyxiate because they'd sailed into completely barren sections of space.

Two centuries after the first failed missions and resulting public relations disaster, an Italian scientist, Marcel Anino, invented the TransLoc gate system. Instead of a single launching point, Anino's gates worked in matched pairs. Once the giant exploration ships arrived at their destination, they would deploy the return TransLoc gate that was built into their ship and return in a much smaller jumper. The entire process took decades to complete and was outrageously expensive, but mankind had once again gained the stars.

Eight centuries later, we'd successfully explored hundreds of solar systems and settled in four of them on a large scale. There had always been talk of the systems we'd abandoned or simply decided to ignore as not being sufficiently profitable. There were even popular conspiracy theories about colonies in far flung systems that had been cut off. Growing up, Nick and I had spent endless hours speculating on the reasons for abandonment and how these mythical colonies might have developed.

I awoke to the alarm I'd set, gently lifted Tabby's arm off my chest and tried to slide out without waking her.

"Where do you think you're going?" she asked, not lifting her head off the pillow.

"We're four hours from Belirand's Terminal One," I said. "It's my shift."

"Wake me when we're an hour out." She pulled her arm back under the covers.

It was hard to leave her as all I really wanted to do was crawl back in with her. I also knew that one thing would lead to another and I'd end up being late to relieve Nick at the helm. I sighed, got ready and took the lift to the galley for coffee. I wasn't surprised to find Marny leaning back in a chair, dozing, with her feet on the mess table. Her eyelids fluttered open as I poured the coffee.

"Want a cup?" I asked.

"Is it that time already?"

"We're four hours out, I'm about to relieve Nick. How about you both catch a couple hours? We'll be coming out of hard-burn in three. No doubt that'll wake you up," I said.

"I'll be up before that, but I wouldn't mind a little rack time." Marny had the ability to sleep just about anywhere and she could jump from completely asleep to fully alert at a moment's notice.

I left her in the combined galley/mess and took the lift back up to the bridge deck. I enjoyed the serenity of the empty *Hotspur* bridge during off-hour shifts. Long, narrow windows on both sides allowed for a beautiful view of the star field.

"Anything to report?" I asked.

"All systems are normal. We're two hours fifty four to our final approach to Terminal One, leading to Bethe Peierls," Nick replied.

I sat down and pulled up the displays on the forward vid screen. All systems were reporting green and I noticed that Nick had added a countdown display. As soon as I took the helm, the display would switch to my own preferences.

"I relieve you," I said.

"I stand relieved," he replied, finishing the formal turnover.

"Are we doing the right thing here?" I asked.

He was confused. "What do you mean?"

"It feels like everyone is blindly following us to Tipperary. What if it's a bust? What if we run into pirates and get everyone killed?" I asked.

"What if we hadn't risked everything and taken *Sterra's Gift* when we did? We would have been on Colony 40 when the Red Houzi arrived and we'd most likely be part of a press-gang or dead. Your parents are miners, Liam. Most of their lives were devoted to working that claim, only to have their ore stolen and their machinery destroyed. This is their chance to start fresh."

"You're right, of course," I said.

"As for pirates. We're never going to escape them. Pirates are just people who aren't willing to work for what they want. They'll always be around." He grinned at me. "That's why we have you and Marny."

"Marny, maybe. Not me." I was uncomfortable being put into the same class as Marny.

"Don't sell yourself short. Both Tali and Marny believe you're a tactical genius. Tali said if you didn't have your own thing going on, she'd have tried to hire you," Nick said.

"Seriously?" I asked.

"Yup." Nick put his hand on my shoulder as he started down the stairs to the bridge. "I'll be back once we drop out of hard-burn," he said and disappeared.

I looked out of the cockpit window wishing I could make out the approaching Bethe Peierls Terminal, commonly called Terminal One. It was one thing I appreciated about *Hotspur*. With our side-mounted engines we could actually decelerate in hard-burn while facing the object we were approaching.

Place a targeting reticle on Terminal One. My AI projected a small rectangular box around the point in space where the terminal was located. I imagined I could see a flicker of light in the center.

I busied myself studying the system we'd end up jumping into. Bethe Peierls was by far the most productive system of any that had been discovered. There were four habitable planets and a large moon, Khayyám, around Vermeer, the largest of the four. It was a shame that our schedule wouldn't give us a chance to stop at any of the planets along the way.

Data moved slowly through the TransLoc gates and I found myself looking at stale TradeNet data. For my purposes, it didn't matter. I wouldn't be setting up any trade routes just yet, but I wanted to get a feel for how things were priced in the different systems. If anything, the availability and margin on shipments were higher than in Sol. Although that was somewhat offset by the higher price of fuel. There were even a few outstanding requests for goods that I was certain I could deliver from Mars and still make up for the TransLoc fuel and gate fees.

"*Transition from hard-burn in two minutes,*" the AI announced on the ship's public address.

"Tabby, you hear that?"

"What?" she replied groggily.

"Two minutes and we're dropping out of hard-burn," I said.

"I'll be right there," she said.

By the time we were twenty minutes away, the bridge was humming with activity and everyone was in their place. Jack and Jenny, who'd ridden the first leg of our trip on *Hotspur*, were on the couch, barely containing their excitement while trying to corral and play with Filbert.

"Hey, Jack, how 'bout putting Filbert into the grav-box?" I suggested. I could handle Jack and Jenny, but if something went sideways, having a frightened cat running loose could be a disaster.

Hail Bethe Peierls Terminal.

A friendly looking, middle aged woman appeared on the cockpit's holo projector. "Greetings *Hotspur*. Belirand Terminus Control here. We've been tracking you for the last forty million kilometers, I trust your trip has been uneventful."

"Roger that, Belirand. I'm accompanied by the *Adela Chen* and *Sterra's Gift*." I wanted to make sure we were being clear with them. Belirand had a reputation of aggressively protecting its assets.

"We've been expecting you and you're clear for approach. I'm transmitting docking instructions as we speak," she said.

A notification popped up on the forward vid screen. There were, indeed, docking instructions but also a turret lockdown requested at a hundred thousand kilometers.

"I see you're asking for turret lockdown at a hundred thousand. Are you secure at that range?" I asked.

"We are, Captain Hoffen. I can also assure you that no ships are within twenty million kilometers, other than Belirand Security. No one is within intercept range of your fleet," she said.

Mute. I instructed the AI.

"Marny, any thoughts?" I asked.

"She's on the up-and-up, Cap. Their scanning technology is the best in the galaxy. If she says no one's close, then we're good," Marny said.

Unmute.

I accepted the turret lockdown for our fleet and looked back at the holographic image of the woman. "Thank you, Belirand. We'll see you shortly. Over and out."

"Over and out," she replied with a curt nod of her head.

We sailed in silence for a few more minutes and watched the terminal grow in front of us. We were approaching one end of what was essentially a triangular prism, its flat top half a kilometer wide and five kilometers long. I'd seen enough vids of TransLoc gates in operation to know that the top was used for launching and receiving ships from fold-space. The V-shaped lower structure was the station itself and where we had been instructed to dock.

Open comm, Loose Nuts Fleet.

"Mom, Ada, are you all set with your docking instructions?" I asked.

"*Adela Chen*, all lined up," Mom answered.

"Good to go, Captain," Ada replied.

As we lined up for final approach, I saw twenty-five ships of different shapes and sizes beneath the terminal. Some of them were in great condition and moderately-armed, although most of them looked like they were barely up to the task of jumping through fold-space. Almost all of them had bundles of mining equipment, containers and pod-jumpers strapped inelegantly around their hulls. Without the *Adela Chen* and her giant barge, we'd probably be in the same shape, trying to bring enough material to the frontier of an untapped asteroid belt.

"You suppose these are all headed to Tipperary?" I asked idly as I let the autopilot guide us in.

"Most of them, I'd think," Nick said. "The expedition is thirty-two ships including us. We're still short seven ships if everything here is going."

"I guess I'm surprised not to see more Belirand ships," I said. "How do they keep up their defenses?" I'd come to expect that pirates would attack just about anyone. A large structure like this had to be a target worth taking.

"Don't need 'em, Cap. Belirand has the backing of NaGEK.

Rumor is they can turn a battleship into rubble from a hundred thousand kilometers with their planetary defense level weapons. No expense was spared when they built these gates," Marny explained.

"How do you want to do security while we're lashed up here?" I asked.

"Let's have an all-hands meeting in the galley. We can run through all of this," Marny said.

"Sounds good, you want to make the arrangements?" I asked.

"Aye, Aye, Cap."

Twenty minutes later we were all packed into the mess of *Hotspur*. It was the single largest, non-cargo area on any of the ships. Even so, it was standing room only.

"We're going to run a single watch from *Hotspur*," Marny started. "I've got all of the ship's sensor arrays linked and a monitoring program running. You need to keep in mind that our turrets are locked down and our best defense is to notify Belirand Port Authority immediately if there's a problem. I've set up a watch schedule for the next five days and will send it to everyone after we're done here."

"How about weapons on station?" Big Pete asked.

"There aren't any restrictions. But keep in mind, Belirand Port Authority is an independent, fully autonomous entity and can mete out whatever punishment they see fit. I wouldn't expect problems, but if you run into something, contact me immediately. Cap, you have anything to add?" Marny asked.

"I do. Thanks, Marny. There are two mandatory meetings with Belirand. The first is for ship's captains. Their requirement is that we have a representative for each ship, although they recommend that anyone who pulls a watch should also attend. Now that we're here, I can schedule that. The second meeting is an informational session on mining in the Tipperary system. Jake, Lena and Jenny, you could probably skip that. Anyone with a claim, however, is required to be there. Finally, every day at 1800, until we take off for Bethe Peierls, Belirand hosts a banquet in honor of the expedition. Everyone's invited. It's not mandatory, but free food might be interesting. Any questions for either Marny or me?" I asked.

"No. Did you see they have a pod-ball court here?" Tabby asked. Apparently, we'd lost her interest somewhere along the way.

I ignored her for a moment and looked to Nick to see if he had anything else.

"It's true. They have three full-sized courts and a standing invitation for visiting teams," he answered.

I sighed. I should have known better. We'd been cooped up for ten days and I was standing between the crew and shore leave.

"I think that's all we have, then," I said.

As the room emptied, Tabby and Ada worked their way over to Jack and Jenny. I had a couple of things to work out with Nick, but quickly became distracted as the four of them kept looking over at me while whispering and smiling.

"I think I need to figure out what's going on over there," I finally said to Nick.

"No problem," he said. We would have plenty of time to talk in the next few days.

I approached the group and asked, "Alright, so what's going on over here?"

"They've got a pod-ball tournament running. It's not too late to join," Tabby said.

"How'd you find that?" I asked.

"Actually, Jenny found it," she answered.

I looked over at Jenny. "Oh?"

"Jack told me the three of you used to be a team. I wondered if the station was organizing any games, what with all the people gathered," she said.

Tabby looked at me, pleading. "Come on, Liam, we have to do this."

"I'm not sure why you're selling me so hard on this. I'd love to play," I said.

"Good, because you're signed up for a pickup match in forty minutes," Jenny said

IT'S ALL FUN AND GAMES...
UNTIL SOMEONE GETS HURT

On the trip out from Mars, I'd had a chance to learn more about Jenny. She was only a few years younger than Tabby and me, but for some reason it felt like a lot more. She'd had a rough time growing up and I figured she was making up for lost time. I hadn't decided if Jack followed her around or if she'd co-opted him. They were always together though.

"Are you going to play?" I asked, looking at Jenny.

"I don't know anything about pod-ball," she said.

"Good time to learn," Tabby said. "We'll find an open court and you can warm up with us. It's not hard to play, but it can get rough at the higher levels. We should see if they have a rec league."

"How about you, Ada? Do you want to play?" I asked.

She shrugged. "Sure. I've only played a few times, but it's fun."

I pulled up the station map on my HUD and found the courts. Two of them were busy, but the third was open. I sent a query and was rewarded with a reservation. "I've got a warmup reservation," I said.

"What's rec league?" Jenny asked.

"I'm surprised they didn't have one on Terrence where you grew up. The rec league is for newer teams, or people who don't want to compete as hard. There are four levels – Rec or B, Double-B, A and Double-A," Tabby explained as we started for the back door.

"Wait up," Marny said. "We'll work out with you."

"Sure. More the merrier," I said.

As we walked through the hallways of the terminal, I was impressed at how clean and well maintained everything appeared. The hallways were wide and painted with a grey deck paint on the floor. The walls were a muted white with a crisp, medium blue stripe running at waist level. Interactive vid panels, inset into the walls at each intersection, displayed a welcome sign for the *Loose Nuts Corporation* and Belirand's itinerary for us while we awaited the departure of the expedition.

"Here we are," I stopped next to the pod-ball arena entrance. Belirand had segregated the area into Red, Blue and Green venues. We'd reserved the Green court, so we entered using the court door, bypassing the one labeled 'gallery.' I wondered how many people their gallery could hold. On Colony 40, most people watched from their HUDs or vid screens as we didn't have many spectator seats.

Once we entered the court, I palmed a panel to sign for a pod-ball. It receded to expose a new looking ball which I tossed to Jack.

"We've half an hour before our match, so we can go over the fundamentals," I said. "If we really wanted to play competitively, we'd keep *Loose Nuts* together. But, by breaking up, we can probably field two Double-B teams by the end of the week. Anyone opposed to that?"

"What are you thinking for teams?" Tabby asked.

"Well, the four of us have good experience, but I think Jenny and Jack would have fun playing together. Ada, Jenny and Jack on one team and Marny, Tabby and myself on the other," I said.

"You'll crush us," Jenny said.

"Not at all," I replied. "I chose Marny because she has the least experience in low gravity. She'll make up for it some because of her physical conditioning, but this isn't a game of strength. It's all about maneuverability. Jenny, you'll be surprised by how much your spacer life will give you an edge."

Marny chuckled, "Aye. Once you turn that gravity down, I'll be no better than a pig on ice."

Ada had counted and looked around. "What about Nick?"

"I don't like to play. I'm the coach," he said.

I tried to imagine what a pig might look like on ice. It didn't make sense, so I let it go. "The rules of pod-ball are pretty straight forward. It's a mix of two old earth games – hockey and basketball. The objective of the game is to put the ball into the goal more times than your opponent. The primary rule that people have trouble with is you can't spend more than three seconds in the blue-zone in front of your opponent's goal. For defenders, the primary rule is that you can't spend more than three seconds in the red-zone guarding your own goal and attackers can't touch the pod-ball if they're in the red zone. Put your face shields up and your HUD will show you those two zones.

"There are a few more rules – like limited contact. If the AI determines you've been targeting other players for contact, you'll be assessed a penalty and have to sit in the penalty box. The AI will give you a warning when it predicts contact, so even if you're not a very good flyer, you'll know that you have to change directions.

"We follow a standard Kokushi formation - a defender and two attackers. The defender's role is to make sure they're always between the attacking team and our goal. For *Loose Nuts*, that was always Jack. For our new team, Marny and I will trade that position back and forth until we figure out who makes more sense. I'd say you probably want Jack to take that on your team, Jenny, since he was one of the best defenders in the league we played in. You and Ada can work out the attack between you. Nick will coach from the gallery and give you strategy.

"At this point, there's no reason not to just play. Your AI will tell you when you're doing something wrong. Any questions?" I asked.

"You think we can really play against other teams?" Jenny asked.

"Absolutely," Tabby answered. "The only way to get better is with competition. I think your bigger problem could be that Jack will have to give up the defender spot. Level B teams aren't likely to score on him, and the AI could bump you up to Double-B if you aren't careful."

Jenny looked at Jack appraisingly. He was easy to underestimate.

We'd already talked through ten minutes of the remaining half hour before our match. I felt guilty abandoning Jack to Ada and Jenny, but I had the ulterior motivation of getting Marny and Tabby some time working together.

"I'll give us a three minute count-down and you have the ball first, okay?" I punched in a three minute countdown to start the match. At one minute the computer would switch the gravity to zero-g.

Marny, Tabby and I jogged to the orange end of the court. "How about you attack first, Marny?"

"Aye. Can do, Cap," she said.

"I've got your back, Marny," Tabby said.

"You might be careful with that, I'm expecting to run into a lot of walls with it," she retorted, which earned her a smile from Tabby.

Twenty minutes isn't a lot of time to play, especially if two of the players are learning the game for the first time. As predicted, Marny had more trouble than Jenny. She was agile, but had a poor understanding of the cause and effect of arc-jet boots and gloves. More than a few times, she slammed into the wall at a high enough rate of speed that we all winced. We'd quickly decided that keeping score didn't make sense. It was fun to see Jenny, and Marny for that matter, learning and gaining skill at a game we'd grown up playing. When gravity was finally restored, we gathered at center court.

"What'd you think?" I asked looking between Jenny, Marny and Ada.

Jenny's face was alight with excitement. She was an enthusiastic, if not overly skilled attacker. "I can't believe I never played on Terrence, it's so much fun. I'll have to figure out how you use all of the barricades, though." Every pod-ball court was set up differently and had different obstacles and barricades between the opposing team's goals. One of the skills you developed was how to utilize different objects to quickly change directions or fake out your opponents.

I nodded and looked to Ada. "What'd you think?"

"I'm with Jenny. It's fun." She grabbed Jenny's hand in a show of solidarity.

"Marny?"

Marny's chest was still heaving from exertion and sweat beaded up on her face. "I wondered when you'd get your revenge on me for those boxing workouts," she said.

Tabby put her arm around Marny's shoulders. "You did better than I thought you would. You just need to spend more time in zero-g so you're not fighting your mass so much."

"Thanks, but I'm toast. I haven't worked that hard for twenty minutes in a long time," she admitted.

"Jenny, what's the level of the match you signed us up for?" I asked.

"Let me look." After a moment she replied, "Double-B."

"Marny, are you up for it? I'm afraid if we put Jack, Tabby and me in, it won't be fair to the other team," I said.

"What level did you guys play?" Jenny asked.

"Mostly A, sometimes Double-A," I replied.

"Sure. Give me a minute," Marny answered.

"You'll have five, which is when we're due on Red Court," Tabby answered.

I returned the pod-ball and we trekked out into the hallway. Lena, Jack and Mom were waiting for us, looking at the different doors.

"Are you guys playing?" I asked.

"No, silly, we want to watch," Mom replied.

"Oh. We're on Red," I said. "Jenny, while you're up there, you should find an open B match."

We entered the court and met the team we were set to play at the center, as was customary. I held my hand out to the first player I met.

"Liam Hoffen," I said.

"Teodorov, call me Tedo," he said. His grip was hard and he tried to crush my hand. I hadn't mined for almost a year, but still had plenty of strength so I resisted and pulled my hand free. He gave me a smarmy grin.

"Are you local?" I asked, ignoring his manner. I'd seen plenty of pre-game ploys to psych out opponents and I figured he was just playing me.

"We represent Oberrhein," he said, with a Russian accent.

I shook the hands of his teammates – Georgi and Mihael.

"Good to meet you. We're part of the *Loose Nuts Corporation*. I take it you're on the Tipperary expedition," I said.

"Enough talk. Are you sure you want to play in this league with your women?" he asked.

Involuntarily, I raised my eyebrows, I wasn't used to people making that type of reference and wasn't sure how to handle it.

"We'll try to keep up," Tabby said and walked toward our goal. I was impressed she hadn't gone off on the guy, but her posture announced that she was looking forward to mixing it up.

"Remember, we're playing Double-B. Just because he's an ass, we can't play too hard," I said when I joined her by our goal.

"Right."

Her one word response was a bad sign.

Formal pod-ball games are broken into three periods. Each period is scored independently. If a team wins both of the first two periods, the match is over.

The first period was a disaster for *Loose Nuts*. The Oberrhein team was better than I'd have expected for Double-B play and with Marny's lack of skill, it turned into a two on three match. I felt bad for Marny because tactically she was able to see that she was the weak link and it bothered her. I'd expected Oberrhein to play like they talked – over confidently. Mostly they just worked us over, setting picks on Tabby or myself and getting Marny alone so they could score.

We didn't lack for our own scoring, but being outnumbered for the entire period caused us a lot of problems.

"I'm sorry, guys," Marny said, as we rested between the two periods.

"You're doing great," Tabby said. "This is a really good team."

"I know, but they aren't having any trouble scoring on me," she said.

Nick, who'd been quiet in the coach's box the entire period, joined us for the intermission. "I looked them up. They're Single-A and Double-A players. Georgi, the fast one, played pro. You shouldn't feel bad. They probably couldn't find another match, so they're playing down."

This perked Marny up a little. "What can we do about it?"

"It's good experience," I said. "You're definitely learning the hard way, though."

"We need to get out of the two-on-three business," Tabby said. "They're leaving Georgi free to score while the others block me and Liam."

"You're right," Nick said. "I say we pull the defense."

I looked at Nick appraisingly. It was a bold move, he was suggesting that we bring Marny away from the goal.

"Won't they just get an easier run on our goal?" Tabby asked.

"Not a lot easier. When Georgi breaks free, the other two are picking up Tabby and Liam one-on-one. Georgi scores on Marny every time," Nick said. I winced at his brutal honesty.

"So, you want me to pick up one of the other two so Liam or Tabby can run down Georgi?" Marny asked.

"It should be Tabby," Nick said. "You need to free her up. She's as fast as Georgi and about fifty percent at stopping him when they're both free. Liam is only about thirty percent."

I shook my head. Only Nick could put that all together from a single period of play.

"I'm in," I said. Tabby and Marny both nodded.

At the beginning of the second period, pulling our defense turned out to be a terrible idea. Mostly because Marny hadn't figured out how to successfully plant a pick on the much faster Oberrhein team. About halfway in, however, she started figuring it out. The player I'd initially talked to, Teodorov, was the slowest player and most often setting up on Tabby. Once Marny figured out how to intercept him, Nick's plan started to work. By the end of the second period, we'd brought the score back to a tie. It was more than I'd hoped for and at least we would be able to play a third period. We were all a little disheartened, as the best possible outcome for the match was a tie, but I, for one, would see it as a victory.

"Frakking Mihael is playing dirty," Tabby said.

"What do you mean?" I asked.

"He's rabbit punching me when we're in a knot. I'm gonna kick his ass if he keeps it up," she said.

"You want to forfeit the match?" I asked.

"Are you kidding me?"

I knew better than to push it.

"You outscored them by five in the last half of the period," Nick said. "Expect them to adjust. I wish I had more advice, but at this point I'd say keep doing what you are."

Marny was losing steam. She was in top physical condition, but her mass got in her way when playing pod-ball. She was exhausted.

I had to ask. "You have another period in you?"

"Aye, Cap. It's a moral imperative."

The third period started off much like the second had ended. Nick's plan was working well. Georgi appeared to be slowing and Tabby was getting stronger. I'd finally shaken off the cobwebs of not playing for a year and having to adjust to my prosthetic foot. I started to feel like we had a nice shot of winning the period.

I saw it happening. I just didn't have the capacity to do anything about it. When flying through zero-g, better players have the ability to use their opponents to change direction and as long as they don't contact them too hard, it's all legal. Where this gets dirty is when the player who gets pushed doesn't have enough time to adjust, getting pushed into contact with one of the obstacles at just the wrong angle.

"Marny, impact!" I yelled through my headset. My warning wasn't going to help. She didn't have the ability to counteract the new forces Mihael had placed on her. She was spinning out of control and her arm snapped across a turnbuckle.

Both Tabby and I rushed over and I watched with disgust as Teodorov picked up the pod-ball and lobbed it into our goal.

Medical emergency. Restore gravity. I said to my AI. Immediately the lights in the court came back up and we all settled to the floor.

"I think it's broke, Cap," Marny said. It was an understatement; her arm was bent at an impossible angle.

Tabby was hot. "He did that on purpose," she spat.

"Careful," I said. I'd seen it too, but it was another matter to accuse someone of trying to hurt an opponent. Mihael had done a nice job of covering his actions.

A medical technician wearing a Belirand uniform and carrying a kit jogged onto the court. He quickly applied a patch to Marny's arm. The relief in her face was immediate.

"Looks like a nasty break, but we'll fix you up. I'm afraid you're done with pod-ball for a few days, though," he said. "Let's take you to the clinic and we'll set that bone."

We stood back up with Marny and started to walk out.

Mihael, apparently not the brightest in the bunch, stepped in our path and put a hand on Tabby's shoulder. "So you forfeit?"

I was a couple of steps away and knew we were headed for trouble. I tried to get to them, but I was too late. He'd have been okay if he hadn't put his hand on her, but it was more than she could take. She grabbed his hand and twisted violently, driving him to his knees. We all heard a pop as she broke something in his arm.

"You bitch! That's assault. You broke my wrist," he said through clenched teeth.

"Get the frak outta my way," Tabby growled, letting go of his arm.

The technician spoke to his AI and my heart sank. He'd called for security and another medical technician. We followed the tech over to the clinic where he started working on Marny after asking us to stand in the hallway.

"Tabitha Masters." Two men approached. They were wearing side arms and had 'Belirand Security' emblazoned on their chests.

"That's me," she answered. I wondered how much trouble she was in.

"You need to come with us."

A BITTER PILL

I'd been sitting in the security office waiting room for two hours when Mihael came in. He was accompanied by another man and a woman, both in their late twenties. Mihael trailed slightly behind the man who had shoulder length black hair. I was surprised when the group walked directly up to me instead of checking in with the officer at the desk. I stood to meet them.

"Hoffen?" The dark haired man asked. He spoke softly and with a Russian accent similar to Mihael's.

"That's me," I said and held my hand out to shake. It was something that Big Pete had drilled into me.

He looked at my hand for a moment and then back up at my face.

"You need to keep a better handle on your crew," he said.

They were here to file a report on the incident. I'd already given my statement and Tabby was being held until they decided how to proceed. According to Marny, penalties from Belirand could be steep.

"I don't believe I know your name," I said allowing my hand to drop to my side.

"I'm trying to decide what we're going to do about this," he said, ignoring my implied question. "I hate to get off to such a bad start, especially since we'll be living so close to each other."

"Petar, we need to punish the bitch. She broke my wrist," Mihael said.

I took a step toward Mihael. "Watch your mouth," I said.

"You would think someone in your position would be more conciliatory. I have the power to cause you a great deal of problems," the one named Petar said. He was clearly the leader as both Mihael and the woman hung on his every word.

I caught myself. I wanted to let him know what I thought about his power, but he was right. If Mihael pushed, it could put a substantial crimp in our plans.

I nodded, accepting his words. "He's talking about my fiancé who, might I add, dropped him like a rock with a simple wrist lock. But you're right. You have some power here. What do you want from me?"

"I want you to keep your *bitch* on a leash," he said looking in my face, daring me to react.

We stood there for thirty seconds staring each other down and I choked back several responses.

"Do we have a problem here?" The security officer on duty had noticed our standoff and approached.

I broke eye contact and responded. "No, officer. I was just explaining to Petar and Mihael how badly Tabby felt for the misunderstanding."

I saw the glimmer of a smirk cross Petar's face. I so badly wanted to wipe it off.

"If she makes an apology, we'll consider this matter closed. I wouldn't want bad blood with our future neighbors," Petar said, still looking at me.

The officer said. "That seems more than fair."

"At dinner tonight," Petar said.

"What?" I asked.

"In front of my crew," he said.

"Are you frakking serious?"

"I'd take the deal, Captain," the security officer answered. "There's a chance the magistrate could refuse to let her traverse the gate."

I looked at him. No way was Tabby going to be okay with this.

"You'll let her walk, now?" I asked.

"Yes. Send me a recording of a sincere apology and I'll dismiss the matter. If she doesn't deliver, I'll have to pursue the matter further."

"I'll make it happen," I said.

"Wait here," he said and walked away.

"We're done," Petar said, looping an arm possessively around the woman whom he'd ignored up to this point.

I turned away and waited for Tabby. A few minutes later she emerged, following behind the officer. She smiled sheepishly and I was glad that Mihael and Petar were already gone.

"What'd you say to them? They said I was going to be locked up for several days," she said, once we were in the hallway.

I steered her in the direction of the ship. We had two hours before the expedition banquet and I thought it would be best if we didn't mix with other crews for a while.

"You're not going to like it," I said.

She stopped and placed a hand on my shoulder. "What?"

"You have to apologize to Mihael."

"Right. That's not going to frakking happen. He broke Marny's arm. Are they going to do anything about that?"

"No, they're not. You know how hard it is to prove that he intentionally redirected her. And, we were playing a Double-B match."

"What's that got to do with it?"

"There's an expectation that you have decent, basic skills if you're playing Double-B," I said.

"So they can play dirty?"

"That's not the point."

"What is?" Tabby's face was getting redder by the moment.

"The point is, they're threatening to not let you continue with the expedition if this doesn't get resolved."

That set her back. "They'd do that?"

"Yes. I don't like it any better than you do, but there are a lot of people depending on us. You need to fix this," I said.

"Frak. I'll do it. But this isn't over."

"Tabby."

"Don't Tabby me. He broke Marny's arm. He'd better stay clear."

"Knock it off. Belirand's watching us now. You're going to stay clear of him."

She turned without saying anything else and stalked down the hallway. I didn't like that I had to be the heavy in this, but Marny had warned us to stay clear of Belirand and we hadn't been able to do that for more than an hour. I didn't like the position Tabby was putting me in. We continued on to the ship, Tabby two meters in front, shoulders set in defiance.

We arrived at the ship having navigated the distance in an uneasy silence.

"My hero," Marny said when we entered the berth deck where she, Mom and Ada were sitting.

"How's your arm?" Tabby asked.

Marny held it up, sporting a solid medical wrap. "Clean break. I'll be as good as new in a week. Did Cap sweet talk 'em out of holding you?"

"That's not what I'd call it," she answered.

I shook my head but didn't rise to the bait. "I'm going to go up and check on Nick," I said.

***

I was in the office next to the captain's quarters researching the trading potential of Tipperary. I already knew there were three habitable planets. They each showed promise, but unlike Vermeer in Bethe Peierls there were substantial negatives to each.

The first, Hipparchus, closest to the system's young star, was named for the ancient Greek astronomer. The planet had a thriving ecosystem which provided an oxygen rich atmosphere. Colonists had found it difficult to set up a permanent location as they struggled against the near constant volcanic activity.

The next planet was Curie. Sixty percent sand, twenty percent ocean and twenty percent tropical rainforest, Curie was by far the most successful and populated planet in the system. Its primary export was precious stones and crystals of all sorts.

The Descartes asteroid belt was located between Curie and Grünholz. It was theorized that the belt was actually formed by two planets or planetoids that had originally shared the solar position and at some point collided, breaking apart into the belt.

Grünholz was the next habitable planet in line. It was larger than earth and boasted a constant cloud cover. It had a thriving biomass, but its primary downfall was the lack of diversity in its terrain. Ninety-five percent of the planet was covered in a shallow sheath of water.

Cool hands slipped down my chest from behind and I smelled the light fragrance that Tabby sometimes wore. We'd been apart for an hour and whatever annoyance I'd felt toward her had dissipated.

"You still mad at me?" she asked with her lips brushing my ear. It was an unfair maneuver on her part, but quite effective.

I reached up, grabbed her hand and swiveled to look at her. "How could I ever be mad at you?"

She threw one leg over the top of mine and sat on my lap, straddling me. "I do appreciate you bailing me out. I just don't think it's fair that I have to apologize to that dick-weed." She slid in closer and looked into my face, interested in my answer. Her physical closeness was starting to make it difficult for me to think clearly.

"I couldn't agree more. I'm always on your side, no matter what, Tabbs. I just need to get us to Tipperary. And I don't think we're done with these jackasses."

She pulled her suit liner off her shoulder and down to her waist and then wrapped her long fingers around my face, pulling me in for a kiss. "I'll take care of it, but maybe we shouldn't talk about this now," she said softly. I think at that moment she could have said anything and I'd have thought it was a good idea.

***

"Cap. Are you two going to come to the banquet tonight?" Marny's voice woke me up. I'd fallen asleep with Tabby snuggled in next to me.

"Oh, right. What time is it?" I asked.

"Jake has watch and the rest of us are headed over. It's almost 1800," she said.

"We're coming. Save us a seat," I said and closed the comm.

"We need to get going." I nudged Tabby. I marveled at how peaceful my fierce little warrior was while she slept naked in bed next to me. I jumped out of bed and into the shower only to be joined by her a few minutes later.

It was hard to leave her in the shower, but I also knew we were only delaying the inevitable. I checked my HUD for information on the banquet's location and saw that they suggested civilian clothing. Apparently, the entire station was double walled and considered L-1 habitation or better. I pulled on my blazer, cream colored shirt, blue jeans and best of all, my cowboy boots.

"Don't you look fancy," Tabby said when she finally got out of the shower. Since I was already dressed, I leaned back on the bed and watched her dry off.

"I wondered when I'd get a chance to wear this," she said, ignoring my lechery and pulling on a thin black dress that made it down to mid-thigh. To say that it was tight was something of an understatement, but I wasn't about to complain.

"Ready?" I asked as I stood up.

Tabby pulled on shiny black high heels and then slipped her arm into my own. We said good bye to Jake who had volunteered to take the watch, and walked out of *Hotspur* and down the attached gangplank into the station.

Music greeted us as we approached our destination. At the door, we were met by an official looking woman holding a reading pad.

"Captain Hoffen and Miss Masters," she said. I felt Tabby stiffen slightly. I suspected she was worried the woman would make reference to the trouble we'd had earlier in the day. "If you'll follow me, I'll take you to your table."

The room was filled with people all seated around tables covered with white cloths. It reminded me of the formality we'd experienced on the *Kuznetsov* when Commander Sterra had hosted a formal dinner. I did a quick estimation. Fifteen tables with an average of six at each table meant there were nearly a hundred people in attendance.

"Here we are," the woman said.

Ada and Celina were seated at the table with a young family. A little girl was seated on Ada's lap.

"Hello, Liam, Tabby," Celina said.

The man, who was in his mid-twenties, stood and held his hand out to be shaken. He wore a welcoming smile.

"Mademoiselle," he said in a thick accent as he shook Tabby's hand. His name was Queletin and he introduced us to his wife, Elsene and daughter, Sevene.

"You'll be our new neighbors," Elsene said with an equally thick accent.

"I suppose that's right. Although the claims are pretty spread out, you could be quite a ways away," I said.

She gave me a quizzical look, which Ada caught. "No, she's right, Liam. Belirand arranged the tables so that people would be seated closest to their neighbors."

"Oh, I apologize. I didn't know," I said looking back to the woman.

She appeared to be older than her husband by a few years. "No apology necessary. You couldn't have known. They announced it once we were seated. Have you much experience as a miner?" she asked.

I smiled, I liked that she didn't mince words. "Roger that. Tabbs and I grew up on Colony 40. My dad," I nodded to an adjacent table where he and Mom were having an animated conversation with another family, "was the miner. But, I suppose he rubbed off on me. How about you?"

"I was also raised in a mining family," Elsene said. "Queletin has never mined before, but he is excited to learn. What kind of equipment do you use?"

For the next hour as different courses arrived, Elsene grilled the table, but mostly me, about our mining experience and techniques, how we would move ore to Belirand, how we'd set up our camp, and nearly every aspect of life on the new mining claims. I wasn't sure why, but I didn't share that we didn't intend to be full-time residents. She seemed driven to get started.

"We've already been approached by Petar Kiirilov from Oberrhein about using their hauling service," she finally said after I'd shared that Ada would be in charge of our ore hauling runs. "They're asking for twenty percent, but they'll also provide security if we commit before we set sail. Have they approached you?"

The mention of Oberrhein soured my stomach and Tabby shot me an annoyed look. "Not yet, although I don't think we'll be interested in that. I'm sure we'll have open space on the *Adela Chen* if you want to consider an alternative. I'm sure Captain Chen can work out favorable pricing for you. Twenty percent seems high to me."

"I thought so too, but we have limited alternatives," Elsene said.

"Dear." Queletin caught his wife's attention. "I believe we should retire for the evening." At some point in the conversation Sevene had fallen asleep on Ada's lap.

"I've been a terrible boor," Elsene said, "I've completely monopolized the conversation."

"Not at all." I stood as Queletin picked up the sleepy Sevene from Ada.

Once they'd left, Celina quipped, "Remind me why I came to a miner's banquet?"

"It wasn't that bad," Ada said. "Sevene is adorable."

"If that woman said mining laser one more time I thought I was going to scream. Let's head back and see if we can get a card game going. I promised Jake I'd bring back dessert," Lena said.

"Tabby, are you and Liam in for some cards?" Ada asked.

"I have something I have to do first, but we'll be back in an hour or less," Tabby answered.

Since we were already standing, Tabby and I walked over to the table where Mom and Dad were chatting with a middle aged couple. A girl, a little older than Sevene, fidgeted in her mother's arms, clearly bored.

"Ah, Liam, Tabitha, meet our soon-to-be neighbors, Frimunt and Annalise Licht. They have quite a tribe. Let's see if I can remember – there's Wilma lying on Annalise. She has twin older brothers, Merley and Ulran. Then there's Ortel and finally, Selig?" Dad said, looking to Annalise for approval.

"Excellent memory, Peter," Annalise said.

"Frimunt and Annalise mined over on Terrence for a time," Dad said.

"Oh? Did you know Celina and Jenny then?" I asked.

"Terrible thing that happened to those two. I'm so happy to see they've made it through. I wasn't completely sure how all that worked out," she said. I felt uncomfortable in the conversation. Lena and Jenny's story wasn't mine to tell and I wasn't about to start now.

"Anna," Frimunt said in a stern voice. "It'd be none of our business."

"Oh, Frimunt. I'm just being friendly," she said.

"It looks like they're all getting along pretty well," I said. Jack, Jenny and what I presumed were the Licht boys were playing a card game at the adjacent table.

From the corner of my eye I caught a Belirand security officer approaching our table.

"Miss Masters?" The man had strong Asian features.

"Yes. That's me," Tabby answered.

"I'm Ryon Sung. Lieutenant Minso asked that I accompany you on your task. Will you comply?" I could tell the conversation made him uncomfortable.

"Of course, Mr. Sung. We were headed there just now. Are you able to help me locate them?" Tabby asked.

Adrenaline soured my stomach. In my mind I could see this going poorly in so many ways.

"Yes. This way, please," he said.

"What's this about?" Dad asked. The appearance of the security officer had perked him up.

"We need to clear up a misunderstanding," I said. "We'll see you back on the ship."

"Are you okay?" he asked.

"We're good, Dad. Thanks," I said.

We followed Officer Sung through the banquet hall which was more than half empty at this point. I searched out and located the full table where Mihael sat. I recognized many of the occupants, but there were a couple we hadn't yet met.

"Tabitha Masters," Petar said as we approached. I noticed that the conversation at the table had stopped entirely as we approached.

"Do I know you?" she asked.

"No, but I'd enjoy getting to know you," he said raising his eyebrows suggestively.

"Right," she said and turned to Mihael. "I'm here to fulfill my part of our agreement."

"Are you so much of a manx that you required a security escort? Hoffen, I might have underestimated your predicament. Perhaps this bitch is too much for you," Petar said. He sounded like he might have been drinking.

"Keep it civil," Officer Sung said, placing a hand on his sidearm.

"Apologies," Petar said, spreading his hands as if he were being gracious.

"Miss Masters?" Officer Sung prompted.

"Mihael Ivov. I sincerely apologize for removing your hand from my shoulder and forcibly driving you to your knees, causing you to scream in pain and for breaking your wrist. I was completely out of line, overpowering you in this way and embarrassing you in front of the entire viewing gallery. I sincerely hope I haven't caused you irreparable emotional distress. I hope you will accept my apology, which I freely give."

"You frakking ... "

Officer Sung stepped between Tabby and the lunging Mihael.

"Mihael," Petar said, raising his voice.

"This isn't done," Mihael said.

I looked to Officer Sung, who shrugged. "That was sufficient. Lieutenant Minso wanted me to tell you that we've revoked your pod-ball privileges for the duration of this expedition, Miss Masters. And, Mr. Ivov, Mr. Kiirilov, Mr. Hoffen and Miss

Masters, you are to keep your distance from each other."

I saw the flush starting to rise on Tabby's cheeks.

"Thank you, Officer." I led Tabby away before she could say anything I would regret.

FRIENDLY ADVICE

Marny broke the watch into two hour shifts. With nine of us available, it wasn't a hardship. My first shift came at 0200 the next day. I was used to early morning shifts and decided to stay awake, playing cards on the bridge. By the time my watch started, all but Tabby and Nick had turned in. Actually, Tabby had passed out on the couch, so she didn't really count. I pulled her legs straight and covered her with a blanket. Her shift followed mine and I didn't want to wake her.

I walked forward to the cockpit and relieved Celina. "Do you want an escort back to *Sterra's Gift*?" I asked.

"I'll be okay. We're the next slip over and the station's security feed has been clear for quite a while," she said.

"Roger that. Ping me when you're on the ship?"

This earned me a smile from the once pirate. "You make me feel bad for trying to bash your head in back on the outpost."

"Who'd have thought we'd end up friends?" I asked.

Celina chuckled. "Not me, that's for sure."

"You're good people, Lena. You deserved better."

"Are you angling for free coffee at the diner?" she asked.

"It sounds like owning a restaurant will be right up your alley," I said.

"Jenny and I used to run Magee's Diner on Terrence."

I knew she was planning to open a diner but didn't know details. "How did you manage the lease, were you able convert Mars Credits into something local?"

She sat back on the arm of the chair. "No. Well, sort of. They're holding an abandoned diner. We have two months to take occupancy. I submitted a business plan, along with the equipment and supplies we're bringing. The lease is free for the first year and they'll ramp up to normal, commercial rates over the second year."

"That's an incredible deal," I said.

"It's risky. If the population of Léger Nuage isn't interested in what we have to offer, we'll be out of luck."

"How many other eating places do they have?"

"Three and they're all bars. We're gambling that people will want a different type of dining experience."

"I hope it works out for you," I said.

Celina stood up. "Thanks, have a good night."

I watched as she walked down the gangplank, through the secure airlock and over to *Sterra's Gift*. As promised, she pinged me once she'd entered the ship.

On forward holo, show Descartes Asteroid Belt and color code the different claims.

I'd done enough security watches to know that I needed something to keep my mind busy as I waited for absolutely nothing to happen. You'd have to be nuts to cross Belirand at their most prestigious terminal. A shoot first, ask questions later approach to EVAs (extra vehicular activity) by Belirand Station Security had pretty much eliminated most of our concerns.

The belt's configuration was becoming more familiar and the highly saturated, colorized asteroids looked like they were straight from a cartoon vid.

Make all of our claims close shades of blue and everyone I've seen associated with Oberrhein close shades of light gray.

Our claims were centrally located in the occupied portion of the belt. The Oberrhein claims spread out starting at one edge and working their way in, past our claims. While we were clumped together, Oberrhein had eight claims that were evenly spaced, with a single non-Oberrhein claim between each of them. Notably, Ada's claim was between Teodorov Tsankov and Vasil Stanislavov.

The arrangement of claims was hardly a problem, but given the interaction we'd had with Petar and Mihael, watching them was in our best interest.

Highlight Carré and Licht family claims.

I was curious about the two families we'd met and was surprised to see two Licht claims. As expected, Frimunt & Annalise, the parents of the large tribe, had a claim, but unexpectedly their eldest son, Selig, had an adjacent claim.

How old is Selig?

"Selig Licht is eighteen stans, four months," the AI responded.

Show proposed site for Loose Nuts Co-Op. Limit field of view to just Loose Nuts related claims.

The display in front of me shrunk so that on one side was Ada's claim and on the other was Nick and Marny's. Big Pete's and my own claim were sandwiched between them. On the border between Nick's claim and mine, an empty spot was highlighted. This was where Nick had proposed we put the co-op. I hadn't spent enough time looking at the layout of the various rocks in our claims, but didn't really think a completely open spot was the best choice for the co-op. I also knew that Nick and Dad would have thought pretty hard about this and I was missing necessary information.

Are there plans to fill this location? If Nick had worked up a plan, he would have used an AI to construct it and I doubted he would keep it secret from me.

"There are three proposed plans for Co-Op construction," the AI responded.

Show end result of each.

The AI cycled through three different completed structures. The first was completely constructed from steel. It was a gorgeous structure, showing housing for dozens of families, a pier with enclosed docking bays and a spacious ore storage and refining platform. I loved it, but there was no way we'd be able to manufacture anything that elaborate, even if we had twenty years.

The next was more practical. A large asteroid, about a tenth the size of Colony 40's P-Zero, had been towed away from my claim, flattened on one side and hollowed out on the other for living spaces.

The final plan showed the same large asteroid, but this time it had been cut in half and the ore handling and refining stations doubled in size. It was an ambitious production design that would take at least three years to complete.

"Which one do you like?" Nick asked as he approached from behind.

"What are you doing up?" I asked.

"Couldn't sleep. I didn't want to wake Marny, so I thought I'd get some work done," he said.

"The first one, but I don't think it's very practical. It would take us forever to refine that much material," I said, answering his initial question.

"I agree. We couldn't start with that," he said. "How about between the other two?"

"I'm not sure about splitting that size of an asteroid, so I guess I like the plan where we flatten one side and live on the other. Getting the co-op up fast is a great idea since the Descartes belt is between two habitable planets. It's not like Colony 40 which was so far from Mars. That particular plan would also keep us true to the mission, specifically not tying us down as full-time miners."

"That was what Big Pete thought too. How do you feel about donating that asteroid? It's the biggest one in your entire claim and according to your dad, it's loaded with iron." he said.

Show remaining asteroids in my claim larger than a million cubic meters with a high iron survey.

The holographic projector showed fifteen asteroids ranging from a million to four million cubic meters. It was more material than I could mine in five life times.

"That works for me. I have no desire to be a miner. I just want to be an old guy who leases out his claim for a bunch of money," I said.

Nick laughed. "Well, you'd get an owner's share of the minerals from the split and then it'd become the property of *Loose Nuts* once Belirand turns the leases into ownership."

"Works for me," I said.

***

My alarm woke me at 1300 so we wouldn't miss the captain's meeting with Belirand. I slid out from under Tabby's arm and forced myself to look away from her naked form on top of the covers. Her synth skin easily adjusted to the minor variations in temperature aboard ship and for some reason she'd decided that au naturale was her default.

"You've got twenty minutes," I whispered and jumped in the shower.

I pulled on a fresh suit liner and my vac-suit. Tabby was still passed out on the bed and would require more work.

"Hey, I need to leave in ten. You don't have to come if you don't want to," I said.

She rolled over pulling the sheet with her and covering up. "What is it again?" she asked with half open eyes.

"Captain's meeting. Not sure exactly what they're going to cover," I said.

"Alright, frak," she said and rolled off the bed, scooping her suit liner off the floor. I winced, the liners did a nice job of staying clean, but I had a hard time putting a liner on after I'd taken it off. She made a quick trip into the bathroom.

"Mom? Ada? Are you ready to head over to the Captain's meeting?" I asked over the comm.

"We're with Lena on *Sterra's Gift*," Mom replied almost immediately.

"Meet on the concourse in five?" I asked.

"We'll be there," she replied.

"Meet who?" Tabby asked as she exited the head. She'd braided her thick, copper colored hair and neatly laid it over her shoulder.

"Mom and Ada." I picked up my heavy flechette and loaded it into the shoulder holster I generally reserved for when I was wearing a coat.

"You think it's a good idea to be packing?" Tabby asked.

"Something feels off. I can't put my finger on it," I said.

"Want me to bring a piece?"

"Up to you. I'm mostly just sending a message to Oberrhein."

"I'm in and don't worry. I won't shoot first," Tabby said.

I laughed nervously. I knew she meant it and I hoped she'd live by it.

We met Ada and Mom on the concourse in front of the gate that led to *Sterra's Gift*.

"Anyone know where we're going?" I asked, joking. I knew it drove Mom nuts when I wasn't organized. She looked at a vid screen embedded in the wall, which had an arrow pointing to the left with the caption, 'Captain's Invitational.' So much for getting lost.

The room was considerably smaller than the banquet hall and had soft chairs lined up facing a speaker's podium. There was a table with cookies and coffee, which sounded like a good idea to me. As usual, we were just in time. Seating was limited, so we had to sit at the front.

A severe looking blonde woman, who was about my mom's age, walked to the front. She wore a blue dress with a Belirand logo over her left breast.

"Greetings intrepid adventurers. I'm Amanda Hoope, station administrator for Bethe Peierls Terminal and I'd like to extend a warm welcome to the Tipperary expedition members. I hope you've found our facilities to be a nice respite from the start of your long journey. For those of you who've traversed the TransLoc gates in the past, much of what I'm about to cover will be repetitive. That said, safe TransLocation is our highest priority."

I'd like to say that I listened to every last detail that she covered for the next half hour, but once she got going I found that she sounded like every other lecturer I'd ever heard. At one point, Tabby jabbed me in the ribs, as I must have started to doze. Thank Jupiter that Tabby had always been an excellent student and had the ability to survive a droning speaker.

"Finally, for those ships without TransLoc engines, we'll temporarily attach a harness to allow the ship to enter fold-space. As that fits most of the ships in this expedition, we've established a schedule for this outfitting process. I thank you for your attention. Are there any questions?" She asked.

"I read that you're requesting we sail between the gates as a fleet. Is this mandatory?" It was Petar who'd asked.

"No, Mr. Kiirilov, it is not. You simply need to arrive at the New Pradesh gate on or ahead of the expedition schedule," she said.

"And if we get to New Pradesh early, will you see us through? We tire of waiting," he replied.

"I apologize for the inconvenience, but no, you will not be admitted early. The TransLoc gates are most efficient when we send a large group through together."

"What about security?" He pushed again.

To her credit Administrator Hoope was unflapped by the questions. "The expedition will be accompanied by the cruiser *Cape of Good Hope*."

"Are you going to require a turret lock the entire trip?" he asked.

"No, Mr. Kiirilov. We only require a weapons lockdown when you are within one hundred thousand kilometers of our TransLoc terminals. But please understand, Captain LeGrande is under orders to aggressively eliminate all threats to the expedition, whether they come from outside the expedition or from within."

"And when will this babysitting end?" Petar asked, clearly not concerned if he was frustrating Administrator Hoope.

"That is not information we are willing to share at this point. I'd be happy to answer any other questions you have if you'd like to make an appointment. Are there questions from anyone else?" she asked.

His questions had caused a stir within the room. At least I didn't have to wonder why I had a bad feeling.

"If that's all, then we're dismissed. Captain Hoffen, would you join me at the front with your crew?"

Since we'd sat in the front row, it wasn't difficult. She looked up as we approached.

"Ah yes, Captain Hoffen. And this must be Captain Chen." She held her hand out and we introduced the entire group.

"Miss Masters. Ah, yes. I feel like I should apologize for your treatment yesterday. I've taken time to review the incidents. Taken out of context, your response to Mr. Ivov was excessive. I also watched the events leading up to Miss Bertrand's accident. Formally, I believe our security personnel handled the situation correctly. Informally, as a former pod-ball contestant, the violation was clear. I understand your reaction and apologize that you were placed in that position."

"Thank you," Tabby said.

"Please don't give me any reason to regret this admission," Hoope said.

"Is there anything else?" I asked.

"Indeed there is. We need your permission to decouple the Adela Chen from its barge and usher the barge through with a Belirand asset."

I looked at Ada and Mom. They had a lot more experience with the *Adela Chen* than I did.

"That's probably best, Liam," Ada said. "We could even lash her to the barge. There's plenty of room."

I looked at Mom who nodded in agreement.

"Would that work?" I asked Hoope.

"I'll bring it up with our engineers. Worst case, we'll outfit the *Adela Chen* with a harness," she answered.

***

Celina traded shifts with Big Pete so he could attend the evening's banquet. She'd emphatically insisted that if she had to sit through another night of listening to the relative merits of a tungsten tip vs. nano-steel, she might end up depositing said tip somewhere it would become uncomfortable.

The seating for the second night had shifted and instead of sitting with Ada, Celina and the Carré's we were with Nick, Marny, Selig Licht and his younger three brothers.

"Selig, have you been mining since you were a kid?" I asked. It felt like we probably had a lot in common, both having grown up on a mining colony.

"Das right," he said. I had difficulty adjusting to his thick German accent. "I was born in our habitation dome."

"Do all you boys play pod-ball?" Marny asked looking around the table at the slightly younger Ortel and the twins – Ulran and Merley.

"We're really good," one of the twins said, excited to be given a chance to talk.

"Dah. Selig doesn't play anymore, but Ulran, Merley and I do all right," Ortel said.

"I saw that you were sitting with Jack and Jenny last night. You all should play together," I said.

"We did," Ulran or Merley said.

"How'd they do?"

"Jack is very good, but the girl, Jenny is new to the game," Ortel said.

"And Selig is sweet on Ada." It was the same twin who'd been doing all of the talking.

"Oh?" Tabby perked up and looked over to the eldest Licht.

"Be quiet, Merley. It is not for you to say," Selig said, but the damage was done and his ruddy face turned a brighter shade of red.

I tossed Selig a lifeline. "I heard they have a pod-ball court at Léger Nuage. I wonder if they'd let us start up a league."

This got Merley back to chatting.

"So Selig, are you going to put everyone on a single claim or split up right away? I noticed you have two claims," I said.

"The boys are very good at flying pod-jumpers, so Ortel and Father will be mining one claim and I'll be mining the other. I understand you might have the capacity to haul ore," he said.

"We do. We're not as serious about mining as it looks. My dad, Big Pete, is the serious miner. We'll be doing a minimum job on the other claims, although I think Ada might be a little more interested than I'd originally expected."

"Oberrhein approached Father with a proposition for hauling. Are you saying you won't be competing with them?"

"Oh, not at all. Captain Chen will definitely be hauling ore," I said. "We just haven't formalized what reasonable profit sharing for hauling is. I've heard Oberrhein is offering twenty percent. On Colony 40 we didn't have a long distance to haul ore, but twenty sounds high to me."

"It was similar on Terrence. Do you know what you'll start at?"

"I don't. Ada will be responsible for that. We'll probably start with some sort of cost plus arrangement. So cover fuel and a small profit," I said. "We've some interest from another family. What would you think about sitting down with them and Ada and talking it out?"

"I'd like that," he said. "This Ada. Is she single?"

"Ooh," Merley said. "See. I told you."

I was impressed at how Merley had ignored the conversation up to that point.

It was too late to save Selig, however, and his face turned bright red.

"I think you'll want to be careful when considering a shipper." I hadn't seen Petar walk up behind me. "I understand that security in the belt can be a tricky thing to guarantee."

Tabby spun toward him and I placed my hand on her arm. She had gone from zero to ready to fight in a heartbeat.

"There's no one in the belt right now. What would you know about security?" Tabby asked, dryly.

"Easy, Tabbs," I said.

"Yes. Reel in your leash. I just don't want Mr. Licht making a decision that he would surely regret in the future," Petar said.

"Get out of here, Kiirilov," I said. "Or would you like me to pass your threats along to Belirand. I believe you've been told to stay clear of us."

"Friendly advice," he said and walked away.

TRANSLOCATION

"Cap. I've got Belirand on the comm. They're looking to set the *Adela Chen* up," Marny called.

It was 1200 with eighteen hours until we'd enter fold-space and travel the hundred and forty seven light years to the Bethe Peierls system. I'd been wondering when they'd want to get us hooked up.

"I'll take it," I said.

"Captain Hoffen? This is Ok Moon Hee with Belirand. Would you be able to meet us at Engineering Bay 301? It's time to outfit the *Adela Chen* and your barge."

"Roger that. I'd like to bring my other captains along as well," I said.

"Understood. Fifteen minutes?"

"Can do. Hoffen, out," I said and closed the comm.

"Mom, Ada, can you meet me outside of *Hotspur*. Belirand is ready to work on the *Adela Chen*."

They both pinged back affirmative. I didn't know if we'd be doing an EVA, so I strapped on my AGBs for good measure.

"Marny, I'm taking Mom and Ada to work on the *Adela Chen*," I said into the comm.

"We'll keep an eye on things from here," Marny said.

Directions to the engineering bay showed up on my HUD. I flicked it open and saw the familiar vaporous blue arrow run out in front of me.

Mom and Ada were waiting at the bottom of the jetway.

"We've been watching them strap these engines onto ships all morning," I said as I motioned in the direction of the engineering bay.

"They better go easy on my girl," Ada said protectively.

I smiled. "Someone said you and Selig sat together at the banquet last night." Tabby and I had skipped the previous night's banquet, not interested in another confrontation with Petar and Oberrhein.

"Loose lips, Captain. Loose lips," Ada said.

"Oh, come on, are you really going to leave me hanging?" I looked to Mom for support. Of course Mom shrugged as if it was the first she'd heard of it.

Ada flashed me her always brilliant smile, enjoying the attention. "I might as well confess. Jenny won't stop talking about it anyway. Selig is every bit a gentleman and we had a nice evening."

"That's not much of a confession," I said.

"I found the Carrés to be nice too. Their daughter Sevene is adorable. Did you know that Queletin has absolutely no experience in mining?" Ada asked conspiratorially. I suspected she was trying to change the subject.

"Elsene seems more than capable though. Don't you think?" Mom asked.

Ada nodded in agreement. "Definitely."

Moments later we arrived at a double wide airlock marked 'Engineering Bay 0301.' I palmed the door, which lit blue and announced. "Please wait for authorized personnel."

The doors slid open and a narrow Asian woman greeted us.

"Captains Hoffen, Hoffen and Chen. I'm Lead Engineer Ok Moon Hee. Thank you for your prompt arrival," she said. We exchanged the obligatory handshakes. "Follow me and we can talk as we walk."

She led us down a hallway into a large hangar.

"Barge traffic through the TransLoc gate is relatively unusual but not unprecedented. The issue is that simply applying the standard TransLoc engine harness to the loosely connected Tug has proven to be unpredictable."

"Define unpredictable," I said.

"The Anino Trans Location system works by communicating a fold-space wave to the Anino TransLoc engines with an extraordinary degree of precision. The engines create a relativity bubble around the ship that allows it to remain on that wave. If any portion of the craft exits that wave, it becomes subject to normal space. Even with our best resources, the effects of those forces are unpredictable. In layman's terms, the result is always bad," she said.

"Define bad." I was pretty sure I understood what bad might indicate.

"Most of the time the ship is pulled from the relativity bubble and breaks apart. The ship and its cargo are spread unpredictably throughout the galaxy."

I nodded. It was a unique, if not well applied, definition of bad.

"And you have a way to make this safe?" I asked.

"We do," she said. She'd led us to the edge of a nearly transparent blue pressure barrier separating the engineering bay from space. We were a few hundred meters away from the *Adela Chen*. "Instead of mating the tug and barge with your traditional linkage, we'd like to build a solid superstructure that mounts to the barge and fits as an exoskeleton around the *Adela Chen*."

"Frak. That'd make sailing her nearly impossible," I said.

"True enough if you were going to sail in normal space. The thing is, in fold-space, your only responsibility is keeping the ship centered along the fold-space wave. We've reviewed Captain Chen's and Captain Hoffen's sailing records and believe they have more than sufficient skill to master this task."

"You're asking Ada and me to sail a rig that could become unstable and spread us over half the galaxy?" I asked.

"No, Captain Hoffen. We would feel more comfortable with Captain Silver Hoffen as the other pilot," she responded.

I looked to Mom and then Ada. It would have been a perfect moment to give me a hard time, but neither of them looked to be in a joking mood.

"I'd want a few hours in the chair to see how it sails," Mom said.

"Wait. We don't need to do this," I said. "We didn't sign up for this." My mind was spinning.

"You are correct, Captain. You have the right to back out," Ok Moon said.

"And undo all of our plans? That's not going to happen," Mom said. "I'll sail her."

"Not without me," Ada said.

Ok Moon gestured toward the ship. "We've already prepared the harness and with your permission I will have it installed."

Both Mom and Ada looked at me and I felt the weight of the position they were putting me in.

"I'd like to reserve the option to back out if we deem the ship too difficult to maneuver," I said.

"Of course, Captain. We will also provide you with a simulation to prepare Captains Hoffen and Chen for fold-space."

"Let's do it," I said.

"Very well," Ok Moon turned to look through the pressure barrier.

A steel superstructure slowly sailed from below us toward the *Adela Chen*. It was carried along by something that looked a lot like a common pod-jumper.

"Cap. There's unusual activity near the *Adela Chen*. Can you advise?" Marny's voice sounded in my ear.

"That's us Marny. Belirand is hooking up a rig for our trip through the TransLoc gate."

"Aye. I hoped that's what we had going on. We'll stand down," she said. I wondered what she might have done if I hadn't explained.

The pilot expertly guided the structure into place. Once set, a welding crew EVA'd from the pod-jumper to make permanent connections.

"We'll remove the structure once you arrive in Tipperary," Ok Moon said. "If I could get the captains to reboard their ship, we'll provide instruction on how we've seen this configuration work the best."

"Let's go," I said.

Mom placed her hand on my shoulder and held me back.

"What?" I asked.

"This will be a hard lesson, but you need to trust your crew, Liam. This is Ada's and mine to deal with."

Ada smiled. She wasn't about to get between Mom and me. It was hard to take. I thought of myself as the best pilot, but if I was honest, when it came to the *Adela Chen*, Mom and Ada both had substantially more experience.

"Okay. Check in once you're done," I said.

Mom gave me a quick side-hug. "Pete said you were growing up. I wasn't sure, but maybe he was right."

***

The hour of departure finally arrived. Mom and Ada had drilled for ten hours with the harness and in the end, their confidence was high. Sailing in fold-space was said to be less disruptive than hard-burn, but just like hard-burn it was the moments around transition that caused the most problems.

Both *Sterra's Gift* and *Hotspur* had originally been designed with fold-space in mind. And according to Weird Wally, *Hotspur* had been designed specifically for travel through the gates. Belirand control walked us through the process anyway. I wasn't opposed to their instruction, although it felt like they went out of their way to describe many things that seemed overly obvious.

The fifty-two hour trip would be relatively easy. Our AIs were designed to keep the ships dead in the middle of the fold-space bubble. Tabby and I split up so we had an experienced pilot on both ships. Me on *Sterra's Gift* and her on *Hotspur*.

Things on the *Adela Chen* would be more difficult. Mom and Ada would swap shifts throughout the entire journey, starting with two hour shifts, then stretching to four. Dad insisted he ride along to help 'keep things lively.'

An interesting benefit of fold-space was that we'd be able to communicate normally with any ship in our bubble. We were in the last of three bubbles. The first two each held twelve ships and our bubble only had five – our three, the Belirand Cruiser, *Cape of Good Hope*, and the Oberrhein ship, *Karelia*.

A few hours before departure, we started a giant lineup. It reminded me of grade school on Colony 40. Only instead of placing my hand on the person in front of me, I was lined up a hundred meters on their aft. The Belirand Terminal was laid out so an entire raft of ships would spool out in a row across the expansive deck and wait for the TransLoc gate to establish communication with its twin in Bethe Peierls. With communication established, a fold-space wave would be harmonized and ships that were part of the same bubble would engage their TransLoc engines.

Watching it happen before experiencing it was both terrifying and exhilarating. Initially, it didn't look like much was happening, with the ships sitting stationary in a line over the platform. When the gates fired up, warning lights raced down the length of the platform. As the lights passed each ship, their TransLoc engines would fire and glow bright orange. By the time the lights arrived at the end of the platform, the ships had simply disappeared.

The concept of fold-space was that ships were taking an alternative route through space, as if jumping through folds of cloth. But, the idea that hundreds of thousands of tonnes of ships simply vanished was hard to process.

"Captain Hoffen, we'd like to synchronize the movement of the final raft of ships onto the Terminal. Will you consent?"

A request popped up on my forward vid screen requesting temporary control of *Sterra's Gift*. I'd already been warned about this, so I complied. Shortly after, I glided along behind *Cape of Good Hope* and *Karelia* onto the Terminal deck. Having already watched it happen, I knew what to expect but it was still nerve racking. According to the briefing, once we were in fold-space, it was our responsibility to stay on the wave and in the bubble. Up to that point, Belirand would be in control.

"*TransLoc engines engaging in 30 seconds,*" *Sterra's Gift* announced. Jake, Celina, Jack and Jenny were all on the bridge, every bit as curious as I was. I pushed the countdown onto the forward holo display.

At exactly zero, the TransLoc engines engaged and the world

turned inside out, or so it seemed. Reading about the experience and feeling it were two different things. I can say with some certainty that it is weird. When transitioning from normal to fold-space it is as if, for a few moments, every bit of matter around you has elongated irrationally. Colors blurred as people and objects seemed to blend together, like we were hot birthday candles smeared together horizontally.

Almost as quickly as it started, the visual dissonance ended. The only thing that indicated we were in fold-space was the movement of the stars, which were now jumping around as if I were blinking my eyes and spinning around. It was unpleasant enough that I decided it wasn't a view I was interested in.

"*Adela Chen*, check in," I requested. We'd been briefed that If there was going to be a problem, it would occur within the first few seconds after transition.

"*Adela Chen*, A-Okay," Ada's cheerful voice replied. "What'd you think of that trip?"

"Not a big fan," I said. "*Hotspur*, check in," I continued. I felt a pulse on my finger under my ring. I was reassured to know that Tabby was doing well.

"*Hotspur*, kicking ass!" Tabby replied. I should have known she would have thought that was cool.

"What do you make of that?" I asked, looking back at the assembled group on the bridge.

Celina and Jake were both seated on the couch, obviously looking out at the stars.

"It's hard to look at," Celina said.

"No kidding," I said.

Jake cleared his throat. "As you probably know, the fold-space wave establishes a non-Euclidian path through the galaxy. Along that path we're literally changing our real or normal location almost constantly. The blinking you're observing is real, although we're actually changing position a hundred times faster than we're able to observe."

"That's going to get old in a hurry," I said.

"No kidding," Celina agreed.

For the next fifty hours we changed shifts every four. The blinking became less annoying as the trip continued, mostly because I made an effort to tune it out.

Arriving at Terminal Two was considerably less disruptive than leaving had been. The only real indication we were no longer in fold-space was that one second we were sailing along, stars blinking, and the next second we'd materialized a thousand kilometers from the station and the stars had ceased their mad dancing. A momentary feeling of deja-vu occurred, as Terminal Two appeared to be an exact copy of Terminal One.

"Incoming hail, Belirand Terminal Two," my AI informed me.

Open comm, I said.

"Greeting, *Sterra's Gift.* Welcome to Bethe Peierls. I'm transmitting instructions for refueling and rejoining the expedition's trek to Terminal Three. Will you need access to station services?"

"Greetings, Belirand. No, we're ready to get going," I said.

"Very well. Safe travels. Belirand out."

I regretted not exploring the Bethe Peierls star system but I also wanted to get on with our journey.

After refueling, we received navigation instructions that would have us join the other ships in the expedition. It was only a forty hour burn to Terminal Three, which would take us directly to the New Pradesh system.

THICK AS THIEVES

Arriving at Terminal Five was a welcome relief. It would take us from the New Pradesh system to our final destination of Tipperary. Belirand had been the model of efficiency, organizing our thirty some ships through the gates, regrouping us each time we exited the even gates to make our way to the next odd-gate for refueling.

"Ready to see your new home?" I asked Celina, who'd taken to hanging out on the bridge when she wasn't on duty.

"It's exciting. I'm probably more excited to stop sailing through fold-space, though," she said.

I laughed, although I agreed with her sentiment.

An hour after our arrival at Terminal Five we lined up once again on the platform. *Cape of Good Hope*, followed by the Oberrhein ship *Karelia*, then *Sterra's Gift*, followed by *Hotspur* and finally the *Adela Chen*.

Celina pointed out the window. "What's he up to?"

The *Karelia* appeared to be having trouble lining up on the platform, fading off to the starboard side. We were moments from trans-locating and the last thing anyone wanted was for a ship to be out of position. At the last moment, however, the *Karelia* slid back in line.

The universe unhinged, lights slid backwards and everything smeared around us. After our first trip, Ada compared the experience to living in an impressionist painting. I had to look up what she was talking about, but after some research, I thought it was about as good a description as could be had.

The second stage of TransLocation was riding the wave of fold-space. I looked out the armored glass expectantly waiting for the blinking stars to start.

"Liam!" Celina shouted at the same time a warning klaxon sounded.

We had barely entered fold-space and *Cape of Good Hope* was already listing heavily to starboard, in front of the *Karelia*. If they didn't adjust back into the wave, the ship would be ripped apart.

"Mayday, mayday, mayday. We've experienced a failure in our starboard TransLocation Engine and are unable to maintain course."

"Hail *Cape of Good Hope*, how can we help?" I asked.

"*Karelia*, we need you to close the distance and make physical contact with our starboard. We're sending instructions for your AI now."

Captain LeGrande was the very picture of a professional. The world as she knew it was breaking up and she was calmly explaining corrective action. A leadership trait I admired.

"Say again, *Cape of Good Hope*." It was Georgi who responded. The holo display showed him turned to the side gesticulating at something outside of the range of the holo transmitter. A moment later, the holo feed from Karelia blinked out.

Captain LeGrande's face pinched. Either she'd received a direct response or drew a conclusion from the *Karelia's* withdrawn feed. We waited for a few moments, watching as the *Cape* continued her dangerous slide toward the edge of the fold-space bubble.

"Captain LeGrande. They aren't answering. Recalibrate with my ship," I said.

Hail Karelia. "Make room, Georgi, I'm coming by on your starboard side."

"That's not advised, Captain Hoffen." The oily voice that responded was Petar.

I snarled. "It wasn't a request."

Show fold-space envelope on my HUD. Project a path to Cape of Good Hope.

There was just enough room to slide by and I accelerated.

"They're not moving," Celina said. She was seated right next to me.

"There's room." I tried to remain as calm as LeGrande.

"Move over, Georgi," Tabby commanded. "If you push *Sterra's Gift* out, I'll launch every missile on this boat up your ass!"

That must have gotten someone's attention as the *Karelia* moved over.

"Captain Hoffen, I need you to back down. You don't possess sufficient thrust to offset our trajectory," Captain LeGrande said.

"We'll see." I just cleared the *Karelia*. She was right, it was going to be tight. *Cape of Good Hope* was getting dangerously close to the edge of the fold-space bubble.

"No, Captain. Do not compound this tragedy. I'm uploading a data burst. Please see that it is delivered to Belirand."

I accelerated. Even without the AI, however, I could see we wouldn't make it.

The starboard side of *Cape of Good Hope* came in contact with the edge of the fold-space bubble and horrifically sheared off, disappearing from view. There would be no recovery.

"I'm sorry, Captain," I said. I wanted to scream, but I would honor her and her crew by respecting their last few moments.

The ship had no capability to stop its slide out of the bubble and unexpectedly, Captain LeGrande spun up her thrusters and accelerated into the void. It was a final act of selflessness.

"God Speed, Captain," I said quietly.

We watched as the ship disappeared, only small parts sailing along in the fold-space wave with us. Without engines to guide them, they'd eventually fall out of the bubble and drop into normal space.

Hail Belirand Terminal.

"Belirand Terminals Five and Six are not within communications range," the AI responded.

I slid *Sterra's Gift* back into the center of the bubble and tightened up the distance between us and *Karelia*.

"You okay, Liam?" It was Nick.

"Yes. How many were on *Cape of Good Hope*?"

"Forty-five souls," Marny said.

"Anyone catch what caused the failure?" Tabby's bust popped up onto the holo display next to Nick.

"No. Just before they declared their emergency, I saw them fade off to starboard and down about ten degrees," I said.

"It had to be Oberrhein," Tabby said. It was the easy conclusion.

"Careful, Tabbs. We didn't see anything like that. It's a big jump from being an asshat to murdering forty-five crew," I said. "Marny, any ideas?"

"No. *Karelia's* behavior *was* suspicious, but they could have just been protecting their crew," she said. "Send me your sensor logs. I'll get the same from *Adela Chen*. We'll see if we can make any sense of it."

"How about our quantum comm device?" Tabby asked. "Should we send a message to Mars Protectorate?"

"I'll send a message and have them relay it to Belirand," Marny said.

"Let's free those turrets. Until we know what happened, I'm working under the assumption that this could have been an act of sabotage," Tabby said.

"Roger that, but let me contact *Karelia*. If we unlimber our turrets, they may not accept our comm," I said.

"Roger, Wilco," Tabby replied.

Hail *Karelia*, I said.

"*Karelia*. What can I do for you, Captain Hoffen?" Petar had denied the holographic and video feeds again.

"Will you share your sensor logs from the events leading up to *Cape of Good Hope's* disaster? We're trying to piece together what occurred," I said.

"What's to be done about it?" he asked.

"That's what we're trying to determine. Will you comply?" I asked.

"No, Captain. We will leave the investigating to Belirand," he said and terminated communications.

Open comm, Adela Chen and Hotspur.

"What's going on, Liam?" Mom asked. Her face was drawn.

"Are you stable?" I asked.

"Roger that. Tell us what's happening."

"Marny, have you found anything new?" I asked.

"No, Cap. *Sterra's Gift* was in the best position for information and with the *Karelia* in the way, we were all perfectly blocked."

"How perfectly?"

"Not sure I understand your question," she said.

"Was *Karelia* blocking *Sterra's Gift's* view of the *Cape's* engine?" I asked.

"Yes. But, to imply that it was intentional would be a leap," she said.

That was enough for me. "We should unlimber the turrets."

"Hold on, Cap. We don't want to be seen as taking provocative action," Marny said. "We are in Belirand controlled space and they've taken a huge loss. They'll be jumpy about things as it is. I'll set up a monitor on *Karelia's* turrets and missile bay. If their status changes we can respond immediately. They won't want to mix it up with three ships in fold-space. Even if they got one of us, they'd have two more to deal with."

"I hope we don't regret this," Tabby said.

"We'll stay alert," Marny assured her. "Pete, I'm going to need your help. I want human eyes on those turrets until we're out of fold-space."

While I hadn't seen Dad on the holo, I knew, just as Marny did, that he was listening. "Oorah," was his one-word response. It was a greeting he reserved exclusively for other Marines. I had to admit it made me proud that he'd accepted Marny as one of his own.

I thumbed my ring and caught Tabby's eye. She held my gaze for a moment. I knew what she was thinking. Someone had murdered those sailors and she wanted to avenge them. Only the slightest thread of doubt kept her in check. But, if the *Karelia's* turrets moved a centimeter, she'd respond instantly.

I closed the comm and stared out the armor glass of the cockpit, trying to process the loss of forty-five souls. I hoped that Oberrhein had nothing to do with what had occurred, but a sinking feeling in my stomach told me otherwise.

Celina, who was seated in the other pilot's chair laid her hand on my arm. "Liam. We'll get through this. What can we do?"

I smiled. It was hard to imagine how far the two of us had come. From enemies to trusting our lives to each other.

"Take the helm?" I asked.

"Of course."

I got up and walked back to Jake. "I know you're already thinking about this, but you probably have a better chance than any of us at figuring out what happened. Any ideas?"

"TransLoc engines are simple. They rely on a high energy pulse transmitted through a resonating crystal. Failure is extraordinarily rare. The fuel is expensive, but again not complex. I wish I could crack that data burst from the *Cape*. I'd bet anything they sent a diagnostic of the engines and critical systems. It'd tell us a lot," he said.

"Any chance you can open it?" I asked.

"Probably not, but I'll try. Those Oberrhein are bastards," he said.

"Let me know if you need anything," I said.

***

"Incoming communication, Belirand Terminal Six," my AI informed me.

I'd been dozing in the pilot's chair, unwilling to leave the bridge of *Sterra's Gift* just in case something changed. We'd been sailing for just under fifty-two hours and were within fifteen minutes of arriving in the Tipperary system.

"I've got it, Lena," I said, trying to regain my alertness.

Open comm with all ships. "Go ahead, Belirand," I replied.

The flickering image of a dark skinned man, with graying hair appeared in front of me. Even as close as we were, I couldn't imagine how they were getting a signal to us. Fifteen minutes in fold-space could put us just about anywhere.

"Captain Hoffen. Station Administrator Atin Emre. We've received a comm via Mars Protectorate that there's been a mishap and we're unable to raise *Cape of Good Hope*. Please advise," he

91

said. At least that's what my AI thought he said. His image flickered and jumped as the AI fought to smooth it out.

I'd been practicing what to say if asked. "I regret to inform you that crew of *Cape of Good Hope*, including Captain LeGrande, has been lost. In short, the ship exited the fold-space bubble and was destroyed."

"Were any other ships involved?" he asked.

I wasn't sure what he meant by involved, so I decided to tell him what I knew without embellishment.

"No other ships were damaged. We have done all possible analysis and can find no cause. Captain LeGrande was able to send a data-burst. We'll start transmitting now, along with our own sensor logs," I said.

"Very well. We're requesting that all ships involved submit to a voluntary quarantine upon arrival until we are able to make a determination as to cause," he said.

"Roger, wilco. Hoffen out."

Marny, Nick and I had talked at length about how Belirand was likely to approach the situation. We had no doubt their requests would turn into demands in short order if we weren't compliant. And to be honest, we wanted to know what had happened as much as they did.

What was different, however, was the complement of two heavy cruisers. These cruisers weighed in at eight hundred tonnes each and stretched seventy meters. In the continuum of ships, they were halfway between a frigate and a corvette. Or more immediately important, two and a half times the size of *Hotspur*. I was glad we'd left the turrets locked down.

Incoming communication, Belirand Terminal Six.

"*Hotspur*, Liam Hoffen," I said.

"Captain Hoffen, Atin Emre. We're enforcing a communication blackout and request that you accompany the Belirand fleet to a holding area," he said.

"I understand. If this is voluntary, why the blackout?" I asked.

"We haven't ruled out an act of aggression. Our team is working diligently to piece together a timeline of the events leading to the destruction of *Cape of Good Hope*. Surely you understand," he said.

"I do and we'll comply. Can you provide an estimate on how long we'll be in quarantine?" I asked.

"Twenty-four hours and we'll have you on your way," he said.

"Hey, Liam. I think I have something," Jake said, not on the comm.

"Mr. Emre, could you hold a moment?" I asked. "We might have information relevant to your investigation."

"Of course," he answered.

Celina followed me back to the crew station where Jake was displaying the starboard TransLoc engine of *Cape of Good Hope*.

Transmit engineering station holo to Atin Emre.

"Are you seeing this, Mr. Emre?" I asked.

"I am, Captain."

"With me is Jacob Berandor. He's a graduate student from Mars Puskar University and has detailed understanding of starship engine technology," I said. "Jake, what do you have?"

"Our sensors did not have a clear view of the starboard engine for most of the time leading up to our line up on the tarmac. I was, however, able to find where we had a brief moment of visibility. I'd like to draw your attention to the highlighted region."

Jake sounded like he was instructing a class. The area he'd highlighted looked the same as everything else around it.

"I'm not seeing it, Jake," I said.

"I didn't either, at first. It's subtle," Jake said. "There are fine particles, almost a mist, inside the TransLoc engine. I'm going to expand them ten times for clarity."

A cloud of particles became evident as soon as they were blown up.

"What would cause that?" I asked.

"Nothing legitimate. To the best of my understanding it is foreign material, unless some part of the engine had been atomized. I believe that the engineers in charge of the investigation could combine this information with data from *Cape of Good Hope*. Anything capable of creating this cloud should have been a recorded event. I've included the time codes in this transmission for that purpose," he said.

"Thank you, Mr. Berandor, I'll see that this information is reviewed," Atin Emre said.

"Jake, anything else?" I asked.

"I'd like to volunteer my services to help with the investigation. I understand that we're under suspicion, but if you keep me confined and just give me a copy of the data, I might be able to help," Jake said.

"Thank you for your offer. We'll get back to you if we decide to take you up on that. Belirand Terminal Six out." Emre closed the channel.

"Nice work, Jake. Any theories?" I asked.

"Simplest answer is an energy weapon that damaged a part of the engine. Problem is, Belirand and everyone else should have picked up on that," he said.

"Even if it was small and focused?"

"I cross-referenced every material, including the fuel, in that engine and calculated the energy required to cause a reaction that could result in that cloud. Not possible. If we eliminate engine malfunction, my best guess is that the particles were added directly," he said.

"How would you do that?"

"Not hard at all. You'd need to have some sort of launch tube and a low velocity accelerant. A puff of air would be enough if there was enough time. Let's say the payload could cause a failure in the engine by simply being there," he said.

"So you just need a material that would do that," I said.

"Magnetized iron - maybe twenty grams."

"Impossible to prove. No sensor would catch twenty grams of tiny iron particles," Celina said what we were all thinking.

"*Incoming hail, Heavy Cruiser Panama.*"

Open comm. "Hoffen, here," I said.

"Captain Hoffen, if you'll accompany us to the quarantine zone." A uniformed Belirand officer appeared on the holo.

"Roger that," I replied and closed the comm.

A navigation path directed us to a location ten thousand kilometers from the station. I engaged the auto pilot.

"Why don't you guys get some rack time," I said to Celina and Jake. They'd been spelling me on the bridge. We were all exhausted, but I was happy to pass out in my chair. They both left without saying much. It had been a difficult couple of days.

I awoke after sleeping for twelve hours straight. If I hadn't needed to use the head so badly, I might have slept even longer. I set a pot of coffee to brew and waited for it to finish while standing in the small galley. The smell of the coffee brewing triggered memories of long flights on *Sterra's Gift*. I felt nostalgic, knowing that we'd outgrown her, but also knowing she'd been the ship that had started it all.

I tipped my head forward, a signal my AI had learned meant I wanted to call up my comm queue. A moderate priority comm was waiting from Belirand.

Captain Hoffen. We'd like to invite you and your command crew to join us on station as soon as you are available. We've lifted the communications blackout and have assigned slips for your ships.

Best Regards - Atin Emre.

I wondered if Tabby had already received the same message. I thumbed my ring. When she didn't immediately respond I realized she was probably still asleep. I wondered how much sleep she'd gotten in fold-space.

I pulled the coffee out before it finished brewing and poured a cup. I grabbed a meal bar and sent a low priority ping to the *Adela Chen* and *Hotspur* to let them know I was up and moving. On the way to the bridge I received ping backs from Marny and Ada.

Open comm, Ada, Marny. Forward message from Belirand.

"Good morning, sunshine," Marny quipped.

"Good morning," Ada responded. I looked at the time. It was 1400 but I decided not to point out their error.

"I'll get on it right now and bring her in to the terminal," Ada said.

"Marny, do you feel comfortable bringing *Hotspur* in?" I asked.

"Aye, Cap. I'm not just pretty," she said. I smiled involuntarily. I couldn't imagine better companions than her and Ada.

"I'd like to take you both with Nick and Tabby to meet Belirand. It sounds like they've cleared us," I said.

"Aye. The Belirand cruisers pushed off a couple of hours back and we're all quiet here. Once we get underway that will change. The kids were pretty wired up when we arrived and it took some doing to get 'em settled down," Marny said.

I grabbed the flight stick and throttled up to accompany the *Adela Chen*. While she was mating the tug to the barge she would be most vulnerable. Belirand had let us know that at ten thousand kilometers they had complete control, but my confidence was shaken.

By the time I arrived, Ada had slipped from the harness and was in the process of connecting to the long tongue of the barge. I stood off two kilometers to give her plenty of room to work.

"All ready," she said cheerily.

"See you at the terminal," I said.

My job of docking was considerably easier than Ada's. I didn't envy her the task of orienting the four hundred meter long barge with the bottom of the V-shaped TransLoc terminal. With that much length, the task was all about planning and small adjustments. I was envious of how easily she executed the maneuver.

I felt a familiar pulse from my ring. Tabby was up. No doubt the ship's movement had awakened her. We'd been apart for less than a week, but I'd grown accustomed to waking up next to her and I missed her. I thumbed my ring.

"What's the word?" Jake asked as he entered the bridge.

"They're not saying much, but they've lifted the blackout and we're no longer quarantined," I said.

"I didn't get any messages. I'm surprised they didn't want some help with analyzing that data," he said.

"Feels like every other corporation I've been around. They don't trust anyone but themselves. There's fresh coffee in the galley," I said.

"Cap, we're all up over here," Marny said. "You could schedule that meeting anytime you'd like."

"Thanks, Marny," I said.

I sent a comm to Atin Emre. He must have already known we'd arrived and immediately responded, requesting our presence. I forwarded his request and proposed that we meet in the concourse outside of the *Hotspur*.

"Pete's got watch while we're on station," Marny said when I approached.

"Great," I said.

I hugged Tabby and we walked down the corridor hand-in-hand. Terminal Six in Tipperary was almost identical to the other five we'd visited. The embedded vid-screens greeted us as normal travelers. They seemed oblivious to our meeting, but instead bragged about the amenities of the station.

We finally arrived on the administrative level. It was impressively appointed, with real wood paneling and railings. Elaborate vid screens displayed scenes from the habitable worlds of the solar system. The scene that caught my attention was of a crystal clear blue lake surrounded by a lush forest.

"Those are live feeds from Tipperary planets and moons." I recognized the voice and turned to see Atin Emre emerge from a doorway and enter the reception area in which we stood. "As you are probably aware, Tipperary is a more verdant system than even Sol, if you count habitable planets and moons. You're looking at Curie's beautiful tropical oasis. In its natural state, it was the most similar environment to Earth that's ever been discovered."

Atin Emre was shorter than I'd expected, but he radiated confidence, similar to Commander Sterra of Mars Protectorate. He was dressed in a stylized business suit that I suspected was actually a vac-suit, although considerably more expensive than anything I could afford to wear.

"I've taken the liberty of setting out some food. I wasn't sure what schedule you're on, but the fruits of Curie are considered a delicacy at any time."

We followed him into a room with a beautiful view of the

unfamiliar star field. An oval table made of a rich brown highly polished wood, big enough to seat at least ten, occupied the center of the room. A side table, covered by white cloth, held an impressive display of fruits, rolls, juice and coffee.

"Please make yourself at home," he said and poured himself a glass of an amber colored juice.

I made a small plate and sat.

"Mr. Emre. Were you able to discern what happened to *Cape of Good Hope*?" I asked.

He sighed lightly and grew serious. "In short, no. We have many facts, but are short on conclusions. You must thank Mr. Berandor for his insight. We believe it was a freak accident. Our best guess is that at exactly the wrong moment a piece of space debris, moving at an extreme velocity, punctured the engine and ultimately rendered it inoperable."

"Wouldn't the Captain have received a warning about that?" I asked. It sounded like a stupid conclusion to me.

"Perhaps, but unfortunately that information wasn't part of the logged data," he said. "We are closing the matter unless new information is presented."

I was shocked. Forty-five people had died and they'd looked into it for all of ten hours. My face must have conveyed my feelings.

"Before you ask, Captain, I understand your feelings. The death of those crew members was tragic. We don't have reliable information that supports any other theory," he said.

"What about sabotage?" I asked.

"We've explored that with a dozen investigators in three systems poring over this data. Regardless, this is an interior matter for Belirand. The reason I requested your presence is to thank you for risking yourselves to provide aid to *Cape of Good Hope*. While your actions were ultimately unsuccessful, your willingness to risk your own ship and crew were most appreciated. We, at Belirand, thank you."

Dramatically, he held his right hand over his heart and bowed his head. To say that I felt uncomfortable was an understatement.

Especially as he held the pose for at least thirty seconds. I didn't know if I was supposed to say something or what. Finally, he lifted his head and looked around the table.

"As to the expedition, we've already sent the first two rafts of ships on to Descartes," he said.

"What of *Karelia*?" I asked.

"Ah, yes, I had heard something about a conflict between your organizations," he said. "How may I help?"

Tabby couldn't hold back. "You don't think they had something to do with this?"

"I see. We had hoped that you'd put the incident in Sol behind you, but I can see that is still a sore spot. To answer your question, no, we don't believe the *Karelia* was involved in this tragic accident. Further, your questions border on libel, I would guard against making baseless accusations."

Emre's features hardened, conveying a sense of displeasure and annoyance.

He was right. There was nothing to be gained by accusing Oberrhein of something we couldn't prove. Tabby needed to back down. "We're just anxious to help as much as we can and get on with our journey," I said.

He smiled broadly. "Understandable. As a token of our appreciation, I've sent a couple of crates of Curie fruit to each of your ships. We are deeply grateful for your assistance in these tragic events. With that out of the way, I know that my brother, J.T., is looking forward to your participation in the construction of Terminal Seven," he said.

"How far behind the rest of the expedition are we?" I asked.

"Ah, yes." He averted his eyes so he wasn't looking directly at me. "They departed five hours ago under the protection of the *Karelia* and her twin cruiser *Kordun*."

"Protection? Where did the *Kordun* come from?" I asked.

A bead of sweat formed on his head and dripped down. "It hails from Grünholz."

"Our agreement was that security was to be provided by Belirand," I said.

"It was to be the duty of *Cape of Good Hope* to provide secure passage and occasional patrols. I've subcontracted this responsibility to Petar Kiirilov's fief within the Oberrhein nation, an action which is completely within my purview."

I shook my head in dismay. "You can't be serious. This is the same *Karelia* who refused to assist *Cape of Good Hope* when they most needed it. Mr. Emre, I hope you haven't jeopardized this entire expedition."

"There's no reason for talk like that. Belirand Security exonerated Oberrhein from all wrongdoing. And let me set you straight. You're in the Tipperary system now and things might run differently than you expect. Belirand is your *only* link back to Sol. If we see fit to hire Oberrhein for security, you'll need to learn how to live with it."

"And if I can't?"

"Check your contract, Mr. Hoffen. You'll owe Belirand half a million Mars Credits. And you'll not be using my gate to return home," he said.

"Your gate?"

"Yes, Mr. Hoffen. The security of Terminal Six is my responsibility. And I alone decide which ships utilize it."

"I see."

"I'm glad we were able to have this conversation and we're looking forward to working with you to build the future of Belirand. I trust we'll have no further problems," he said.

"I'm not sure what problems you're referring to," I said as dryly as I could manage.

He smiled ironically, "It sounds like we've come to an agreement."

"I believe our agreement calls for fuel and I imagine you'd like to retrieve the superstructure that was installed on our barge," I said.

"We'll make arrangements for the superstructure at a later date. We're currently short on available engineering crews. You may refuel at your leisure," he said and abruptly left the room.

"That's shite," Tabby said.

Nick held up his hand. "They're likely recording the conversation in this room. I'd say we should retire to our own ships," he said.

"Right. Let's fuel up and get out of here," I said.

LÉGER NUAGE

"I'd like to keep the same crew configuration. If we run into trouble, I want Ada, Tabby and myself in the chairs."

"You're short a gunner on *Sterra's Gift*," Marny said.

"We'll make do. I'm sure Jake can handle the missiles and I wouldn't bet against Lena in the crow's nest," I said.

"That should work," Marny agreed.

Our first stop would be Grünholz, fourth planet from the FD-40307 star (commonly called Tipperary). Grünholz, perpetually covered in clouds, is a planet thirty percent larger than Earth and covered almost entirely by a shallow layer of fresh water. The atmosphere is naturally breathable by humans.

Originally, the most promising aspect of Grünholz - its ready access to water, turned out to be its largest impediment. For decades German engineers tried to sink pylons into the soft soil beneath the bog, never to find bedrock. In the end, the Germans gave up on colonization. They left behind several small cities they'd cut out of the thick overgrowth that was a permanent feature of the bogs. The largest city was Nannandry and the second largest, the domed city of Solnste.

While the Germans had been slaving away, trying to tap the promising potential of the surface, the French had laid claim to the skies. Built above the ever present clouds, they'd constructed the cloud nation Nuage. Our ultimate destination, Léger Nuage, was one of eighteen of these cities, all recognizable by the 'Nuage' somewhere in the name.

Hail Adela Chen. "Ada, can you reconfigure for hard-burn? We'll put on fuel and set sail for Léger Nuage," I said.

"Can do, and it's your mom," Mom said. "Ada is getting coffee. Are we staying here for anything?"

"Only if you need something," I said.

"No, I think Pete's going to bust if we don't find him a rock to bash pretty soon," she said.

"I'll send you my latest comm with Belirand. That might not be the only thing he wants to bust," I said.

"Oh no. That bad?"

"We'll be okay, but it's annoying. I've sent you a rendezvous. Once you're fueled up, we'll meet there."

"Understood. What about the fold-space harness?" she asked.

"Belirand is too busy to mess with it for now. We'll remove it once we get to the claim," I said.

"For a company short on nano-steel, I'd think they'd want to reclaim it."

"Agreed." I waved goodbye and closed the comm.

I set the auto-pilot to take us in to the fuel depot and built a navigation plan from Terminal Six to Léger Nuage. We'd need to conserve fuel until we started actually bringing in credits. Nothing would shut down a mining operation faster than lack of fuel.

Belirand had a program that would allow us to buy fuel in exchange for ore. Iron ore sold for about the same as what we got on Colony 40, but Nick explained that the deal was considerably worse. We'd eliminated the middle-man and delivery now depended on us expending both time and fuel.

If the entire deal had hinged on the efficiency of working with Belirand, we likely would have passed on it. But Nick believed Tipperary was three years from becoming a major trading system, much like Bethe Peierls. Growth in the system would drive demand for ore higher and higher and we weren't exclusively locked in with Belirand, other than to fulfill annual quotas for two years.

That all sounded great, but I wanted to get out and explore the galaxy. I'd be happy to put in time mining, if that's what it took, but it would happen on my schedule.

***

What could have been an eight day trip turned into twelve, due to an overly efficient burn plan. At half a million kilometers away, the giant planet started to grow in the armored glass of the bridge. At fifty thousand kilometers, the gorgeous grey-blue planet completely filled our view.

Hail Nuage Air Defense, I said. I was excited to finally be at this point in our long journey. We'd traveled a thousand light years to get here.

"Unidentified ship, please add frequency FA04Q to your transponder signature." I admit to being a little more than pleased to hear the woman's faint French accent. To this point, I'd read a lot about the French settlement of the cloud nation and her accent made it seem that much more real.

Add frequency FA04Q to Loose Nuts Fleet transponders.

"Thank you, *Sterra's Gift.* Are you travelling in convoy with *Adela Chen* and *Hotspur*?" she asked. I was sure our company registration showed this information, but I didn't mind answering the question.

"Roger that, Nuage Air Defense. This is Liam Hoffen of *Loose Nuts*. We're requesting clearance for Nuage Airspace," I answered.

"What's the nature of your visit, Captain Hoffen?" she asked. She lit up the holo transmitter and I experienced that disconnect I sometimes felt when I saw someone that I'd only previously talked to. In my mind, I saw her as a young woman and she was clearly my mom's age.

"Trade and emigration. I've contracts that confirm this." I was prepared to blather on, but if Nick had taught me anything it was to take a breath once in a while.

"Well, then, let me be the first to welcome you to our beautiful cities. I'm Lieutenant Sonia Lafaille. I've marked your ships as neutral and if you'll register with the security office on Léger, we'll upgrade that status to probationary," she said.

"Thank you."

"I've informed Léger of your pending arrival," she continued. "I'm uploading a list of contraband, please run it against your current cargo."

"I'm prepared to upload our manifests," I said.

She chuckled and I mentally kicked myself. Nick would give me a hard time for oversharing. "That won't be necessary. Make sure if you ever visit the capital city of Nuage Gros that you stop in and visit. Nuage Air Defense out." She closed the comm.

Open comm, Adela Chen.

"Go ahead, Liam," Mom answered.

"We need to hold the *Adela Chen* in geosync above Léger Nuage. I'll put together a shore leave schedule, but I need you and Dad to take the first shift," I said.

"Not necessary, son," Big Pete answered. "We're staying on the ship. There's too much riding on the barge for us."

"Roger that. Our plans are to be in the city for fourteen hours. Mom, if you'll set your orbit, *Hotspur* will sail in close and pick up Ada," I said.

"Copy that, *Adela Chen* out," she said.

Open comm, Hotspur.

"Heya, lover. You don't call much anymore." Tabby appeared on the holo in front of me. She was biting her lip suggestively. It was a reminder of our separation I didn't need.

"Mom and Dad are staying with the ship, could you pick up Ada and follow me in to Léger?" I asked.

"Copy that," she said.

Half an hour later, Ada was aboard *Hotspur* and we were descending through the thickening atmosphere. When we'd closed to within forty kilometers, three small, identical yellow ships emerged from the heavy cloud cover. They were boasting swept back wings that made them more maneuverable, as well as efficient, in the atmosphere.

"*Incoming hail, Nuage Air Defense*," the ship's AI said.

Accept. "Captain Hoffen," I said.

"Greetings, Captain. Squadron Leader Gray here, we've been expecting you." A dark haired man seated in the cockpit of one of the three ships appeared on my forward vid screen.

"Greetings, Mr. Gray. I was about to request permission to land for *Sterra's Gift* and *Hotspur*," I said.

"Permission granted. You're both cleared on pad 2404. We'll see you on the deck," he said and closed comm.

Landing instructions appeared on my vid-screen and I locked in the auto-pilot.

"Tabbs, did you get landing instructions?" I asked.

"Roger that, hot stuff. We're less than two minutes behind you," she said.

In the distance, I could just make out an asymmetrical white cylinder-shaped city. It was tapered slightly at the top and hung just above the clouds. As we approached, the shape became more defined and lost some of its regularity. Its design was as artistic as it was clean.

"Look at that," Celina said.

"Leave it to the French," Jake said.

"How's that?" I asked. I didn't know much about French culture, other than to appreciate the accent.

"If a spacer had built that, it'd be a big metal box. It's just nice they made it something to be proud of," he said.

"True enough. So what do you think of your new home, Celina?"

She was smiling. "It's exciting. A fresh start, our own diner. I can't wait."

"When do you think you'll be up and running?" I asked.

"Well, I should have brought it up before now. Any chance we could use the construction bot for a few hours before you take off?"

Ugh. I didn't want to delay Big Pete too long. "How much time do you think?" I asked.

"Program says six hours. One other thing?" she asked, grimacing guiltily.

I chuckled at her expression. "What's that?"

"I was hoping to use your industrial replicator for a few items. I'd pay for the materials, of course, unless you wanted to take it out in trade."

"What kind of trade?" She had my attention. We didn't have credits, but we had lots of materials.

"Fair exchange for food... and excellent service, of course," she answered.

"Why not? We're not taking it to Descartes in the first load. How about this – you can use the machine for free as long as you're not reselling the items. You pay us retail for material and we pay you retail for food and service," I said.

"Deal," she said.

As we'd been talking, *Sterra's Gift* had slowed significantly and bucked slightly in the unpredictable winds that swirled around the floating city's structure. A round landing pad extended from a vertical column that ran the entire height of the city. Large bright numerals displayed 2404. If I'd insisted on sailing by hand, I'd have been uncomfortable with the unfamiliar surroundings and shifting winds. The AI shared no such reservations.

"Well, I guess that's that," I said.

Ordinarily, with a full load, Marny would want us dressed in armored vac-suits, but it wasn't the impression I wanted to make. I decided to strap on a thigh holster with my heavy flechette.

"Looks like we have company," Celina said, gesturing out of the armored glass of the bridge.

Sure enough there were half a dozen people in brightly colored clothing standing inside a large arched opening, looking out at us expectantly.

"Well, we shouldn't keep them waiting," I said.

Lock flight controls. I instructed as I exited the bridge. It would take one of the regular crew to get us going again. Down the hall and to the right I pushed my way through the first of the two airlock doors. The ship had already equalized our cabin pressure with that of the city and the door opened easily. I punched the button to extend the stairs and waited impatiently for them to lower.

Just as I reached the bottom of the stairs, *Hotspur* approached and neatly set down next to *Sterra's Gift*. I had to hold on to the railing to steady myself from the gust of wind she'd caused. Right behind her, a single golden Nuage ship swooped up from below the platform. I panicked when I realized he was expecting to set down, yet there wasn't even close to enough room. Worse yet, he'd overshot and was hanging off the edge of the platform. My heart jumped as gravity won and the ship nosed over. What I hadn't seen, however, was that the ship had deployed a clamp that locked it onto the edge of the platform and while it was hanging vertically from the side, it was quite secure.

On the underside of the ship, which was now the side pointed toward me, a hatch slid open. Squadron Leader Gray grabbed a bar at the top of the hatch and swung his legs out, neatly depositing himself on the platform. I shook my head in amazement. If it had been his intent to impress me, he'd been more than successful.

"It's a lot less dramatic if you're expecting it," he said, holding his hand out in greeting. We had to shout over the wind.

"Nice to meet you, Mr. Gray," I said, shaking his hand. I noticed he had Captain's bars on his shoulders.

"Call me Luc," he said. "That's quite a pair of ships you have there, Captain."

"I'll call you Luc if you call me Liam. We've been fortunate," I said. "Your patrol ships are gorgeous. And they're so nimble, are they space worthy?"

When he didn't immediately answer, I followed his eyes to *Hotspur* where Tabby, Marny and Ada had exited the ship.

"Mon Dieu," he said under his breath. I understood how he felt. They were each beautiful in their own way and as a group, more so.

"I believe that's an understatement," I said with a slight raise of my eyebrow.

"My apologies. Yes. The Falcons are primarily suited to atmospheric missions, but can be utilized in limited engagements in vacuum."

"I understand there's a registration process for crafts, as well as for those emigrating to Léger," I said.

"Of course. We can perform the craft registration later if you would prefer, but it is sometimes difficult to find the correct personnel," he said.

"What's involved?" I asked.

Tabby gave me an overly enthusiastic hug and a kiss. I was overpowered by her and had no choice but to go with it. Luc Gray looked away, only slightly embarrassed. Fortunately, Marny and Ada introduced themselves.

"I missed you too," I whispered.

"We need to sell one of the ships. I don't want to keep splitting up," she said.

"I hear you. There might be some other options. First, let me introduce you to Captain Luc Gray," I said. "Luc, this is my fiancé, Tabitha Masters."

"A fortunate man indeed," Luc said, taking Tabby's hand and kissing the back of it. She gave me a triumphant waggle of her eyebrows.

The rest of the crew had disembarked and were milling around.

"Hey Marny, I'm going to work with Mr. Gray to register our ships. Let's get people headed in to the station. We need to fill out forms and check in with customs."

"Aye, Cap. I think Nicholas is already on it." She looked over to the arched doorway where Nick was shaking hands with the group of colorfully dressed individuals. "Will you and Tabby stay with the ships until we get back?"

"Will do," I said.

Marny herded our group toward the arched door and the noise diminished dramatically.

"Quite a group you have there," Luc said.

"Best ever. How can I help with registration?" I asked.

"First, I need to inspect both ships, cargo holds and living spaces," he said.

"What are you looking for?" I asked.

"Contraband and smuggling holds. I assume you've run your manifest against our contraband list," he said.

"Sure have."

"There's nothing illegal about smuggling holds, but we want to know if a ship has them. Depending on the contraband, we have the option of holding it and returning when you depart or, if it's especially egregious, we'll seize it."

"Not sure I follow," I said.

"We mostly have problems with slavers. We won't allow a ship to leave with slaves on board," he said.

"Got it. I'm sure we're clean," I said.

"The easiest way to do this is for us to walk through the ship. My scanner will compare your ship's design with the actual open spaces. I'll ask you to open any smuggling holds and we'll want to make sure those items are accounted for on your manifest or are at least legal."

"Sounds like a fairly intense registration process," I said.

"You haven't heard the hard way. That's where we take your ship to Nuage Gros and run it through a ship scanner. If we find anything amiss, we hold your ship until we resolve whatever issues might have come up." His face had grown hard. He was ready to take whatever path I chose.

"If you walk through, are we then registered?" I asked.

"We recommend you reflag your ships to Nuage. By doing so, you will have the protections offered by our nation while in our airspace."

"Great. Let's do it," I said. Nick and I'd already talked about the advantages of reflagging. It was by no means a permanent commitment, but we would be setting our base here for now, so it made good sense.

Tabby and I led Luc through the two ships where he allowed a finger sized autonomous bot to flit around, gathering information and making comparisons to the exterior dimensions. Finally, we ended up on the bridge of *Hotspur*, having completed the walkthrough.

"Everything checks out," he said. "I've submitted your probationary status and as long as you have no major infractions within six months, your permanent registration will automatically kick in. You're free to land at any of our cities as long as you check in with our automated air control. Swipe here." He held out a small pad and I swiped my hand across the top of it. It had taken us half an hour to finish the entire process.

"Great. Thank you," I said.

"Nuage Air Defense would appreciate reports of security issues you might encounter around the Nuage cities. Unofficially, if you find yourself at Nuage Gros, you should look me up for drinks. I'd be happy to give you an insider's view of our beautiful nation in the clouds," he said.

"Perfect, expect a call. I imagine we'll be on Nuage Gros after we settle in the Descartes belt," I said.

Tabby and I showed him out and watched as he swung into the bottom of his small ship. The hatch slid closed and before you could blink an eye, the ship's clamps retracted and it slipped downward, falling toward the planet below. After gaining sufficient speed, the ship gracefully arced out of its dive and sailed away from the city.

"There you are," Marny said walking out from under the archway.

"Where'd you think we'd be?" I asked.

"I hailed *Sterra's Gift* and no one was home," she said. "If you head down to level twelve, they're pretty fast at getting you through. They'll ask if you're looking to naturalize, you probably want to say no. They're happy to give us automatically renewable two-year visas."

Tabby and I walked through the arched door and I felt a slight pressure change. We'd passed through a transparent energy barrier. It was a nice change from having my ears constantly buffeted by the wind.

My HUD's vapor trail showed that we were to continue directly into the center of the city following a wide, carpeted passageway. There were a few unoccupied retail spaces and things appeared dusty, as if this level didn't see much traffic.

We stopped at four vertical transparent tubes which were clearly elevator shafts.

Call elevator. I said. One of the four immediately pulsed red at both the ceiling and floor. A moment later the pulse changed to green and an opening appeared in front of us. We stepped into the elevator and dropped to level twelve.

"That was fast," I said.

"Seriously?" Tabby looked at me. "These guys float entire cities and you're impressed with their elevators?"

"Ah, right," I said.

The office we were looking for was only a few doors down from the elevators.

A woman greeted us as we entered. "You must be Mr. Hoffen and Ms. Masters." Our clothing must have given us away. It was different from the colorful, baggy pieces we saw on everyone else.

"I understand from the application you've provided that you're interested in obtaining a visa. Do you believe you'll be applying for naturalization?" she asked. I remembered Marny's warning.

"Visas would be great," I said. Tabby nodded in agreement.

The woman looked disappointed.

"If you'll step onto the scanner, we need to make sure you are who you say," she said.

We both complied.

"Almost there." She held out a swipe pad. "Just need your signature and you'll be on your way. Your visa is good for two years, and can be automatically renewed if you're here during its renewal period. Do you plan to stay long?" I caught a slightly wistful look.

"Miners and traders. We're hoping to set up a permanent base here, though," I said.

Her face brightened. "Then let me be the first to welcome you to Léger Nuage."

IT ALWAYS COMES DOWN TO CHICKEN

"Nick, we're headed up, where are you?" I asked.

"Level-23. There's a loading terminal. It's totally empty except for us. Ada just brought *Sterra's Gift* around. If you want to bring *Hotspur*, there's room," he said.

"I thought we were on twenty-four," I said.

"Yup. The loading terminals serve three levels. It's well done. You'll like it," he said.

"We're on our way," I said.

"This way." Tabby jogged away from the elevator banks.

I chased after her and we got strange looks. We were already dressed oddly for this place, so we would have gotten the looks either way. Tabby paused at the edge of the city, where the outside walls swept around in a wide arc. She pointed at metal stair treads welded into the wall and painted to perfectly blend in.

"You want to run up twelve levels?" I asked.

"Try to catch me," she said.

I knew I didn't stand a chance, but needed the exercise all the same. I lunged for her, but she easily avoided me, turned and started running up, three steps at a time. It was a feat I quickly became incapable of, catching my toe on the fourth set and sprawling forward onto the hard surface.

I heard Tabby land lightly, with her feet straddling my hips. She pulled me up to my feet. Since her time in the tank, Tabby's physical strength and agility had continued to increase to the point where I wasn't remotely in her league.

I touched her nose. "I caught you."

"So cheap," she said and slid around me, racing back up the stairs.

I dug in, taking two at a time. I felt like I was keeping close, but

Tabby was soon out of sight. By the time I made it to level twenty-one, my lungs were burning. But I had to admit it felt good.

"Nice job," she said, waiting for me on twenty-four.

"Don't ... patronize ...," I said, between breaths.

She put her arm around my back and walked me out to the ship. I was breathing regularly by the time we slid into the pilot's chairs.

"Good to have you back on board," Tabby said.

I looked over and smiled, but inside I worried that I'd never be enough for her.

Navigation path to Level 23 loading terminal, I said.

I pulled up on the flight stick, lifted off from the pad and sailed lazily around to the opposite side. The open bay beckoned and I slid us in nice and slow, landing next to *Sterra's Gift.*

"Hey, you okay?" Tabby asked.

"Absolutely," I said. There was no way I was going to let her see me feeling sorry for myself.

While we were in the armory changing into armored vac-suits, I received a ping from Nick.

"You going to open up?" he asked.

"Almost there," I said, sliding my heavy flechette into the chest holster that I preferred. Tabby was already holding a blaster rifle.

"Any trouble out there?" I asked.

"Nope," Nick replied.

Lower the rear cargo ramp, I instructed. I did a quick scan through the ship's sensors and could only pick up Nick.

"Where is everyone?" Tabby asked as we walked down the ramp.

"Up on twenty-four," Nick said. "They're all checking out Lena's new diner. You mind staying here until we're unloaded? That way I can organize our warehouse as the crates are delivered."

"Sure. How do you get there though?" I asked.

"It's a sweet layout. We are directly below the end of the warehouse. A three meter lift loads items from the ship directly up and into the back of our warehouse. We might want to invest in a stevedore bot. I was able to rent one, but I had to exchange Mars Credits," he said.

"How expensive?" I asked.

"We're spending two thousand for today," he said.

I whistled. I wouldn't have expected to pay more than four or five hundred. "Is the exchange rate that bad?" I asked.

The system currency was confusingly called a credit and was an agreement between Nuage and the two nations on Curie and Hipparchus. As far as we'd heard, Oberrhein didn't participate in the exchange. "The exchange rate is bad. For goods, a Tipperary credit is about half as valuable as the corresponding Mars credit. For example, we had been paying three Mars credits per kilogram of fuel. Fuel here is six and a half credits per kilogram. Worse, there's very little call for Mars Credits here," he said.

"Good to know," I said.

"Let's unload Lena's and Jake's crates first. She wants to get rolling on her diner. Did you know Jake leased a bar?" Nick asked.

Nick poked a button on his reading pad and a stevedore bot lifted from the ground and jetted toward *Sterra's Gift*.

"We talked about it on the trip out," I said.

"How's he going to trade?" Tabby asked. "He doesn't have a ship."

"I guess he'll hire it out," Nick said, shrugging. "Oh. We've agreed to let Lena use a small part of our warehouse. You okay with that?"

"Well. We agreed to let her use the Industrial Replicator as long as she paid for materials," I said.

Nick laughed. "She mentioned it. Wanted to know when we'd have it set up. She has a sign for her diner she wants to manufacture."

"Why wouldn't she just hang a vid screen?" I asked.

"She said it wouldn't be authentic. Something about neon lights."

"Sounds fun," Tabby said.

The stevedore bot finished stacking half a dozen crates and settled down on top of them.

"That's my ride. I'll send the bot back down once we've unloaded the lift," Nick said.

He walked over to the stack of crates and gestured on his pad. He and the crates were lifted through a widening hole in the ceiling.

Two and a half hours later, we'd finally unloaded the last crate. Tabby and I changed into normal vac-suits and locked down both *Sterra's Gift* and *Hotspur*. We hadn't seen a single person the entire time we'd been unloading, but I turned on *Hotspur's* sentry program regardless. It wouldn't apply lethal force, but it would cause quite a ruckus if ignored.

We rode the lift up to the warehouse. Most of the items we'd carried in the ship's hold had belonged to Jake and Celina and they fit easily in the large space.

With everything loaded in the warehouse, Nick instructed the construction robot to set up the industrial and medical replicators against the wall. We would move them out to Descartes once we had outpost warehouse constructed and the defensive systems set up.

"Come see this," Ada said. She'd been picking items out of a crate and handed us each a bundle to carry to Lena's. We made our way through the warehouse, into the connected storefront space and finally into the main hallway.

"She's to the right, toward the center," Ada said.

"Just put those bags on the counter," Lena said as we walked through the front door of her diner.

The restaurant had a row of booths running down one side. A long countertop separated the booths from a service area on the opposite side. Patrons could sit on stools at the counter or in the booths.

"Lena was able to get them to build it out to her specifications. She just had to bring her own ovens, preps and hydrators. Her kitchen is back here," Ada said, pushing through a gate that led into the service area. She turned to walk through a tall set of swinging doors, which was where we found Jack and Jenny, loading foodstuffs onto the wire shelving.

"Where are Nick and Marny?"

"They're helping Jake set up his bar," Jenny answered.

"How do we get there?" I asked.

Jenny pointed at an open door at the back of the kitchen. "That hallway links up a few of the businesses. His back door should be open."

"Thanks, we'll go check it out."

"I'm staying here," Ada said.

It was a short walk through the narrow hallway. We heard Marny and Jake's voices and followed them into a storage room.

"There they are," Marny said when she saw us walk in. "You'll never believe what Jake's got on tap."

I shook my head not understanding. "What's that?"

Incoming comm, Silver Hoffen. I held up my hand to let Marny know that I was getting a comm.

"Mom. What's up?" I asked.

"We might have some trouble up here," she said.

"What kind of trouble?"

The room grew quiet.

"Two small cruisers have pulled up on us. Oberrhein registration," she said.

"What do they want?" I asked.

"Nothing yet."

"We're on our way," I said. I looked at Marny and gave her a curt nod.

Quickest route to Hotspur. The familiar blue contrail snaked out in front of me and I jogged after it with Tabby, Marny and Nick in tow.

"Nick. I need you to get Ada and follow in *Sterra's Gift*," I said. My gut said that more ships would be better, but I knew I could get there more quickly with *Hotspur*.

"Can do," he said and peeled off.

"What's up, Cap?" Marny asked.

"Two cruisers on the *Adela Chen*," I said. "No comm yet, but they're making Mom nervous enough to make a call."

"Aye."

Without the AI, I'd never have found my way back, but I palmed my way into the warehouse on a dead run.

Open hatch and raise lift to halfway up. It was an obscure command and I hoped my AI could figure out what I meant.

When we got to the back of the warehouse, the hatch was open, meaning the lift was rising. It would be a three meter drop, but I was in a hurry. Without hesitation, Tabby jumped off and landed gracefully, allowing her legs to absorb the impact, squatting deeply. Marny and I jumped at the same time. I bent my legs allowing myself to roll on impact. My suit absorbed enough of the shock that it was merely painful. I appreciated that Marny also opted for a roll, although her recovery was better than my own. We took the second drop to the loading terminal where our ships sat.

"Tabby, Marny, suit up and I'll get us out of here," I said.

They both acknowledged monosyllabically.

Display Nuage controlled space on forward holo, Hotspur cockpit.

I'd just cleared the airlock, well behind Tabby. She'd kicked open the door leading into the berth deck, even though she hadn't yet entered. I passed by the armory, through the back door and onto the lift.

Display navigation path to Adela Chen.

Filbert looked up from where he'd been lying on the couch. I slowed my movement, knowing he'd bolt if I approached too quickly. He lazily rolled over on his back, looking for a rub.

"Not this time, killer," I said, scooping him up and petting his fur flat. I gently slid him into the grav-box. He gave me an annoyed chirp, but settled in, all the same.

I slid into the cockpit seat and pulled on my combat harness.

Prepare for emergency departure.

The forward vid-screen reported 'All Systems Nominal.' It was not our routine takeoff sequence, rather something we'd worked up for this type of event. The ship would close down all external hatches, look for critical systems that were non-operational and inform all occupants that we were about to take off.

I simultaneously lifted on the right stick and pushed forward on the left throttle. I couldn't afford to get too aggressive this close to the city, but I'd push it nonetheless.

There were only four ships in the vicinity of the city and none in our path. I accelerated as quickly as I felt was reasonable.

"Mom, how's it going?" I asked.

"They're demanding an inspection. They say we're in their airspace and they are looking for contraband," she said.

Tabby leapt over the back of the starboard cockpit chair and pulled on her combat harness.

"Marny, how close are you for a combat burn?"

"Go, Cap. I'm in," she said. I could hear her footsteps running.

Combat burn. I pushed the throttle down and was thrust back into my chair.

"Tabby, look at the holo. Can we get *Adela Chen* into Nuage Controlled space?" I asked.

"Too low, she'd never escape the gravity."

"Frak."

At our current rate we'd arrive in two minutes. Good thing too, we were burning a frak-tonne of fuel.

"Mom, stall 'em. We're almost there," I said.

Her voice was tense. "Pete wants to burn for Descartes."

"They'll fire on you. Give me two minutes," I said.

"They must have picked up on your approach," she said. "They're forming up, getting between us."

I pulled back on the throttle and dropped out of the combat burn. We were going fast enough that we'd catch up soon enough.

Identify cruisers.

The ship's registrations were *Kordun* and *Stenka*. *Kordun* had been the name of the cruiser Oberrhein sent to help the *Karelia* take over security of the mining expedition as it left Terminal Six. I couldn't imagine that was a coincidence.

"Incoming hail, *Kordun*," the ship's AI informed.

"Marny, how far out is *Sterra's Gift*?"

"Two minutes behind us, Cap," she replied.

Accept hail. "*Loose Nuts*, Liam Hoffen," I said.

"I'll need you to stand down, Captain Hoffen. If you continue on your current course we'll consider your actions to be hostile."

"Cruiser *Kordun*, you're illegally interfering with my ship in open space. I'm requesting that you stand off fifty kilometers," I returned.

"Request denied. You're in Oberrhein space. Comply with my order or be fired on," he said.

Terminate comm. Open Loose Nuts command channel.

"Marny, you with me?" I asked.

"Aye, Cap. You'll want to split them up, they'll try to trap us," she said.

"Mom, go ahead and start your burn," I said. I was gambling they wouldn't destroy the load they were clearly trying to hijack.

"Nick, warm up your missiles. We'll focus fire on the *Kordun* if it comes to that. Ada, make sure you're hit and run. Don't get too close to those turrets," I said.

"Copy that," Ada said.

I veered off to the side at twenty degrees looking to flank the *Kordun* but also give the appearance of heeding his requirement.

"Ada, try to keep *Hotspur* between you and *Kordun* if possible," I said.

The *Kordun* moved between us and the *Adela Chen* while the *Stenka* positioned itself five hundred meters directly in front of the barge.

"You can make that, Silver," Ada said. "Cut your burn and pull up to dip the barge's nose down, let your inertia carry you past."

"Copy that. I've got it," Mom said, her voice strained.

I put a burst of speed on. I needed to at least keep their attention divided. Ada caught up and slid in to formation next to me. It was a good sign they hadn't fired on us up to this point.

We all held our breath as we watched Mom maneuver the *Adela Chen*, dipping the front end of the barge beneath the *Stenka*. On her current course, the tug would collide with the cruiser once the barge had fully passed beneath.

"You're almost there," Ada said. "Once the barge is seventy percent past, drop forty meters, but don't overshoot."

"Gah. That's tight," Mom said.

"You've got it, Silver."

It was difficult to watch. Why did it always come down to a game of chicken? On schedule, she dropped the *Adela Chen* downward. The majority of the mass of the barge was already past the *Stenka* and as Ada had predicted, Mom neatly slipped beneath, narrowly avoiding collision.

On the other side, Mom pulled the tug back into line with her original trajectory and fired its powerful main engines. Engine wash bucked against the *Stenka*, which in any other situation would have been considered a major breach of safety protocols.

"Stay tight, Ada," I said.

The *Stenka* moved to escape the turbulence and I saw an opportunity to outmaneuver the slower cruisers. For the moment, the *Kordun* stood between us and the *Adela Chen*, but with the *Stenka* moving into our lane I would use it just like I'd set a trap in pod-ball.

Ada stayed tight as I rolled under the larger ship and accelerated toward the *Adela Chen*. The pilot of the *Kordun* responded as I'd hoped and shifted to cut us off. He realized, too late my move had been a feint. I reversed our roll and accelerated at full combat burn directly at the *Stenka's* bow. The *Kordun's* and *Stenka's* pilots attempted to adjust but lacked the necessary coordination. The trap had been sprung and we sailed around the floundering ship and watched with satisfaction as the *Kordun* executed an emergency braking maneuver to keep from colliding with its companion.

"*Incoming hail, Kordun,*" my AI said.

We weren't completely out of the woods. The cruisers could overtake the *Adela Chen* and if they decided to go hostile we'd suffer significant losses.

I accepted the hail.

"Captain Hoffen, you're making a big mistake. You don't want to be an enemy of the Oberrhein nation and your actions today amount to an act of war."

"The only hostile action I've seen is your attempt to illegally seize one of my ships and threaten me and my crew," I said.

"We were only interested in an inspection to provide assistance to a ship that appeared to be in distress. You've overreacted," he said.

"Please accept my apology in that case. We are not intimately familiar with the local regulations. We are, however, sailing under the Nuage flag, so if you'd like to file a complaint with them, I'm sure they'd be willing to provide redress."

There was a long pause that made me think there was a discussion occurring that we weren't privy to.

"You are new to this system, so I'll give you a pass this time, Captain. Next time, I'll not be so forgiving."

"Roger that. Hoffen out."

SETTLING IN

In order to keep up with Mom we had to enter hard-burn, though neither *Hotspur* nor the *Adela Chen* struggled. After an hour of no pursuit from the Oberrhein cruisers she relented and reduced her acceleration enough that we could communicate.

"You all okay?" Mom asked.

"No shots fired. I think we're good," I said. "And that was some pretty hot-stick sailing back there. Same with you, Ada. Without those maneuvers, I believe things would have turned out differently."

"Any idea what that was about?" Tabby asked.

Nick answered, "It was just what it looked like. They were looking to plunder the barge and didn't expect us to show up."

"Even so, we're poorly matched for two cruisers, even small ones. If they'd wanted it bad enough, I think they could have forced the issue," I said.

"Registering our ships with Nuage saved us," he replied. "Oberrhein and Nuage have a trade agreement and from what I can see, it's been a bloody path getting to that point."

"If they keep that crap up, it's going to be a bloody path with us too. And, I don't intend to be the one bleeding," Tabby said.

"Nothing we can do about it now," I said. "Nick, what about Jack? I'm guessing he got left behind on Léger. I'm sure I could get back there and pick him up."

"Not necessary. Lena offered him a job in her diner and he wanted to stay," Nick said.

"Okay, let me come up with a burn plan that gives us some deviation, just in case anyone's following us," I said.

A navigation plan popped up on my vid-screen from Ada. It had a slight dog-leg that would take us ten thousand kilometers out of our way. I put a time code on it so we could all sync and sent it to the other ships.

"See you all in a couple of days," I said.

A moment later we transitioned to hard-burn. We were five days from the Descartes belt.

I sat back in my chair - a little despondent about the turn of events. Back on Mars, Tipperary had felt like such a good idea, full of possibility and adventure. Much of that shiny, new feeling had been scraped off before we'd even started. I wondered what Mom and Dad were thinking.

Having sailed for weeks to get to Tipperary, a five day journey seemed like a drop in the bucket and I was glad to finally be on the same ship with Tabby again.

"Can you take the helm, Tabbs?" I asked.

"Copy that," she said.

I opened the grav-box and lifted a sleepy Filbert out. He chirped, not liking to be awakened, but I cradled him and smoothed his fur and he grew content. I sat at Nick's now vacant workstation chair, next to Marny.

"What's up, Cap?" she asked.

"Sorry about splitting you and Nick up. I didn't have a lot of time to think and I wanted to have you on the turrets," I said.

"It was a good call. I've missed having you on board," she said.

I leaned back and put my feet up on the console. Filbert jumped down, awake and ready to explore. He rubbed against Marny's leg and gave a pitiful yowl. I looked at her with raised eyebrows.

"Little rat's figured out I have an access panel to the tween deck under my station," she said.

"And what? He wants you to open it?" I asked.

"Aye. He believes there is evil to be vanquished," she said dramatically. She slid a panel in front of her legs open and unsealed a small pass-through hatch in the floor. Filbert gracefully jumped into the dark space.

"At least he has a choice about it. You think we'll ever be done chasing evil?" I asked.

"Nay. There will always be those who fill the vacuum of space with their greed and ambition. Mind you it's a small group, but their ability to muck it up for the rest of us is the stuff of legends. I have to admit that I'm impressed with how quickly you flushed them out, though.

"Yeah, real impressive," I said.

"Nothing to be glum about. Good to have 'em out in the open. It'll save us from wringing our hands about being polite later," she said.

I laughed. The image of Marny wringing her hands, worrying about what someone thought of her, struck me as funny. "Okay. Enough moping then. Coffee?"

"Not for me. I've got a date on the track unless you need me to take a watch," she said.

I cut the next two and a half days into even, four-hour watch schedules. It was easy to fall into a familiar pattern of watches, exercise, cards and sleeping. I wasn't overly fond of a three person watch, as it guaranteed that Tabby and I had to split sleeping shifts with each other. But for such a small duration we could survive.

As was our tradition, we paused at the mid-point of our journey. Technically, we could simply flip over and fire up the engines again, but Marny wasn't having any of that. One thing she enjoyed was hosting a feast. We were far enough into the journey that we were short on fresh food, but that hardly slowed her down. She pulled item after item out of the freezer and worked with the minimal tools in our galley.

Tabby and I set the table, poured wine, and generally did whatever Marny instructed. Her timing was excellent as Mom and Dad walked in at just the moment she was placing a large pan of lasagna on the table. Nick and Ada followed shortly behind.

After hugs and greetings, we took our places at the table. I always felt nostalgic when we got together, thinking of how often we'd repeated this particular ritual. So much had changed and really so much hadn't. One change I was especially thankful for was that Tabby was on this journey, too.

For her coup de grâce, Marny served chocolate cupcakes with frosting. It wasn't the first time she'd picked this particular dessert and I hoped it wouldn't be her last. There was something about chocolate and coffee that I especially enjoyed.

"What's the first order of business once we arrive?" I asked of the table. I knew Big Pete was ready to get going and would have a list ten meters long of tasks to be accomplished.

"Silver and I have located our home asteroid so we'll be digging our habitation dome in," Pete answered.

"Do you always do that?" Ada asked. "I thought habitation domes were made to be set up on the surface."

"I'd recommend it for any structure. It's more work, but these new claims are going to have a lot of rookies working them. Breakaway debris will be commonplace and you need to be protected," he said.

"We're moving the big co-op asteroid to its new home," Nick said. "We'll need your help with that, Ada."

She nodded her understanding.

"I thought Liam and Tabby might clear cannon emplacements. Marny and I will set up *Sterra's Gift* as a temporary control room," Nick said. "Since it will take Ada a solid week to move that asteroid, we should have all three cannons online and be ready to start clearing the ore shelf once she arrives."

We continued to talk about the details of the operation, but most of it was rehashing or fine tuning. Finally, it was time to start the final sixty hour deceleration burn to the Descartes asteroid field.

***

"Area is clear, Cap," Marny reported. *Hotspur* had arrived an hour before the other two ships to make sure we'd be in good shape.

"Tabby, you want to take us to our claim and check out the co-op rock?" I asked.

It was the largest asteroid on my claim, which I considered to be just as much Tabby's as my own and I wanted a good look at it.

"Copy that," she said. Tabby accelerated and gracefully wove us through an unclaimed section of the belt.

"The light is crazy," I said to no one in particular. Descartes occupied the same solar position as Mars did in the Sol system, but the Tipperary star was twenty percent brighter and had a whiter light than our Sun. The end result was more light and heat than we were used to, even on Mars.

"Should be good for hydroponics," Marny said. "I think Nick bought plans for a hot-house."

"That sounds like Nick. Did he bring along any seeds?" I asked. It was the one thing you couldn't replicate on anything we could afford.

"Aye, Cap, he has a load of seeds," she said. Personally, I didn't care much for produce. Given sufficient bio-mass, I could replicate meal bars all day long.

Tabby slowed the ship as we approached the asteroid. While it wasn't anywhere near as big as Colony 40's giant iron egg, it was bigger than anything I'd ever mined.

"Hard for me to imagine we're going to move that anywhere," I said.

Tabby slowly sailed around the rock. We already had a good general survey of the claim, but were missing detailed surface scans that the ship was able to gather close up. The rock was roughly the shape of a short work boot, or it would be that shape once we leveled off the 'sole.' After that, we'd hollow out the 'heel' for a permanent control room and the 'ankle' for the habitat and a series of docking bays. To say we had big plans for this hunk of iron was an understatement.

"How long will it take to clear off the top of that thing?" Marny asked.

"Several months, I'd think," I said. "But, we won't do it all right away. We'll clear forty thousand square meters to give us enough room to stack a full load of unprocessed ore for the barge. There's a spot in the middle that's mostly flat already, so we'll start there. It should only take a couple of weeks."

"We should do a fly-by on the Licht and Carré claims," Tabby said.

"Sure, be nice to let 'em know we're in the area," I said.

We'd become friends with the Licht and Carré families and at least acquaintances with most of the rest of the expedition during the nightly banquets on Terminal One.

Tabby pulled the claim map up on her vid-screen and drew a navigation path that would take us on a tour of our immediate neighbors.

Open comm, Elsene Carré.

"Greetings, Liam Hoffen. It is good to hear from you. When you didn't rejoin the expedition the rumors started to fly. Is everyone safe and sound?" she asked.

"Greetings, Elsene. Roger that. Everyone is well. We're late because we had a stopover planned on Grünholz. We're just checking out the area, waiting for the rest of our company to arrive. Do you mind if we sail over your homestead?" I asked.

"Certainly. We'd love to see you. You should stop in for tea," she said.

"We can't at the moment. Mind if we take a raincheck?" I asked.

"Yes, that's fine," she said, sounding disappointed.

"I see their ship," Tabby said off-comm. She redirected *Hotspur* so we'd sail over the Carré's work site.

"We're sailing up on you now, you should see us just above the horizon of your ship," I said. I fired up our ship's powerful search lights.

Elsene was outside of their ship. A laser drill lay at her feet as she cleared a pad for a habitation dome. She waved as we sailed above her. Her husband, Queletin, and young daughter, Sevene, however, were nowhere to be found.

"We'll send a comm once we get settled. Let us know if you run into any problems," I said.

"Will do," she said.

The next claim belonged to the Licht family. They had two, the other owned by their eldest son, Selig. The distance between the claims was enough that it took a few minutes to leave the Carré's.

Open comm, Frimunt Licht.

"Frimunt," he answered tersely. I wasn't sure which family member I should contact. Frimunt wasn't much for talking.

"Hi, Mr. Licht. Liam Hoffen here. Do you mind if we sail over your claim? We're just checking out the area," I said.

"Hello, Liam." His accent was thick enough that it sounded more like he'd said hah-low. "Yes, you are permitted."

I turned our search lights back on so they'd be able to see us approaching. Otherwise, *Hotspur* was difficult to see.

Unlike the Carré homestead, the Licht's was buzzing with activity. They'd chosen a large asteroid and I counted the arc of three laser drills firing deep in a man-made cavern. The motion of a grav-sled caught my attention as one of the younger twins, either Ulran or Merley, was flying it pell-mell at a large pile of unprocessed ore. They were digging out a location for their homestead and making excellent time of it.

The grav-sled driver paused after dropping off his load at the ore pile and spun around to locate us. His ability to immediately locate us suggested that we'd been spotted by another family member and the information had been shared.

"Comm request, Annalise Licht."

Accept comm.

"Hi, Mrs. Licht," I said.

"Please, Liam, call me Annalise. You make me feel old. And, you must stop in," she said.

"We can't right now. We've only just arrived and are waiting for our other ships. We'll touch base after we're settled," I said.

"I'll keep you to that," she said.

I smiled, knowing she would.

"Are you all doing okay? It looks like you've made progress," I said.

"Frimunt said we've had a couple of equipment breaks and wondered if anyone had a Class C replicator available," she said.

"Our big replicator is over at Léger Nuage, but we've a significant parts supply. Can it wait? I can check our inventory if not," I said.

"Liam, we broke three P12 cap-spans. Must have gotten a bad batch," Selig Licht cut in. "We don't have much to trade right now and I'm hoping not to have to make a run back to Belirand. Their credit rates are bad and it'd be a waste of fuel."

It was tough luck. A miner could go an entire year without breaking a cap-span. The explosive charges wouldn't work without them. It was a real problem, as they couldn't clear the ore efficiently.

I punched up our inventory and saw that we had two full crates of cap-spans, and the P12s were by far the most common. They weren't inexpensive – about two hundred fifty credits each if you were in the Sol system. In Tipperary, I had no idea what we'd charge for them.

"I've got a load of P12s coming on *Sterra's Gift*. We can probably get 'em over to you in the next couple of hours, but I can't tell you what we want for 'em. That'll be Nick's headache. I'm sure we'll make you a good deal, though," I said.

"They're worth a lot if they save us a trip," he said.

"We'll be fair, don't worry. How many do you need?" I asked.

"We'd be interested in replacing all three of them," he said.

"Roger, that. I'll see if I can get Ada to run 'em over."

"Uh... That'd be great," Selig said. I could tell he was wondering if I was going to make a smart ass remark. But just hearing him stutter a little at hearing her name was all I needed.

"Cap. I've got *Adela Chen* on sensor and they're hailing us," Marny said.

"Selig. We need to go. Talk later," I said.

"Be safe. Licht out," he said and closed the comm.

Tabby and Marny had already worked out the location of the *Adela Chen* and *Sterra's Gift* and Tabby was accelerating through the asteroid field on an intercept course. I could hear Marny filling them in on the security status.

"Nick, you there?" I asked.

"Yup. What's up?" he asked.

"Where are we setting up the barge?"

We needed to disconnect it from the *Adela Chen* so we could start moving the big asteroid over to its new permanent home.

"We'll set up next to where we're going to drop the co-op rock. We can use it as our base of operations. There's plenty of room to land *Hotspur* and *Sterra's Gift* and we can unload supplies," he said.

"Until we get one of the cannons operational, I'm going to want to keep *Hotspur* close to me and Tabby," I said.

"Agreed," he said.

"Ada, you up for making a delivery?" I asked.

"What do you mean?" she replied.

"Lichts need some P12s," I said. "I told Selig you'd drop 'em off once we got settled, you up for that?"

"Sure. I'd love to," she said.

***

Six long steel containers loaded with gear and a newish pod-jumper were the extent of Mom and Dad's equipment. They'd loaded the containers back on Mars and once we'd come to a stop, they hadn't wasted any time chaining the containers together and setting off for their new home. I knew from experience that Dad would be drilling holes into rock within the hour. He'd have a difficult time resting until they had their homestead protected by the iron laden shell of an asteroid.

"You ready for this?" I asked, looking at Tabby.

I suppose I was a chip off of the old man's block. I'd already grabbed a mining laser and explosive bags and was sailing them and *Hotspur* over to our first cannon emplacement.

"I thought you didn't want to be a miner," Tabby said.

"I don't."

"You sure seem to be enjoying this."

I hadn't used a laser drill in over a year, but it felt good in my hands. I'd always taken a measure of pride in being fast and accurate and it was easy to fall back into the comfortable pattern. We'd estimated it would take three hours to clear a shelf off of this fifty cubic meter rock and I wasn't about to miss my first deadline.

Tabby had spent enough time around mining operations that she was good help. We didn't need to talk a lot as I punched horizontal drill holes into the surface of the asteroid and set up for a single sluff. I wasn't quite as fond of horizontal clearing as it required more quilting to keep the ore from flying off. At exactly two hours thirty minutes, we'd loaded the explosive bags into the drill holes, stretched the quilting out and fired up the gravity retainers.

"Blow it when you're ready," I said.

"It should be your honor," Tabby answered.

Even so, she picked up the virtual plunger, twisted and compressed it. I could feel the vibration of the gas expanding rapidly in the explosive bags, in turn, fracturing the ore away from the asteroid.

"I'll pack up the equipment, get the grav-sled and drop the ore on the back side. We'll come back for it later," I said.

"Copy that," she said.

Technically, it had taken us three and a half hours to clear the shelf. But, I felt okay with it.

"Marny, we're clear on the first cannon emplacement," I said.

"Okay, Cap. We're almost there," she said.

Locate Sterra's Gift.

My AI outlined a position in space with a translucent reticle.

"Want a ride?" Tabby asked.

She'd finished dropping off the ore and was headed back to *Hotspur's* open cargo hold with the grav-sled. I jetted over and sat down on the sled's large bucket. I noticed that it wasn't just *Sterra's Gift* sailing in, rather, there was also a pod-jumper with one of the large cannons awkwardly strapped beneath it.

"Want to do another one? I bet we could get it cleared in less than three hours this time," I said.

"Why not," she said.

ULRAN AND MERLEY

By the time we cleared the second cannon emplacement asteroid, Marny and Nick had the first cannon up and running. The single gun was able to run in a standalone mode, but we'd linked it into the sensor strips of our three ships to effectively extend its range. There were a multitude of ways to defeat a single gun, but with the extended sensors we'd given it, you'd need to bring your A-game and we'd have a lot of warning. Colony 40 had been protected by a single cannon, not much bigger than one of our three. That said, we'd lived through the failure of that approach and weren't excited about repeating history.

"I haven't been this tired in a long time," I said.

We were seated at the galley of *Hotspur* drinking a pouch of electrolyte water and eating a meal bar.

"You and Tabby are fast with that mining gear," Ada said.

"That's all Liam," Tabby said. "I just try to stay out of his way."

"Not true, clearing that rubble and ore is a big deal. Mining is mostly moving material and you're killer on that grav-sled," I said. "If you stuck with it, you'd get better fast. The horizontal shafts are the hardest. It's a lot easier drilling into the face of an asteroid than trying to drill across. Speaking of making progress. Ada, did Selig think those cap-spans were going to work for him?"

"Yes. He was delighted to get them," she said.

"Bet that's not the only thing he was delighted with," Tabby said under her breath, but loudly enough for everyone to hear.

It was hard to see a blush on Ada with her dark skin, but I knew her well enough to see a slight reddening.

"You're naughty," Ada said.

"I was thinking of offering them a trade for labor," Nick said. "Do you think they'd be interested?"

"Selig did say they'd be interested in working out some sort of a trade. They won't have Tipperary credits any time soon. They're hoping to trade all of their minerals with Belirand for food, fuel and new gear. I think they spent everything they had to get out here and are working on a shoestring budget," Ada said.

"They're living the dream, though. Scratching out their livelihood on a new frontier. I think it's romantic," Marny said.

"From what I've seen, they're really getting after it. They've got quite a pile already, although it didn't look like they had a pre-sift, so it's going to be lower quality," I said.

"Pre-sift?" Ada asked.

"A lot of the ore you pick up is just uninteresting rock, no real concentration of mineral. The pre-sift machine grinds it up and tosses out the junk. Tailings," I said.

"You have one of these?"

"Roger that. We have three," I said. "We'll need one for our refinery. The other two we'll either rent or sell."

"How are you going to staff a co-op?" Ada asked.

"To start with, it will be an occasional thing," Nick said. "We probably won't run the refinery or forge for quite a while. The co-op will just be a place people can pile their ore for delivery to

Belirand's Terminal Seven. Once we get enough for a delivery, we'll load it onto the barge and make a run."

"How are you going to figure out the cost for delivering ore?" Ada asked.

I took that one. "That will end up being your problem in the long run."

"Mine?"

"Sure. It's no different than any other load. Figure the cost of fuel, wear and tear on the ship, O2, paying the crew shares, etc.," I said.

"But how do I do that without knowing the value of anything?"

"I'll help," Nick said. "It's not as simple as Liam is making it sound, but we'll figure it out."

"So, tomorrow?" Marny asked.

"Finish installing the cannons and build a rig to mate the *Adela Chen* to the co-op rock. The sooner that thing is moved, the sooner we can start shaping it," Nick said.

"0600?" I asked. That would give us eight and a half hours of sleep.

"Geez, you really are your father's son," Tabby said.

I stood and pulled her up with me. "Let's get you into the shower, grumpy girl."

Reluctantly at first, Tabby followed me to the lift. Once in our room, I shucked my vac-suit and suit-liner and dropped the liner into the suit freshener. The vac-suit could probably use a cleaning, but that'd have to wait for another day. I turned the shower to a hot spray and let it knead the muscles I hadn't used in so many months.

Tabby slid in next to me. It was cramped quarters for two, but I wasn't about to complain. She massaged my shoulders from behind and for a moment I almost forgot that she was completely naked and pressed up against me. Almost. After our shower we fell asleep holding each other.

At 0530 the next morning I woke easily, my mind whirring with the tasks of the day. Tabby wasn't awake yet, so I snuck out of bed and pulled on a clean suit liner and my vac-suit. About halfway down the lift I smelled strong synth-coffee brewing. Marny was already at the mess table, drinking a cup and looking at her translucent reading pad.

"Whatcha looking at?" I asked.

"Morning, Cap. Sensor logs show we had a flyby from one of those light cruisers," she said.

I was surprised I hadn't gotten a warning. "How close and which one?"

"Not that close and they had their transponder disabled. They were just on the edge of our sensor range in an unclaimed area of the belt," she said.

"What do you think they were up to?"

"I imagine they were checking us out. They didn't get close enough to trigger a security perimeter warning, but I'm sure they saw the cannon. By design, it has a pretty significant sensor signature," she said.

"We knew it would happen sooner or later," I replied. "I'm just glad they didn't decided to push it. I was tired last night."

"I'm with you, Cap. There's something about physical labor that's different than exercising. It's a lot harder on the muscles," she said.

Nick walked out of their room, adjacent to the galley, his hair still wet from a shower.

"Any chance I could get you to draw up your plans for the control center?" I asked him. "I was thinking that Tabby and I could start drilling out a tunnel from the back side."

I knew he intended to place the control center for the co-op at the edge of the asteroid and the habitation, storage and docking bays would be stacked behind that.

"Already done," Nick said.

He pinched the plans off and flicked them at me. He'd drawn out thirty rooms of different sizes with a large oval-shaped atrium connecting them in the center. At one end was the control room and the other end joined up with five docking bays. The sheer number of cubic meters of material he was looking to remove was astounding.

"Never accuse you of dreaming small," I said. "That's probably three years of work for one person."

"Forty months, if you use the standard calculations. And that's just the main level. I figured it's best to have a plan. All I want is for you to clear a large enough space for the bots to reconstruct the warehouse we took from the pirate base and a hallway over to the control center," he said.

"How long will that take?" I asked.

"By yourself eight weeks, but I talked to Selig last night. He's interested in trading the twin's labor for parts and equipment rental. He said they've been mining since they were six."

"How long do you have them for?"

"They'll be helping for the foreseeable future. Selig wants to rent a pre-sift, pod-jumper, four containers, and another laser drill."

I whistled. "That's a lot. What about school, though?"

"They're only available from 1200 to 1700. Annalise does school in the morning with them and they have chores at home."

"You're too chipper for this time of the morning," Ada said, stumbling into the mess and sitting down with her knees drawn up tight against her chest for warmth.

Nick poured a cup of hot water and slid it and a bag of tea across the table to her. We'd learned that while she would drink coffee, she preferred tea. She smiled brightly at Nick for his thoughtfulness.

I heard the lift drop and watched as Tabby slunk over to the table. When she arrived, she sat on my lap and grabbed my coffee.

"Ada, you up for delivering more equipment to the Licht's?" I asked.

"I can. What am I delivering?" she said.

"Nick has a list. What about Ulran and Merley?" I asked, looking at Nick. "How soon can they start?"

"Selig said they were available today," he said.

"I'd say, take a pod-jumper out to their claim and bring them back. They can load up the equipment and run it back," I said.

"They're all of twelve stans. Ulran and Merley have no business flying pod-jumpers around full of equipment," Marny said.

Nick and Tabby exchanged a look.

"What?" Marny asked.

"When you grow up on a mining colony, the first thing you learn to do is fly a pod-jumper," I said. "I was delivering ore to the refinery when I was ten. It's just something you do."

Marny looked to Ada for support with raised eyebrows.

"Maybe I could fly with them a few times. Selig did suggest supervision, right?" Ada asked.

"Sure." I shrugged. "It's probably best."

"How long until you get the second cannon installed?" I asked.

"Two hours," Nick said. "The first was the hardest. Now that we know what we're doing it should be easier."

Half an hour later, Nick, Marny and Ada disembarked and we sailed *Hotspur* to our last emplacement.

Very similar to the setup at the pirate outpost where we'd obtained the cannons, we'd laid them out in a close triangle. Each cannon's range overlapped the other two by fifty percent. The layout significantly reduced the range of our defensive perimeter. The tradeoff was that an attack on one of the guns forced the attacker into range of the other two. We'd seen firsthand the results of medium-sized ships caught in their lethal kill box.

My muscles complained as I moved the mining machinery around the rock. It was a good feeling and I was surprised to discover that I'd missed the serenity of working in the dead calm of space. We easily finished the job by 1000.

"Nick, we're off to the co-op rock," I said. "We'll start on the harness."

"Yup. We're just finishing up here," he said.

The big asteroid's current location was well outside of the reach of the cannons, although I didn't expect any trouble. We'd only had a single flyby from one of the three Oberrhein cruisers. And while I had a bad feeling about the long-term implications of their involvement, there wasn't much we could do about it now.

It was pure serendipity that Belirand had decided to leave the tug's harness, which we'd used to get through fold-space, on the barge. It would save us from manufacturing something else with the limited supplies available to us. Nick would detach the four connecting posts from the barge and then Ada would fly it over and lower it into holes Tabby and I were to drill out in preparation. We'd sink the heavy legs of their harness twenty meters into the surface of the asteroid. The great thing is that it was already perfectly fit to the *Adela Chen*. There was some risk that if Belirand ever wanted the harness back they'd feel bad about our alterations to it, but it was too convenient to ignore.

"Frak," I said. I'd been looking at my HUD and using the AI's calculations of where the legs of the harness were to be placed. When I overlaid the proposed plan, I discovered a good sized hill right where the nose of the *Adela Chen* would be resting.

"What?" Tabby asked.

I flicked the plan to her and she groaned in appreciation. The hill would take at least twenty hours of labor to remove.

"Not much to be done about it, but we're going to need more gravity generators. That's going to be a big pile. We'll put it in that swale." I circled my fingers around a low spot to highlight it on my HUD then flipped it over to Tabby so she could see what I was talking about.

"I can't imagine clearing the entire top of this thing. It'll take forever," Tabby said.

"Don't think of it like that. This is all good ore on here. Think of it as excellent mining," I said.

"You think there's any precious?" she asked.

"Hard to tell. We'd need a pre-sift machine and a hundred meters of ore to get a good idea about that," I said. "There's always a chance, but it looks like it's mostly iron."

We laid out our equipment and started drilling. The hill was big enough that I was able to get both Tabby and myself working on it at the same time. It was good practice for her as sluffing off the face of a hill required less accuracy than trying to make a flat, horizontal cut.

We were ten percent into the hill when Ada raised me on the comm.

"You need anything before I drop off the boys?" she asked.

"I didn't think they were coming until later," I said.

"It's 1300, Liam," she said. "We've already delivered the equipment to Licht's claim and are headed back with Ulran and Merley."

I looked at the time on my HUD – 1312. We'd been drilling on the hill for three hours.

"Right. Sorry. Lost track of time. We need some equipment. I'll send you a list," I said.

I hastily punched up a list of what I figured we'd need to finish the job and sent it to her. We already had a sizeable pile of ore from the hill and needed grav generators to hold it down, along with another drill and grav-sled. I wasn't ready to start processing the ore since my real goal was to knock down the hill and get the shafts for the harness legs drilled.

An hour later the shadow of an approaching ship caught my attention. I found it odd to work in the bright illumination of the Tipperary system's star. On Colony 40 it was always our sensors or lights of the approaching ships that caught our attention. I looked up and saw one of our pod-jumpers on approach carrying the harness from the barge.

"Liam, can you anchor one of the legs?" Ada asked.

She pushed the nano-steel structure down toward the asteroid. I grabbed an impact hammer, stakes, and a loop of cable and jetted over to where she would touch down. After a few minutes, Tabby and I had it secured. I jetted up beneath the pod-jumper and freed Ada from the harness.

"You're free, Ada," I said.

She gently lifted away and landed next to the hill where we'd been working. I'd always been impressed with her light touch on the controls. Puffs of atmo escaped and three shapes exited the spindly craft. I mentally corrected myself, as I noticed it was one of the boys who'd actually been flying.

"That was a nice bit of flying, Merley," I said. My AI was generous in supplying the name of the boys on my HUD as they approached.

"Thank you, Mr. Hoffen," he said.

"What else are you good at?" I asked.

"Pod-ball," Merley said.

I laughed. "I bet, but I was wondering what mining equipment your Dad lets you use?"

"I can do the drill and the bags," Ulran said.

"You do not. Dad doesn't let anyone do the bags, except Selig," he said.

"Does too."

"Does not."

"Hold on boys," I said. "For now, you'll run the grav-sled and stretch out the blankets. If you do a good job with that, I'll check you out on the drill. Okay?"

They both agreed, but sounded disappointed. I understood. The grav-sled was the least interesting piece of equipment to run, but it was critical in removing the broken up material from the work area.

"I've got to go," Ada said. "Nick and Marny are waiting for me to come back for the *Adela Chen*."

"Merley, you want to run her back?" I asked.

"Yes sir," he said enthusiastically.

I showed Ulran where we were depositing the ore and started him on the grav-sled. As expected, he was quick about it and expertly started moving the loose material. He even re-arranged the gravity generators as the pile grew.

Tabby and I started drilling again and the three of us figured out a rhythm. It wasn't particularly difficult, drill holes, drop in the explosive bags, cover the face with a dampening quilt, blow the bags, pick up the rocks, rinse and repeat.

When Merley returned I called Ulran over and asked him to demonstrate his drilling skills.

"This is a nice drill," he said, lifting it into position on the ridge of the hill.

"We lost all of our equipment on Colony 40," I said. "It has less than ten hours on it."

"Merl, you're gonna love this thing," he said.

He completed the hole, moved over and drilled another. His movements were efficient and precise. No doubt he had plenty of hours with a drill.

"Merley, we'll switch every hour," I said.

It was impractical to have more than two drills running on the face of the hill, so I left Tabby and Ulran drilling and Merley cleaning up with the grav-cart. I started working on the shafts for the harness's legs. It was amazing how much faster we were able to work with the help of the boys. By 1700, when it was time for them to go home, we'd demolished the hill.

"I'd say that's a good point to stop," I said. "You boys are good help."

"Thank you, Mr. Hoffen," Ulran said.

"Let's load up in *Hotspur* and I'll get you snacks while Tabbs runs us over to your homestead," I said.

"We get to ride in that?" Merley asked, pointing at *Hotspur*.

"Sure. You can even sit in the pilot's chair if you want," I said.

Suffice it to say it didn't take much to get them moving after that.

A LINE IN THE SAND

By 1200 the next day we'd successfully attached the harness to the asteroid and set the *Adela Chen* in place. Nick had assured me that the forces on the harness were well within the nano-crystalized steel leg's tolerance, but when Ada fired up the tug's powerful engines and we didn't start moving, it felt like this might be a bad idea.

Fortunately, it was time for us to pick up Ulran and Merley. I had no problem admitting I was happy to leave. I didn't want to watch the epic struggle between the irresistible force of the tug and the immoveable asteroid.

"What are we working on today, Mr. Hoffen?" Merley asked. He and Ulran were squeezed between the pilot's chairs looking out the armored glass of the cockpit.

"We're working on the bottom side. We're going to bore a hundred forty meter corridor over to where we'll locate our security control room," I said.

"A hundred and forty meters? Do you actually have a bore?" Ulran asked.

"No. We'll use drills. It's not that hard, you just have to be accurate and check your depth. It won't go as fast as the hill," I said.

"Why do you need a security control room?" Merley asked.

"We're not just mining this asteroid. We're setting up a co-op and a place where people can stack ore. We may even set up a refinery," I said.

"What's that got to do with a security room?"

I loved how innocently he looked at the universe.

"We need to protect the co-op's equipment," I said.

Apparently, that was an invitation for them to start peppering me with questions about our equipment and other plans. Top on their list was if we had any intention of constructing a pod-ball court. Fortunately, I recognized it for the trap it was. If I suggested it was a possibility, I'd never hear the end of it.

When we returned, I was pleased to see that the *Adela Chen* hadn't spun off into the asteroid belt. It remained firmly attached to the asteroid. I read a slight delta-v from its original null velocity. It was moving, albeit slowly. If anyone but Nick had come up with this plan, I might have thought it was ridiculous.

Our goal was to burn around the clock. Much of our engine burn would be dedicated to changing direction as we attempted to weave through the asteroids. Without the AI, it would have been impossible to plan. The asteroid, once moving, would take hours to slow or change directions, even slightly. In the end, it had to arrive at the desired location, be pointed in the correct direction and be at a null velocity. Most people wouldn't come close to accomplishing this without a much larger ship. As it was, we were going to burn forty thousand credits of fuel to get it all done.

On the fifth day, we'd finished the three meter hole which ran from the front side of the 'ankle' of the upside-down boot to within six meters of the 'heel' where we'd locate the control room. It was tedious work and if I never had to bore a hole like that again, it would be too soon.

The control room turned out to be just as annoying. Nick had given us a very precise drawing of what he wanted us to clear. The problem was we'd ended up over clearing the room, but if it bothered Nick, he wasn't dumb enough to say anything.

"Don't you want a view of the outside?" I asked Nick.

"Not until we get our armored glass panels," he said. "I want the security room to be L2 space. We'll need three panels spaced at least two meters apart to accomplish that."

Six meters of separation from the vacuum of space was more than just a little protection. Like most things Nick was involved with, it was substantially over-designed. The material of the asteroid was rich in iron, which would nicely protect future station inhabitants.

"Well, you have your room now," I said. It wasn't news to Nick, as we'd already brought him down to show off the completed work.

"I've got enough panels to put an airlock back here. Are you going to be able to start on the docking bays, now?" he asked. "I thought we'd set up the warehouse in the first bay once you get it clear."

"We'll start tomorrow," I said. We'd stopped working at 1600 but with shifts on the *Adela Chen* eating into our sleep, I was getting cranky.

We resumed work the next day on the first docking bay beneath the 'arch' of our boot-shaped colony.

On the fourteenth day of our burn, the *Adela Chen's* engines finally spooled down. The asteroid was in its final resting place. Nick had thoughtfully oriented the co-op so that the star's rays illuminated the control room and habitation area. In the future, when we added armored glass, we'd be able to flood the interior with bright, natural light.

For the last two days we'd slowly been approaching our final destination. Impatience had overruled our initial safety concerns and we'd set the construction bot to the task of assembling the warehouse in the cleared docking bay. We'd started on a second docking bay, even though we knew we'd abandon it in favor of clearing the topside ore storage platform once we were at rest.

"How many meters are you planning to clear up here?" Merley asked. The 'sole' of the asteroid, to which he was referring, was eight hundred meters at its longest point and two hundred meters at its widest.

"Eventually we'll clear the entire thing, but for now we're just looking for forty thousand meters in the middle. See how it's flat through there?" I asked. "We're thinking that's only sixty thousand cubic meters to move."

"Only." Ulran scoffed. He was right. In the last two weeks we'd only moved ten thousand.

"It'll be a lot easier without having to worry about walls and corridors," I said.

"You're still talking about three months of work," Merley said.

"True enough. But we have you, don't we?" I asked.

"Slave labor, if you ask me," Ulran said.

It was a complaint he'd voiced a couple of times. The first time I'd felt bad, wondering about the morality of these kids working off their family's debt.

"Not like you wouldn't be mining at home," I said.

"Yeah, stop complaining, Ulran," Merley said. "At least we get to run the drills here."

"Got me there," he said.

It turned out that Merley's guess of three months wasn't that far off. The saving grace was that Nick, Ada and Marny all joined in. We spent initial time training Ada and Marny on the drills and while Nick had no interest in drilling, he didn't mind being relegated to running a grav-sled. Mostly because of her lighter build, Ada struggled more than Marny to begin with. But, after a couple of days both she and Marny were able to do a lot of the work, as long as I reserved the really difficult cuts for myself and the Licht twins.

When you spread three man-months of work between seven people, it gets done pretty quickly and two weeks later we had a big pile of sifted iron ore and a small pile of tailings. The last two days were spent without Ulran and Merley as they'd finally worked off what their family owed. To say that I was impressed with the rug-rats was an understatement.

I was glad to be done with the initial setup. We had man-years of work left to fully complete the co-op, but we'd accomplished much of our original plan.

"We should have a picnic," Marny announced.

"Where?" I asked.

"The warehouse. We could invite the entire expedition and have a pot luck," Marny said.

"That's a great idea," Nick said. "We could advertise it as a swap meet. We've been getting inquiries about equipment."

The swap meet quickly took on a life of its own once we sent out a comm to the rest of the expedition. Ian and Sylvia Folkson, a couple originally from Earth, volunteered to provide live music. Several other families requested reserved spots to set up tables where they could show off their wares. We considered charging for spaces, but for now, at least, we figured it made more sense to establish the community rather than try to make a small amount of money. Throughout the next week, requests and offers continued to come in and it was shaping up to be a great event.

One day before people were scheduled to arrive, we'd successfully cleared the warehouse by moving our extra equipment and supplies into the corridor and control center. We decided not to move the missiles, but instead used habitation dome panels to construct a locked room around them. According to Marny, moving them was safe, but not recommended.

"Cap, Nick, we have a situation," Marny said. Her AI had been monitoring a constant feed from the control room.

"On my way," I said.

Tabby and I were in the warehouse, helping arrange the shelves that held the equipment we'd brought from Mars for the purpose of trade.

"Belay that, Cap. Let's get you and Tabby into *Hotspur*," she said.

My heart raced.

"Tabbs?" I said as I made my way to the warehouse's airlock.

"On your six," she said.

We cycled through the lock, jetted to *Hotspur* and slid through the energy barrier and into the hallway. I knew Marny would prefer us to be in our armored vac-suits, but we'd lose minutes changing clothes and anything that could punch through the armor of *Hotspur* wouldn't struggle to crack armored vac-suits. I looked for Filbert and saw that he was asleep in the grav-box.

We jogged through the bridge and spun up the engines as we pulled on our combat harnesses. We worked through the abbreviated checklist we used for emergency situations. Fortunately, we were showing green.

Prepare for departure, I said. The AI would close the airlocks and if there was someone on board that we were unaware of they'd be notified. It would also cause the clamps to release our landing gear.

"Green?" I asked Tabby.

"Green," she agreed.

I pulled back on the stick and gently lifted *Hotspur* away from the asteroid. We'd taken to mooring it on the station side of the rock. Eventually we'd have our own docking bay cut out, but for now, we had installed temporary clamps to hold the ship in place.

"We're up, Marny. Where are we going?" I asked.

The forward holo jumped to life and I saw three small cruisers lined up on the edge of our security perimeter. In my mind, I might consider taking on one of the cruisers in a pinch. Each ship was thirty percent larger than *Hotspur* and carried the same weapons compliment. But, that also meant we'd be faster and more maneuverable. What the cruisers gave up in speed, they more than gained in armor. With three ships, they'd easily pin us down if we weren't careful, and you could forget about us lining up for any offensive maneuvers.

Not surprisingly, the ship's registrations showed up as I'd expected – *Karelia, Kordun* and *Stenka*.

Show defensive perimeter coverage zones on forward holo, I said.

"Marny, sit-rep," I said.

"Twelve minutes ago, our defensive perimeter sent an automated announcement to the three ships requesting a turret lockdown. When they failed to comply, we informed them that entering our space with weapons hot would be interpreted as a hostile action," she said.

"Have they responded?" I asked.

"No."

"I see. Stay on the comm. I'll attempt to make contact," I said.

Hail Kordun.

"Captain Hoffen. You need to turn off your defensive systems. We're here to fulfill our obligation to the Belirand Corporation," I recognized the voice of the person who'd tried to board the *Adela Chen* near Léger Nuage.

"Please identify yourself," I said.

"Captain Miles Benesch, Oberrhein."

"Captain Benesch, please state the obligation with Belirand that allows you to invade our territory with turrets hot," I said.

"As you've been informed, Oberrhein has a security contract with Belirand. We provide patrols of their interests in the Descartes asteroid belt."

"Wait one," I said.

Mute comm.

"Nick are you catching this? Are we obligated to allow them to sail through our space, fully armed?"

"There is nothing in the contract. Generally, however, claim holders have the right to defend their territory from all trespassers. Belirand is allowed to manage the claims for the NaGEK consortium, but I'm not able to find anything that supports an extension of Belirand's authority to our claims," he said.

"Got it," I said.

Unmute comm.

"Captain Benesch, your request is denied. We welcome your presence on our claims as long as your weapons are restricted in accordance with an accepted lockdown protocol," I said.

"I'm afraid that isn't your call to make, Hoffen," he said. "We're coming in. If you fire on us, it'll be a fight you can't expect to win."

"We're not bluffing, Captain Benesch. We're taking your threats against my family and company very seriously. If you cross that boundary our cannons will engage you as a hostile entity. I don't know why you insist on escalating, but we will stand firm," I said.

Close comm.

The three ships started to slide forward.

"Cap. What do you want me to do?" Marny asked.

"What would you recommend?" I asked.

"I don't think we can afford to roll over. If we do, they'll own us," she said.

I looked to Tabby.

"You know what I think. Personally, I'd draw them in deep enough to make sure we can take 'em all out," she said.

"Marny, we're going dark. Once all three of the ships are completely inside our perimeter, fire a warning shot and if they engage, you know what to do," I said.

"Aye, Cap. Stay safe," she said.

Engage silent running.

The holo projector popped off at the same time the lights of the bridge extinguished and vid screens blacked out. I also knew that our turrets had been covered by an armored cowl and missile ports were closed. We'd lost our offensive capacity, but with nine turrets lined up on us, we really didn't stand a chance from our current position.

I rolled *Hotspur* up and to the portside using a minimum amount of thrust, but still headed in their direction. With three ships and a recent, known location, they might be able to track us. It all depended on the fidelity of their sensors.

"You getting any movement on their turrets?" I asked Tabby.

"They had aligned on us, but they're no longer tracking," she said.

I saw friendly cannon fire cross a hundred meters in front of the advancing ships, drawing a line in the sand. I accelerated and sailed in their direction. With a gentle stick, I turned the ship so that we were directly behind the *Kordun*.

"This could get messy. You ready, Tabbs?" I asked.

"You're one crazy frak, you know that? And heck yah, I'm ready. All I need is two seconds to open the ports on the missile bays," she said.

"Okay, I want you to do that, but don't fire unless they fire on us," I said.

"Oh geez, I hope they fire," she said. That's my warrior-girl.

If they did, it would be a mistake on their part. In our current position, our missiles would shred the small cruiser's engines and likely knock out power to the entire ship.

"They're open," she said.

Their turrets swiveled to orient on *Hotspur*. Our position was such that without moving their ships they'd have a difficult time getting a good shot.

Hail Kordun.

"Captain Benesch. We've been more than polite. You need to back off, unless you want me to put an end to this right now. You need to stand down your turrets and move out of *Loose Nuts* controlled space. Do you read me?"

For a tense moment I wondered if he would actually comply. Then the ships finally changed direction enough that they were no longer heading into our space and their turrets returned to a more neutral position. I knew they could easily swivel right back, but for the moment we'd been successful.

"This isn't over, Hoffen," he said.

"It doesn't have to be this way, Captain Benesch. We're not looking for a fight. We're just here to make an honest living."

"Pretty words, Hoffen. You're in our space now and we'll see how you feel when you're not hiding behind your big guns," he said.

I terminated the comm and sailed back toward the co-op. There would be no value in mixing it up with this guy.

"Nicely done, Marny," I said.

"Thanks, Cap. I think you rattled his cage with that backdoor move. I'm afraid he's right though. This thing isn't over."

"We need to take these jerks out," Tabby said. "We're not getting anywhere being nice and one of these days they're going to catch us in the open."

"It's a fine line, Tabbs. If we attack, unprovoked, we open ourselves up to legal problems. We really need them to flinch first," I said. "Marny, we're going to be out of comm for a couple of hours. I want to see where these guys are headed."

"Aye. Stay frosty," she replied. "Tabby, you might get your wish yet today."

I engaged the ship's silent running mode again and turned back toward the three Oberrhein ships. We followed them as they tracked toward another claim. I pulled up the owner's information on my HUD and discovered it was the Jance family, who we'd only talked to in passing.

As the trio of warships passed over the homestead, they turned on their bright search lights and illuminated the claim, completely washing it in harsh light. We watched in silence as the Jance's put down their equipment and turned around to look up at the three ships.

"I'm gonna frakking kill these sons of –" Tabby said.

"Hold on there. Technically, they're not doing anything illegal," I said.

"Whose laws? We're not under Mars Protectorate or even NaGEK for that matter. This is intimidation, pure and simple and I could stop it with a couple of well-placed missiles," she said.

"Intimidation for what purpose?" I asked.

"Does it matter?"

After a few minutes of the treatment, the Oberrhein fleet moved on. I hung back long enough to watch the Jance couple embrace and walk back to their habitation dome, holding hands, leaving their equipment behind. It was disheartening.

We followed the ships and observed them repeat this behavior time and time again. It was a disgusting display, but I also knew how effective it had to be. The miners would feel cut off and alone. They couldn't hope to stand against the power being displayed.

"Do you suppose the Lichts, Carrés and your family received a similar visit?" Tabby asked.

"No idea," I said.

The ships had arrived at a new claim and fired up their lights, looking to draw out the claim holders. I had my AI search for the owner's name, not having memorized where people were located. It looked like whoever it was still lived on the ship that brought them to the claim. Finally, my HUD displayed one Dave Muir, an older, single man, in his mid-sixties. We'd met him at the banquet - a crusty old fart. He'd been mining his entire life and wanted nothing more than to be left alone. According to him, he'd figured one couldn't get further away from all of the a-holes than by going to Tipperary. Tabby and I watched as he shouldered a blaster rifle and plinked away at the ships.

"That dumb-ass! He's going to get himself killed," Tabby said.

The *Kordun* returned fire. Three shots laid down in front of him.

"That's it!" Tabby said.

"No! Hold it," I said.

When the debris cleared we could see that he'd been knocked down, but was still moving. I suspected they were talking to him on the comm. To his credit he lifted himself up to his knee and shouldered his weapon and fired.

"They're going to kill him," Tabby said.

"Wait," I said.

The *Kordun's* turrets swiveled, locked on the old man's ship and opened fire. After twenty seconds it exploded, sending shrapnel in all directions. Fortunately, old man Muir had dived behind the low hill he had been working on.

"Convinced yet?" Tabby asked.

"Yes. We can't win this fight but we can save that man's life."

We held back and waited for the ships to move on. They sat for a few minutes waiting to see if Muir would get up, which he didn't. A few minutes later, they slowly moved on, not bothering to lend him aid.

"Watch my back," I said.

"What are you doing?" Tabby asked.

"I think he's alive. I'm going to go check," I said.

I ran down to the armory, pulled on my armored vac-suit and loaded up my favorite flechette. Given the circumstances, I wasn't sure why I'd chosen to carry a weapon, but Marny would have chastised me later if I hadn't.

"We clear enough to open the side airlock?" I asked over the comm.

"Roger, that, they've moved out of sensor range," she said.

I fired up the energy barrier, which would allow me to leave the hallway pressurized, and slipped out next to the ship. We were a few hundred meters from Muir's claim and I arc-jetted over to his last known position, keeping low to his asteroid.

Establish line of sight comm channel with David Muir, I instructed the AI.

I popped over the small hill and took a blaster round to my shoulder. I spun away involuntarily as my shoulder erupted in pain.

"Frak, Liam, are you okay?" Tabby broke radio silence, possibly giving away our location.

"Clear the channel, Tabbs. I'm fine," I said. I'd lost the use of my left shoulder, but it was a temporary affliction.

"What do you want?" Muir asked, standing on a hill looking down at me with his blaster rifle squarely aimed at my chest.

I raised my one working hand. "Peace, Mr. Muir. We saw what Oberrhein did to your ship and wanted to offer aid," I said.

"Does it look like I need help?" he asked hotly.

"Yes. Frankly, it does. Unless you have another place to stay," I said.

He remained quiet but didn't lower his weapon.

"If you really want us to, we'll leave, but I think you need some help. Can you lower that weapon?" I asked.

"Shite," he said and lowered the gun.

I popped up and massaged my shoulder. Feeling was starting to be restored.

"I don't know if they're coming back. We should grab whatever we can from your claim and clear the area for now," I said.

I followed him over to the burned out husk of his ship. It was a total loss.

"Frak," he swore softly. "They got it all."

"Not your drill and most of your mining equipment," I said.

"A lot of help that'll be," he said.

"Liam, they're coming back," Tabby said. It was a devil's choice she had to make. Her comm would likely alert them to our presence, but if they were coming back to the claim, we'd be stuck down here.

"Time's up. We have to go now," I said. I recognized the old man's slowness. He was experiencing shock, trying desperately to figure out how to piece his world back together.

I wrapped my arm around his waist and lifted off with my arc-jets. It wasn't impossible to fly while holding another person, but it was awkward. Initially, I overshot the hatch into the ship but quickly adjusted and slid Muir through the energy barrier in front of me. I helped him to his feet and swung the door closed.

"Tabbs, get us out of here," I said.

HUBRIS

"Are you okay, Mr. Muir?" I asked. I hadn't exactly asked his permission to abduct him from his asteroid and throw him into our ship.

He just looked back at me.

Scan Muir for injuries.

"Look, I've got to get back to the bridge. If they've seen us, we could be in for trouble," I said.

I didn't wait for his answer and jumped through the energy barrier between the hallway and the Berth Deck.

"David Muir's blood pressure is elevated and there are no visible injuries," my AI informed me. I'd rather have scanned him with a medical device but there wasn't time.

"Sit-rep," I said, jumping into the chair next to Tabby.

"I think they see us," she said.

"I don't know, they're pretty far off," I said. "Head toward that asteroid twenty degrees off-port and see if they follow."

"Frak, that. Let's see if they want to play with the big boys and girls," Tabby said.

I pulled my combat harness on and hoped that Muir would find a soft spot to hold on to. Tabby was in the chair and it was her call. I pulled the weapons display up on my HUD and instructed the targeting system to acquire a soft missile lock. Their systems wouldn't know I had a lock. I'd have to upgrade before I fired unless we were at point blank range, which with Tabby wasn't out of the question.

The asteroids in this part of Muir's claim were dense enough that the Oberrhein ships were unable to sail three abreast. Tabby was pressing our advantages of both speed and agility. In open space, the three cruisers would tear us apart, but in this part of the field they'd have a difficult time getting a line on us. If they wanted to play a game of dash through the boulders, I'd be up for that.

Tabby hit the combat burn at what felt like a full hundred percent and we accelerated at a mad rate. The strain of acceleration made it difficult to concentrate on their lead ship, *Stenka*, and I struggled to dial in a firing solution with the turrets.

My HUD displayed three individual blue outlines of firing yokes in front of me. I swept my hand across, combining the yokes into a single firing plan. Unlike Marny, I had no chance at controlling two turrets independently and as it was, at these speeds, I'd be firing in what Marny referred to as the 'spray and pray' pattern.

A warning klaxon sounded moments before the *Stenka* fired their forward laser blasters. Tabby's response was immediate and jarring as she pushed down hard into the asteroid field. It felt like a blind maneuver and for a moment I was worried that Tabby might not know what was directly beneath us. I quickly pushed the idea out of my mind as I realized she was giving me an opportunity with our two top turrets. I didn't waste it and laid on the trigger. The turrets responded with their muted staccato thwupping.

Don't watch your bolts. Marny had drilled this into me. It was a common mistake for new gunners to watch their rounds streaking towards the enemy and ignore the targeting reticle. I didn't release until the *Stenka* became obscured by a passing asteroid.

Engage silent running, Tabby commanded.

My virtual turret controls flashed yellow. I'd have to unlock them to override Tabby's command. It wasn't difficult to do and it would also be the wrong answer. Tabby's aggressive run at the Oberrhein ships had given us enough delta-V in our trajectories that it made their chance at finding us infinitesimal.

"Feel better?" I asked. I was glad that Tabby hadn't decided to fully engage them.

"I'm disappointed you didn't toss a couple of missiles their way," Tabby said.

"I'm not sure if we're that kind of friends yet. I felt like they were holding back and I wasn't looking to escalate," I said.

"They didn't fire more because they didn't have a better firing solution," Tabby said. "These guys aren't any different than the Red Houzi."

Tabby turned her head slightly as we heard the lift operating at the back of the bridge.

"Geez, I hope it isn't that bad," I said. "I hope these guys are better business people than that. Nobody wins if we're shooting at each other."

"Don't be an idiot, kid," Mr. Muir's rough voice caught me off guard. "They'll be by your claim soon enough to shake you down. After your performance here, I'd guess they'll do to you what they did to me - without the benefit of the speech."

"What'd they ask for?" I asked.

"Does it matter?" he responded bitterly.

"Humor me," I said.

"Five thousand meters of premium ore every month," he said.

"In exchange for?" I asked.

"Think before you open your trap, kid. What do you think?"

"I suppose so they'll leave you alone," I said.

"Right. You might as well have left me there. They blew up everything I had and I'm too old to start over," he said.

"You always been a miner, Mr. Muir?" I asked.

"What's it to you?" he asked. He'd taken a seat between our two chairs and was staring at the floor of the bridge.

"Mostly just curious," I said.

"I was a Marine and did a few tours. After that mining sounded nice and quiet," he said.

"Same with my Dad," I said.

"Yeah. We talked."

I couldn't imagine they'd talked for long.

"You want another shot at those dickheads or are you all used up?" Tabby asked.

Muir looked over to her and shook his head. "Too young to be an officer."

"I didn't realize that Marines gave up when they got old," she said.

He looked at her flatly. "You're about to cross a line."

"What? You're not dead yet? Answer the question. You want another shot at em?" she asked.

"You think this little plinker can stand up to three cruisers?" he asked.

"Listen jackass," she said. "This ship just saved your life."

"Hold on you two," I said. "First, we're not headed back to your claim anytime soon. Not, at least, while those cruisers are there. Second, like it or not, we're on the same side out here."

"And?" he asked.

"And, I've got a proposition for you," I said.

"This ought to be good."

"You come work for me on my claim. I'll give you twenty percent of the net on the ore you mine," I said.

"Yeah, that's real generous. I get a hundred percent on my own."

"Hear me out. I'll supply fuel, equipment, food and a habitation dome. Once you're back on your feet, you can do what you want, no strings attached. In return, you'd need to put in some shifts, help out around the warehouse, taking watch, that sort of thing."

"What about Oberrhein?" he asked, staring into the grav-box at Filbert, who was sleeping comfortably.

"We've three General Astral 65mm Long Range Blaster Cannons set up. Defending our home isn't a big problem," I said.

He grunted, which I took as a grudging sign of respect. I reached over my chair, unlatched the grav-box and pulled the sleepy kitty out.

"What'd you bring a damn cat into space for?" he asked.

"We collect strays. What do you say? Any interest?" I asked.

Filbert looked Muir up and down, purring and nudging the man's hand.

"Stupid animal," he said.

I caught Tabby's eye just as she was about to pounce and got her to hold off on what was sure to be a good tongue lashing.

Filbert had pushed his way onto Muir's lap and, contrary to his words, he gently scratched the cat's neck.

***

Getting Muir set up wasn't difficult. We had extra habitation domes and mining equipment available. I shared with him the plans for one of the four remaining docking bays and by the next morning he'd started removing material. It was hard to watch him work as he moved slowly. That said, he had an efficiency to his movements that showed a long familiarity with the task.

By 1500, forty-five of the ninety-two members of the expedition had shown up for the swap meet. It was a better turnout than I'd expected, given the threatening nature of the Oberrhein ships. On the other hand, swap meets were critical to most colonies, as exactly the wrong type of equipment had a habit of breaking at just the right time.

The warehouse was littered with equipment and crates as people showed off items they'd brought to trade. Overall we were at max capacity for the warehouse, so it was probably good more people hadn't shown up.

"Did you get a visit from Oberrhein?" I asked Dad. We were standing in a small knot of people and it was the first chance I'd had to talk to him.

"We did. They're offering protection for about a quarter of our monthly production," he said.

"What'd you tell 'em?"

"I didn't answer. I figured they'd said what they needed. Frimunt said they got the same visit," he said.

"You hear about Muir?" I asked.

"Marny told me. Old nut shouldn't have fired on them," he said.

"True, hard to blame him though."

Selig and Ada had found each other and were talking. It might be completely innocent, but no doubt much would be made about it after the party.

"You still owe us a visit for tea," Elsene Carré said, as she approached holding a very wiggly Sevene.

"Hello, Sevene," I said and looked up at Elsene. "You're right, we need to do that soon. How are you getting along with the mining?"

"Queletin isn't much with a drill, but he's coming along okay with the grav-sled."

"Equipment holding up?" Dad asked.

"I'm having trouble with my drill. Not all the time, but sometimes," she said.

"What kind of trouble?"

"It's this ridge I've been working. The drill keeps sliding off. I originally thought it was Queletin being a rookie, but I've got the same problem."

Dad scratched his chin and thought about it for a moment. "Frimunt, you have a minute?" He called over the elder patron of the Licht family.

Frimunt picked his way over and nodded his head in acknowledgement. "Pete. Liam," he said and turned to Elsene. "I don't believe we've been introduced."

"Elsene Carré, meet Frimunt Licht," I said.

"Elsene was describing a problem she's been having with her laser and I wanted to hear what you thought," Pete said.

Elsene described her problem again. Dad and Frimunt exchanged a knowing look and Frimunt nodded seriously.

"Annalise, would you bring Wilma over?" Frimunt said. It was noisy enough that his AI would have had to pipe it to her suit.

A moment later, Annalise worked her way through the crowd with Wilma. Frimunt and Annalise exchanged a look and then Frimunt made introductions.

"I was just about to let Wilma have a cupcake. Is that something you'd allow Sevene?" Annalise asked Elsene.

Elsene hadn't missed the nonverbal communication. "Yes, of course." She set Sevene on the ground.

"We only need a few minutes," Frimunt explained apologetically to his wife.

Annalise smiled and knelt down so she was at the same level with two little girls. "How about it girls? Is it time for cupcakes?"

"What's this all about?" Elsene asked.

"Not here," Big Pete said.

"*Hotspur's* just outside," I said. I thumbed my ring and caught Tabby's eye across the room. I preferred that she knew where I was. She smiled and I felt the familiar ping back on my finger.

"Yes," Frimunt agreed.

"So, the big secret?" Elsene asked again once we were all standing in the combined galley/mess on *Hotspur*.

"Frimunt?" Big Pete asked.

"There is only one thing that will deflect a laser drill like you've described and that's a sizeable gem," he said.

"Gems with a high refractive index," Big Pete said. "Most likely you're onto Hematite, it's common on these iron asteroids. But don't mistake common with not valuable. A kilo of Hematite is worth a hundred Mars Credits, and I've seen formations where there were thousands of kilos. On the other side of the spectrum, you could be on to Diamond. I don't believe I need to spell out what that could mean."

"If you can't drill into it, how do you extract the gems?" Elsene asked.

"*Communication request, Dave Muir,*" my AI informed me through my earwig. I stepped away from the group and lowered my face shield.

Go ahead. "Hello Muir, what's up?"

"Thought you might like to know, there's someone lurking in the corridor that leads back into the asteroid," he said. It had to be the corridor that led to the control room. We hadn't had time to manufacture any monitoring devices, so it was possible.

"Roger that, Muir. Appreciate the heads up. You should join the party, there's beer and cupcakes."

"For frak sake! Nobody drinks beer with cupcakes," he said and closed the comm.

"Marny, who's in the control room?" I asked.

"Nick. What's up Cap?" she asked.

"Muir said he saw someone headed down the tunnel," I said.

"Meet me at the entrance. I'll warn Nick," she said.

"I'll bring a blast rifle for you," I said.

"Aye."

"Tabby, we have something going on in the control room. Can you find a flechette and position yourself by the front door of the warehouse just in case something's going down?"

"Got it. I see Marny headed out the back of the warehouse. I'll warn Silver and Ada," she said.

"Copy that," I said.

I was right by the armory and palmed the security panel to enter. I slipped a shoulder holster on, equipped a blaster pistol, plucked a blaster rifle from the rack and stepped back into the short hallway separating the armory from the exit hatch.

"What's going on, Liam?" Dad stood in the doorway that led back onto the Berth Deck.

"Not sure. Reported intruder in the control room," I said. "Mom's still in the warehouse, you might bring her a flechette."

"No need, she's got her Ruger," he said. It surprised me, but I didn't have time to talk about it. I knew Mom owned a Ruger laser pistol, but I hadn't seen her carrying it.

I popped through the energy barrier of the external hatch and fired my arc-jets. *Hotspur* was clamped on the side of the asteroid less than ten meters from the front of the warehouse. I landed behind the warehouse, just out of visual range of the corridor.

Marny had a flechette drawn and holstered it on my approach. I handed her the blaster rifle.

Establish tactical channel with Marny and Nick.

"Sit-rep," I said.

"Three armed in the tube, eighty meters in." Marny said.

"Nick, what's your weapon status?"

"Flechette," he said. I mentally kicked myself. I couldn't imagine why we'd been so confident that no one would breach an open hole behind the warehouse that we hadn't secured it at all.

"Focus, Cap," Marny said. Somehow she always knew when I was getting distracted.

"Simple plan. I'll confront them, no weapons drawn and see if I can de-escalate," I said.

"That's risky," Marny said. "What if they decide to fire on you?"

"We don't even know who these guys are. It could be kids for all we know. But, if it's an attack on the control room, I'd like to know that before they get to Nick. They're in the open right now and that gives us leverage," I said. "Nick, contact Dad and get him back into the warehouse, and send Tabby out. I'd like another body out here."

"Will do," he said.

"Marny, cover me," I said.

"Aye."

While I had confidence in Marny's accuracy with a blaster rifle at eighty meters, I knew that if everything went to crap, I wasn't going to be in the best spot. I wished I'd had time to pull on an armored vac-suit, or at least grab a riot-shield.

The corridor was three meters across and roughly squared out. I entered it and laid into my arc-jets. My HUD displayed the three figures who'd made it another twenty meters and were getting too close to Nick's position for my comfort. Their suit lights popped on and they turned when I got within thirty meters. I slowed my approach and flipped over, keeping my feet towards them. It was common courtesy for spacers to orient themselves when in zero-g but I wanted to present the smallest possible target.

"Identify yourselves," I said, flipping on my own suit lamps.

The middle figure raised a blaster rifle and aimed it generally in my direction.

"Marny, not yet," I said. I didn't want to be the first to fire. I could imagine her annoyance and was glad that Tabby wasn't behind me yet. My directive would have been lost on her.

"You first, bitch." My AI recognized the voice and displayed the name Teodorov Tsankov. He'd been one of the pod-ball players from Oberrhein. He was a nasty player and very fast.

"Put your weapons down, Tsankov. You're trespassing," I said.

"You first," he said.

"I don't have a weapon pointed at you," I said.

"Maybe I'm not talking to you," he said.

"That's not going to happen," Tabby's voice came over the channel. "You want to get out of this in one piece, you put it down. Otherwise, I'm drilling for gold in that ugly dome of yours."

Uncontrollably, I rolled my eyes. Somehow Tabby and I were going to need to get on the same page with our approach. That said, her reputation of being a hothead had some benefit. Tsankov lowered his blaster so it wasn't pointing directly at me. It was something at least.

"We were just looking for the head and got lost," he said. "Do you treat all of your guests like this?"

"Lay your weapons on the ground," I said, still not holding my own. My HUD showed the tactically chosen targets. Tabby had Tsankov, Marny had the guy on his left and they'd tagged the woman on the right as my target.

"Not going to happen," Tsankov said.

"We'll give 'em back when you leave. Your weapons aren't allowed on our station as was clearly communicated," I said. "This isn't negotiable."

"Liam, we have a problem in the warehouse," Dad said over a separate comm channel.

As long as I preceded communication with a name, my AI would correctly route the comms. "Dad, emergency or under control?"

"Under control, but needs attention," he said.

"Roger that, we'll be there shortly," I said, then turned back to the problem at hand. "Tsankov, whatever you had planned didn't work. The warehouse is secure. Put your weapons down or we'll do this hard."

There was a long silence. I'd zoomed in on Tsankov and could see that he was talking to someone over a private comm. I used the distraction to pull out my own blaster, but held it in a neutral though easy to point position. Nick had come out of the control room and had targeted Tsankov also.

The three let go of their weapons and allowed them to float

slowly toward me. It was a provocative move. I knew that with their pod-ball experience they'd be able to recover them quickly if necessary.

"Drop your AGB boots," I said.

"You're mad," he said.

"Do it."

They complied. I directed them to fly slowly out. Most of a person's thrust when using AGBs came from the boots and by removing them, I'd left myself with a significant advantage. When we reached the end of the corridor, Marny removed their gloves and zip-tied their hands together while Tabby held a blaster rifle on them.

"What are we going to do with them?" I asked. I'd expected we'd just release them.

"We've a situation in the warehouse," Marny said. "We can't deal with them right now."

"Right you are," Tabby said. She grabbed Teo and pulled him upward as she pushed off with her boots. At one hundred meters she zeroed their delta-v with the station and left him.

"What are you doing?" I asked.

"Temporary brig," she said.

I shrugged, it wasn't a bad idea.

"Nick, take their weapons and hole up in the control center," I said.

"Can do," he said.

I grabbed the second male, whom I was able to identify as Mihael Ivov, the one who'd injured Marny and had his wrist broken by Tabby. I set him ten meters away from Tsankov as Tabby dropped off the third, a woman I recognized as Petar's girlfriend, although I didn't know her name.

Add Big Pete, Mom and Ada to tactical channel.

"Dad, we're on our way in. What's going on?"

"You'll see," he said.

We cycled through the airlock. The warehouse had transformed from the festive environment we'd left. A dead silence hung in the air while people quietly packed up their belongings. Mom was standing by the front airlock with her shiny silver Ruger laser pistol in hand. She smiled grimly at me and nodded toward a stack of shelves, behind which we'd stored all of the items that weren't part of the swap meet.

As we walked through, the families we'd had such a fun time with just half an hour ago avoided making eye contact. I couldn't imagine what had changed in such a short period of time.

Behind the shelves, I found Big Pete and Ada standing behind Petar Kiirilov and two others that I recognized as Oberrhein. The three had their hands tied behind their backs and were kneeling on the floor of the warehouse.

"What's this about?" I asked, looking to Dad.

Petar spoke first. "You should kill me now, Hoffen. As far as Oberrhein is concerned, you and your family are all dead."

Big Pete stepped forward and bashed the back side of Petar's head. For a moment I thought he'd killed him, but movement convinced me otherwise.

"What the frak, Dad?" I said.

"Sorry, just really getting tired of hearing that from him," he said.

"You want to fill me in?" I asked.

"Ask her," he said. "She seems to be his second."

He nodded to a woman who I'd seen at one of the Belirand banquets. She was compact with dark olive skin and short black hair. Her scarred face suggested a hard past. I noticed that she had several blades strapped to her vac-suit.

"You are who?" I asked.

"Bacheva," she said. "Petar may have underestimated you, but it will not change your fate. Your family has been marked as enemies of the Oberrhein nation. We have informed the rest of the expedition that if they continue to fraternize with you they will be granted a similar status. We are not without compassion, though. We're allowing for a short period of amnesty for those who have chosen the wrong side. You will now see who your friends truly are."

"Care to tell me why?" I said.

"So naïve. We are Buccaneers. We take what we want from who we want. If you stand against us then you are our enemies. You could have avoided all of this if you had simply complied. Your hubris will be your end. Did you really think you could stand against an entire nation?"

SLOW RIDE

In the end, we asked everyone to leave. The Lichts were the last to go. While emotionally tough, there wasn't a choice to be made. They had no capacity to stand up against Oberrhein.

We'd decided to release Petar and his crew. We had no capability to hold them and there was no court with jurisdiction over the asteroid belt. I'd like to say that it didn't cross my mind to simply space the entire group, but as vile as they were, they hadn't earned a death sentence.

"We'll collect our items and stay on the station for a while," Dad said. Originally, he'd wanted to tough it out on their claim, but Mom convinced him that was a bad idea.

"Marny, if Oberrhein is still in the area, how should we approach getting Mom and Dad's stuff? I don't want to get caught off-guard again," I said.

"You and Tabby in *Hotspur* with Pete and Silver. Ada and I will provide backup from *Sterra's Gift*, but we'll stay within the defensive perimeter. Nick stays in the control room," she said.

"Any objections?" I asked.

We'd all changed into armored vac-suits. I wasn't completely sure what to think about our predicament. Was I causing all of this? Was it all hubris? Should we have stayed safe back at Sol? I pulled myself back to the present, knowing that Marny would bust me for reveling in non-productive thoughts when I was needed in the present.

Prepare for departure, I said. The AI keyed on those words and unclamped, making sure we were locked up tight. It also forwarded the message to all inhabitants of the ship.

Mom and Dad both reported back a green status from Marny and Nick's workstations.

Engage silent running, I said. I couldn't fathom just how valuable the stealth capacity of *Hotspur* had become to us. I remembered being somewhat ambivalent about it when we'd talked to Weird Wally.

I pulled us away from the surface of the asteroid and exited the defensive perimeter in the opposite direction of Mom and Dad's claim. Marny transmitted *Sterra's Gift's* full sensor package data stream on an encrypted channel, effectively overcoming the fact that *Hotspur* could only use passive sensors while running silent.

We slowly approached their claim and I was relieved to see that all the equipment was neatly ordered and laid out just like it always had been when I was growing up.

"Looks clear, Dad," I said. I swung the ship around so that the armored glass panel between the two crew stations was directly aligned with his claim.

"Keep sailing, Liam," he said quietly. The intensity of his voice alarmed me.

"What do you see?" I asked.

"I'd hoped it was nothing. Shortly before Oberrhein arrived at the warehouse, I lost contact with my system," he said.

"How do you know it's trouble?" I asked.

"Take us back, son. Let's get to a safe location before we discuss it," he said.

I heard Tabby take a sharp breath and looked back at the habitat. Everything still looked good to me. Nonetheless, I gave a short punch to the throttle and sailed on past.

"What?" I looked at Tabby.

"Just get us out of here," she said.

Without any ships nearby, I throttled up and sailed back to the station. I held my questions until we'd all gathered in the warehouse.

"What's the word, Pete?" Marny asked.

"Explosive charges rigged on the habitation domes, I assume they'd done the equipment too," he said. "I didn't get a great look, but I saw enough to do us in a few times over."

"I didn't see it," I said.

"Not unexpected. You don't have any experience destroying buildings. I was looking for it," he said.

"You have experience destroying buildings?"

"More than you'd expect," he said with no hint of sarcasm in his voice.

I gave him an appraising look. He wasn't much for joking, so I put it in the back of my mind to be followed up on later. "Can it be salvaged?" I asked.

"Depends on what type of trigger they have. It looks like they were trying to hurt someone. We might be able to disarm them with the right kind of bot," Marny said.

"Nothing we can do right now." Pete slumped into a chair, defeat on his face. Oberrhein was taking his life's work away - again.

"So, what? We hunker down and wait for our supplies to run out?" Tabby asked provocatively.

"*Hotspur* doesn't have any problems moving around. We could retreat to Léger Nuage," I said.

"That's what they want," Nick said. "Did anyone really think we wouldn't have to fight for what is ours?"

"We're seriously outgunned," I said.

"We don't have to outgun anyone," Ada said.

She was the last person I expected to step into the conversation. I wasn't alone in my surprise, as the whispered side conversations stopped and the room grew quiet. We all looked at Ada.

"Space is big. All we need is a forty minute head start and even the *Adela Chen* can't be caught," she said.

"What are you proposing?" Silver asked.

"We make an ore delivery. If you count Licht's pile, we're two-thirds full," she said.

"Don't you think they'll want that back?" I asked.

"No. I already asked Selig," she said.

Things began to click in my mind and a plan began to form.

"Nick, does Belirand buy ore for Tipperary credits?" If we were going to be in the Tipperary system very long, we needed the local credits.

"They do, but it looks like they're charging a fifteen percent premium. We can offset that by buying supplies there. Belirand's price on fuel, O2 and most supplies are actually better than what we got in Sol - as long as you're trading for ore," Nick said.

"What do you think about Ada's idea, Marny?" I asked.

"We'd have the element of surprise. We just need a good distraction," she said.

"Silver and I could sail the tug," Dad said. "It's not like we have anything else to do."

I caught Ada's eye and could tell she wasn't interested in being left behind.

"What about mining? I'll make you a pretty good deal if you'll work for me," I said.

Dad laughed sardonically. "Ouch. You'd be my boss now?"

"Nothing like that. We need the co-op hollowed out and someone to man the control room. How about you cut me in for twenty percent of the net on the ore you mine and work with Marny to keep the perimeter secure," I said.

"We could do that," Pete said, sitting up straighter.

"Aye. I already consult with Pete on station security. It'd certainly free me up to travel," Marny said. "Plus, Oberrhein won't be expecting us to leave so soon. It's a risk, but then what isn't."

It had been a long day, although I couldn't imagine sleeping. "Dad, you can take over *Sterra's Gift* or build a habitation dome, really it's up to you. If you could make sure that Muir doesn't run out of food, that'd be good. He doesn't like to talk much, so I don't think he'll bother you," I said.

"So, it's a plan?" Tabby asked.

I looked around the group and realized they were waiting for me to make a decision.

"It is. We set sail in three hours," I said.

"Don't you think you all should get some sleep first?" Mom asked.

"I couldn't sleep right now if I wanted to. Tabby and I will load fuel and consumables for both ships. Nick and Marny, can you check Mom and Dad out on station security?"

"What about me?" Ada asked.

"We need a navigation plan that gets the *Adela Chen* out of the belt as quickly as possible and a meetup spot for *Hotspur*," I said.

With tasks handed out, the meeting broke up.

Tabby and I arc-jetted to the top of the asteroid and grabbed a grav-sled. We'd use it to move fuel to the ships.

"I've a bad feeling about this," Tabby said, as we picked up our first load of fuel and flew over to *Hotspur*.

"A bad feeling about this trip? That's not a hard call," I said.

"Not just the trip. Something feels off and I can't put my finger on it," she said.

"What? Aside from being named an enemy of one of the two nations we've come in contact with in the system?"

"It's more than that. Tell me, why would Belirand pay to have us come out here, just to put the squeeze on us? We have one of the few ships which can transport ore. It's like they don't want Terminal Seven to get built."

"Maybe Oberrhein doesn't. That doesn't mean Belirand doesn't," I said.

"So you're telling me that Belirand, the company that runs TransLoc terminals in four solar systems, isn't smart enough to figure out that Oberrhein is a threat? How many billion credits do you think they've got at risk?" Tabby asked.

I didn't have an answer. She had a good point, though. We'd seen Belirand's fleet and it was hard to imagine any small country wanting to tangle with them.

"Who's riding with Ada?" Tabby asked.

"Probably me," I said.

"Yeah. I don't think so," Tabby said with a finger on my chest. " Ada can sail *Hotspur* just fine. I'm not taking another two week trip by myself."

I smiled. I suppose for others, Tabby's possessive side might be a little much. But, I'd spent so much of my life just hoping she'd pay attention to me that I enjoyed it.

"Sure. The AI does all the hard work anyway," I said.

"Ada," I said opening a comm line.

"What's up boss?" she asked.

"I'm going to load ore onto the barge and wondered if you wanted to ride along," I said.

"I'll be right there," she said. "Go ahead and hook the barge up."

Tabby and I jetted over to the *Adela Chen* and hooked up. I was careful to follow all of the steps on the familiar list. By the time we were ready to go, Ada had poked her head into the cockpit.

"Don't you guys ever sleep? Aren't you tired?" she asked.

Tabby looked at me and waggled her eyebrows.

"Oh, that's enough of that," Ada said in mock disgust.

I walked Ada through what I intended to do and she agreed. My first task was to orient the barge to be upside down in relationship to the ore storage on the flat side of the station. Going slow was the key to working with a barge and I turned us over and then twisted the long barge around to line up correctly with the asteroid.

"Something to consider is how you might have made both of those rotations in a single move," Ada coached. "It's a little more difficult, but you could get an AI assist. It would put less strain on the couplings."

I nodded. I'd thought about it, but I was getting tired.

Navigate to ore storage for pickup, I instructed the AI.

A navigation path showed up on the forward vid-screens and *Adela Chen* crept forward. The barge sailed closer to the top of the asteroid than I was comfortable with, but it was a necessity for a gravity transfer like we were about to do.

A message popped up on the vid-screen and requested permission to disengage the gravity generators that held the ore in place on the asteroid. I accepted the request and we all watched as the ore flowed onto the barge in a perfect wave as we slid forward.

"How does it do that without sucking us in?" Tabby asked.

"The rear-most grav-generators on the station are repulsing us and the ship is using that as a fulcrum. We're actually generating downforce," Ada said.

"You ever do that manually?" I asked.

"Always wanted to, but Mom wouldn't have it," she said.

"You think she'd like what we're doing?" I asked.

"She would. She was a risk taker and liked to see the solar system. She'd have loved coming to Tipperary," she said.

"I wish I'd known my mom," Tabby said.

Ada placed her hand on Tabby's arm in support and I saw alarms going off in Tabby's eyes. No doubt she hadn't intended to share that last part with Ada. I was glad she had. Ada was as safe a person to share your feelings with as anyone I knew and I wanted them to be better friends. Tabby still saw Ada as competition.

I decided to rescue Tabby. "Ada, what would you think of Tabby and I taking the *Adela Chen* out to Terminal Seven and have you be principal pilot on *Hotspur*?"

"That makes sense," she said. The ship continued to slide forward as the ore was transferred.

"I was thinking you could make a stealth run down by the Oberrhein claims and see if they'll follow you. It'd give the *Adela Chen* a chance to get a decent burn going," I said.

"They probably won't fall for that twice," Ada said. "But it should work this time. What burn plan are you using?"

"Class E. We need to conserve fuel," I said. "It'll take us twelve days. We'll only burn for the first eighteen hours. We should consider leaving now, though."

I looked between Tabby and Ada. Tabby just shrugged.

"Nick, you awake?" I asked.

"Yup," he said. I knew it was the truth because, like Ada, he was slow to wake up.

"We're about done loading the *Adela Chen* and were thinking that maybe we should get going," I said.

There was a short pause, no doubt he was talking to Marny.

"We're short a pilot or two," he said.

"We're on our way over to *Hotspur*. We need to grab our vac-suits. Otherwise, we've topped off all of the consumables on both ships," I said.

We left the *Adela Chen* where she sat and arc-jetted over to

Hotspur. Tabby was feeling playful and tagged my butt on the way by and I jetted after her. We surfed around for a minute, finally popping through the energy barrier.

Nick and Marny weren't on the ship yet. They'd been working with Pete and Mom, familiarizing them with control room operations. By the time we'd changed into our normal vac-suits and grabbed our go-bags, they'd arrived on the bridge with Ada.

"If you don't hear from us in thirty minutes, assume you're clear," Ada said.

I looked to Nick and he gave me a quick nod. Ada must have already shared the bait-and-switch strategy of luring the Oberrhein fleet away so we could escape with the *Adela Chen.*

"Let's do it," Tabby said.

By the time I arrived on the *Adela Chen,* Ada had a navigation path and burn plan waiting for me. We'd meet up in five hours. I sent a quick comm to Mom and Dad, letting them know of our imminent departure.

"You want some coffee?" Tabby asked. Waiting thirty minutes wasn't something she'd do easily.

"You know where it is?" I asked.

"How many places could it be?"

Twenty minutes later I heard her climbing back up the ladder. She dropped a cup of coffee into the console next to me, leaned over and gave me a kiss. Her still damp hair was loose and fell into my face. She smelled fresh and it made me conscious of the fact that I hadn't showered for at least a couple of days.

"Ready?" I asked.

"Let's do it," she said, taking her seat next to me.

We hadn't heard from *Hotspur,* which was what we wanted. They were to draw off the Oberrhein fleet and put distance between us. The route Ada gave us would have us clear of the asteroids shortly and we'd be able to start a hard-burn.

Engage navigation plan.

The ship started moving slowly forward. We lifted carefully from the surface and spun over in a maneuver that I would have found difficult to execute without the AI. Pushing the huge sled full of ore took patience, as we were slow to adjust to course corrections.

I breathed a sigh of relief when we cleared the belt. Our massive engines caused the ship to shudder as they spooled up. My ears popped at the sound cancelling wave the ship generated to eliminate the noise within the ship's living space.

"Five hours," I said. We weren't out of danger, but we would be shortly.

"What do you want to do?" Tabby asked suggestively.

I shook my head. "I need a shower."

"That'll work," she said.

After I'd showered, I pulled the sheets off the bunks in the ship's only sleeping quarters. We wouldn't need both beds, but I figured I might as well clean them.

"Anything shaking?" I called up to the cockpit.

"All's quiet," she answered.

I was surprised when she gently nudged me awake. I'd rejoined her in the cockpit and hadn't intended to fall asleep.

"Frak, sorry," I said.

"No sweat. You get the next shift," she said. We'd been sailing for four hours and would meet *Hotspur* in less than one.

"Do you want me to wake you when we meet up?" I asked.

"Only if there's a problem," she said and lay her head back.

"I made the beds in the cabin. Why don't you go down there? It'd be more comfortable," I said.

"Maybe," she said and proceeded to fall asleep next to me after grabbing my hand.

An hour later the engines spooled down and Tabby rustled awake. With the large engines, it was nearly impossible to ignore them when they changed cadence. At a minimum, the noise-abating sound wave caused your ears to pop uncomfortably.

"There they are," I said. *Hotspur's* transponder illuminated brightly on my vid screen. Visually, I tried to locate them in the star field in front of us, knowing that it was a fool's errand. Even without being in stealth mode, its light absorptive armor was impossible to see from five hundred meters, much less five hundred kilometers.

"Incoming comm request," the ship's AI softly informed me.

Accept. "How'd it go?" I asked.

"That girl would give you a run for you money, Cap," Marny said.

"Oh? Did it get dicey?"

"Sure did, but she made this old girl dance. Nearly took out two ships by getting them to run into each other," she said.

"Sweet. Anything else shaking?" I asked.

"Nope. See you in a hundred hours," she said. Marny was referring to the point in the journey where we'd turn around and start decelerating.

"You making cupcakes?" I asked.

"Guess you'll just have to wait and see," she said.

"Hey, Marny, you know what time it is?" I asked.

"It's about 0230."

"Nope."

Connect to Hotspur public address. Queue Foghat's Slow Ride, I said.

"Oh, no," Marny groaned.

What sounded like people stomping and the growl of an ancient electric guitar filled the ships.

"Slow ride, take it easy —"

"Slow ride, take it easy —"

SNAKE OIL

We had specific instructions from Belirand on the acceptable velocity at which we could enter their controlled space and at what distance we were required to establish contact. As a result, we dropped from hard-burn a full six hours from Terminal Seven.

Hail Terminal Seven.

My vid-screen showed an acknowledgement from Belirand's comm equipment, but it took several minutes before we received a response.

"Greetings, *Adela Chen*. This is Ensign Jeeker. Please state your business."

We didn't have a holo projector on the *Adela Chen*, but I saw a man about my age on the forward vid-screen. His uniform vac-suit was not fully sealed and looked like it could use a good cleaning. A half-naked woman realized she was in direct view of the camera and jumped out of the frame. If I hadn't been paying attention, I might not have caught it.

"Greetings. *Loose Nuts Corporation* with an ore delivery from the Descartes belt. We're sailing in tandem with the sloop *Hotspur*," I said.

There was a small delay before he replied. "Oh, I see *Hotspur* now. We're not getting much of a signal on her, but her transponder is coming through loud and clear."

"Roger that. Not much of a signature since she's not an ore hauler," I said.

"Right. We were wondering when you'd get here," he said.

I wasn't completely sure what he meant by that since I knew we hadn't registered our navigational plans with them.

"Would you like us to head over to the refinery to unload?" I asked.

"Won't do you any good," he said. "They're only working a single shift and won't have anyone available until 1000. But I'll go ahead and assign you a mooring."

Moments later a location showed up on my vid-screen.

"I'll leave a message for the foreman. Have a good night," he said and closed the comm.

"Ada, you get all that?" I asked.

"I did, Liam. I'll make a run in and get you a clean route. It appears Jeeker doesn't have much experience directing barges," she said.

"Thanks, Ada,"

Tabby and I watched the red outline of *Hotspur* move across our vid-screen toward the markers representing Terminal Seven and the refining platform. Ten minutes later, a navigation path popped up on the vid-screen and I directed the AI to follow it.

We passed by a hodgepodge structure that the AI labeled Terminal Seven. Unlike the other six Belirand terminals we'd seen, this structure was made up of dozens of rectangular steel and armor glass boxes. The welding scars were still present from a hasty assembly. According to Nick, Belirand had shipped the nuclease of the terminal from Mars and assembled it onsite. It was a twentieth of a completed terminal's size, but held all of the technology required to run the TransLoc gate. Over the next few years, Belirand construction and engineering would manufacture and assemble the rest of the terminal.

Ada's navigation path was perfect and we twisted around as we passed the main terminal and headed toward the refining platform. Unlike the terminal, the refining and manufacturing plant was nearly complete. On one end was the refining platform with a wide apron for accepting large piles of ore. The clean surface of the apron suggested it hadn't seen any use yet. In line with the refinery was an assembly line of manufacturing modules that branched out like the limbs of a tree. I'd seen a similar design at the plants we delivered ore to back on Mars. Each module had a specific purpose and Belirand's design was as large a plant as I'd seen.

"Wellington," Tabby said.

"What's that?" I asked.

"They shipped a lot of those modules up from Wellington. It's written on the side," she said.

It felt odd seeing the familiar corporate logo so far from home.

The *Adela Chen* slowed to a stop and a shudder rippled through the ship as the grav-anchors fired out and grabbed on to the platform.

"Ada, where'd they drop you?" I asked.

"They've got a mooring camp up here," she said. "We're two kilometers to your aft and up a quarter."

"We're going to lock it down. It sounds like the refinery won't get going until mid-morning," I said.

"Sweet dreams," she replied and terminated the comm.

"Whatever are we going to do until 1000 tomorrow?" Tabby asked.

It was 0200 and the prospect of eight uninterrupted hours of sleep was compelling. Trading shifts back and forth between Tabby and me for twelve days had been difficult. When we'd first started out on *Sterra's Gift*, Nick and I had slept through shifts, but with all of the problems we'd run into, that no longer seemed wise.

For all her bluster, Tabby must have been just as tired. She didn't even bother to take off her vac-suit, but spread out on the bed. She hadn't left me much room, but I knew that was because she expected me to slide in close.

The sound that woke us up wasn't the alarm I'd set for 0900, but an incoming comm request. I pushed Tabby's arm off and sat up in bed. I'd gotten seven hours of sleep, but would have liked another two.

"Liam Hoffen," I answered denying the request for a video feed.

A red-haired man seated in an industrial looking room popped up on my HUD. "Bob Holly, refinery operation chief. Good morning, Mr. Hoffen," he said.

"Good morning." I wasn't doing a very good job of keeping the sleep out of my voice. I stumbled out of bed, grabbed the ladder railing and started climbing up to the cockpit.

"Looks like you've a load for us. I've got to say, we're excited to see this equipment fire up for the first time," he said.

"I wondered if we were the first. That platform looks shiny," I said.

"Virgin voyage. I'd like your permission to launch our scanners. We run more automated than back in Sol, not so many restrictions on autonomous bots here in Tipperary," he said.

"Copy that. Permission granted," I said.

Tabby slid into the cockpit chair next to me and handed me a cup of day old coffee. Old or not, it was hot and fully leaded. I accepted it appreciatively.

"What'd I miss?" Tabby asked.

"They're launching the ore scanners," I said.

As if on my cue, two dozen bright yellow spherical bots, a third of a meter in diameter, popped out of three ports in the topside of the refinery's apron. In a choreographed swarm, they flew over the top of the barge, passing back and forth like a school of fish in vids I remembered watching as a kid. As soon as they reached one side of the barge, they'd flash over, re-form a new wave and sweep back. Ten minutes after emerging, they disappeared, the ports in the top of the apron closing back up.

"You're running a little light, aren't you, Captain?" Mr. Holly asked.

"We are. Call it a payroll run," I said.

He laughed appreciatively. "One point eight two kilo tonnes?" he asked.

"Right on the money," I said.

"I'm transmitting your batch yields. You had a strong iron concentration and a little precious, fourteen hundred grams gold, twenty-four hundred grams platinum and forty-four kilograms silver. We're not taking precious yet, but we'll have the ingots for you in less than an hour," he said. "Do you want to review the slips and sign off?"

"Roger that, give me a minute," I said.

"Take your time, we're not going anywhere," he said.

I forwarded the mining slips to Nick on *Hotspur* and compared them to what our pre-sift machines had reported. The Belirand scanners were several orders of magnitude more accurate than our machines, but I had experience reconciling the differences. If anything, the ore we'd shipped was richer than expected.

A signature request appeared on my vid-screen and I signed off on the ore-receipt slips.

"Do you want us to execute a grav-dump?" I asked.

"Nothing so crude around here," he said, "just keep your hands and feet inside the ship for a few more minutes and we'll have you unloaded."

Tabby looked at me quizzically. I wasn't exactly sure what he was saying, but his intent was plenty clear.

"Roger that," I said.

From our vantage point, we had a clear view of both the barge and the refinery's apron. On the opposite side of the apron, four large panels pulled back and another fleet of bots emerged. These were something of a mix between a grav-sled with the large bucket on the front, and a compact stevedore bot. Similar to the ore scanners, these bots flew in what could only be described as chaos. They dipped down and picked up giant scoop-fulls of ore and deposited them in neat piles. Before they had finished, the closest piles of ore were already being pulled into the refinery for processing.

In all, it took twenty minutes for the bots to complete their job. It was impressive, but I still thought I could have dropped the ore more quickly if I'd sailed over the top and done a grav-dump. From watching the movements of the bots, however, it was clear they had used the ore-scan data to organize their piles by some measure of quality or density.

"Captain Hoffen, do you have refueling instructions?" Bob Holly asked.

"Are you able to do that while we're docked?"

"That we are. We have the ability to load all supplies directly from the platform. Our objective is to get you in and out as quickly as possible once we're fully operational," he said.

"Perfect. We're looking for a full load plus twenty tonnes on the deck," I said.

"Safe travels, Captain. We'll have your fuel and precious metals delivered shortly," he said and closed the comm.

"Nick, Ada, we're about done here," I said. "I believe they've been in contact with the business office, so you should be able to refuel and pick up supplies."

"Yup. I was just notified and we're headed there now. We also have a meeting scheduled with the station manager, J.T. Emre," Nick said.

"What's that about?"

"He agreed to meet with us and talk about the issues we're having with Oberrhein," he said. "He's sending a shuttle to pick you up."

"Understood," I said, and closed comm.

"I'm coming too," Tabby said.

I hadn't had enough time to process and had conflicting emotions about Tabby coming along. I trusted her with just about everything other than keeping her cool when people were being dishonest. J.T. Emre's brother, Atin, had felt pretty greasy to me and I suspected J.T. might be much the same.

"Sure," I said.

"You don't sound too convinced," she said.

"You have as much invested in this as I do. I just need you to keep your cool, okay?" I asked.

"I'll do my best," she said. I'd annoyed her.

We didn't have long to wait as a comm request came in fifteen minutes later and a shuttle pulled up next to the airlock. It was Jeeker, the same Ensign who'd been on watch the night before.

"Mr. Jeeker, you certainly have a lot of duties here. I'd have thought you'd be asleep after pulling a late shift," I said as Tabby and I found seats on the hard metal benches that ran the length of the shuttle.

"Yeah. About that. I'd appreciate it if you didn't tell J.T. that I wasn't completely alert when you arrived," he said.

"In the Navy, falling asleep at your post is a court-marshal offense," Tabby said.

Jeeker looked back at us nervously, but didn't say anything.

"We have your back, Jeeker," I said.

"Thank you. What are you meeting with J.T. about?" he asked.

"Claimholder stuff," I said. "We're still working out some of the details."

"Oh good," he said relieved. I wondered if he'd volunteered to come pick us up so he could have this conversation.

He landed in a docking bay that held several other shuttles and led us into the main station.

The finish of the interior of the station was considerably nicer than the exterior, although still not up to the other Belirand terminals. We met up with Nick in a reception area.

"Mr. Emre will be out in a few minutes," Jeeker said and excused himself.

"Did you take a shuttle over too?" I asked Nick.

"No, we're tied up here. Marny and Ada are loading fuel and supplies. I asked them to drop off the ingots on *Hotspur*, you okay with that?" Nick asked.

"That's probably better. We don't have a lot of interior storage," I said.

"Ah, Gentlemen. Ma'am."

A younger, handsomer version of Atin Emre emerged from a pair of double doors. He had a wide, welcoming smile and I found it difficult to dislike him as we traded introductions.

"Come in, come in. You'll have to excuse the mess. Most of my meetings are about the construction project and I'm not set up to receive visitors," he said.

"Thank you for agreeing to meet with us," I said.

"Absolutely, have a seat and I'll clear off some space."

The walls in his office were covered with vid screens that displayed all manner of information about Terminal Seven. I even caught the refining station's report on our recent delivery. In addition to a desk, J.T. had a table surrounded by comfortable chairs. Both flat surfaces were covered by transparent reading tablets of varying sizes. In the center of the table stood a replica of a finished TransLoc Terminal and the refining station we'd visited.

"You've set off quite a chain of events around here," he said. "I've already got department heads squabbling about who gets the priority on the finished products. So how can I help you?"

I smiled despite myself. The man exuded confidence.

"The corporation you hired to provide security for the expedition has leveled threats against our company and other claim holders," Nick said.

"Oh? I'm not familiar with that arrangement. Let me take a look," he said, picking up a reading tablet. After a few minutes of searching he finally asked, "Oberrhein?"

"Right," Tabby answered.

He creased his eyebrows and nodded his head appreciatively. "I see here that we contracted them to escort the expedition to Descartes, but I don't see that they are still in our employ. Could you share more specifically what's going on? This is most disturbing." he said.

"Do you mind if I use one of these?" Nick asked pointing at a vid-screen on the wall.

"Go right ahead," he said.

Nick displayed several video sequences starting with Oberrhein trying to inspect the barge while we were over Grünholz. Next, was the sequence where the three cruisers attempted to breach our security perimeter. And finally, Nick ended with the destruction of David Muir's ship, the armed invasion of our station, threats to the other colonists at the swap meet and their direct threats to *Loose Nuts*.

"I certainly understand your concern and I assure you that Belirand does not condone this activity. I guess I'm not sure how I can help," he said.

"In our contract, Belirand agreed to provide secure transport and periodic patrols of the claim," Nick said. "When we asked your brother about this, he indicated that Oberrhein was fulfilling this obligation. I'm having a difficult time reconciling what you're saying with what he said."

"I think it's pretty clear. When Atin communicated that, it was true. We have since revoked Oberrhein's contract," he said and slid a reading pad across the table to Nick.

"How will you fulfill your obligation to provide periodic patrols?" Nick asked after reading the pad.

"As you witnessed, *Cape of Good Hope* and her forty-five crew died heroically discharging their duties. It will take us time to replace both the ship and her crew. I'm sorry to be so blunt, but that is the simple truth of the matter," he said.

By bringing up the lost ship and crew, he'd successfully made me feel guilty for questioning why things weren't going the way I wanted. I knew it was wrong, but I had to admire his tactics.

"I feel like I need to be equally blunt, then," Nick said. "The threats against our company and crew are real and we'll be taking all necessary measures to defend ourselves."

"Of course you will and I would expect nothing less," he said.

Tabby started to speak, but Emre held his hand up to hold her off.

"You know what, we're really approaching this the wrong way. I can see here that you've worked hard and under difficult circumstances. We here at Belirand like to foster that pioneering spirit of tenacity and hard work. Certainly, you all have demonstrated those characteristics in delivering on your contracts ahead of schedule. To that end, I believe a bonus is in order. I'll be adding a twenty-five percent performance incentive to this and your next load. Now, I know you're busy and so am I. If there isn't anything else, I'll have Jeeker see you off," he said and stood up.

"One quick question," Tabby said while shaking his hand, refusing to let go.

"What's that?" he looked amused, as if they were sharing an inside joke.

"What role was *Cape of Good Hope* to fulfill once she arrived in Tipperary?"

He smiled, as if entertaining a simple question from a child. "Security, of course."

"Was *Cape of Good Hope* transporting Belirand personnel to

either Terminal Six or Seven?"

He pulled his hand back from her and looked scandalized. "I'm not sure what you're implying. There are always transfers on Belirand ships."

"I guess I've never bought the accident story and wondered if there was another reason someone would have wanted *Cape of Good Hope* destroyed," Tabby said.

"A thorough investigation was performed and nothing suggests anything but an accident. The people on that ship were my co-workers and I'd appreciate it if you didn't tarnish their names with wild speculation," he said. "Now, if there's nothing else, I have other business to attend to."

"That man is a snake," Tabby said as we loaded into the shuttle with Jeeker.

"Not here, Tabby," I said.

"You should be careful talking like that," Jeeker said. "Mr. Emre and his brother are very powerful men."

"You're right, Jeeker. Sometimes it's hard not to get annoyed, though," I said. "By the way, I was meaning to ask. You mentioned that you'd been expecting us. How'd you know we were coming?"

"Lucky guess. We knew someone would be coming," he said.

"I don't mean to be a prick about this, but I think you owe us a little since we didn't tell about your sleeping on duty and all," I said.

"Frak. You can't tell anyone where you heard this, but Mr. Emre told the chief engineer that you were coming. I heard about it from someone …else," he said.

"Wouldn't have been that cute little gal we saw you with last night would it?" I asked.

"Maybe. But, you're not going to say anything about that are you?"

"It'll be our secret."

SPACER'S DREAM

"Ada, I'm sending a navigation path for our trip back," I said.

"What's with this dogleg at two hundred thousand kilometers?" she asked. "It looks like you're headed to Grünholz."

"That's the idea. It's been awfully convenient that Oberrhein and Belirand both seem to know where we're going before we get there. Remember, Oberrhein ships found the *Adela Chen* when we went to Léger Nuage instead of Descartes. Now, somehow, Belirand knew when we left Descartes. You have to ask, how'd they know?" I said.

"I don't think Oberrhein has anywhere near the tracking capabilities Belirand does," Marny had been listening to the conversation. "Makes me wonder just what agreement they have."

"You know, just because you're paranoid..." Ada said chuckling.

"Finish the saying," I said.

"What do you mean?"

"The saying is 'just because you're paranoid, doesn't mean they aren't after you,'" I said.

"Oh. You're just burning an extra twenty-five hundred in fuel," she said.

"Roger that. I want anyone who's tracking us to believe we're headed to Grünholz. I'm hoping to get those small cruisers out of Descartes before we get back," I said.

"Well, I hope it works," Ada said. "I assume you're going to let me scout the area before you try to sail back to the claim."

"Roger that," I said.

The first leg of the plan I'd sent her would take us eight hours to execute. At that point, we'd take a twenty degree turn away from Grünholz and head directly over to the Descartes asteroid belt. By turning at two hundred thousand kilometers away from the new Terminal Seven, we'd be well out of range of their sensors.

"Are we really going to keep playing cat and mouse? I'm not a very good mouse," Tabby said.

The autopilot on the ship had been navigating us out and away from the Belirand structures and we were awaiting the short burn to engage.

"More like a mouse with claws," I said. "No. We learned important things on this trip. Oberrhein isn't operating under contract with Belirand, so we can retaliate without any expectation of repercussions. We just need to get this ship back to safety and then we change our arrangement with Petar."

"I like the sound of that," Tabby said.

"I thought you might. *Hotspur* is an even match against one of those cruisers inside the asteroid belt. In the open, however, we'd have a hard time getting close enough to do much damage, except possibly with our missiles," I said.

"What happened to the Liam who needed to be shot at first?" she asked.

"Still here. I'll give them a chance to back down," I said.

***

"Liam. Get up here," Tabby called. We were six hours into the journey and I was in the galley making a fresh pot of coffee.

The urgency in her voice caused me to throw the loose items into a drawer and lock it closed. I climbed the ladder as quickly as I could, cursing under my breath at the inconvenience of my prosthetic foot on the ladder.

"What's going on?" I asked.

"I've got sensor contacts, closing in from the aft," she said.

"Are they on intercept?" It was mostly a stupid question. At the speeds we were travelling the odds of meeting up with any ship without it being intentional were literally astronomical.

"I'm taking the helm," I said. If we'd been in *Hotspur*, I'd never have superseded her, but I had a lot more experience sailing the tug than she did.

"Roger that," she said. "Bringing weapons online."

Tugs, in general, didn't have much for offensive weapons and the *Adela Chen* was no different. We had a single large blaster with limited range.

"Can you get any resolution on them?" I asked. Under hard burn the *Adela Chen's* sensor package had a difficult time overcoming interference generated by the engines.

"No. But there are three of them. I don't think it's hard to guess who it is," she said.

"Delta-V?" I asked.

"We're cornered, Liam. They're coming in hot, and we've no hope of outrunning them. They'll overrun us in three minutes. We could extend to six if we ramped up to max burn," she said.

"Frak."

"We can't keep burning. We need to get maneuverability," Tabby said.

"It won't work. If we do, Ada will come back and take them all on. *Hotspur* will get shredded," I said.

The cabin grew quiet for a heartbeat.

"*Hotspur* just cut their burn," Tabby said.

I followed suit. Immediately, the cruisers popped up on the vid-screen in full resolution. They'd be on us in a hundred forty seconds and Ada had beat me to the punch, powering down and jumping between us.

I lifted up on the *Adela Chen's* flight stick and twisted, causing the ship and barge to circumvolve. Under normal circumstances the task would take six or seven minutes, time we didn't have. I torqued it hard and would accomplish it in one.

"Ada, one pass with missiles and then you have to go silent running," I said.

"Don't be stupid, Liam," she said.

"Put everything you have into *Stenka*," I wasn't going to argue. She would either do what I asked or she wouldn't.

"Marny, can *Hotspur* take a single pass from two cruisers?"

"Aye, but not much beyond that," she said.

"Liam, maybe we can, but the *Adela Chen* can't," Ada said. "They'll shred you."

I accelerated as hard as the *Adela Chen* would allow and closed distance with *Hotspur*. Tabby's calculation hadn't considered that I'd be dumb enough to turn around and head at our pursuers and the vid-screen displayed the rapidly closing distance between the five ships.

"Roger that. You need to drive *Stenka* upward with your fire," I said. "Let me stay close on your six. Dive beneath the ships at the last minute. But tell me when you make your break." I turned to Tabby. "I need you to trust me."

"With my life."

"Get in the life-pod and hold on," I said.

"I'm not going without you."

"You have to trust me. I can't argue with you about this. Too many people are going to die," I said.

"Frak you, Hoffen. Don't do this," she said.

"Trust me, damn it. GO!"

The life-pod was at the back of the cockpit, just over the ladder that led down to the galley and sleeping quarters. Tabby jumped from her seat and grabbed my face, giving me a fierce kiss, tears running down her face.

"You better have a good plan," she said.

I laughed, although it sounded more like a cough as my throat was too constricted from the swirl of emotions.

"I do. Don't give up on me," I said.

She clambered back over the hole that opened up to the ladder leading to the galley and sleeping chambers and climbed into the now open life-pod. As soon as she was in it, I overrode its controls and closed the door. I'd pay for that later… if I was lucky.

The deep dark of space exploded in a brilliant show of lights as the cruisers opened fire.

Return fire, target Stenka. I said.

The *Adela Chen's* heavy blaster blurped a single shot that the Stenka easily avoided. I'd been hopeful that I'd actually hit them, but I knew any decent pilot would see that coming.

I twisted slightly to lift the starboard leading edge of the barge upward. Ada immediately recognized the move for what I intended and allowed me to place the barge protectively over *Hotspur*. The move only provided a shield from one of the approaching ships, but it was all I could hope to do.

Unfortunately, this left the *Karelia* with nothing to do but fire at me. On the positive side, we were only ten seconds from passing beneath the approaching ships.

Blaster fire ripped at the *Adela Chen* and my suit closed up moments before the cabin's atmosphere was violently and instantaneously exhausted.

Hotspur surged forward, all three turrets pouring their fire into the *Stenka*. Their armor was holding, but taking a terrible beating. Marny's discipline with the missiles was legendary. She wouldn't have time for a reload so she was waiting for the optimum range to ensure a hit. Even with the pounding we were putting onto the *Stenka*, we couldn't hope to take it out with only two missiles.

I adjusted my flight path to keep the *Stenka* centered as much as possible. Her pilot made small adjustments that I mirrored and we settled into the final seconds of our tilt.

"Now," Ada yelled into comm.

A million things happened all at once as I pushed down hard on the flight stick. I saw the puff of missiles launch from *Hotspur* as she dove beneath the *Stenka*. The *Stenka's* pilot correctly assumed that *Hotspur* would dodge down, out of the way. What he or she hadn't understood was that *Adela Chen* would not be dodging beneath with her. It really wasn't even a possibility, given the location of my engines. By pushing down on the flight stick and with the *Adela Chen's* massive engines still accelerating as hard as possible, I pushed the barge's front end into the path of the approaching cruiser.

I punched the escape pod's release, flinging Tabby out into space, safely beneath the pandemonium caused by the colliding ships. I also hit the emergency release which should have freed the *Adela Chen* from her burden, but I was too late. I'd timed it incorrectly and the barge had been driven back into the tug and wasn't letting go.

A peace filled me.

Show Tabby's escape pod.

It would be okay, she was safely headed away from the carnage. I could live with that... well, sort of...

I felt a tug on my ring and smiled. It was poignant that my last thought would be of Tabby.

The ship disintegrated around me as the forces of the collision became too much for its structure.

And then a most wonderful thing occurred. The ship broke free of the barge and we were flung off at an odd angle. I say we, because at that point, my only strong relationship to the tug was the fact that I was tacitly inside of a now, mostly open structure.

On pure instinct, I dove down into the cluttered passage leading to the galley and sleeping quarters. My objective was to locate my AGBs. I'd made it three of the four meters when blaster fire lanced through the cockpit, obliterating it entirely. Well, I suppose it might not have obliterated it as much as relocated the vast majority of atoms that had originally been coalesced into the form of the cockpit.

Reduce suit emissions, I'm under attack, I said. My AI was certainly smart enough to make appropriate adjustments.

I didn't stop moving. Space battles were usually over in seconds. First one to pop the weasel almost always won. And I'd been popped. I couldn't afford to hang around and see what came next. The lack of continued fire led me to believe that my attackers were coming around for another volley. Ada must have stealthed out, as the cruisers wouldn't be taking out their aggression on me if *Hotspur* was still available.

More fire lanced through the ship. So much for a break. The gravity generator had long since given up, in fact it appeared that no other power systems were still operating. I used my hands and legs to scrabble through the wrecked structure. The sleeping quarters were open to space, but my boots and one of my gloves were right where I'd left them in a perfect little corner of the room that seemed completely unaffected by the chaos around me. I snapped the glove into place, followed by the boots.

Firing the boots as hard as I could against the tattered wall, I passed through a wide-open rent in the hull. I shut the jets down, straining my neck to get a good look around. It wouldn't do to escape the ship, only to rip my suit open on a metal shard. That said, I also had no intention of giving away my location to the Oberrhein ships by flashing my arc-jets.

Almost too late, my HUD identified a long cable whipping back and forth in front of me. It was spewing some sort of gas and sparks arced from a live electrical connection. My mind whirled, as I tried to determine the periodicity of the cable's snaking path. My AI showed a collision, but I was out of time.

It didn't seem right to use the word 'fortunate' in such a scenario, but it was true; I was fortunate to have been struck by the cable. First, the sheer force of the strike knocked me out. The arcing cable didn't actually end up grounding on me, which should have been obvious. The collision, did, however, put me on a new path; one that the ships that were looking for me couldn't track. It was either that, or the fact that I was floating lifelessly away from them that did the trick. Turns out, I had no idea what actually happened, because I was unconscious for the next two hours.

I awoke to a low oxygen alarm. To make matters worse, I was floating in space with nothing in sight - no ships, not a thing. I wondered if I was dreaming. It was a common enough dream for any spacer, common enough that we have a name for it; the 'out of O2 dream.' Yeah, I know, not very creatively named, but then neither is the 'I have a test and I'm naked dream.'

Let's be clear. I love the deep dark of space. I love free floating, except when I have absolutely no idea where I am. When I awoke, I was suffering from concussion. So on top of a splitting headache, all I could remember was that something really crappy had happened. I determined that I wasn't dreaming and needed to deal with the fact that I only had ten minutes of O2 left. Admittedly, at that point, I was completely freaked out.

O2 was the first problem. I had a choice. I could stay put and conserve oxygen or try to find help. My boots and glove had a small amount of O2 in the reaction matter that might give me an additional twenty minutes. Since I couldn't see any place that I could jet to in my remaining ten minutes, I directed my AI to deplete the O2. So much for going anywhere.

Slowly my recollection of how I'd gotten into this predicament came back to me.

Hail Adela Chen.

I reasoned that with only thirty minutes of O2 left, if Oberrhein was still in the neighborhood they couldn't do me any worse than had already been done.

"There are no communication relays within range," the AI informed me.

I suspected that might be the case, but I'd been hopeful. I just prayed it didn't mean *Hotspur* had been lost - frak - Tabby. I hoped they found her. I'd sent her last known trajectory to *Hotspur* when I released her, but who knows what might have happened.

I sighed. I'd come so far and I'd die a spacer's death; alone in the dark and out of O2. I twisted so I could look toward the Tipperary star. It was a gorgeous sight. This part of the galaxy had an amazing cluster of nebulas that were visible just over the horizon of the star. I'd first noticed them when we'd been on Léger Nuage.

The view calmed me and I focused my thoughts on Tabby. I recalled her horrific trauma at Colony 40 and was grateful that, this time, it was me who was in trouble. I was also grateful that I hadn't been torn up like she had. I couldn't imagine surviving that. For me, death would come as I slid off to sleep, probably not the most horrific thing that could happen.

I smiled as I felt the familiar tug on my ring. Tabby must be thinking of me.

I wish I didn't have to admit that this act of salvation didn't immediately occur to me. I simply thumbed the ring in response, more to comfort her or to let her know I was thinking of her in my last moments. Yup – maudlin.

The tugs on my ring became frantic and I responded. It was then that I actually recognized the immeasurable utility of these rings.

"Cap, come in." Marny's alto voice filled my helmet.

"I'm here," I said. "Come get me."

"Cap, can you read me?" She said again.

"I'm here, Marny!"

I realized how ridiculous I was being. Of course they couldn't hear me. *Hotspur* had a much more powerful transmitter than I did. My signal couldn't possibly reach them.

"Liam. Hit your ring twice if you can hear me," Tabby said.

I complied.

"Oh babe, we've been worried sick. I love you," she said. I wished I could respond. "Are you hurt? One ping for no, two for yes."

I gave her one ping.

"How is your oxygen? Give me a count of minutes," she said.

I looked at the HUD. I was down to four and counted them out to her.

"We're coming for you. Tell us where you are," she said. "Nick. How!" Tabby sounded frantic.

"Hey buddy," Nick's voice was calm. "You're in a pinch and we don't have a lot of time. I'm going to give some instructions to your AI and then you're going to punch in the numbers it displays. Got it?"

I pinged back twice.

"Good," he said and then instructed my AI to display a sequence of celestial coordinates.

My HUD showed three, three digit numbers. It didn't seem like enough information, but I was down to a hundred twenty seconds.

"First number, Liam." I punched in a four and heard Tabby relay four.

"Give me a ping if that's right," Nick said calmly.

I looked at my display and the air was down to a hundred seconds. We couldn't possibly get through the entire sequence and

I could hear Marny yelling at me to stay in the moment. I had no idea if it was real or imagined.

Start transmitting emergency beacon, I said.

I watched myself punch in the next number, and the number following that …

ROGUE

I watched *Hotspur* approach. Nick and Tabby jetted through the pressure barrier on the starboard side of the hull. I'd always liked the particular blue hue our pressure barriers emitted. The color reminded me of the vids of the oceans on Earth. To be honest, at that point, things had become somewhat fuzzy in my head.

Someone's arms wrapped around my chest from behind. I breathed in deeply and was rewarded by the faint smell of fruity shampoo. I rolled my head to the side and saw Tabby's braided pony tail resting over my shoulder.

"You smell nice," I said.

"You're a bastard," she said. She might have meant it, but she also held me closer.

"You need to work on your bedside manner," I said.

My head was clearing and I discovered that I was lying on Tabby's lap on the bridge couch. Marny and Nick were standing over us.

"How's your head?" Nick asked.

The mere mention of my head seemed to light it on fire. It felt like my brain was too big for my skull.

"Not good," I said. Disregarding the pain, I pushed ahead. "But that went well, right?"

"You should have died," Nick said. "It was a terrible plan."

"Where's Ada?"

"Right here, Liam," she said. My back was to the cockpit where she was seated.

"Sorry about your tug," I said.

"That was a very brave and asinine thing you did. Mom would have been proud," she said.

The mention of her mom, the woman I'd only talked to over the

199

comm and namesake of the *Adela Chen*, made me flash back to when we'd rescued Ada from an attack on the Chen family tug.

"You guys keep saying that, but my plan worked perfectly. Just tell me I took out the *Stenka*," I said.

"Aye, Cap. The *Stenka* is no more," Marny said.

"Anyone hurt?" I asked.

"Negative," Marny said.

"*Hotspur*?" I asked.

"Armor is compromised in three locations on the port side towards the aft. We probably can't take another hit back there, but it's holding. Barring combat, we should be fine," Nick said.

My head was pounding and I was outrageously tired, so I closed my eyes and snuggled back into Tabby. We'd done it. We were all alive and that was all that mattered for the moment.

"We're headed to Nuage Gros," Nick said. "They've a repair facility that will fit us in."

"Cool," I said. I wasn't really listening. Tabby was warm and with my eyes closed, my head didn't hurt nearly as badly as it did when they were open.

"I'm taking him back to bed," Tabby said.

Marny's voice sounded far away. "I'll bring in a medical monitor."

Nick helped Tabby get me to my feet and for a few steps it seemed to be going all right, but then my legs buckled. The bands of Tabby's muscles tightened as she kept me from slouching. Then she did something that caused me no small amount of confusion. She swept her left arm under my knees and lifted them so she was carrying me in front of her. I decided I'd need to be okay with it, since she wasn't asking. Furthermore, I wasn't in any shape to argue.

"I'm going to have to take your suit off, Liam. I'm worried you have injuries we're not seeing," she said as she lay me on the bed.

For whatever reason, this did *not* cause me the same level of confusion.

"I'll help," Marny said.

Yeah, I was pretty sure I'd had this dream before.

When I awoke again, I was hungry and had to use the head about as bad as I can ever remember. Marny had probably put a hydration med device on me, although upon inspection I couldn't find one. I also discovered I was completely naked. I tested out my limbs and felt pretty good, so I got out of bed.

Before I made it to the head, Tabby entered the room. She must have set a monitor on me.

"How are you feeling?" she asked.

"If you help me take a shower, I'll show you," I said.

"That sounds promising…"

***

"Tell me you thought about the fact that we could have just given them the *Adela Chen* by abandoning her," Nick said. We'd always had the ability to talk honestly.

"I did. There wasn't much time to think. Sitting here now, I wonder if it was the best move. I know how close I came to biting it back there," I said.

"It's not a fair question," Marny said. I was surprised to see her step between me and Nick this way.

"How do you figure?" Nick asked. As usual, he wasn't perturbed, he just didn't see an issue with the question.

"You're asking Liam to judge his actions based on the now known outcomes," she said. "The question implies that abandoning the *Adela Chen* would have been a better decision."

"Respectfully, I disagree," Nick said. "I want to know that Liam saw both avenues and made a decision with that information."

"It feels like second guessing to me," Marny said.

The stress of our relocation to Tipperary had been building for weeks, especially since the problems with Oberrhein kept getting worse. It was understandable, but hard to see my two friends sniping at each other. I wished Nick had decided to start this discussion in private. Having just survived a near-death experience, I was in a different state of mind. I couldn't think about anything except how grateful I was that we were all alive.

"I think you're both right," I said. "Nick has spent the better part of his life second-guessing my crazy maneuvers. Sometimes I find it annoying, but he deserves an explanation. I also agree with Marny. What's done is done. But we'll all trust each other more if we're completely honest.

I laid my hand on Marny's arm. She started to object, but quieted. I needed to make things right for her too.

"Ada, why don't you join us for this conversation? I owe it to you all," I said.

Ada, who was at the helm, could easily hear us from her chair, but came down and joined us on the couch.

"You've all probably done your own research on this, but since I made the call, you should hear what I knew or believed. The *Adela Chen* was forfeit the moment those three ships came into sensor range. There was no outrunning them. The only question was would we survive. In my opinion, that encounter could very well have killed us all. The only way any of us could survive was if *Hotspur* ran. I don't believe for a minute that any of you would have abandoned Tabby or me.

"Of course not," Ada said, momentarily caught up in the drama.

I smiled and continued, "To Nick's question, there was no way I was going to hand that tug over to Oberrhein if I had any other choice. We were under hard burn and moving between ships wasn't feasible. Once we'd dropped out, there might have been enough time, so I briefly considered abandoning the *Adela Chen*. The plan I ended up going with allowed us to take out a cruiser while leaving *Hotspur* intact."

"I feel like you didn't value your own life enough," Nick said. "I don't know what we'd do without you."

I hadn't ever seen Nick cry, but his eyes were red and glossy.

I sighed. "You'd keep going. There are families in the Descartes asteroid belt that need us to deal with these Oberrhein bastards. Mom, Dad, Ulran, Merley and even frakking Muir. It's bigger than us now," I said.

"Don't forget *Cape of Good Hope*," Nick said.

I cocked my head to the side. I wasn't sure why he was bringing that back into it. "What do you mean?"

"How could Oberrhein know where we'd be exactly?" Nick asked.

"Frak me, you're right," Tabby said. "Only Belirand would have sensors that would pin us down that accurately. That's proof that Belirand is in on it."

"Or at least the Emre brothers," Nick said.

"What motive?" Ada asked.

"Maybe we're looking at this wrong. We've been thinking about this as a territorial power struggle between us and Oberrhein. There's a big problem with that; they've been coming at us from the beginning, before we even knew who they were. Why all the hostility right out of the box?" I asked.

"We've also assumed that Petar Kiirilov represents Oberrhein," Nick said. "Just because he says it, doesn't make it so. I'm not sure how we could contact Oberrhein directly, but we might want to try."

"I've an outstanding offer for drinks with one Captain Luc Gray on Nuage Gros," I said. "Maybe he could shed some light on Oberrhein. Or, maybe he can help us with a contact."

"Who's that?" Ada asked.

"He's the squad leader who accompanied us the first time we visited Léger Nuage," I said.

"Oh, I loved those little ships they had. The Nuagians certainly have a flair for color," she said.

"I don't think you should refer to his ship as little. He might get offended," Tabby said.

"Oh, you're naughty, Tabby," she said. It felt good to laugh and release some of the weight we'd been carrying.

"Any chance we'll be going by Léger on the way to Gros?" I asked. Ordinarily, I'd have been the one setting the navigation plans, but that had changed since I'd been indisposed.

"Why?" Ada asked.

"I know that Jake had been sitting on a pile of beer. We might be able to line up a delivery for him," I said.

"If we're going to do that, we should take out a bond that is respected in-system," Nick said.

He was right, if we wanted to haul cargo in Tipperary, we needed to be bonded.

"I hate to ask, but after paying for repairs, how will we look for credits?"

"A hundred fifty thousand after repairs," Nick said. "I was thinking of a seventy-five thousand credit bond."

"So, if you count the *Adela Chen*, the barge, fuel, repairs and missiles, what did that encounter cost us?" I asked.

"Seven hundred thousand, give or take," Nick said. "Revenue from ore was about two hundred fifty thousand credits, so the loss was half a million."

Marny sighed. I could tell she didn't like the idea of attributing a specific cost to our defense. I needed to bail Nick out.

"What'd it cost Oberrhein?"

"Those small cruisers are probably worth one-point five million each," Nick said. He looked relieved to have received the question.

"That's got to seriously piss someone off. They sailed *Karelia* in from Mars. I'm guessing that's because small cruisers aren't available in-system. I wonder if they'll be so cavalier with the remaining two," I said.

"I don't care if they hide," Tabby said. "We're not even."

"Nick, I'll get back to you on the bond. I'd like to see if I can get a load from Léger to Gros that's worth our trip," I said.

***

I received word back from Jake that he was indeed interested in a delivery to Nuage Gros. Overall, Léger's primary exports to Gros were items they manufactured from raw materials gathered from the Grünholz city of Nannandry. Nannandry was unaffiliated with Oberrhein and, more importantly, it was located directly beneath Léger Nuage.

We purchased a fifty thousand credit bond from a reputable bond holder on Curie. There wasn't enough material to completely fill the hold, but after fuel, we would clear four thousand credits and I nearly had a return trip that would be just as profitable.

It was a ten day trip from Terminal Seven to Grünholz, just about the same amount of time as it took to travel to Descartes. We were careful with our burn plans, as fuel was taking a significant amount of our budget. I missed the days back on Mars when fuel consumption didn't matter as much.

I preferred to be in the chair when we arrived at port and this trip was no different. As we approached Nuage airspace, I hailed the automated system.

"*Incoming hail, Nuage Air Defense,*" the AI informed me.

Accept hail. "Captain Hoffen, *Hotspur*. Go ahead," I said.

"Liam Hoffen, Captain Gray here, we're in the area and going to do a flyby," he said.

"Greetings, Captain Gray. Any issues we need to be aware of?" I asked.

"Nothing critical," he said. "We're working on an elevated security condition and require visual inspection of all ships entering our airspace."

"Roger that, Captain," I said. "Did you get my invite?"

"That I did. Any chance you're bringing your crew along?" he asked.

"We're a thirsty bunch. If you're up for it, it'll probably be the entire group," I said. "Are you able to share what the security condition is about?"

"We've had unregistered warships in the area. It happens from time to time, we just like to keep everyone honest," he said.

"Small cruisers?" I asked.

"Could have been. We didn't get detailed sensors on them, but we believe it was a pair of ships in the three to six hundred tonne range. Transponders were not operable," he said.

I saw a squadron of the bright yellow atmospheric ships sail up on our position. The five ships were flying in a wedge formation.

"I see you off my starboard," I said.

"Your ship does not register well with our sensors. I'm not sure we'd be able to see you at all if your transponder was turned off," he said.

"Old blockade runner. She's built for stealth," I said.

Illuminate all bulkhead lights, I directed.

"Thank you, Captain Hoffen. We have what we need. We'll see you in a couple of days on Gros," he said.

The squadron turned tightly and swept across the bow of *Hotspur.*

"What was that?" Tabby asked, sliding into the starboard pilot's chair.

"That was Luc Gray. I think we're on for drinks," I said.

"He came all the way out here to tell you that?"

I shook my head. "No, apparently they've had unidentified ships in their airspace and are doing visual flybys for all contacts."

"Think it was Oberrhein?" She asked.

"Sounded like. Not sure why they'd come through unidentified though. Oberrhein has a treaty with Nuage."

"I bet he'll tell us more over drinks," she said.

"He wanted to know if you and the rest of the crew would be there," I said.

She winked at me. "I'll wear the red dress."

"Ada's right. You are naughty."

"Don't you forget it."

The approach to Léger was just as beautiful the second time. The gleaming white city sat nestled on a thick blanket of gray clouds. Lightening flashed below, illuminating a storm on the planet's surface.

We lined up on our docking bay and I allowed the ship to negotiate the landing. It didn't feel like home yet, but it was familiar and I was grateful for that.

"How many hours are we down for, Cap?" Marny asked. We'd gathered on the bridge.

"Fourteen," I said. "Are we keeping a watch?"

"Negative, Cap. Léger gave us full access to this bay. The only other ships allowed have long established relationships with Léger. We'll run a security program and keep things locked up."

"It's 1800 local. We can't load until 0600 tomorrow. Tabby and I are going to grab a meal at Lena's Diner. Anyone care to join us?" I said.

Forty minutes later we stepped off the elevator on Level 24. We followed the smell of coffee and the sounds of people talking.

"Will you look at that," Marny said.

A sign that read 'Lena's Diner' hung above the opening to a very busy restaurant. It was the same sign our industrial replicator had been working on several weeks ago, only now it was lit with bright neon tube lights. Lena had mentioned she was doing a retro theme and that the coral and sea foam colors she'd chosen would make sense when I saw them. I had to admit that it was quite a look and certainly grabbed my attention.

I caught Jack's eye as he entered the area behind the counter from the kitchen. He smiled, dropped off the two plates he was carrying and wiped his hands on a towel he had hanging from his belt. He placed his hand on Celina's shoulder and pointed at us.

"Come on in," she said.

After we'd greeted each other, Celina pointed to a corner booth along the wall that was deep enough for all of us. Her restaurant was more than half full, but there were only a few choices left for such a big group.

"Looks like you're doing well," I said.

"The response is better than I could have hoped for. I told Jake you were here. He said you should stop over after you've eaten," she said.

I saw what people liked about her diner. The food was fresh and she and Jenny worked the crowd with a friendly patter. In the end, I suppose that was what people wanted from a restaurant.

Jake's bar, now named Startron Lounge, wasn't anywhere near as busy when we finally made it there at 2300, after closing down Lena's Diner.

"What brings you through Léger?" Jake asked.

"Yeah, you've been kind of tight lipped about that," Celina said.

I looked around the bar. A couple of other tables had some late night drinkers, but they were well out of earshot.

"Your place was pretty busy, Lena" I said. "I don't mind sharing, but I was waiting for a little more privacy."

It was well after 0100 the next morning by the time we'd explained what we'd been through.

"If you get me access to the *Karelia*, I bet I can prove her involvement in the destruction of *Cape of Good Hope*. There's no way they can erase what they did," Jake said.

"I need two favors," I said.

"Didn't you hear? That's my new job," he said. "What kind of favors do you need?"

I laughed. The real Jake Berandor had finally emerged.

"Information. We need to know who was on the *Cape* and if there'd be any reason for the Emre brothers to kill them."

"Not sure if I can help with a motive, but the information shouldn't be too hard to come by. What else?" he asked.

"They booby-trapped Big Pete's habitation dome. We need something to disarm their explosives,"

"Do you have any information on the trigger?" he asked.

"We have the information we gathered from *Hotspur*. It's almost completely visual," I said. "We were running silent at the time."

"Depends on how sophisticated the explosives are. It'll probably be enough," he said.

"How much?" I asked.

"For what?"

"All of it. Your help getting the information out of the *Karelia*, the information about the crew of the *Cape* and the explosives disarmament." I said.

"Well, I'm just getting started so I'm running a special. Cost plus fifty percent for the information and the explosives work. You get me access to the *Karelia* and I'll do that for free. I'm not a total rogue," he said.

"Yet." I added to punctuate his declaration.

He nodded with a wry grin. "Agreed."

LIPSTICK ON A BULLDOG

0600 came too early. One of our customers had requested to load first thing and I wasn't about to turn them down. I had intended to load on my own, but I found Marny in the galley with her running clothes on.

"I'm loading some crates this morning. I don't think we'll get in your way, though," I said.

"I'm running outside today," she said.

"Where?"

"Level-15 has a track around the outside. It's open to the public," she said.

"Sign me up next time," I said. "I've downloaded a new prosthetic for running."

"I wondered when you'd start branching out. Your combat prosthetic is good all-round, but nothing beats a task specific tool. When's your next load after this one?" she asked.

"0830. For some reason the Parton Mill likes to start early," I said.

"What are they shipping?"

"Nothing special, just flour. Someone grows wheat in a bubble farm on the surface. The bubbles are all about keeping the rain off the plants and amplifying the effects of light that makes it through the clouds. Apparently, the star has really great light for growing plants. More intensity in the visible range than the Sun," I said.

"Learn something every day. How about I'll help you load the flour and then we can run together?"

"I'd like that."

I had to use a new armored vac-suit, as mine had been lost with the *Adela Chen*. It adjusted to my body as I pulled it on. The fitting process was disconcerting, but fortunately it didn't last long. I strapped a heavy flechette to my chest, grabbed a transparent reading pad and brought up the bill of goods we'd be loading. It looked like four tonnes of flour and a tonne of something I didn't recognize. I looked it up and discovered it was basically sugar extracted from what the original settlers of Grünholz called a syrup tree.

Marny, who had also changed into an armored vac-suit, joined me at the end of the cargo bay as we dropped the loading ramp.

An elegant older woman with blonde hair pinned up in a bun behind her head approached us from the elevator shaft. She wasn't dressed in the same loose clothing we'd come to expect from the Nuagians.

"Mr. Hoffen?" she asked in a higher, lyrical voice.

"You must be Ms. Parton," I said. "You're right on time."

"I apologize for the hour, but it's a baker's life to be up early in the morning. I'm afraid it has rubbed off on my business transactions as well," she said.

"No apology necessary. The life of a spacer is filled with shifts at all hours. I believe you have six tonnes of baking ingredients for Nuage Gros," I said. I held my tablet out and she obliged by tapping it with her own. My program struggled to work with the unusually formatted data, but it eventually found what it was looking for.

I looked around, wondering when the stevedore rep might show up.

"Is there a problem, Captain?" she asked.

"No, I was just expecting to see the stevedore representative," I said.

"Oh, we don't always use them here. You have access to a stevedore robot on this level. Here, I'll show you. I'd forgotten you aren't local," she said.

I found it only a little embarrassing that she had to show me how to call up the stevedore bots. They were the smaller units Nick had arranged to use when we'd first arrived. Getting our own bot was a detail I needed to take care of, as the station charged us a small fee to use theirs.

Once moving, the bots loaded the crates in fifteen minutes.

"Do you mind if I ask you a question, Ms. Parton?"

"Dorothy, please," she said.

"How do you ship your grain up from Grünholz? We might have occasion to visit the surface," I said.

"We have a contract with the grower. But, I'd be willing to put you in contact with them. I'm sure they'd like an alternative shipper," she said.

"Much appreciated."

"Ready for that run?" Marny asked after we were alone again.

"Sure am."

We quickly changed, me into a suit liner and Marny into shorts and a loose top. An hour later, I was sweating profusely and perversely appreciated that Marny was just as winded.

I woke Tabby after a shower and enlisted her help in loading Jake's beer and preparing for the other vendors I'd contracted with. We had a tight schedule, mostly because the city was well set up for delivering crates. Initially, I'd been concerned about being able to organize so many individual contracts, but the crates and their representatives showed up precisely on schedule and we finished loading by 1030.

"All hands prepare for departure," I said. "All stations check in."

"You mind if I take this?" I asked.

"All yours," Tabby replied.

I gently nudged *Hotspur* out of the docking bay. The strength of the wind was more than I'd expected, but I adjusted and allowed the ship to fall into the clouds. The view was exhilarating as we accelerated. I pushed forward on the stick to increase our thrust and felt the stubby wings catch the air. I pulled back on the flight stick to trade some of our speed for elevation. I had minimal experience in atmosphere and it was always fun to play around with something new. I tipped the stick over and barrel rolled. In space, it wasn't much of a maneuver, but with wind beneath the wings it was thrilling.

"That's all, Nick," I said, leveling out our flight.

"Thanks," he grunted. I knew his hands had been gripping the side of his station, knuckles bare from exertion.

By staying within the atmosphere, we avoided the fuel expense of exit and re-entry. If not for the rush of wind past our cockpit, I'd have felt we were just crawling along. Unlike sailing in vacuum, while in atmosphere, we had to keep a small amount of thrust going to continue at the same speed. It was only a four hour trip to Nuage Gros.

Not unexpectedly, the airspace around the Nuage capital grew progressively busier as we approached. It was nothing like Mars, but we counted several dozen ships of differing sizes and shapes by the time we arrived.

Nuage Gros was breathtaking in its size. In pure volume, it was ten times the size of Léger. Much different than Léger, it also had what I could only describe as thin outrigger towers. The outriggers were only thirty meters across, two hundred meters tall, and hung from the sides of the main city by catwalks at several levels.

"Just when you think you've seen it all," Tabby said.

"It's gorgeous," Ada said. She'd knelt between the two pilot's chairs and was looking out the armored glass. "You know they have really great shopping here, too."

"Like what?" Tabby asked.

"Are you kidding? Clothing, of course. This nation was founded by the French," Ada said.

I looked from Ada to Tabby. Shopping? I had no idea what they were on about.

"I'm going to need some credits, Liam," Tabby said.

"I heard that," Nick said. He was seated at the couch working through something on a reading pad. "I've paid out everyone's share of our delivery to Terminal Seven and rented a suite in the Star-Side tower."

A notification showed up on my HUD. Nick had created an account for me with the Nuage banking system and had a pending deposit of fifteen thousand credits. I acknowledged receipt and authorized creation of the account. Nick had explained earlier that he needed to distribute money proportionally depending on how much of the corporation each of us owned. At the completion of each trip, he wanted to pay out some of our earnings.

"Thanks, Nick," Ada said. "I think it's more than it should be."

"You're welcome. And no, it's exactly what you're due for a captain's share. I also paid out a small dividend since we're all new in the system," he said. "It's nice to have money in the accounts."

"Now I'm going shopping for sure," Tabby said. "And you're coming with us, Liam. Marny, are you guys in?"

"We might tag along for a while, but I'm not looking for anything new right now," she said.

"Humor us?" Ada asked.

I could hear Nick and Marny whispering and finally Marny answered meekly. "Sure. I'm game."

Notify Nuage Air Defense of our arrival and request landing permission and navigation path to Level-42 loading bay 4205, I directed.

A notification popped up on my forward vid-screen and the familiar blue contrail of a navigation path appeared on my HUD.

Engage auto-pilot.

Our approach to Gros took us to the opposite side, giving us a great view of the entire city. Like Léger, the docking bay didn't have a lot of vertical clearance for *Hotspur* and I allowed the auto-pilot to bring us in. I didn't mind flying us out, but we had to back in and that maneuver would have caused me a good deal of stress.

"We won't need everyone to help unload. I'll stay back, I just need one more," I said.

"I'll stay, Cap," Marny offered, probably too quickly.

"You're not getting out of shopping that easily, Marny. Nick can take Ada and me over to the hotel. We'll wait for you there," Tabby said.

Marny wasn't a complainer, but I heard her groan quietly as the ship came to rest in our designated loading bay.

We only had a quarter of our hold filled. But on short notice it was a nice pickup. We'd met a number of potential new customers in Léger and we'd meet just as many on this side. I'd keep track of their names and make sure to inform them when we'd be coming through in the future.

Marny and I switched into our standard armored vac-suits and by the time we'd lowered the loading ramp, two of our eight vendors were already present. They seemed to enjoy talking with each other and I had to wait until they finished to actually get started.

"You appear to be expecting trouble, my young friends," a short, older woman said. She was dressed in the expected loose Nuagian clothing, albeit her preferences tended toward a more conservative color palette. She introduced herself as Sophie Fillium.

"Liam Hoffen. We're new to the system and not entirely sure what to expect," I said.

"Don't listen to her. She's just disappointed you're not wearing those tight fitting suits like your friends." Her companion stepped forward, offering his hand. "Personally, I like the enhanced look of your muscles beneath all that armor."

He introduced himself as Thounerlin, but I wasn't sure if that was a first or last name. I felt awkward knowing we were being ogled by people at least thirty years our senior.

"Oh, now you've done it, Thoun. You've made him blush," Sophie said. She pronounced his name Thee-ooh-en.

"Which of you would like to unload first?" I asked. I had no doubt I was blushing.

Sophie produced a reading pad and bumped it against mine. She had half a dozen crates loaded with textiles. As was the routine on Nuage, I recognized it was my responsibility to call the stevedore bots. I'd need to make sure I had their costs loaded into future transactions. They weren't expensive, but it was cutting into our expected profit margins.

"Will you be on Gros long?" Sophie asked. She had an easy manner about her.

"Five or six days, I believe," I said.

"You should stop by my shop. I'd like to dress your girlfriend there," she said referring to Marny.

"Oh, she's not..." I stopped myself. "She doesn't like shopping."

"Bring her along. I'll make it worth your while," she said.

The stevedore bots had her crates loaded onto the cargo lift.

"I'll see what we can do," I said.

Sophie nodded with a tiny smile and waved goodbye as the lift closed.

Thounerlin had eight crates, including two of the beer that Jake had brought from Mars.

"You should take her up on her offer. You won't be sorry," he said.

"I'll be sure to pass that along to the crew."

"What's that?" Marny asked. I couldn't help but notice Thounerlin's awe as he appraised Marny. I chuckled to myself. I'd grown used to her powerful presence, but I still remembered how I felt the first time she'd entered my bridge near Baru Manush.

Just then a new group of people arrived, which I assumed to be the rest of our shipping customers.

"I'll fill you in later," I said and moved to introduce myself to the new group.

We worked quickly and finished forty minutes later.

"I need to take the ship to the shipyard. Feel free to take off from here," I said to Marny when we were finally standing in an empty cargo hold.

"I'll come along for the ride," she said.

Negotiate arrival with Meerkat Shipyard, I directed the ship's AI.

Marny and I stripped out of our armored vac-suits and hung them in the armory.

"I guess we're down to civvies," I said.

"What do you think Ada and Tabby have in mind?" Marny looked worried.

"I think they'd like to upgrade your wardrobe," I said.

"Lipstick on a bulldog," Marny said as I stepped on the lift to the bridge.

It was one of her favorite sayings and I was dismayed she saw things that way.

"Would you mind a personal observation?" I asked as she joined me in the cockpit.

"What's on your mind, Cap?"

"I believe you'll dismiss what I'm about to say, but I'd really like you to take it to heart."

"Oh, this must be bad. Spit it out, Cap. I can take it," she said.

"I'm not sure you can."

She turned to me, no longer working through the quick checklist we used for short flights.

"Now I'm concerned," she said. "What's on your mind, just say it."

"You've got to stop denigrating yourself. I feel like you believe it," I said.

"Don't take that too seriously, Cap. I think I've got a pretty realistic view of myself," she said.

"You're a beautiful woman, Marny. We all see it and it's a common belief that you don't."

"I think you're making too much of this."

"Do me a favor, then," I said.

She chuckled. "You're a funny man, Liam Hoffen. What's the favor?"

"Humor Ada and Tabby when you're shopping," I said.

"You're too much. Eight days ago you were minutes from dying and today your biggest concern is that I have low self-esteem. If it'll make you feel better, I'll let the girls dress me," she said.

"It's a start."

We finished the checklist in silence. I knew I'd made things awkward between us, but there was nothing to do about it now.

I gently lifted the ship from the floor of the loading bay and slid out the door. Like Léger, the loading bays were designed for smaller ships than *Hotspur* and I only had four meters of total vertical clearance, so I had to be careful.

The shipyard was located on the lowest level, just above the antigravity devices that held up the entire city. Raw power radiated from the machinery and I could hear a deep hum as well as see a distortion of the airspace beneath. I didn't think it would be a very good idea to fly directly beneath the city.

"Captain Hoffen, you're right on time." A man in a bright red jumpsuit stood inside the open bay and was motioning to us. The HUD showed an outline around him, letting me know he was the speaker.

"Roger that, where do you want us?" I asked.

He made an exaggerated tossing motion and instructions popped up on my vid-screen. I swiped them over to the auto-pilot and let go of the controls.

Marny hadn't said anything while we'd made the short trip down to the shipyard. She stopped me before we got on the lift.

"I appreciate what you're trying to do, Cap. It means something to me that you're concerned," she said.

I gave her a side hug as we approached the lift.

We met the Meerkat foreman and exchanged security protocols. Nick had set up the appointment and we were on our way to the elevator almost immediately.

Our destination was Level-53 on the Star-Side, which was just eight levels below the top of the city. According to my AI, Nuage Gros was home to fifty-five thousand inhabitants and unlike Léger, it was close to fully occupied.

The elevator was busy and we stopped twice on the way up to add passengers. I paid special attention to what people were wearing, as I knew Tabby and Ada wouldn't let go of the shopping idea anytime soon. We really did stand out like the aliens we were with our Sol-styled clothing.

"Where are you in from?" A man asked as we continued the ride upward.

"Most recently, Mars," I said.

"Welcome."

It was a common interaction. Overall, the Nuagians were more outgoing than the people of Mars. I wondered if it had anything to do with the fact that the Léger nation's entire population was less than two percent of just the city of Puskar Stellar.

Level-53 reminded me of Léger Nuage in design and overall styling. There were more people, of course, but the wide hallways spoked out from a central core just like Léger. Residences and businesses were immediately accessible from these hallways.

What was different, however, was when we got to the Star-Side tower. A five meter long cat-walk joined the main city with the slender outrigger tower. I discovered that the Star-Side designation meant that this particular outrigger was oriented toward the Tipperary star. When we stepped onto the cat-walk we were bathed with bright, white light and a gust of fresh air.

We stepped through a transparent pressure barrier and into the lobby of the hotel where Nick had made our reservations. Glass extended ceiling to floor, which gave the feeling of floating as I looked out over the clouds.

A man in a hotel uniform approached us. "Mr. Hoffen, Ms. Bertrand, we've been expecting you. I see you're traveling light," he said. "If you'll follow me."

The lobby reminded me of the resort we'd stayed in on Coolidge; brightly colored wood tones and comfortable seating groups littering the floor. Nuage Gros was a trading hub for the eighteen Nuage cities and I imagined the hotel had quite a lot of business from visiting traders.

"What do you all do for fun around here?" I asked, making conversation as we descended on a smaller elevator.

"If it's one thing we enjoy, Mr. Hoffen, it is entertainment. There are plays, musical performances, art shows and fine dining on Nuage Gros. If your tastes lean toward the more active, we have first class pod-ball competitions with Double-A class athletes. The hotel also boasts a beautiful spa with luxurious swimming pools that are an experience you'll never forget," he said. "We also have the finest shopping establishments in all of Nuage."

"Right, speaking of, do you know where we'd find Sophie Fillium?" I asked.

This stopped him. "Your taste surprises me, Mr. Hoffen. Ms.

Fillium is a high-end designer. It might be difficult to get an appointment with her on short notice. But to your question, Flair Fillium is located in the Lee-Tower, on Level-32. You can't miss it."

"You may be getting in over your head, Liam," Marny said, smiling.

"It comforts me to know that you'll be right there with me," I said.

"And here we are," the bellhop announced as he swung a beautiful high gloss, wood-grained door open. I felt bad that I hadn't even learned his name.

He held a small reading pad out suggestively to me and I accepted it. One of the things I appreciated about my AI was that it recognized when I didn't understand a common social norm and provided prompts. The bellhop was asking for a tip and my AI presented me with three options, which it had somehow identified as appropriate. I chose the middle ground, tipping him ten credits which amounted to roughly five Mars credits. It seemed like a lot for walking us to our door, but he smiled appreciatively when I handed it back.

"There you are," Tabby said, greeting me at the door with a hug. She'd changed into jeans and a tight, short-sleeved black top.

We walked into the central room of the suite where there was a living room styled group of couches and chairs. Ada had her legs draped sideways over a chair and was staring out at the clouds and the many passing ships visible through the floor to ceiling glass.

"What a view," I said.

"You better be talking about the clouds," Tabby said with a warning note in her voice.

I looked at her, confused, and then back to Ada, who was wearing a sleek, blue dress that accentuated her lithe form. I jerked my head back, realizing it had been a trap.

Tabby looked at me sternly for a moment until she and Ada couldn't contain their laughter. Somewhere along the way, I'd missed their transformation from competitors to friends.

"Very funny," I said.

GUESTS

"The bellhop said something about a pool. Anyone want to go?" I asked.

"Don't even think about it," Tabby said looking between Marny and me.

"Thanks, Cap, but I don't think they're going to be distracted that easily," Marny said.

Ada popped up from the chair. "Aww, don't be like that, this will be fun."

Ada looped her arm through Marny's and leaned in to the bigger woman. The warrior presence Marny almost always commanded had abandoned her and in its place stood a woman who looked completely lost to the moment.

"Where do you want to go first?" Tabby asked.

"I'd really like to get into those full length jumpers everyone here is wearing," Ada said. "Can you imagine Marny with that one we saw on the way up here?"

Tabby grabbed Marny's other arm and turned her back toward the door we'd just entered.

I moved over to the couch where Nick was and started to sit down.

"Don't even think about it, Hoffen. And you too, James. Get your asses up and don't be whining. We've been cooped up for months eating meal bars and swabbing decks. It's time to spend some quality shopping time," Tabby said.

"I was just helping Nick up," I said, extending my hand to help Nick out of his chair. "I might even have an idea of where we could go."

"Not sure I want to hear this, Hoffen. We're definitely not going to a commissary or chandlery or anywhere they sell bulk food with their clothing," Tabby said already through the door.

"I'll have you know, I made friends with one of the city's top designers," I said defensively. Sophie Fillium was hardly a friend, but she *had* suggested we stop by. Not only that, she hadn't been able to take her eyes off Marny.

"Seriously?" Ada asked.

"Level-32, Lee-Tower, you'll see," I said.

Whether to prove me wrong or otherwise, Tabby led the way through the lobby and to the center of the city where we took the elevator down to Level-32.

"You better not be trying to slow us down, Hoffen, 'cause we're doing this either way, even if we are out all day," Tabby said.

"No, no," I said. "Have some faith."

With the help of the AI, we found the breezeway that led from the main city over to the Lee-Tower. It was on the opposite side of the city, but it felt nice to get out and walk. Tabby was wearing red high heels and I couldn't imagine how she was able to walk so easily. I knew that her synthetic skin had superior wear characteristics and as a result she wouldn't likely get blisters, but even so, it was like she was tiptoeing the entire way. I had to admit that I liked how it caused her to sashay when she walked.

Level-32 in this tower was clearly one of the shopping districts. We passed jewelry stores, shoe stores and even an electronics store. We pulled up and stopped in front of Flair Fillium. Compared to the other stores, it was understated and caused me to remember Sophie's gray pantsuit that was considerably less flashy than others I'd seen around town.

Inside, the décor was simple – wood plank flooring and textured gray walls that I suspected were actually built in vid-screens.

"May I help you?" A woman in her early twenties asked. She was slightly built, tall, wore a simple dark-grey dress and had dark straight hair cut to hang at an odd angle. She exuded what I imagined 'fashionable' might represent on just about any world.

"I met Sophie this morning and she recommended we stop in. Is she around?" I asked.

"I'm not sure. She's very busy so... I'll be right back," the girl said.

"You get two points for actually remembering where this place is and having her name right," Tabby said. "You might even get another point if she comes out and talks with us."

"What a delightful surprise." I recognized Sophie's soft voice as she appeared. "I do hope you've come to at least try on a few things. Tell me your name, dear."

She'd walked straight up to Marny who had that deer-in-the-headlights look again.

"Marny Bertrand," she said.

"You hide in the company of delicate beauties, hoping to not be seen for who you are, my dear," Sophie said.

Marny raised her eyebrows not knowing what to say so she opted for the safer, "Pardon?"

"Do not be coy. You're a warrior princess but you dress like a man. You must let me fit you," she said.

"She's already agreed to it," Ada said.

Ada pulled Marny forward into the alcove where Sophie was standing. Up to that point, I hadn't realized the function of the different alcoves in the room. Now, I saw them as locations where a store representative could show customers the different fashions that were being offered.

"Are you shy, my dear?" Sophie asked.

Marny paused and Ada stepped in, "She'll need a modesty screen."

Sophie nodded her head and a semi-circular transparent panel emerged from the floor stopping just below the level of Marny's collarbone.

"Please remove your clothing," she said.

"I have under clothes that I will keep on," Marny said.

"We'll see. It is impossible to construct a great work with a poor foundation," Sophie said.

Her helper had re-entered the room and pulled comfortable bench seats from the floor. Apparently, this was meant to be a spectator sport.

"I can see from your body language that Mr. Hoffen is not your other half. Is it this gorgeous, unassuming, but poorly groomed man here?" she asked, looking at Nick.

Marny smiled and started to speak.

"No! Keep it to yourself. Your smile is all I needed. Pauline, make an appointment for Ms. Bertrand's lovely man to have his hair styled. Use Terrie," Sophie said. "Now, off with those dreadful rags, my dear."

Tabby looked at me with interest. I think her question was if I was going to watch as Marny removed her clothing behind the screen. I just shrugged. I'd seen Marny in tight fitting clothing for most of the time I'd known her. I didn't believe we were about to cover new ground.

Marny reached out to stack her belongings on the provided shelf. First, her quarterstaff, which was a flat, third of a meter-long stick. Next came the nano-blade and then her neatly folded civilian clothing. Marny had worn the faded jeans and loose top for her civvies since the first time we'd met.

I discovered it was one thing to casually see someone in tight clothing on a regular basis and another thing entirely to know they were almost completely naked and only obscured by a thin screen. I realized I was in trouble and looked over at Nick.

"Okay, Buddy. I don't think I'm going to stick around for this. How about we go get that hair-cut?" I said.

Tabby guffawed. "Is there a problem?"

"Maybe. I don't see how this is going to go well for me," I said.

"Mr. Hoffen. Your reaction to this beautiful female form is completely natural. I'd offer that no one in this room is not similarly affected. I would prefer if you stay," Sophie said. "Ms. Bertrand, are you uncomfortable learning that your Captain finds you attractive."

"Hey, wait," I started to protest. I'd leapt without thinking of where I was going. I didn't appreciate being singled out and needed to get out of the hot water Sophie had dropped me into. But what could I say? Marny was attractive, I'd always thought that. It didn't mean I wasn't committed to Tabby… I hoped.

"As entertaining as it is to watch your internal conflict, please be seated Mr. Hoffen," Sophie sighed. "To be so young as to believe we actually control how we feel."

I sat back on the bench. My face burned and I wished everyone would just look away. Tabby rested her hand high on my thigh and squeezed suggestively. I just shook my head in embarrassment.

"I'll reward your loyalty later," Tabby whispered in my ear, allowing her hand to cross the line between suggestive and naughty as she withdrew it.

"I'm afraid this won't do," Sophie continued.

I was glad for the privacy screen, as in a single deft movement Sophie removed Marny's bra and flung it across the room. Pauline, predicting the event, handed her something black and lacy. Sophie put it on Marny, swatting at her hands as she tried to help.

"I thought we were keeping that," Marny said.

Sophie smiled but didn't answer. "Quickly now, dear," she said, urging Pauline as she disappeared through a panel that doubled as a door. Her urging was unnecessary, as Pauline reappeared almost immediately with a stack of bright red and gold cloth.

"I quite understand your need to be intimidating when fulfilling your work functions, but you are also a woman and we should celebrate your individual beauty," Sophie said, while handing Marny the clothing. "Your current garb seeks to hide that form and I find it offensive. But, I also don't want you to look cheap. This ensemble will meet that careful line."

She nodded and the privacy screen dropped back into the floor. The change was dramatic. Sophie had constructed an outfit that resembled the colorful, loose Nuagian clothing we'd seen throughout the station, but was also significantly different.

The pants were loose through the hips and flowed down to Marny's ankles where they were gathered tightly. The red material was overlaid with a muted beige design and the wide cummerbund around her waist and the cuffs around her ankles were decorated with an ornate gold pattern.

Marny's rippled abs were visible for several centimeters before the top started, which was made of a similar, although stiffer material. The top was strapless and it showed a small amount of the black, lacy bra that had been the first to go on.

It was fair to say that Sophie had captured both Marny's strength and beauty. It was a big change, however, and I wondered what Marny's reaction to it might be.

"What do you think of it?" Sophie asked.

"I cannot see it," Marny immediately responded.

"Of course you can. Look at your friends and tell me how it looks," Sophie said. I had to admit, I was beginning to think she was just a little nutty.

Nick stood up, approached and whispered in Marny's ear.

"No secrets, Ms. Bertrand. What did your dear man say?"

Marny looked at Nick who nodded almost imperceptibly and answered. "He asked if I would wear it for him a few times and if I didn't like it after that, I could go back to whatever I liked."

"Very politic and wisely said. There is just one more piece I'd like you to try on," Sophie said. Pauline handed her another red, patterned bundle. "This is for more formal environments, where you might like to be more circumspect. It is meant to be worn over the top."

Marny pulled out what amounted to a knee length dress cut up the sides. Small gossamer threads allowed the sides to split open, but applied enough tension to mostly keep it together.

"It's perfect," Ada finally said, unable to hold back.

Marny nodded her head in acceptance.

"Now, for the rest of you," Sophie said. "Pauline has laid out ensembles for you all."

"How?" I asked.

"My dear, Mr. Hoffen. You're in my city now," she said.

"I hate to be crass, but can we afford you?" I asked.

"A reasonable question. You will each pay me a thousand credits. It is significantly less than what I normally would charge, but I am not giving you all a choice. I assume this is not a problem?" she asked.

I had that feeling I got when someone was backing me into a corner on a deal. I'd spent more than that on Tabby's clothing in the past and I'd probably be willing to pay it just for the moral boost.

"It sounds more than fair," Tabby stepped forward and shook Sophie's hand.

I smiled. I guess I'd have to do my thinking faster next time.

An hour later, we left Flair Fillium, all more colorfully dressed than when we'd entered. The women all had variations of what Marny was wearing. What Nick and I had was less complex, but still loose fitting. We were all carrying matching pullover tunics which, according to Pauline, we would need for more formal engagements.

"What do you think about the clothes, Marny?" I asked.

"Better now that you're all wearing them. I'd have stuck out like a peacock, otherwise," she said.

"What are we doing for dinner?" Ada asked. It was late in the afternoon and the smells of the nearby restaurants were compelling.

"We're meeting Captain Gray for drinks in forty-five minutes. We should drop our stuff at the hotel and head over," I said. "Do you think we're supposed to wear the formal top?"

"What part of bar says formal to you?" Tabby asked.

"Right."

The bar Luc had chosen was called *de Laroche* and was in the main city on Level-23. As we approached, it became immediately obvious as to why he'd chosen it. The walls were covered by ancient looking airplane props and old airframes hung from the ceiling.

"Who do you suppose de Laroche was?" Marny asked. My HUD immediately showed a reference to an old Earth French aviator, Elise Deroche, the first woman to fly an airplane.

"May I help you?" A server asked as we walked into the bar foyer.

"We're meeting someone. Do you know if Luc Gray is here yet?" I asked.

"He just arrived. Follow me," he said.

"I almost didn't recognize you outside of your vac-suits." Luc Gray stood up as we approached.

"You already know Tabby, but let me introduce you to the rest of the crew," I said and introduced everyone.

"I maintain my earlier statement. I cannot imagine how you remain sane, sailing a ship filled with these beautiful women." He paused and looked into Ada's eyes as he kissed the back of her hand, something he'd done more quickly with Marny and Tabby already.

"You're a flirt, Mr. Gray," Ada said.

"I hope I've not offended."

"I didn't say I didn't like it," she replied.

"Game on," Tabby said.

"What are we drinking tonight?" I asked as we sat.

"I've heard that there's a new brew in the city. I suspect, however, that it might have been you who brought it in," he said.

"You'll need to make sure you try the Guinness if you haven't had it," I said.

"I'll do that. Let me order the first round," he said.

"Only if we can pay for it," Nick said.

"I got a report from Meerkat Shipyard today," Luc said. "They're concerned that the repairs they're performing are the result of combat."

I smiled. He didn't have any problem getting right to the heart of an issue. I preferred his straight-forward approach to games.

"How much do you want to know? We've been having some problems getting our goods delivered," I said.

"In Nuage airspace?" he asked, alarmed.

"Not the really hairy stuff," I said. "We did have a run in with Oberrhein just off Léger Nuage a few weeks back."

"Define 'hairy,'" he said.

"We lost our tug in an attack by three Oberrhein cruisers," I said.

"A Nuage flagged ship?"

"No, our tug wasn't flagged yet, but *Hotspur* was. *Hotspur* received the damage while defending the tug. I've got a combat stream you can look at if you want," I said.

"I'm compelled to inform you that I'm an officer of Nuage Air Defense. If you show me something that implicates you in a crime, I'll have no option but to report it," he said.

I looked at Nick who nodded.

"We've committed no crimes," I said.

"You seem very calm for someone who lost a ship," he said.

"Don't mistake calm for lack of resolve," Tabby said.

"No offense intended," he said, holding up his hands.

I pinched the data stream that I'd prepared in advance, just in case he asked for it, and flicked it at him. A round of frosty mugs filled with amber liquid arrived and we all sat back while Luc reviewed the ten minutes that I'd spliced together.

When he finished, he looked up and grabbed his beer thoughtfully. He was visibly agitated after watching the presentation.

"You took out a cruiser with your tug? What possibly could have possessed you?" he asked.

"There was no escaping," I said. "Oberrhein had us caught in the deep dark and the crew on *Hotspur* would have sacrificed themselves trying to protect us."

"Merde," he said. "Only one thing that doesn't add up for me."

"Only one?" Tabby asked with an ironic laugh.

"You keep saying Oberrhein, but Oberrhein doesn't have any cruisers," he said. "It is outside of our treaty with them."

"Their transponders sure read that way," I said.

"Show me."

I extracted one of the many interactions we'd had with them and forwarded him the partial combat data streams that contained the transponder signatures.

"It's no secret that we've had a difficult truce with Oberrhein. I'll need to forward this to my superiors."

"How can we be sure they're really Oberrhein?" Nick asked.

"Who else would they be?" Luc asked.

"We were hoping you might have some ideas," Nick said.

"You've only heard half of the story."

"There's more?"

"How much time do you have?" Tabby asked.

"I find my evening's schedule has suddenly opened up," he said.

Over the next hour and with fish tacos and chips, we recounted the events starting with the destruction of *Cape of Good Hope* and ending with our encounter after the delivery to Terminal Seven.

Nick, Marny and I had talked about the dangers of telling Nuage about our problems and it had come down to the recognition that we needed an ally in the system. Luc's response wasn't unexpected and I was glad that he had taken us seriously.

"That's a lot to take in," he said after we finished. "Can you back it all up with data streams?"

"Certainly," Nick said.

Gray stood suddenly as an older woman approached. "Admiral Marsh, it's unexpected to see you this evening." He looked like he was trying to decide between saluting and shaking her hand.

"At ease, Mr. Gray. We're all just out for a nice dinner, aren't we?" Her tone implied anything but what her words indicated.

"Yes. Of course, Madame," he said.

"You should introduce me to your friends and invite me to join you," she said.

"Of course, my apologies," he said. He introduced us all in turn.

"I received some rather disturbing news from Colonel Festove this evening. I have to admit, I'm surprised I don't see him down here, given the nature of his message," she said.

Gray remained quiet. A question hadn't been asked and he'd wisely not offered an opinion. I noticed that while he was sitting down, he remained bolt-upright in his chair.

She continued. "Tell me, is it your opinion as an officer that this information is credible?"

"I am not sure exactly what Colonel Festove sent you, but the information presented to me by this crew seems too astonishing to make up. Yes, I believe the preliminary reports present a credible threat," he said, stiffening.

"Very well. Mr. Hoffen, Mr. James, I am sorry to ruin your evening plans, but I'd like to request that you and your crew accompany me back to the command center," she said.

"Are you detaining us or requesting our assistance?" Nick asked.

Marsh visibly stiffened. I suspected she wasn't used to being questioned.

"You are guests of the Nuage nation and we are requesting your assistance in an urgent matter," she replied.

"Certainly," Nick answered.

PRIVATEER

I called the server over and swiped the charges for the evening. We'd spent four hundred credits and I had to remind myself that every credit here was roughly equivalent to two Mars credits.

"Mr. Gray, will you accompany our guests to the Gasser Planning room?" Marsh asked, although it felt like more of an order than a request.

"Oui, Madame," he replied. My AI provided the translation of his affirmation.

Admiral Marsh turned on her heels and left without further conversation.

"Were you expecting that?" I asked Gray.

"I cannot say I'm surprised. Admiral Marsh is a proactive leader," he said. "We should be on our way, as she is also not particularly patient."

"Will she be conducting the interviews?" Nick asked.

"I would not think so, but it is not up to me," Gray responded.

We followed him to the elevators where a car stood open. The lights inside the car were a blue hue and I wondered if that was some sort of indication of official business. Once we entered, the doors closed and we started moving. Gray had not offered any visible instruction. The ordinarily transparent walls of the car were obscured and the elevator dropped more floors than I could keep track of.

The doors finally opened to a reception area that shouted military; clean, white walls, tight gray carpet and minimal furniture. We were met by two uniformed guards who saluted upon seeing Captain Gray.

On the single table that occupied the reception area was a small square basket.

"Greetings, Captain Gray. We'll need everyone to place weapons and communications devices into the basket before we take you back." The speaker was a sturdy looking soldier.

Gray looked at me, clearly wondering if this was going to be a problem.

"As long as we get them back, I don't see a problem," I said.

I pulled off my earwig, withdrew the small flechette I had strapped beneath the loose fabric of my new pants and placed them into the basket. I slid my fingers into my waistband and withdrew the small nano-blade that I carried. It wasn't a full-sized blade, but in a pinch could be very useful. In truth, I was intimidated by the blade's ability to do damage without providing much feedback.

As expected, the basket provided was too small by a fair margin and the soldier had to retrieve another, larger basket after Marny and Tabby unloaded. Probably the most surprising to me was Ada, who I didn't believe normally carried anything. She contributed a slender laser blaster and a stun device I'd never seen before. The device caught Gray's attention and he looked at Ada with raised eyebrows.

"Girl never knows what she might run into," she said with a grin.

"Those aren't strictly legal," he said.

Ada practically simpered. "I won't tell if you don't."

Gray just shook his head.

"We're this way, Captain." It was the smaller of the two guards. Without my HUD, I wasn't able to get a lock on his nameplate.

We followed him down a wide, nondescript hallway into a larger conference room. For all of Nuage's care towards the aesthetic, their security establishment had adopted the same austere design as Mars Navy. The room was utilitarian, with a center table and functional chairs. On the opposite side of the room was another door with two guards standing on either side.

We were first joined by five officers who didn't introduce themselves but simply took their spots at the table. Two minutes later the guards opened the door again.

"Attention," one of the guards said crisply as the door opened and Admiral Marsh entered. The officers all stood in response. I wasn't surprised to see that Marsh had changed from her civilian clothes to a uniform, although it was impressive how quickly she'd been able to make the transformation.

"At ease. Please, everyone take a seat. Ensign, secure the room," she said and proceeded to the head of the table.

After we were seated, she continued. "Captain Gray, you're to be commended for bringing this matter to our attention. Ordinarily, I'd dismiss you from the conversation based on your role in Air Defense and not in Central Security Services, but given your relationship with our guests from Sol, I've requested that you remain. Colonel Festove has agreed as long as it doesn't interfere with your normal duties. Is this amenable to you?"

"Yes, Ma'am," he said. I noticed that he'd changed from a French affirmation to standard speech.

"Mr. Hoffen, Captain Gray has identified you as the spokesman for your crew. As such, I'll be addressing my questions to you. Is this appropriate?"

I looked back at her. She had cold gray eyes and exuded the same type of command presence I'd seen in many other officers.

"That will work, but to be honest, it will depend on the question," I said.

"By all means, I'd prefer we are honest," she said.

If her statement was meant to put me on the defensive, she'd have to work harder than that. I returned her stare and waited for a question. I felt like she was measuring me and we waited for a full minute before she continued.

"Would you introduce yourself and your crew?" she asked.

I introduced everyone, starting with Nick and ending with Tabby. When I finished, she introduced the four other officers who had entered with her. Colonel Festove was the only name I recognized and without my HUD, I had no hope of recalling any of the other names.

After introductions, she started right in. "Captain Gray reported that three cruisers identifying themselves as Oberrhein attacked your small fleet in open space. Would you elaborate on this?"

"If I could have access to a reading pad, I've prepared several vid sequences that summarize our interactions with the Oberrhein ships," Nick said. Apparently, he wasn't off-put by her attempt at formality.

Festove cut in before Marsh could answer. "How do we know these vids aren't fiction?"

"A reasonable question. Mr. James, are they fiction? And, what were the circumstances in which you presented this information to Captain Gray?"

"Captain Gray asked about the nature of the damage our ship, *Hotspur*, had taken. Apparently, Meerkat Shipyard filed a report suggesting that they'd been asked to repair combat damage," Nick said.

"Did you?" Festove asked.

"Take damage in combat? Yes. Our sloop and tug were attacked by three, four-hundred tonne cruisers at roughly fifty million kilometers from Belirand's new Terminal Seven project."

"And, you expect us to believe that a three hundred tonne sloop and a tug succeeded in combat against three larger cruisers?" Festove asked. I was starting to wonder how much of the video Gray had forwarded or at least how much Festove had actually watched.

"We're not asking you to believe anything," I said. "Captain Gray asked us a relatively simple question about the nature of the damage to our ship and we told him as succinctly as possible. I don't believe we've broken any Nuagian laws by being fired upon."

"No, but don't play the simpleton, Mr. Hoffen. Your accusations threaten a fragile treaty between Nuage and Oberrhein," he responded.

I wasn't about to take the bait and jump into the argument. He hadn't asked a question and I wasn't about to defend our actions.

"Let's be clear, Colonel," Tabby said. "We're not making any accusations."

"Mr. James, would you be open to an audit of your data streams?" A thin, dark skinned female officer asked.

"With some limitations to keep our company records private," he said.

"Aswa, is this something you could start on right away?" Marsh asked.

"Yes, Admiral. If Mr. James would provide access, I will execute an audit. To your question, Mr. James, I will set up the parameters to avoid exposing corporate information. We only desire to understand the veracity of the data streams. The nation of Nuage respects all people's right to privacy," Aswa answered.

I had no idea if it was her first or last name and didn't appreciate not having my HUD available. She stood and walked around the table to where Nick sat and placed a mid-sized reading pad in front of him. I recognized the interface to our ship's systems. Nick gestured and typed, finally holding the pad up to Aswa.

"Hold on to that. Now that I have access, I'll run my audit as you present the information requested," she said, returning to her chair, leaving the reading pad with Nick.

"Colonel Festove, any objection to us proceeding?" Marsh asked.

I was interested in the Nuage military hierarchy, I'd assumed that Admiral was above Colonel in their reporting structure, but Marsh was deferential in her treatment of Festove. It reminded me of how much I didn't like bureaucracies.

"No. I believe Ms. Nilovila's audit will address the issues I have with the truth of the presentation," he said.

"Mr. James, please proceed," Marsh said.

Nick swiped a video sequence that I was starting to become overly familiar with. He'd reorganized it and was starting with our sensor data that showed the trace elements we'd tracked entering *Cape of Good Hope's* engines. He'd artfully caught *Karelia's* transponder signature, showing Oberrhein as the flag issuer.

"Hold on a minute," Festove complained. "You're not even in Tipperary. How is this relevant?"

Nick paused the playback and I sat back in my chair. It was going to be a long evening.

Two hours later we finished getting through the ten minute sequence. I'd started to understand Festove's general issue. He was in charge of Nuage Air Defense and they'd only enjoyed a decade of peace with Oberrhein.

"Is there any reason to believe those ships aren't Oberrhein?" Marsh asked, looking at Festove.

"Ms. Nilovila, are the signatures confirmed?" he asked.

"Yes, Colonel."

"It would be a dangerous game for anyone to pretend to be Oberrhein without their permission, even if it were technically feasible, which it shouldn't be," he said.

"Mr. Stephano, have you heard back from the Oberrhein ambassador?" Marsh asked. We hadn't heard a single thing from the final Nuage officer who was seated at the table.

"Formally, no. Informally yes," he said.

Marsh sighed. "What did they, informally, say?"

"My contact has requested a meeting with Mr. Hoffen and Mr. James in the neutral location of Nannandry," he said.

"Explain," she said.

"My apologies, Admiral. For the sake of our guests, I'll have to cover ground that you already understand. With your permission?" he asked.

"Understood," she said.

"Hold on. We should not be including outsiders in our internal discussions," Festove said.

"Unfortunately, Oberrhein has made that decision for us," Stephano answered.

"Colonel, let's give him some latitude," Marsh said.

Stephano continued, "To grasp our current issue, you need to understand how Oberrhein is organized. Unlike Nuage with our centralized government, the Oberrhein nation resembles ancient feudal Europe. That is, each state of the Oberrhein nation is generally referred to as a fiefdom and overseen by a lord. Within their own fiefs, the lords are left to govern as they see fit.

"I've heard rumors of a new fief emerging, one that is space-bound and not planet-bound as is the rest of Oberrhein," Stephano said.

"Didn't you think Air Defense should be informed about a new threat?" Festove asked, fighting to keep his composure.

"With respect, Colonel, until today, I've not had any verification of this rumor. I believe what we're seeing is this emerging fief and that Petar Kiirilov, is the lord of that fief. His actions against *Loose Nuts* are consistent with other Oberrhein encounters," he said.

"How does this impact *them*?" Festove asked looking directly at me.

"Mr. Turnigy, Oberrhein's ambassador to Nuage, has requested a meeting with Mr. Hoffen. It seems that Lord Kiirilov has overstepped his authority."

"What could Turnigy want with *them*?" Festove asked. His use of the word 'them' was starting to grate, as if we were some sort of pariah.

"Perhaps you should have read the memo I published about the arrival of this small company – *Loose Nuts*," Ambassador Stephano replied.

"Forgive me. Perhaps I'm behind on my reading related to emigration. I hardly see how it could be relevant to Air Defense," Festove said.

"Ordinarily, I would agree with you. But in this case, the company *Loose Nuts* was one of only three corporations awarded a Letter of Marque by Mars Protectorate in the last sixty years," Stephano said. "Their recent history reads more like a work of fiction than anything else. If I hadn't vetted the information myself, I would not have included it in my rather lengthy memo to the senior leadership."

"What are you saying, Stephano?" Marsh asked.

"It is quite simple, really. We should do the same thing Mars Protectorate did. We should invite *Loose Nuts* to sign a Letter of Marque that we would issue on behalf of the nation of Nuage," he said.

"What in Curie's damnation is a Letter of Marque?" Festove spouted. His AI obviously picked up the question because I could see his eyes scanning text in front of him. Inwardly, I chuckled and tried not to let it escape.

Wait for it …

"You want to give them license to take out pirates in the name of Nuage?" Festove asked. His face was beet red.

Stephano's voice was calm as he replied. "I believe they've identified themselves as buccaneers, as opposed to pirates. But, either way, that is exactly what I'm recommending. By signing this letter, *Loose Nuts* would be obligated to present any prizes taken to Nuage. Think of all the intelligence we'd be able to gather from those ships. Everyone benefits and it costs us nothing."

"And if they attack innocents?" Festove asked.

"If it happens within our airspace, we prosecute them. Otherwise, we bring criminal charges to the Tipperary Criminal Tribunal on Curie, just as we would without the letter. Frankly, I'm surprised you're not more interested, Breshev. It's a brilliant system that gives us complete deniability. There is almost no risk to us," he said.

"What do *they* get from it?" Festove swept his arm indicating the five of us.

"Legal ownership of the prizes. Think of it this way, they are incentivized to remove the bad elements of space so they can grow stronger and more prosperous. Instead of running from these buccaneers, they will want to eliminate them. Our influence would spread into the Descartes asteroid belt without a single credit of capital being expended."

"I don't like it," Festove said.

"You don't need to. We would run the program through the intelligence and diplomatic branch," Stephano said.

"We certainly won't make a decision tonight," Admiral Marsh said. "Mr. Hoffen, Mr. James, Ms. Bertrand, Chen and Masters, we are grateful for your help this evening. I feel compelled to tell you that everything we've discussed in this room must remain confidential and I would greatly appreciate it if you refrained from sharing it with others. As you are not citizens, we cannot legally compel you, but I can say that it could affect your visa status with Nuage. Captain Gray, would you escort our guests back to their hotel?"

As annoyed as he'd been, Colonel Festove shook our hands as we left, as did the rest of the senior officers. He even thanked me personally for bringing the matter to their attention. To say that it was a confusing moment is to understate it. I would never understand politicians.

"Are we hot-tubbing?" Marny asked after we'd collected weapons and earwigs and stepped onto the elevator.

"The spa is beautiful," Ada said. "Luc, are you joining us?"

"I have to be up by 0800 this morning," he said. I looked at my HUD and was surprised to see that it was 0200. It had been a five hour meeting.

"You could stay for an hour..." Ada said and looped her arm into his. He was a goner. No one could resist Ada when she wanted something.

"No fair," he said.

"I believe your Admiral wanted you to have eyes-on for as long as possible. I'd have to wonder if you're actually duty-bound," Marny said, making me smile.

When we arrived at the hotel lobby, I requested that the concierge replicate swim suits for all of us. Tabby chose a pattern that I would have shied away from as it felt pretty revealing for the women, but I certainly wasn't going to object.

"We can change in our suite," I said, handing the suits out.

"These look pretty small," Marny said.

"I believe the French invented the word 'risqué,'" Tabby answered. "And besides, we'll be in an aerated tub."

Marny smiled, recognizing she'd been played.

The suits covered more than I'd originally expected, although to be fair, it was just barely more than what I might have thought to be the minimum. I'd seen Marny and Ada in vac-suits that left little to the imagination, but these suits were a whole new level.

"Don't be getting too distracted," Tabby said as she slunk in behind me. I turned to look at her and my breath caught in my throat. I'd seen her undressed plenty of times, but it never really got old. She placed her hand under my chin and pushed my mouth closed. "And for the record, that's the right reaction."

Tabby playfully grabbed my hand and we half ran down to the spa area, leaving the rest of the crew to follow.

The hotel's spa took up an entire level in the Star-Side Tower. The deck was translucent, as if someone had melted pockets for water to sit in on the large circular surface. It was late enough that we had the entire room to ourselves, although it looked like it could easily host forty or fifty bathers.

I jumped into the central pool behind Tabby and realized I had no idea how to swim. I recognized my trouble immediately and thrashed around, trying to bring my head back to the surface. Nothing I did had any affect, or so it seemed. I managed to get back to the surface a couple of times, but still choked on the water.

I felt a strong arm grab me from behind and fought against it. I couldn't be drawn back down. The arm, however, was inflexible. It wrapped around my neck, pulling me. When I broke the surface and was dragged back to where I could stand again, I calmed. It was Marny standing behind me.

"I guess that answers the age old question, Cap," Marny laughed as she pushed me to the side of the pool.

"What question is that?"

"If Tabby jumped off a cliff, would you follow?" Marny said.

"I don't know what I was thinking."

"I'm guessing you were allowing other parts of your anatomy to do your thinking," she said.

"Frak, what happened, Hoffen?" Tabby asked as she swam up to me.

"Can't swim. I guess I forgot," I said.

"Oh, babe, I'm so sorry! Are you okay?"

"Roger that. Marny pulled me out," I said. I hoisted myself up and sat on the edge of the pool. "Hot tub?"

"We need something to drink," Tabby said.

"There's room service," Nick said. "What do you want?"

I noticed that he hadn't jumped in the pool either.

"Just something. I'm mostly hungry, but wine would be nice," she said.

"Beer for me. Wine gives me a headache," I said.

"I've got it," Nick said.

"Where's Ada?"

"They're over there," Marny said, pointing to a hot tub on the very edge.

Tabby placed her hands on the side of the pool and lifted herself out in a single motion.

"When did you learn to swim?" I asked.

"I was in the Navy. Everyone in the Navy swims," Tabby said.

"You were in Mars Navy," I said.

"Tell that to my C.O."

We walked over to Luc Gray and Ada. "Mind if we join you?" I asked.

"Sure," Ada said.

The tub had been built into the wall and we had a spectacular view of the stars above as well as an amazing view of the clouds below, which from this vantage point appeared to be glowing.

"Why do they glow?" I asked.

"It's only fully dark for six hours. We're high enough that Tipperary illuminates the clouds, causing the glow. It's just starting now and it'll break above the horizon in about two hours.

"Everything about Nuage is gorgeous," Ada said.

"It sure is tonight," Luc said.

He stayed with us until we agreed to break it up at 0400. As it was, he would only be getting three and a half hours of sleep. I felt guilty as Tabby and I lay back in our luxurious bed. I might have had a difficult time sleeping after the meeting, but the spa and drinks had done their job.

At 1300, I awoke to the smell of food. I pulled on my new civvies and slipped out into the common room. Marny and Nick were at a high table, next to the window, looking out over the clouds.

"Sleep well, Cap?" Marny asked.

"Not sure I even rolled over once," I said. "You run already?"

"Aye, and a little weight lifting. They have a great workout center. I was thinking, perhaps we should do a little swim training with the two of you," she said.

I glanced at Nick who had the look of someone who had given in to the inevitability of the moment.

"Sure. But I'm starving," I said.

"I received a comm from Ambassador Stephano," Nick said.

"What'd he want?" I asked.

"He'd like to drop by and talk with us," he said.

"What do you suppose he wants?"

I heard a knock at our door.

"You can ask him yourself. I think that's him."

I was closest, so I opened the door. It was indeed Ambassador Stephano. He was wearing a more formal looking uniform than he had the night before.

"Good afternoon, Ambassador. Please come in," I said.

"Greetings, Mr. Hoffen. Thank you so much."

"To what do we owe the pleasure of your visit?" I asked as I led him over to Nick and Marny.

"I wanted to find you right away so that I could extend to your company the offer of a Letter of Marque from the people of Nuage," he said.

"Did you find any issues with my last set of changes, Jacques?" Nick asked.

"No, Nicholas, you've a keen mind and your changes are fair," he said. I wanted to roll my eyes at the excessive buttering up.

"Liam, are you good with this?" Nick asked.

"I've always thought of myself as a privateer."

NANNANDRY

"Try to relax, you need to float in the water. Remember, most of your body needs to be submerged," Marny explained for the millionth time.

I'd spent most of my life floating in zero-g and the concept didn't even remotely resemble what she was trying to get me to do in the water. It was our fourth swimming lesson and at least I could swim enough to keep my head above the surface while taking a breath.

"It's harder for spacers," Tabby observed. "The planet-born were all much better swimmers. You'll get it eventually. At least you won't drown."

"Aye. Not in a pool, he won't. Perhaps we could stay away from oceans, lakes and the like," Marny said.

Marny was an excellent swimmer. In the Marines, it had been part of her physical fitness regime to swim a few kilometers on a daily basis. It seemed she could swim forever under the surface of the water, ending up ridiculous distances away from us when she finally surfaced.

"What's wrong with oceans and lakes?" I asked. "Wouldn't it work the same?"

"That it does, but the water moves in the oceans and even the best of swimmers meet their match in an angry ocean," she explained.

"I think I'll stick to space," I said, pulling myself out of the pool. "It's much more forgiving."

Marny laughed. "Only to a spacer, Cap."

"What do you think about Ada and Captain Gray?" Tabby asked the question generally, but I knew she was fishing for Marny's answer.

"He's a handsome man. I just don't know if he's a free enough spirit for our Ada," Marny said.

"Have you heard something?" Tabby asked in a hoarse whisper.

We'd moved poolside where Nick had taken up residence on a chaise lounge and looked to be asleep.

"They've been out every night. There's something going on," Nick said without opening his eyes.

"What about Selig?" Tabby asked, sitting sideways on a lounge.

"Ada doesn't seem the miner's wife," Marny said. "No offense to Silver, Cap."

"Did you get a load to Nannandry settled?" Nick asked. We were changing the subject.

We were due to set sail tomorrow and had a clandestine meeting with Oberrhein's Ambassador Turnigy in the afternoon at Nannandry.

"Sort of. We're going to be light and barely cover fuel to the surface. On the flip side, however, I've a spec load of raw materials. The market rate is excellent," I said.

"How are we paying for it?" Nick asked. "I didn't think folks in Nannandry took credits."

"They don't, but we've a nice load of precious - nearly eighty thousand credits of the stuff. We can darn near fill the hold with raw materials for that," I said.

"Aren't you going to flood the market?"

"Not even close. Trade between Nannandry and Nuage cities is almost all bartered goods. Nannandry supplies raw materials for Nuagian refined goods. We're offering a material Nannandrites don't have access to. There's almost no mining done on Grünholz so they're willing to trade over market price for gold, platinum and even silver," I said.

"Show me," Nick said.

"Certainly." I flicked the research I'd done and the orders I'd put together.

"Nicely done," Nick said. "This could really be a thing for us."

"Agreed. We could even open it up to the rest of the Descartes belt once we deal with Oberrhein," I said.

"You mean Petar," Nick said.

"We'll see..."

We awoke early the next morning at 0500. Well, most of us did anyway. Ada had to be prodded to get moving. I'd heard her come in only a few hours before we got up and she was dragging badly. It was unusual to see her without her normal level of enthusiastic energy.

Level-1, Meerkat Shipyard, I instructed the elevator car.

Like most cities, there were a few people up at the early hour, but for the most part we were alone.

"Coffee?" Ada squeaked, looking at us with bleary eyes.

Tabby let go of my hand and wrapped a long arm behind Ada's back, which she accepted gratefully.

"How about you get some rack time while we sail over to Nannandry? You can take watch once we're down there." Tabby said.

"You're a saint," Ada said, closing her eyes.

"It'll cost you. I'm going to want a full accounting," Tabby said.

"Nuh-huh," Ada said. I couldn't tell if she was agreeing or not.

"Are we square with the yard?" I asked Nick as we stepped off the elevator. *Hotspur* was sitting to the side, taking up a good portion of the main hangar area.

"We're square and we'll get a walk-through of the fixes. Most of the damage was to the armor," he said.

"Any problems getting the armor replicated?"

"No, ironically, we paid through the nose for nano-crystalized steel," Nick said. "They bring it in from Curie."

"It'll be a long time before we'd be able to produce nano-steel," I said.

"Agreed. But at the prices we paid, we might want to push that schedule," Nick said.

"I bet Big Pete would love that conversation."

A man in a Meerkat shipyard uniform approached.

"*Hotspur*?" he asked.

"Roger that. Liam Hoffen," I answered, extending my hand.

"They call me Bing. Would you like to inspect the repairs?" he asked. It was mostly a formality as the repairs were electronically logged.

"Sure thing. You mind if the crew gets loaded while we take a look?" I asked.

"Suit yourself," he said.

"Count me in, Cap," Marny said.

Meerkat had a grav-lift that easily accommodated the three of us and Bing lifted us up to the first repair location. The damage had been perfectly repaired, at least to the naked eye.

"We had to replace the entire panel," he explained. "That armor is tricky to work with."

"You get many Oberrhein ships in here?" I asked.

"We'll get an occasional Oberrhein freighter, but they're always old and beat up. Since they don't trade credits, it's hard for their captains to pay," he said.

We moved to the next repair location.

"Any warships?"

"Treaty doesn't allow their fighters in our airspace, but they never had much anyway," he said.

"I was under the impression there'd been quite a war between Nuage and Oberrhein," I said.

"Sure was. Airships aren't their strength though. What they've got are great floating ships that can shell the cities from the surface," he said.

"Sounds like you might have had some experience with that," Marny said.

"It was hard times and we didn't know if we'd make it through. Hate to see us back in that mess again," he said.

"Well, you have a beautiful city and you've done a great job on our ship," I said.

"Much appreciated," he said, finally depositing us near the exterior hatch on the starboard.

"Like what you saw?" Nick asked when I passed him on the bridge.

"Can't tell there was ever a problem," I said.

"Yup. They're expensive, but if they do a good job, it's worth it," he said.

"Agreed. Tabby, you want to run us topside to the loading bay?"

"Course is laid in, and all sections are reporting green," Tabby said.

"Nicely done, helm is yours," I said.

Tabby gently lifted *Hotspur* from the floor and glided slowly through the pressure barrier. A sharp updraft immediately caught our wings and we easily drifted up to the docking bay where we'd pick up the small load we had for Nannandry.

"Cap. Can you and Tabby handle the load?" Marny asked.

"Roger that," I said. "What's up?"

"Breakfast run," she said.

"Heck yah."

***

"Heya, sleepyhead," Tabby said, looking over her shoulder.

I hadn't heard Ada's approach from behind us and when I turned I could see she was gingerly sipping a cup of tea.

"If I didn't know better, I'd say you have a hangover," I said.

"Shhh," she said.

"Luc?" Tabby asked.

"Yeah."

"You two seem to be awfully cozy," Tabby said. "How's that going to work out with Selig?"

"Selig and I aren't that serious," Ada said.

"You're gonna break his heart," I said.

"Don't say that. I like Selig."

"Are you okay staying on board? Or we could lock up while we meet with the Ambassador if you want to come along," I said.

"Please. My head is pounding. I don't know how they drink so much wine," she said.

We'd been sailing, well, technically flying for the better part of the morning and would soon need to drop through the heavy, perpetual cloud cover.

Negotiate landing with Nannandry terminal, I instructed the ship's AI.

"There are no channels available for Nannandry," the AI replied immediately.

Identify Nannandry landing protocols.

"No protocol available."

"What do you think of that?" I asked, looking at Tabby.

"Sounds odd to me, but I'd heard they have limited tech on the surface. Something about the electrical storms," she said.

"Nick, you have any thoughts on a landing solution?" I asked.

"Yup. There's a landing strip, but the shape of it changes constantly due to the wild-growth of the plant life. I'm sending you coordinates now," Nick said. "You'll have to do a visual approach."

"Roger that. Okay everyone, let's buckle up."

I nosed the ship over and punched into the thick cloud cover. The heavy clouds looked like they should provide a lot of resistance, but we simply dropped in without any issues until the ship started bucking. To date, we'd experienced very light turbulence in the high altitude of Grünholz and what we found now was a completely different experience. Without being able to see anything through the clouds, the constant dropping and shaking was extremely concerning.

"Frak." Tabby said in response to a jagged lightning bolt that illuminated the clouds in front of us. She was having to talk loudly due to the noise generated by the uneven air rushing past the skin of the ship. "I'm not getting a good read on elevation."

"Roger that," I said.

Terms like elevation, ceiling and visibility all of a sudden jumped from being obscure to having relevance. I couldn't imagine how people flew regularly in this crap. I hated the idea of not being able to see out the window.

When we broke free of the clouds, things hardly got better. The clouds had blocked most of the light, but below them we passed right into a heavy rain and lightning storm. For a space-borne it was almost too much to bear.

"Port, twenty-five degrees," Tabby all but yelled due to the rain hammering against the hull of the ship.

"Is that hail?" I asked concerned, looking at the chunks of ice sliding down the armored glass.

"Sensors are back," Tabby said pointing at the vid-screen in front of me.

She was right. *Hotspur* was showing an instrument panel on the vid-screen. We'd exited the clouds at twenty-five hundred meters and were dropping at fifty meters a second. I pulled back on the stick and traded speed for elevation. I banked to the port and centered the targeting reticle on my HUD so that we were lined up with Nannandry. We'd leveled off and were flying at three hundred meters per second. It seemed too fast for the weather conditions, so I pulled back on the thrust.

"Shouldn't we see lights or something? We're only two hundred kilometers away," I said.

"Stay above five hundred meters until we get closer," Nick said. Ordinarily, I'd be able to hear him from where he was sitting, but I had to boost the volume in my earwig to catch it all.

"Why's that? I didn't think there was any civilization until we got to Nannandry."

"Some of the vines are able to reach three hundred meters during electrical storms," Nick said. "They're actually trying to get struck by the lightning, but they'd take us down just the same."

"I'd like to see that," Tabby said.

I had to agree with her and joined Nick at five hundred meters.

"You see that?" I asked.

Sheet lightning intermittently illuminated the sky around us like the Tipperary star couldn't. It wasn't until the heavy rain started to diminish that the reality of the lightning vines became evident. Giant vines reached up from the surface that boiled in response to their thrashing.

"There's one!" Tabby said as a bolt of lightning struck one several kilometers ahead. The nearby vines became agitated, as if irritated they'd been overlooked by the lightning gods.

"Liam, you need elevation," Nick said urgently.

I didn't hesitate and pulled back on the stick and jammed the thrust forward. A huge tentacle towered above us and I realized we had no chance to climb away from it. I rolled to the side and it adjusted with us, somehow recognizing that we were avoiding its destructive swing.

I heard the rapid fire thup, thup, thupping of the blaster turrets letting loose with a barrage.

"Marny, no!" Tabby said. "They're drawn to the electric discharge."

Indeed, the area flooded with hundreds of monstrous arms, seeking out the source of the blaster fire, like kittens to their mother.

Silent running, I commanded and pulled the thruster back, switching to arc-jets. The arc jet's power alone wasn't enough for us to climb quickly, but our emissions would be reduced to virtually nothing. I was taking a gamble.

We lost elevation and were soon flying just above the deck at forty meters, where the bases of the huge, seething plants were anchored. Each base was at least ten meters across and, at this elevation, had little capacity to flex. Contrary to common sense, it was considerably safer down here than up around their flailing arms.

"Nice call, Tabbs," I said.

"That was crazy," she agreed.

A tense twenty minutes later we exited the field of lightning vines and caught a glimpse of the dim lights of Nannandry. It was like no city I'd ever seen, rising up from the surface of the murky water, carved from the thick overgrowth of century old leadwood trees. Unlike the clean lines of a space station or the sprawl of the bazaars of Puskar Stellar, Nannandry was a loose collection of platforms connected by ladders or narrow paths.

"It's like they barely have power at all," Ada said.

"That's true," Nick said. "Grünholz actually repels technology. Electromagnetic waves are naturally generated by a phenomenon that's never been identified. It's like a low level electrical magnetic pulse is released every few minutes by the planet. Between the constant EM and the rain, tech just doesn't survive for more than a few years."

"Lightning vines, constant rain and no tech? Why would anyone live here?" Tabby asked.

"A constant twenty-two degrees, potable water, digestible bio-mass and an atmosphere that's a perfect match for human life," Nick said. "On paper, it's paradise."

"Yeah, except they never see the light of the star," Ada said.

"It's just a little less than most mining colonies," Nick defended.

We were close enough that I needed to look for the landing strip in earnest. I had the coordinates and needed to gain a hundred meters from our current altitude.

"Tabbs, see if you can locate the strip," I said as I flipped on *Hotspur's* powerful search lights.

It wasn't until we were perfectly lined up with the coordinates Nick had given us that I finally saw a narrow clearing with faded markings that heralded our destination. I waited until we were completely over the strip before I spun around and lowered us to the platform. There were no other ships, but I made sure to snug up next to the edge, leaving as much room as possible without allowing us to be blocked in. The intertwined growth of the vines and trees continued skyward, eventually rejoining above us. I wondered how long it would take without human interaction before Nannandry simply disappeared, swallowed by the verdant growth.

"When are we meeting with Ambassador Turnigy?" I asked, joining Nick and Marny on the bridge.

"We're to go right away," Nick said. "He's been expecting us."

"Ada, are you still okay with this?" I asked.

"Copy that, Liam," she said. She appeared more alert and I suspected she'd applied a hang-over med-patch.

"I've started a security subroutine. It won't fire on anyone, but the bottom turret will track entities that approach within four meters. It's more of a visual deterrent than an actual threat, but you'd be surprised at how effective a blaster turret tracking your every move can be," Marny explained.

Ada smiled and nodded her understanding. Maybe she hadn't taken a patch after all.

We'd switched to our vac-suits enroute and I pulled on a shoulder holster, loading it up with a small flechette. I'd found that the larger flechette was uncomfortable in the shoulder holster, and I didn't like the look of a chest or hip mounted holster for a supposedly friendly meeting.

"You know where we're going?" I asked Nick doubtfully as I opened the exterior hatch on the starboard side. Rain dripped down the pressure barrier. I wasn't looking forward to stepping out into the storm.

"Yup. Just go, you big chicken," he said.

I ratcheted up my courage and stepped out into the warm rain and thick atmosphere. Immediately, my legs complained at the 1.3g and for the first time in a long time, I felt the pinch of my prosthetic foot as I climbed down the stairs to the landing strip's deck.

The first thing I noticed was that the deck wasn't flat, rather it was entirely composed of logs that had been laid next to each other and scraped flat on one side. Gaps as wide as my hand could be seen where the logs didn't perfectly line up. In some places the gaps had been filled in by debris. In others, the water simply escaped to unseen levels below.

"Smells like the Amazon," Marny said as she joined me at the bottom of the stairs. "At least we don't have to worry about swarms of autonomous, killer drones."

"They say it's always raining on Grünholz. The locals have over twenty different words to describe the different types of rain," Nick said.

"I'd go with wet," Tabby said.

My HUD projected the familiar blue contrail that directed me to the opposite side of the strip. I could just make out an opening in the vegetation. The uneven surface of the strip took some getting used to. My boots had reasonable grip for most surfaces, but the soles had a difficult time shedding the small, wet particles we picked up along the way.

Through the opening at the back of the strip, narrow stairs led down a winding path. Small trails exited from the well-traveled corridor and I caught glimpses of the shorter, thicker Nannandrites going about their business. They appeared to embrace the wet environment, wearing neither rain gear nor shoes for that matter.

We exited this main stair onto what my HUD indicated was one of the larger markets. Thatched huts, with narrow countertops formed many aisles. And unlike our descent, this area was bustling with activity. The burly locals dickered with each other as they traded their goods. I was particularly interested in the vendors who displayed varieties of the local animal population.

One particularly gnarly woman with long, stringy hair caught my eye as I looked at her display of dead reptiles. "What have you to trade, pigeon? It's all freshly killed today," she said. Her voice was surprisingly melodic, not matching her rough outer visage.

"Just looking, nothing today," I said.

"You could use some meat on those bones, boy," she said.

I nodded politely and kept moving, barely avoiding running into a small boy racing through the street.

On the other side of the market, we re-entered the dense vegetation through a much narrower path that led upward. I had a difficult time getting enough traction on the slick logs and had to take it more slowly than I would have liked. The downpour had all but stopped and in its place, a drizzle remained. If we were going to spend much time here, I'd want to learn more names for the precipitation.

Solid walls of thick plant growth rose up on either side of us, broken here and there by passageways kept open with primitively cut timbers. Each opening was the same; a short set of stairs ending in a crude doorway. It occurred to me that the only purposes the doors might serve was for privacy or security, as they appeared to allow atmosphere and moisture to freely pass. As we climbed and passed into a more affluent area of Nannandry, the doors became nicer and more refined.

Finally, my HUD indicated that we'd arrived. The path took a slight turn and a wider stairway led up to a recently hewn set of double doors. Like its neighbors, the entry wasn't sealed to the elements. In contrast to the first homes we'd passed, the doors and surrounding timbers were heavy, giving a strong sense of security.

I turned back to my companions as I mounted the stairs. I was about to ask if we should knock. To my surprise, Marny had drawn her flechette and was pushing Nick to the side and around the corner. Tabby had also drawn and was moving to take cover. I was committed to the stairs. To retreat would paint a target on my back, so I spun around and faced the doors. I ignored my pistol, since it was encumbered in my shoulder holster and drew my half meter long nano-blade.

MESS WITH A BULL

My heart sank as the scene unfolded in front of me. Petar Kiirilov stood at the center of a well-armed group of thugs. Unlike his normal crew, they were all significantly shorter and bulkier - obviously locals.

"What are you doing here?" Petar snarled, his blaster pointed at my chest.

"Lower your weapon, ass-clown," I said. "We have a meeting with Ambassador Turnigy."

"I'm afraid he isn't available," he said. I had to wonder what was keeping him from blasting a hole in my chest.

"How did you get here?" I asked. "We didn't see any other ships."

"Gentlemen! There is no need for weapons." A short, stocky man, who I recognized from a vid as Ambassador Turnigy, pushed his way through Petar's cohorts. Dressed in deep green robes that shimmered as he walked, he placed himself between the two groups.

"What's the meaning of this?" I asked. I moved my nano-blade so it wasn't directly pointing at Turnigy.

"It is a simple matter of unfortunate timing," Turnigy said. "Lord Kiirilov dropped by for an impromptu visit and was just leaving. Am I correct, Lord Kiirilov?"

Petar glared at Turnigy's back. I could tell he wanted to do something, but was resisting the urge.

"This is not over," he said.

I imagined he was speaking to me and started to reply when Turnigy cut me off.

"You have delivered your message most forcefully, Lord Kiirilov. I will convey it with all haste to our Monarch," Turnigy said, still facing me. "If you would like the continued hospitality of our embassy, I'll be happy to accompany Captain Hoffen and his crew to an alternate location."

"You should not be meeting with these criminals. They are enemies of Oberrhein," Petar said.

"And yet, I have been directed to meet with them. The nation of Oberrhein has extended an invitation to *Loose Nuts* and they will be peacefully met. Such is the nature of diplomacy," Turnigy said. "Mr. Hoffen, if you would retract your blade, we will retire to another, more suitable location."

I looked from Turnigy to Petar and made up my mind. If he was going to shoot me, it wasn't like my nano-blade would stop blaster fire. I flicked the blade so it disappeared and slid it into a small pocket at my waist.

"That won't be necessary. We were just leaving," Petar said.

He lowered his pistol, but didn't holster it, and pushed past the Ambassador. I stared him down as he passed. He wanted to say something, but to his credit, he didn't. I wasn't sure what I'd done to him, but I could see in his eyes how much he loathed me.

I was tense as he and his four henchman reached the bottom of the stairs where Tabby, Nick and Marny were standing with weapons lowered. I knew that this could turn ugly quickly and rested my hand on the grip of my flechette.

"Until next time, Red," he sneered at Tabby as he walked by.

"More than happy to do this right now, worm," she said, taking a step toward him.

Two of his group closed in to intercept, but he stopped them, laughing. "Soon. I'll take great pleasure in showing you how a lord trains a woman for service."

I didn't have to see her face to know that it was the perfect bait for her. Fortunately, Marny also understood the impact of his words and stepped between them.

Petar kept walking and soon disappeared from sight.

The rain picked up and large drops splashed against the ground, the water now falling faster than could be drained away.

"Welcome to Nannandry, Captain Hoffen," Ambassador

Turnigy offered his hand cordially.

Out of reflex, I accepted it. While he was significantly shorter than even Nick, his hand easily enveloped my own.

"Thank you, Ambassador. Would you care to explain what that was all about?" I asked.

"Perhaps we could step inside. I know it's unusual, but I find that I prefer to talk inside, out of the rain," he said.

Nick, Tabby and Marny joined us on the landing at the top of the stairs and we followed the Ambassador into the embassy or his home - I wasn't sure which.

In contrast to all of the primitive building materials we'd seen since arriving on Nannandry, the foyer's floor was covered with ornate red tile and the walls were a light gray, smoothed flat but rounded at the arched entry ways and around corners. It was an elegant look.

"Cap. I'm going to let Ada know she might have company. Maybe a few of us should go back. If Petar has his cruiser here, she'll need help," Marny said.

"Petar arrived in a shuttle and if anything, he would fear discovery by your ship," Turnigy offered.

Marny nodded and stepped aside so she wouldn't interrupt our conversation as she made contact with Ada.

"Eloá, your timing is perfect," Turnigy said. A small woman appeared from the hallway and handed out plush, bright white towels. "We'll be meeting in the den. Would you escort the young lady when she finishes her conversation?"

"Yes, Mr. Turnigy," she answered, bowing her head slightly.

The humble exterior of the home did not accurately reflect the beauty we found inside. Turnigy led us down a long hallway and through a pair of glass paneled doors. Colorful wood furniture with soft cushions littered the room in several seating groups. Turnigy beckoned for us to join him.

"Eloá will be along shortly with refreshments," he said.

"What was Petar doing here?" I asked.

"Lord Kiirilov is a member of the royal court of Oberrhein and as such had business to discuss," he said.

"That didn't look like a friendly discussion."

"No. I don't like to talk about our business out of turn, but I believe he intended to murder me this day," he said.

"What stopped him?" I asked as Marny entered the room.

"I believe you did," he said. "Whiskey?"

He picked up a tray from a side table. On it was a crystal bottle filled with an amber liquid and several matching glasses.

"Whiskey sounds good. Tell me, Mr. Turnigy, why would Petar Kiirilov want to kill you?" I accepted the heavy glass with a centimeter of whiskey in the bottom.

"Let us drink first. There is much to discuss," he said, handing out the glasses. Once distributed, he held up his glass. "To new friendships."

"New friends," I agreed and took a generous drink. I knew I was in trouble as the liquid burned the second it hit my lips and didn't stop until it was well into my stomach. I'd never had straight whiskey before and was unable to stop myself from gasping and wheezing.

"Nothing to be ashamed of, Mr. Hoffen. There are few things Grünholz makes well. Whiskey is one of them," he said.

I coughed and smiled, still embarrassed. I caught Tabby's eye, which sparkled with humor at the involuntary admission of my lack of experience with alcohol.

"To hospitality and a dry home," Marny offered.

Turnigy nodded to her appreciatively and raised his glass. This time I was more careful and while the whiskey still burned, I was able to avoid gasping.

"You asked a reasonable question, Mr. Hoffen. Now that we've shared a drink, we are all friends. Let us sit as friends and talk. Lord Kiirilov is a disturbed young man with sights set well beyond the length of his arms," he said.

I wasn't completely sure what he meant, but felt like I had the general idea. "Is Kiirilov from here? Is that how he became a lord?"

"No. You must understand, Mr. Hoffen, the economy of Grünholz is in a precarious position. We are rich in biological diversity, but very poor in minerals. Lord Kiirilov approached Lord Benesch, who until very recently commanded two cruisers executing trade through the gates," he said. "Kiirilov was to join Lord Benesch and establish trade that would result in the expanded delivery of minerals to our economy. In short, he was granted his title so he could expand this trade."

"He owes me a ship," I said flatly.

"That is not how he sees it, of course. As you might imagine, he has painted you and yours to be a villainous crew, bent on the destruction of Oberrhein," he said.

"How does this result in him attempting to murder you?" Nick asked.

"He learned of our meeting and I believe he feared what we might discuss. It was a desperate move on his part," Turnigy said.

"Could he kill you without repercussions?" I asked.

"With the limited technology of Nannandry, his trip would have gone unnoticed. It says something that he stood down when you and your crew showed up. He must not have felt he would survive," Turnigy said.

"That's because I was prepared to drill a hole in his head," Tabby said.

"His assessment was correct. He held the high ground, but his crew wasn't professional," Marny agreed.

"Ambassador Stephano said you requested this meeting. What did you want to talk about?" Nick asked.

"Ah, right to the point. I suspect if you were to replay his words, you would discover that he suggested that I would be interested in talking with you. As it turns out, it was Ambassador Stephano who suggested that you might have information critical to the wellbeing of Oberrhein. But, let us not get distracted by semantics. Lord Kiirilov's visit, in combination with Ambassador Stephano's communication, leads me to believe you have a compelling story that needs repeating," he said.

"It's a long story," I said.

"I'll ask Eloá to make sandwiches. And, please, start at the beginning. I do enjoy a good story."

As a group, we'd become quite adept at recounting the facts, so much so that we knew when to pause and allow someone else to pick the story up. After an hour, Eloá appeared with a platter filled with small sandwiches and finger-sized desserts.

"It is your contention that Lord Kiirilov and Atin Emre destroyed *Cape of Good Hope* and her crew, that they are subverting the construction of Belirand's Terminal Seven, and are attempting to enslave Belirand's mining colony in the Descartes asteroid belt?" he said.

"Your words, Mr. Turnigy," Nick said. "But your analysis of these events is close to our own."

"We have no direct quarrel with Oberrhein," I said. "We do have an issue with Kiirilov and indirectly with the Emre brothers. We believe in right and wrong and if we can prove they had anything to do with the events leading to the destruction of *Cape of Good Hope*, we will, of course, bring this to the proper authorities."

"I am glad you are able to separate the actions of Lord Kiirilov from that of Oberrhein. There is still the matter of your destroying our ship, *Stenka*. This has allowed Lord Kiirilov to present you and your crew as outlaws to the king and the other lords. What would you say to them?" he asked.

"It is a simple matter to prove that your three ships hunted us down in open space. It is equally easy to prove that we acted in self-defense. The fact that we defeated a cruiser with a tug speaks more to the ineptness of your captains than it does any amount of aggression on our part," I said.

"How would you prove this?" he asked.

"We turned our data streams over to Nuage Air Defense for a complete, forensic audit. We have authorized their release to Oberrhein," Nick said.

"So you have. Even so, there are those who believe we should make an example out of you," Turnigy said. "That your company represents a real threat to Oberrhein's sovereignty simply by standing up to us."

"Kiirilov painted us into a corner. We reacted to his aggression and have taken no provocative action against him or Oberrhein. We have a saying where I come from; 'if you mess with a bull, you get the horns,'" Marny said.

"Most aptly spoken, Ms. Bertrand," he said. "Is this how you all feel?"

"The *Kordun* and the *Karelia* might outgun us, but we have something they don't."

"What is that, Mr. Hoffen?" he asked.

"We're fighting for our family. We cannot afford to lose," I said.

"Very well. It is important to know the level of your dedication. You have given me much to think about. Will you be staying in the area for long?" he asked.

"We have goods to pick up and deliver to Léger," I said. "After that, we were planning another trade mission."

"Please check in with me before you depart Léger. I will contact King Kostov and relay what you've shared."

"Answer one question, Ambassador?" Nick asked.

"What is that, Mr. James?"

"What happens to Oberrhein if Belirand discovers that your nation aided Atin Emre in the destruction of *Cape of Good Hope*?" Nick asked.

"I would be careful about spreading that particular lie around, Mr. James. Oberrhein would take great offense to that accusation," Turnigy said.

"I agree, Ambassador. Only a rogue operative would be involved in such an operation," Nick said.

"I believe we understand each other," Turnigy agreed, standing up, his hand held out.

I'd seen this particular maneuver enough times to recognize that we were dismissed and indeed, ten minutes later, we found ourselves standing outside the front of Ambassador Turnigy's home.

"What was that last bit about a rogue operation?" Tabby asked looking at Nick.

"If it were to become known that Oberrhein attacked a Belirand ship, imagine what Belirand might do," Nick said.

"So, why don't they just turn Kiirilov over?" Tabby asked.

"It's one thing to think Kiirilov did something and another thing entirely to know it. King Kostov has a problem," Marny said. "Without proof, he can't move against one of his lords. His problem is that he didn't vet Kiirilov very well."

"And now it's our problem," Tabby said.

"It sure is," I said. "We learned some important things, though. Oberrhein isn't directly out for us and if we can prove Kiirilov acted against Belirand, we can finish this. Let's hope Jake found something."

We'd made it back to the main market. The rain had lessened enough that it felt like a light mist.

"What are you expecting from Jake?" Tabby asked.

"Motive," I said. "Why would Emre want to destroy that ship? It's a house of cards. The Emres and Kiirilov are in this together. I believe that something on that ship threatened one or both of them."

"Don't you have a load to pick up here?" Nick asked. There were enough people around that I suspected he wanted to cut the conversation short.

"You're right. Let me see who we're supposed to talk to," I said.

I pulled the information up on my HUD and discovered I was to talk to one Haik Torigan. His location was identified as 'Marketplace, Nannandry,' hardly a definitive address. I walked up to a vendor, an old woman, who'd been eyeing us since we'd come down from the Ambassador's home.

"Would you direct us to Haik Torigan?" I asked.

"What do you have to trade for this information?" she asked.

I was taken aback. "I'm afraid I don't have anything on me that I could trade," I said.

"Wealthy off-worlders always have something to trade. Come back when you have something," she said.

"You give Nannandry a bad name, Narod. Torigan is back on the third aisle. His wife wears blue robes," another vendor said. He had small, intricately carved items spread out in front of him. Some items appeared to be wooden and others made of bone.

I turned to him. "Thank you Mr. ...."

"Hapet." He finished my sentence for me.

I was drawn in by the carvings. It was hard to imagine a person laboring over such a task, when a replicator could so easily spit them out. That said, their very imprecision made them interesting.

"Your work is beautiful, Mr. Hapet."

"Blessings to you, off-worlder. The real beauty can only be felt." He held out a small, carved lizard to me. "This is the Blue Lagarto, carved from its own bones. A hunter carries its likeness for luck and protection. The great Blue Lagarto is a most feared predator."

The bone felt warm to the touch, which surprised me.

"Ah, you feel it do you? You must be a great hunter yourself," he said.

I smiled. The wily craft of a master trader was never lost on me. I wondered what he did to keep the carvings warm. It was a neat trick. I found it difficult to take my eyes off of the gorgeously crafted carving.

When I attempted to hand it back, Hapet held his hands up to stop me. "No. It is yours. Consider it a gift from Nannandry to you. May your trade always bring you profit."

"I can't take this from you," I said. "But, I really don't have anything to trade. We'll be coming back, though, is there something I could trade with you?"

"My knives grow thin from sharpening. I would trade much for new knives," he said.

"Show me one."

He held up a short knife. Its blade was indeed narrow. I nodded and placed the Lagarto carving back onto his table.

"You hold this for me," I said.

"As you wish."

We walked down toward the third aisle as he'd indicated. I was struck by how impoverished the traders seemed to be. Nannandry was definitely not a great place to live.

"You've such a soft-heart," Tabby whispered in my ear, grabbing my arm and pulling in close. "He totally played you."

"I know. But, his carvings were one of a kind," I said.

"Simple to replicate, too," she said.

"That's what makes them interesting. Who would put that kind of work into something like that? I think people might be interested in them."

"You'd have to sell thousands of them to make it worth your while," she said.

"I know. It's just hard, seeing how they scrape by here," I said.

"Well, keep your wits about you. Desperate people sometimes do desperate things. Don't look, but we're being followed," she said.

"By who?"

"Whom," she corrected. "Mostly children, but they're doing a very good job of staying hidden."

"What could they take?" I said as my eyes caught on a solid looking woman, resting in a colorful, comfortable chair, wearing dark blue robes.

"Just be careful," she said.

I nodded and we approached the vendor stall where the woman sat.

"Haik, come forward! Your off-worlder friends have arrived," she said looking at me and smiling. "Haik will be here momentarily."

A short, thick set man appeared from behind the stall. He had a quick smile and wore blue robes, similar to his wife. We exchanged introductions.

"Sybilla, please offer our guests some of that delicious red berry juice," he said while arranging several chairs for us. "I trust your meeting with the Ambassador was positive?"

I wasn't surprised that he knew of our business with the Ambassador. Nannandry was probably like Colony 40, where everyone knew everyone else's business.

"A very polite man," I said. "I'd like a chance to inspect the goods before we load."

"Certainly," he said. "My stores are close by."

I'd done research on the types of material that would trade well on Léger Nuage and had even gone to the effort of constructing an inspection subroutine that would verify we were getting the right stuff and in the right quantities.

We followed him up through a small gash in the curtain of vegetation at the back of the Market platform. It would be easy to become disoriented in the tall material.

"How do you keep the paths clear?" I asked as we climbed up the uneven surface. My prosthetic foot had been rubbing against my leg due to the uneven terrain and the high gravity. It was becoming increasingly sore.

"We cut them with long knives. It is a daily exercise," he said, arriving at a door just off the path. "Every young person on Nannandry knows how to tend a path."

The lighting inside his warehouse was poor and I pulled my helmet up so that I could have the benefit of my lamps. Haik brought his hands up to shield his face from the bright light.

"My apologies, Mr. Torigan. My eyes are not used to the dim light of your world," I said.

"It is to be expected. Not only have our ancestors adapted to the heavy gravity, but our eyesight has adapted to the lower light," he said.

"How did that happen?" Nick asked. "Three or four centuries isn't enough time for an evolutionary change."

"It is not something we think about much. But, there are rumors of genetic manipulation," he said.

"That's illegal," Tabby said.

"Perhaps."

The pallets in front of me were stacked with biological material. Some of it was stranded for textile production, some pulped and then there were vats of not-so-great smelling stuff. I inspected twenty of the forty crates and found that the differences were well within tolerance for what I was looking for.

"How will you deliver this to the ship?" I asked. I couldn't imagine how they would lift the crates in this gravity and move it up or down the path we'd just traversed.

"Our trade will have a very positive affect on this week's economy within Nannandry. I've hired our strongest porters to move the material and they will carry the pallets to your ship on my say so," he said.

"It appears you are a few crates short of what we agreed upon," I said.

"Not to worry, my friend. I was required to purchase the balance from one of my competitors, but you will have what we bargained on. Now that I have shown you my material, I would very much like to confirm your payment," he said.

"Certainly. Let's meet at the ship in two hours and we can conclude our business," I said.

We shook hands at the door and left him at his warehouse, returning the way we'd come. My AI had already figured out that we were returning to the ship and provided small directional clues through the HUD.

"I saw you sampling the material. Did it all check out?" Nick asked.

I pinched off the AI's analysis of what we'd seen. If anything, the material was a higher quality than I'd been promised. We would make a better profit than I'd originally expected.

"Look out," Tabby said as a small kid darted in front of us. He was being pursued by a heavier, older kid.

"Thanks," I said to her.

I watched as the small, unusually thin kid ran, taunting the older one. He was allowing the heavier kid to stay within range, but not so close as to allow him to be grabbed. They were running directly at a heavy wall of vegetation and I wondered if the small kid actually saw a passageway that I didn't. We all watched as he put on the brakes and slid toward the wall. At the last moment he slid up a curved vine and did a backward vault over his pursuer. It was an unexpected maneuver and the heavyset youth crashed painfully into the wall of vegetation.

The younger of the two turned and asked the older if he'd been hurt. To my eyes it hadn't looked like play, but the kid was definitely concerned for his playmate.

"I'll kill you," the older youth bellowed.

This got the attention of the smaller kid, who turned in a panic and rammed directly into Marny.

"Whoa there, little man," she said, chuckling. "What's this all about?"

Nick, wasn't having any of it and pulled his flechette. He growled, "Take it somewhere else."

"Oh, there's no harm here, Nicholas. Put that away," Marny said.

"I believe his friend there means to do him in. You," Nick said, indicating the larger one. "Go on, get out of here or we'll be calling the police."

"Constable," Tabby corrected.

"Fine, Tabby. Get out of here or we're calling the Constable," he said.

The older youth stalked away, not at all happy with the events.

"Sorry for that. He gets moldy some days, but he'll be clean in a few minutes," the smaller kid said. "Sorry to bother you."

"Stay safe," Marny said.

"What's with all the hostility, Nick?" I asked.

"We've been followed since we landed," Tabby said. "That might not have been as innocent as it looked."

"Hah! That little shite swiped my nano-blade," Marny said.

"Want to chase him down?" I asked.

"Never happen," Tabby said. "He'd know every hidey-hole and back alley in the city. He'll no doubt hole up until we leave."

I shook my head. It wasn't a big loss, but a kid with a nano-blade could be a problem.

Once we were back on the ship, we checked in with Ada. There'd been no activity, so we had a couple of hours to kill.

"I think I'd like to go back to the market and see about trading with that carver," I said.

"Aye, Cap. We'll oversee loading of the material. Nick already sent me all of the pallet signatures."

"Hopefully I'll be back before then," I said.

"I doubt it."

"Why?"

"They've already started stacking behind the ship," she said.

"I can stick around."

"No, we have it," Nick said. "You and Tabby go. Just be careful, though."

It took twenty minutes to find and replicate a suitable carving knife set. It wasn't anything special, but the handles were made of easily graspable material and the blades of strong steel. It wasn't nano-crystalized steel, but it would be more than enough for carving wood and bone. I wrapped the four blades in an oil infused cloth.

"Ready?" I asked Tabby.

"You really are a dope. But, that's what I love about you," she said.

"I know. But, the guy just has one knife and I really did like that Lagarto carving," I said.

As we exited the ship, the rain intensified. I almost turned around, but then thought of Hapet and kept moving. I noticed the residents, who had all been milling about when it was misting, had moved inside. The porters must have dropped off the first load of crates because a big group appeared behind us, crossed the market and went up toward the shop to fetch the next load. It looked like they had four people for each crate.

"That's going to take a while," Tabby said, yelling to overcome the noise of the rain.

"No kidding and in this rain? They're tougher than I am," I said.

Tabby nodded. The stairs down to the market were better covered than the landing strip, but the rain found us just the same. I suspected it was a matter of everything being saturated at all times.

"Blessings to you, trader," Hapet said as we approached.

"Liam and Tabby," I said, recognizing my gaffe at not giving our names on our first visit.

"Thank you. The Lagarto pulls on your spirit, does it not?" he asked.

I smiled. I wasn't ready to jump off that cliff yet.

"I have a proposition for you," I said.

"What is that, Mr. Liam?"

"Would you find this valuable?" I asked, placing the smallest of the four knives I'd replicated on the counter in front of him.

He picked it up and turned it over in his hands. He then picked up the piece he'd been working on and dug into the wood, deftly removing the material.

"A fine blade. You listened to Hapet. Your knife is worth more than the single Lagarto," he said. "It is worth ten of my carvings."

"How many carvings do you have already finished?" I asked.

"Perhaps fifty," he said.

I rolled the cloth out in front of him, exposing the remaining three knives. I was delighted at his excited reaction, picking each up in turn.

"Would you trade your stock for this collection?" I asked.

He looked at me and then back to the knives. He was struggling with something and I wasn't sure what it was.

"Is that not a good deal for you?" I asked.

"Hapet would be taking advantage of Mr. Liam. I would like to do this trade, but I would feel bad about it after," he said.

I extended my hand. "If Hapet would gather his carvings, I would be most pleased to make this trade."

MOTIVE

"You love that, don't you," Tabby said.

"What? Trading two credits worth of materials for two hundred credits of local art?" I asked defensively.

"You did that because you liked him" she said. "Like you need the hassle for two hundred credits."

"Win, win, if you ask me," I said. She was right, of course, but I wasn't about to admit it.

"Don't ever lose that instinct to do what's right. It makes me want you just that much more," she said grabbing a handful of my behind. I wasn't expecting it and I jumped.

The rain hadn't let up by the time we got back to the ship. I found Marny standing beneath *Hotspur's* port-side wing, overseeing the loading of the pallets.

"Nick is meeting with Torigan in the galley," Marny said when I approached.

"You okay out here?" I asked.

"I never thought I'd find a place as wet as the Amazon, but this place beats everything," she said.

"I'll help, Marny," Tabby said.

I ducked under the ship and climbed up the starboard-side stairs and through the hatch. I could have entered from the cargo bay, but the porters were busy carrying their heavy loads and I didn't want to get in their way.

"All set, Mr. Torigan?" I asked when I entered the galley. I noticed that Nick had offered him a cup of coffee and they were both seated at the table.

"Your business partner has us all squared away. If you come across more of the silver and gold, I'd sure like first crack at it," he said.

"What of iron ore, steel ingot or steel sheet products?" I asked.

"Ore, not as much. Steel ingot and sheet I could find a home for. Any nano-crystalized steel?" he asked.

"Not yet, but you never know," I said.

"Very well. I feel fortunate that we've had a chance to meet under such favorable circumstances," he said. "I look forward to doing business with you in the future."

We shook hands and passed Marny and Tabby coming in through the hatch as we saw him out.

"We're secure, Cap," Marny said.

"If we hurry, we might be able to arrange for a delivery," I said. "I'm dying to see this deal all the way through."

"I don't know about any of you, but I want a warm shower and a dry suit," Tabby said. "Sorry that you have to fly us back and can't join me in the shower." Her tone was mocking as she dragged her finger suggestively across my chest.

I joined Tabby on the lift. At a minimum, I was ready to get cleaned up. The vac-suits had kept us dry, but my hair was sopping wet.

"How'd it go?" Ada asked. She was stretched out sideways on the starboard pilot's chair.

"Hard to know who to trust, but the Ambassador was very interested in our encounters with Petar and the Emre brothers. He definitely doesn't want Belirand to blame Oberrhein for any of this mess. I think he's sharing that with his boss now," I said.

"Luc said the politics of the Oberrhein Kingdom were complex and we needed to tread lightly," Ada said.

"I'm not sure how lightly we can tread with Petar. But, we'll try to play it straight with Oberrhein and see if we can have one less enemy shooting at us," I said.

"What was in the load?" Ada asked.

"All bio-materials. I think I have it all sold on Lèger. How are you holding up?" I asked. "It worked out well having you hold down the fort."

"I'm tired, but at least I'm not dripping all over everything," she said.

All hands prepare for departure.

Ada swiveled in her chair and together we checked off our list. Regular maintenance was really paying off as *Hotspur* was ready to go, with a full charge of energy in her batteries and a nearly full load of fuel.

Nick and Marny checked in and I slowly lifted us from the landing strip. For a moment, one of our claw feet resisted and we started to list to the side, but once I applied more pressure, we tore free from whatever was holding us. I filed the information away for the future. We might have trouble sinking into the natural materials of the Nannandry flight deck if we stayed too long.

The clouds were heavy and the rain constant, but as soon as I cleared Nannandry, I pushed up into the atmosphere. I'd had enough of the rainy planet for the day and looked forward to the relatively clean, dry environment of Lèger.

The light from the Tipperary star was nearly blinding as we finally broke through the clouds only a hundred kilometers away from Lèger. I turned back to our home base.

Open comm, Yolande Ardouin.

"Captain Hoffen, I've been hoping you'd call today. It's getting late, but perhaps we could inspect your goods this evening," she said.

It was 2100 and I appreciated her willingness to take care of things today.

"Greetings Ms. Ardouin. We're ten minutes out. Where would you like to meet?" I asked.

"I'm currently on Level-12. Would you be able to meet at the landing parapet?"

"We'll be there," I said and closed the comm.

"You need to clean up," Ada said. "I'll bring us in. At least wash your hair."

She was right. I could feel grit on my face from where the water had dried. I wasn't sure how I'd gotten dirty, but suspected it had something to do with the water washing through the canopy of Nannandry, picking up detritus along the way.

"The helm is yours," I said.

As I passed by, I said to Marny, "I'll meet Yolande on the parapet and bring her back to the hold."

"Aye, Cap. I'll get *Hotspur* opened up. We've a bit of a smell going in there," she said. "But then, so do you."

"Geez. You too?" I asked.

"Low hanging fruit, Cap."

I shook my head and started releasing my vac-suit. I couldn't smell anything, but dropped the suit into the cleaner once I got back to my quarters all the same. A few minutes later, I hopped out of the shower and wiped down my prosthetic foot. The stub on the end of my leg was red and angry looking. I was clearly not a big fan of heavy gravity. I applied a thin med-patch and pulled my foot back on.

Instead of a vac-suit, I chose the new clothing I'd purchased on Nuage Gros. The loose, shimmering cloth pants, tighter shirt and belted tunic had become familiar to me. I liked how the outfit felt and looked on me. One of the things I really appreciated was that I was able to strap my heavy flechette beneath the tunic, easily accessible and also out of sight.

My timing was good. *Hotspur* made positive contact with the landing parapet as I walked onto the bridge.

"Cap, your welcoming party just arrived and are walking out from the city. The pad is otherwise clear and I'm lowering the ramp so we can get some fresh air in there," Marny said.

"Copy that, Marny. Nick, you want to join me?" I asked.

"Yup," he said.

"I'm coming too," Tabby said.

The three of us squeezed onto the lift that was designed for transporting two and dropped down to the Berth Deck where we found Ada coming out of her bunk room, dressed in civvies.

"Where's the party?" she asked.

"Meeting a trader. You're welcome to join us," I said.

"Maybe I'll help Marny."

I nodded and walked through the pressure barrier into the short hallway that joined the armory, Berth Deck and cargo hold to the starboard exterior hatch. Marny had already extended the stairs. The clean smell of the thin, Grünholz atmosphere was a welcome change from the soupy environment of Nannandry. The smell was similar, but nowhere near as intense.

Three Nuagians stopped half-way between our ship and the grand, arched entrance to the city. We approached and I recognized the woman in the middle from a vid-chat we'd had when I was on Nuage Gros. One thing I found interesting was how little information a video feed actually provided. Sure, I recognized her face, but I'd expected someone tall, like Tabby. The woman was actually small, although well proportioned.

"Captain Hoffen, it is good to meet you in person," she said as I approached and we exchanged introductions.

"I'm curious, Ms. Ardouin, what do you do with all of this bio material?" I asked as I led her around the port side of the ship toward the cargo bay.

Movement on the starboard side caught my eye and I saw a small figure running at high speed away from *Hotspur* carrying a bundle. Marny ran out the back of the bay and gave chase for a moment. She was twenty meters behind and barked something I couldn't quite make out.

"What was that all about?" I asked when Marny came back to the ramp.

"I think we had a stowaway," she said.

"How did the AI miss that?" I asked.

"Not sure. With all the biological material, whoever it was might have been well hidden," she said.

"We can look into it once we're done here," I said.

"Count on it, Cap."

"Ms. Ardouin, may I introduce Marny Bertrand, our chief of security?" I asked.

"Please, Captain, call me Yolande. It is nice to meet you, Mademoiselle Bertrand," she said. "You emptied dear Haik's stores, Captain. You must be a very fine trader indeed to get that rapscallion to part with such a load."

"Does it meet with your approval?" I asked.

"Frieda?" she asked, looking to one of her companions.

"Yes, Madame. Preliminary scans show a high quality. I believe there is more stranded red-bamboo than we need, however."

"Thank you," she said and turned back to me. "There is a public loading bay on Level-14. Will you be staying the evening so that we could unload in the morning?"

"We'll be here for a couple of days at least," I said. "We will be docked on Level-23. Is that inconvenient?"

"Many pardons, Captain. Are you a local trader?" She paused and a look of recognition flitted across her face. "I am so sorry. You must be the crew from Sol who just moved here. I'm not sure why I was so slow to put this together," she said.

"No offense taken, Ms. Ardouin. We have not been in the city for very long," I said.

"Your graciousness is refreshing. Level-23 is most convenient. Would 0800 be too early?" she asked.

"Not at all. I believe we'd appreciate being able to offload this material as soon as possible," I said.

"Frieda, would you have Jans meet them on Level-23 with an eradicator? I'm afraid our new friends may have had more than one unexpected companion," she said.

"Yes, Madame," Frieda replied.

"Eradicator?" Tabby asked.

"Of course, I can't believe I forgot," Marny said. Her face had lost most of its color. "This much material will have snakes, lizards and other creepy crawly stuff in it."

"I'm afraid it is part of the business," Yolande agreed. "Fortunately, you have a positive seal between your living quarters and the hold."

"I don't think so," Tabby said. "We only run a pressure barrier when not in combat."

Yolande pinched something from her HUD and flicked it at me. "You'll want to call this man. He will help you rid your ship of its unwanted passengers."

I shook my head. It was always something unforeseen that got us.

We finished with Yolande and traipsed back into the ship. Tabby made a big show of pulling the hard doors closed between the hold and the Berth Deck. When we arrived on the bridge, I was surprised to see Ada perched on the back of her pilot's chair. Pinned to the console by a dozen flechette rounds was a very colorful, meter long snake.

"I don't like snakes," Ada said through clenched teeth.

"Nick, you want to give him a call?" I asked, tossing him the contact for Thomas Ulrich. His business name was long, but descriptive – 'Thomas, Remover of Unpleasant Beasts and Things That Go Bump in the Night.'

"Yup. And, I vote we sleep on station tonight," he said.

"I'll second that," Marny agreed.

Upon landing in our docking bay on Level-23, we hastily gathered our items and exited the ship. Ulrich had already agreed to clean the ship once we'd offloaded the pallets. Jans arrived with a small bot we set up at the back of the hold, which upon turning on, fired three small blaster rounds, its specially tuned sensors locating things I chose not to inspect further.

"That was officially disgusting," Tabby said to Ada as we got on the lift to our warehouse on Level-24.

"You don't get that with ore," Ada agreed.

"Drinks?" I asked. "First round's on me."

It was late and Celina's Diner was closed as we walked by, but Startron Lounge was open for business. The lights were low and there were half a dozen patrons seated at tables and a couple at the bar. I didn't recognize the bartender and didn't see Jake, so we just grabbed a table large enough for the five of us.

"What's our next move?" Ada asked after we'd been served our drinks.

I didn't immediately answer. I had several ideas, but hadn't formed a complete plan.

Nick finally answered, "We need to get back to Descartes. Big Pete says things have cooled down and they haven't seen the cruisers. I think we know why that is. Hopefully Jake was able to get a pattern so we can disarm the explosives Kiirilov planted on

Pete and Silver's claim," he said.

"It's true. If Dad can get the refinery going, we could haul ingots instead of ore. And if we could find a buyer, we could afford a new tug in four or five loads," I said.

"Better find a space station to deliver that to," Ada said. "You'll tear up *Hotspur* if you land her with a full load of iron ingots on Grünholz very often."

"Meerkat had some interest in sheet, even more so if we had nano-crystalized," Nick said.

"We won't be set up for nano for a long time," I said. "Maybe we should skip the pig iron ingots and go straight to sheet material."

"We need to take out Kiirilov and trade his ship for a decent tug," Tabby said.

"We got lucky with the *Stenka*. We're not an even match for even one of those small cruisers," I said. "We can't think about what we lost. We have to think about what we have and how best to use it."

"Geez, don't jump down my throat," she said.

I leaned over, tried to kiss her and she gave me her cheek. I'd need to figure out how to be more circumspect in my answers in the future. I wasn't going to let her pout, though, so I climbed onto her lap, facing her and lightly kissed her until she gave in.

"Okay, get off," she said, laughing.

"She's got a point, Cap. Petar's *Karelia* is the linchpin to this entire problem. Without it, we'll never be able to prove their involvement in the *Cape's* destruction," Marny said.

"What's going on over here?" Jake Berandor's deep baritone voice cut through the quiet of the bar.

He grabbed a chair and pulled it around to the table, smiling broadly.

"Delivery," I said.

"Word is, you brought a nice load of crawlies with you too," he said.

"Seriously? How did you hear that?" I asked.

"Not many secrets in a small city," he said. "You should try the blue ale. It's from Curie and it's delicious. Jerico, bring us a round of Curie's Blue."

"How's business?" I asked.

"I've got to say, I love these people. And actually, that's why I'm here. I have updates for you and I think you're going to like it."

"Do tell," I said.

He set a small device on the table and my ears popped. I'd seen a similar device deployed before and knew it was designed to keep our conversation private.

"Never can be too careful," Jake acknowledged. "First, I sent the data you had on the explosives at Big Pete's claim to Professor Coffman. She sent a pattern for a small bot that should have a better than seventy percent chance of disarming the charges."

"That sounds good. How about the other question regarding who was on the *Cape of Good Hope*?" I asked.

"It's different than what we were thinking, but just as damning," he said. "And before I tell you, you need to know this was expensive to get. I do think you'll find it worthwhile."

"We'll pay," Nick said.

"They had an audit crew on board. Apparently, Emre's reports haven't been adding up," he said.

"Why wouldn't Belirand just send a heavy cruiser through the gate and remove Emre?" I asked.

"According to my source, Belirand didn't have enough information to isolate the problem. By destroying the ship, Emre stopped movement through Terminal Six for the time being. His engineers reported that a flaw in the TransLoc gate is what caused it to fail. At a minimum, he bought six months to cover up whatever he's been doing," Jake said.

"That's motive enough," I said. "We just need to prove it now and that's on us. What do we owe you?"

Jake slid a pad over to me. Twenty-two thousand credits. I whistled when I saw the number. "Do I want to know how you got this information?"

"You do not," he said.

I signed the transfer of credits.

The next morning, I awoke in the apartment that had been furnished with our warehouse. It wasn't elegant, but we had enough beds for everyone to sleep in. It wasn't like any of us would be sleeping on *Hotspur* until it had been cleared of bugs and reptiles.

Marny and I quietly exited the apartment and took a lift down to the loading bay where we'd left *Hotspur*. Both Frieda and a man I didn't recognize were already there.

"Thomas Ulrich," the man introduced himself. "I understand you have a pest problem."

"We do. First time hauling from Nannandry and we weren't careful with the doors," I said.

"A mistake you won't make twice, I'd be willing to bet," he said with a chuckle. "I'll assemble my crew and once you're unloaded we'll get it all cleaned up."

"Great. My pilot took this one out, any idea what it is?" I pinched the picture of the snake Ada had shot and flicked it to him.

"Call that a King Coral. Less deadly than it sounds, but if you don't get its bite treated within the first fifteen minutes or so, you're a goner," he said.

"That's not deadly?" I asked.

"Not compared to the chimera beetle. That little bugger will kill you in less than three minutes," he said.

"And you can get it all out?" I asked.

"We're very thorough, but just to be safe, I can sell you a critter gitter. It'll patrol your ship and look for pests," he said.

"How much for that?" I asked.

"Twelve hundred," he said. "But, since we're doing a full treatment today, I'll sell it to you for eight hundred."

He was probably getting the better end of the deal, but I wasn't going to argue. We needed to feel secure.

"I'm in," I said.

When we opened the ramp, the smell of Grünholz hit us in a heavy wave. On the floor of the hold, there were no less than twenty lizards, snakes and miscellaneous things I couldn't quickly identify in front of Yolande's bot.

"How hard is it to get the pattern for one of those?" I asked.

"They're not expensive," Frieda answered. "I'd be happy to forward you a reference."

"Please do," I said.

"Cap, are you sure this is a good business for us?" Marny asked.

"I'll tell you after I square with Frieda," I said.

Frieda flashed a smile and held out her reading pad for me to bump. The offloading process proceeded smoothly, only occasionally interrupted by the flash of the small blaster from the tiny pest sentinel that stood guard.

After Frieda disappeared with her final load, I checked out numbers. We'd grossed twenty five thousand credits. Thomas would take three thousand and we'd burned another two thousand in fuel. As disgusting as it was, it had been a very profitable run.

"Ready?" Thomas asked.

"For what?"

"Just open your hatches, and you'll see," he said, standing with his hand on the edge of a crate that he'd brought up on a small grav-sled.

I dropped the pressure barriers and opened the hatches. "All yours," I said.

With a flourish he opened his crate and a swarm of small, autonomous bots flew, jumped and slithered out.

"Give 'em an hour and you'll be one hundred percent critter uncluttered," he said. "I also offer a cleaning service. Looks like your hold could use a good scrubbing."

"Sign me up," I said as I chuckled and shook my head.

TOUCHING BASE

Two hours later, we bade Thomas Ulrich farewell. He represented an unexpected cash outlay, but he'd been good to his word. The hold was spotless and the invasion had been stemmed. He left behind a small, mechanical centipede that was the length of my hand stretched out. Its only objective was to crawl around the ship and look for and disinvite unwelcome guests.

"Nick, Tabby and Ada are having breakfast at Celina's," Marny said. "You want something?"

"Sure, whatever they're eating is fine," I said. "I'll be along in a second."

"I can wait," she said.

I ran up to my quarters for the bag of Hapet's carved statuettes.

"Any thoughts on how we deal with two cruisers?" I asked Marny as we took the private lift into our warehouse.

"I know that we don't take them on at the same time," she said. "We took a heck of a pummeling with just a single pass from them."

"The foundry and forge will make dealing with them less critical for us, but what about the other claim holders? How will they survive if Terminal Seven isn't a safe place to deliver their ore?" I asked.

"One step at a time," she said as we rounded the corner to Celina's Diner.

The restaurant wasn't busy and we joined the rest of the crew at the largest table in the back after greeting Celina with a hug.

"Where are Jack and Jenny?" I asked.

"Not sure. They're cooking up trouble somewhere, though. They went tearing out of here just after breakfast rush," she said. "Coffee?"

"Please," I fished out a bone carving of a rodent. "Hold on a sec before you go. Do you have any interest in these?"

She picked it up and inspected it. "What's it made of?"

"That's hand-carved lizard bone," I said.

"What do you want for it?"

"I don't know. I bought fifty for nearly nothing," I said.

"I could probably sell them for ten credits apiece," she said. "How about we split the profit and I'll see how they do?"

"I'm keeping one, but you've got a deal."

"Are you ever not working?" Tabby asked.

"That isn't work. That's just having fun," I said.

"I finished replicating that bot pattern Jake got for us," Nick said. "I'd like to get back to Descartes and drop off fuel, food and the machinery. It sounds like Pete and Muir have everything all laid out for the refinery."

"Fine by me," I said. "The ship's all cleaned up."

"Are you sure?" Ada asked.

"Not a hundred percent, but Thomas did leave a guardian behind. He unleashed quite the little army of killer robots. I'll spare you on how much they actually pulled out. Suffice it to say, we need to keep that hold locked down when we have biological material on board."

"What about the eradicator robot that Yolande put in the hold?" Tabby asked.

I nodded. "We should probably replicate that before we go back to Nannandry."

"Are we taking the industrial replicator out with us?" Ada asked.

"We'll have to," Nick said. "We need to manufacture a lot of parts for the refinery. We don't have enough steel to do it here."

"We should advertise that we have it on station. I was talking to Selig last night and they've broken some equipment," she said.

"Aren't they concerned about repercussions from Petar?" I asked.

"They are, but keeping Petar happy doesn't do them any good if they can't actually mine," she said.

"I'm looking at a departure of tomorrow morning," I said. "Anyone opposed?"

"Why not take off now?" Ada asked.

"Does someone miss Selig?" Tabby asked, with a lilt in her voice.

"You be good, Tabitha Masters," Ada said.

"I'd like to contact as many of the claim holders as possible and see if any are in need of supplies. They've been out a long time and I don't imagine that Petar cares much for how they're surviving," I said.

"I'd be willing to organize that," Ada said. "How will they pay, though?"

"We can trade for ore, fuel or extra equipment. Let them know we'll be discreet," I said.

"And the co-op will extend credit for O2 or food," Nick said.

I nodded my agreement

"We can split up the list," Tabby said, "I'll help. You want Lichts?" I smiled at her inability to let it go.

"That's fine," Ada said.

"We need to reload ship stores," Marny said, "I'll get to that."

We all went our separate ways until late in the afternoon when I met up with Tabby and Ada. They had a list ten kilometers long of supplies requested by the claim holders. Most of them had little to trade other than ore. Nick and I decided that if we ever wanted the co-op to be successful we'd have to make that work.

We gathered on the bridge, mentally exhausted from making deals and arranging deliveries.

"We're out of cash," Nick pronounced after making his final order from his workstation.

"Ugh," I said.

I knew we were getting close. We'd be betting the business by running our cash down to zero. But we were the best shot most of the Descartes claim holders had at survival. If we turned our backs on them now, they would go flat broke, sitting on a pile of ore they couldn't move.

"You suppose that's part of Petar's plan? Let them mine all that ore, wait until they leave, then take it from their abandoned claims?" Ada asked.

"I'd bet that crossed his mind," Nick said.

"Ada would you send a comm to the claim holders. Anyone who's nervous about staying on their claim can take up residence on top of the Co-Op. They'll have to bring their own hab-domes, but we'll even give them work mining out the station," I said. "You okay with that, Nick?"

"With everything that's owed us, sure. It's a good idea," he said. "Marny, what about security on something like that?"

"I need a security door on the control room. Otherwise, I think between Big Pete, Silver and Muir, we can keep things moving along. I suppose it depends on how many people take you up on it," she said.

"Any chance you can get a security door pattern with Mars credits or free?" I asked.

"Shouldn't be a problem, the idea is straightforward enough," she said. "I'll ask Pete to give me some measurements and I'll get something designed."

"I'm going to give the Ambassador a call. Let me know if anyone thinks we can't make it out by 1000 tomorrow," I said.

"Copy that, Cap," Marny said.

Tabby followed me back to the small office next to our quarters and took one of the two seats. She clearly wanted to hear what Turnigy had to say. I didn't blame her.

Open comm, Ambassador Turnigy, I said.

"Young Captain Hoffen. I was wondering when you'd be calling," he said.

"We're prepared to set sail in two days," I said. Tabby lifted an eyebrow at my obvious untruth. "We're headed for Nuage Gros. You'd asked for a heads up."

"Right you are and I thank you for your courtesy," he said. "My presence has been requested by King Kostov. He suggested that he would like to meet you. Would you be interested in accompanying me?"

"That's a problem," I said. "We've nearly a full hold of goods that won't keep. Is there any possibility of pushing this off for a week?"

"If that means you'd accompany me, a week is quite acceptable," he said.

"Will the king guarantee our safety? I'm under the impression that we're not exactly welcome by many of the lords," Tabby asked.

"Ah, Ms. Masters, a perceptive question. King Kostov has granted your company temporary immunity for the duration of your trip. Any faction within Oberrhein that attacks this diplomatic mission will be acting against the crown. It is not a guarantee, but it is also a death sentence to any who might violate it," he said.

"We'll be in touch," I said and closed the comm.

"You really don't trust him, do you?" Tabby asked.

"I don't know who to trust. We could certainly use his help though," I said.

"When did life get so complex?" she asked.

"No kidding."

We all worked well into the night, receiving loads from the different vendors of Lèger. I found it ironic that I ended up purchasing back some of the bio material, albeit processed, from Yolande for our medical and food grade replicator. Fortunately, the neat little dry packages she provided no longer carried little crawly passengers.

The next morning we were up early again, tearing down the industrial replicator and loading it onto the ship. By 1000 we pushed aboard the last of the O2 crystals and extra fuel. I'd never seen the hold so tightly packed. I hoped we wouldn't run into any problems on the way out. We were running heavy and if we got holed, the loss would be catastrophic.

All stations prepare for departure, I said.

Ada had requested to take the helm on the way out and I helped her through the checklist.

"Schedule-B burn?" Ada asked.

"Roger. We're in a hurry," I said.

"Ooh, I love it when we light it up," she said.

I laughed. I'd always thought of Ada as being reserved, but in the end she was just like Tabby and me. She liked to go fast and turn hard.

"Helm is yours, Captain Chen," I said.

I enjoyed sitting in the chair when either Ada or Tabby had the stick. Their skills were different. Ada was a minimalist when launching. Each move was specifically orchestrated to perfectly move the ship on exactly the right heading. Tabby loved to push the corner of every turn, eking out every meter of freedom to pile on the speed. It was difficult not to learn something from them by observing.

I faded out a little, tired from the hectic schedule of loading the ship, and was surprised to see the familiar yellow Nuage Air Defense ships as they twisted into formation to the starboard of *Hotspur*. I no longer thought it was coincidence that Ada had requested the helm when I caught the tail number on Captain Gray's bird.

"Hey, isn't that Luc?" Tabby asked, she was sitting on the couch of the bridge looking out through the armored glass windows.

"Weird, huh?" I said sarcastically.

If Ada heard us, she was ignoring it. I heard her chatting with Luc and then we watched as his squadron executed a perfectly synchronized roll, and headed back on their assignment.

"Alright, you little old ladies, bring it on," she said.

"What?" I asked innocently and walked back to join Tabby on the bridge.

The rest of the short trip went without incident. The Schedule-B burn rate put us in Descartes in just under seventy-two hours. I'd arranged to have the helm when we arrived and brought us in under silent running.

"Looks like a couple of folks have taken you up on your offer," Marny said as we passed under the bottom of the asteroid.

There were ten new habitation domes set up, although it was 0200 and we didn't see anyone milling about.

"*Incoming hail, Loose Nuts Co-Op,*" the ship's AI announced.

"Hoffen, here," I said.

"Good to hear your voice, Son," Big Pete said.

"Are you in the control room at this hour?" I asked.

"Negative. We've a terminal set up in our dome. It's a little complex, you'll have to see," he said.

"Roger that. Would you rather we tie up for the night and see you all in the AM?" I asked.

"Probably best. No need to wake your mom. There's a slip open for you in the middle docking bay. We've grav generators running," he said.

"I copy. See you in the morning," I said.

As I pulled up to the large asteroid, I could see evidence of a considerable amount of work. When we'd left, there'd just been enough room for the old pirate outpost's warehouse. Now, three of the ten docking bays had been opened up and they'd strung landing lights in the center bay. I slid in and allowed *Hotspur* to settle.

"I'd say we get a few hours of shuteye," I said to Marny.

I'd tried to get her to sleep while I brought us home, but she wouldn't have anything to do with it. The idea of being caught flat-footed bothered her a lot and I certainly didn't mind the company.

At 0600 my comm alarm went off, waking Tabby and myself. I knew it was Dad and simply picked it up.

"You ready to get going?" he asked.

"Be right down. You have any coffee?"

"I'm in your galley, talking to Marny. She said I had to wait until six and yes, we have coffee. Your mom even made sweet rolls," he said.

We exchanged hugs and I sat in the galley while my body adjusted to being awake. The coffee and rolls helped.

"Nick says you have a full load of supplies. Good thing too, people are getting mighty nervous out here," he said.

"Did Nick fill you in on what we think is going on?"

"You mean that Oberrhein and Belirand are trying to choke out this mining colony?" he asked. I could tell he was steamed.

"We're not sure it's really Oberrhein or Belirand directly. But yeah, factions within those two," I said.

"Bunch of crap. If it were North Americans or Mars, we'd own up to it," he said.

"Like we did in the Amazon?" Marny asked with an arched eyebrow.

"Not our finest moment, but you know I'm right," he said.

"You're right of course, Pete, but even in the Amazon, it took someone to out those corporate asshats who started it all," she said.

Marny was the only person in the world who could talk to my dad that way and get away with it unscathed. I'd sure have loved to know what they talked about when they were alone.

"So what are we going to do?" he asked.

"We need to drop this load and get back to Grünholz," I said. "We're going to meet with King Kostov from Oberrhein. If it's going to be a long road, we'll need credits. The only way we're going to get those is if we start producing something that someone other than Belirand will buy."

"Like what?"

"Ingots, preferably steel and sheet materials," I said. "If I had nano-crystalized steel I could sell every ounce of it at five times what you'd expect. Silver, gold, platinum, rhodium are all on the table too. Nobody can process ore, but anything else and we're good to go."

"Just like Mr. James relayed it," Dad said. "Well, let's get it all unloaded. I'll give Muir a call."

"I thought he was a loner," I said.

"He is. Doesn't mean he's ready to roll over and die though. You just need to know how to talk to him."

"What about that harness we used to transport the barge though the TransLoc Gate. Seems you could sell that," Mom said.

"Isn't that Belirand's?" Tabby asked. She cut off her words as they came out. "Frak, yeah. I'll take Ada over and we'll cut it up. It's got to have seven or eight thousand credits worth of nano-steel."

"Try twenty-five thousand, Tabbs," I said. "There's a huge shortage of the stuff. Closest manufacturer is off-planet Curie and apparently it's just a small operation."

"Damn, I wish we'd set up for that," Pete said.

"One thing at a time, Dad," I said. "You get me some steel ingots and I'll turn 'em into credits faster than you can stamp 'em out."

"I'll take you up on that. We've a shite-tonne of ore stored up," he said.

Unloading was always easier than loading and this trip wasn't any different. Dad knew right where he wanted everything and he ordered us around like a drill sergeant. By 1100 the hold was empty and Nick and Marny were setting up our two replicators in the warehouse. I joined Ada and Tabby and we set about cutting up the nano-crystalized steel I-Beams and loading them into the hold.

When we finally sat down for dinner, we were all exhausted.

"What else do we need to do?" I asked, leaning back in my chair.

"I don't mean to beat this drum too hard, but we need to get this thing with Oberrhein resolved. You come back in two weeks and we'll have a stack of ingots for you to sell. But, that's just a bandage on the problem. People need to be able to trade their ore," Dad said.

"Any reason not to take off first thing?" I asked.

"Nope," Nick answered.

"Pete, will you take care of installing that security door on the control room?" Marny asked.

"Aye. Muir and I will put that top of the list," he said.

"One last thing," Nick said. "An explosive disarming bot is being manufactured on the replicator right now, should be done first thing in the morning. You might want to drop it off on your claim some time."

"Fantastic," Dad said.

TRUST IS EARNED

We loaded extra fuel into the hold and burned hard back to Grünholz. I'd never met King Durko Kostov, but if rumors were to be believed, being late wasn't the first impression we wanted to make.

On the way, I searched for a load from Léger to Nannandry and ended up finding a small one that would clear a thousand credits. It wasn't much, but would pay for fuel to the planet and a little more.

Incoming hail, Celina Dontal.

I was surprised by her call as we'd just let her know that we'd be stopping through for dinner. It was a nice perk of having let her burn through our replicator supplies that we pretty much had a free meal every time we were in port and would for the foreseeable future.

"What's up, Lena?" I asked.

"We've an emergency, Liam, how close to the city are you?"

"Two minutes, if we pick up the pace," I said.

"There's a boy climbing on the outside of the city, he could be in trouble," she said.

"Roger that. What's going on?"

"Tough to explain the whole thing. He was being chased by thugs, we think he's going to try to climb the outer wall on the star-side," she said.

"Understood, we're almost there."

I pushed forward on the thrust stick and swooped around the city. The entire crew had heard the exchange and were standing by for action.

"Tabbs, grab your AGBs and head back to the hatch, we might have an emergency EVA," I said.

"Copy that," she said and jumped up, heading back to our quarters.

"Marny, Nick, can we get detailed plans?" I asked.

"Mr. Hoffen, it's Jenny," a new voice said. "I put a tracking beacon on my friend. I'm sending the registration."

"I've got it," Nick said.

Add Jenny Dontal to bridge comm.

"He's outside, right now," Jenny said. It was unnecessary information as we could see a blinking blip on the holographic image of the city.

Engage targeting reticle on tracked object, I said.

Just as we should have had view of him, the blinking signal disappeared back into the safety of the city.

"He's safe," I said. "He made it inside."

"No! You don't understand," Jenny said. "They're chasing him and they're going to hurt him. They already killed another boy."

"Who, Jenny? Who's doing this," my mind raced, could Petar be behind this? What could he gain from it?

"She's a slaver, trying to take him back to Nannandry," Jenny said.

I winced. Jenny had once been taken as a slave and I knew this added a level of urgency to the situation.

"Who is she?"

"I don't know. Priloe's from Nannandry, but he's been hiding here with his little sister and the bad woman is trying to force him to go back. She's very dangerous," she said.

"Okay. We'll do the best we can," I said. "Where's he going?"

The tracked signal had moved back into the center at the highest level of the city and with no other destination, I could only continue to circle around or head back to the public landing.

"He's headed for the pod-ball court," she said.

"I'm not sure what we can do."

"It's at the top, please, Mr. Hoffen. What if he goes outside again?" she said.

I didn't think it was very likely, but I wasn't going to ignore her since he'd already been outside at least once. As dangerous as it was, I knew anything was possible when you were being chased.

I pulled back on the stick and sailed up toward the top of the city.

Just as we arrived, I saw with horror the glass of the top room blowing straight up. There must be a substantial pressure differential between the interior space and the exterior.

"Frak. Tabbs, someone blew the glass out. We might need that EVA," I said.

"I've got it, Hoffen. Just get me close enough," she said.

"Can you talk to him, Jenny?"

"I am. He knows you're there."

I hit the emergency override and dropped the cargo bay loading ramp. Tabby would have a difficult enough time negotiating the city's gravity and gusty winds, I wanted to give her the largest return landing zone possible.

I heard Marny jump onto the lift, executing an emergency drop onto the Berth Deck. No doubt she wanted to make sure she was on hand if Tabby needed her.

"I'm off," Tabby said.

I watched Tabby's flight on the vid screen as she sailed between the ship and the top of the city, smacking into a small boy, wrapping him up with a single arm and spinning around, back toward the ship.

"She's got him!" Jenny cried.

I swung the aft end of the ship to line up as closely as possible with Tabby's return arc. She flew back into the wide open bay and landed easily.

"We're in, Love," Tabby said over the comm.

I directed the ship to close the cargo hold and turned my focus on getting us back to our landing bay. Before I knew it, I heard Tabby approaching from behind.

"Nicely done, Tabbs. I couldn't have done it better myself," I said.

"Captain Liam Hoffen, meet Priloe," Tabby said.

I turned, not expecting to see the boy standing directly behind my chair.

"Good to meet you, Priloe. Just a second and I'll get us landed."

"I agree," Tabby said.

"On what?"

"You definitely couldn't have done that better."

Upon landing we were met by a worried group of people. Jenny was holding a small girl who reached for the boy when we got close.

As we walked back to the diner, they excitedly replayed the events. Apparently, Jenny had been right. Some woman had tried to abduct Priloe and his sister. In the process, the abductor had killed one of Priloe's friends from Nannandry and nearly succeeded in killing Priloe.

A city security officer was waiting for us when we arrived back at Lena's Diner and Celina peeled off to speak with her. I could read their body language and was relieved that the conversation seemed to be going in the direction that Lena wanted. Finally, they parted and Lena rejoined us with a smile.

"Everything okay?" Jenny asked.

"Yes. We have some legal hoops to get through and we'll need to see what Priloe would like to do, but they're not going to send him back to Grünholz," she said. "Now, I believe we've a ship-load of people who need a good meal. Jenny, why don't you show Priloe how to make up some of that meatloaf we had today. Jack, would you set the big table and put out some of that Blue Brenton Ale we just got in?"

Jenny put the small girl down and the three ran back into the kitchen. Apparently, they had all become friends at some point. Lena bent over to pick up the small girl who'd become fascinated, staring at Marny.

"I think you have a fan," Lena said, looking over at Marny. "Her name is Milenette."

Marny didn't miss a beat and held her arms out. Milenette turned back, suddenly shy, burying her head in Lena's shoulder. Lena wasn't fooled, however, and coaxed the small girl into Marny's arms. I wasn't entirely surprised to see that Marny had an easy way about her with the girl.

In short order, the table was set and steaming food delivered.

"Priloe, what would you like to be when you grow up?" Tabby asked between bites.

Priloe had a difficult time keeping his eyes from Tabby and I knew she recognized the attention. I chuckled to myself as I considered what I'd have thought, at his age, if someone who looked like Tabby had rescued me.

"I don't know," he said, clearly uncomfortable being the center of her attention.

"Don't know, or don't want to say? Everyone has dreams," she said.

"You'll think it's stupid," he said. It had the effect of quieting the table which made him look down, into his lap.

"Not if you don't," she said. "Try me. If I laugh, you can punch me in the shoulder as hard as you want."

He looked up, startled. "I would never."

Tabby smiled at him. It was a smile I loved receiving. She didn't look away and after a few minutes Priloe realized he wasn't getting out of the conversation.

"I want to live in the stars. Somewhere where there's no stupid rain and people are nice," he said.

"Maybe someday you can come visit our station in the Descartes asteroid belt," she said.

"Really?"

"It's not ready for visitors right now, but someday it will," she said.

I caught Celina stifling a yawn and realized she probably had an early morning in front of her.

"You've gone above and beyond, tonight. Thanks for dinner, Lena. We've an early morning tomorrow and I bet you do too," I said. "Could you send the bill for dinner to me and we'll get out of your hair?"

"Not sure I feel good about billing you after what you did today," she said. "Besides, you still have credit for the materials we burned on the replicator."

"How's your cash flow?" Nick asked.

"I won't lie, it's tight right now. We've expanded quickly and had lots of one-time expenses," she said.

"Send him the bill. We don't need to be paid back on the materials immediately. We can settle up over time," Nick said.

She looked sheepish when she responded. "Well ... okay, it would help," she said.

"How are those carvings doing?" I asked.

"Really well. I only have ten left. We sold twenty in the first day," she said.

"What are you selling them for?"

"Started at ten credits, raised them to forty on day two and then sixty on day three," she said. "Seems like sixty is the right price, since we're still selling them. Can you get more?"

"Sure. I'll let the artist know we're interested," I said.

We helped clean up the table and headed back to the ship.

"Did you find a buyer for the nano-steel?" Nick asked as we arrived at *Hotspur*.

"No. I thought we'd offload it into the warehouse," I said. "We've a small load for Nannandry, but I'd rather not drag that steel all over."

"We can do that now," Marny said.

"Sure. I'll grab the grav-sleds," I said.

I had no desire to deal with it right then, but it would allow us to sleep in the next morning and I was all about that. I'd contacted Ambassador Turnigy earlier in the evening. We were to meet him on the Nannandry landing strip at 1400 the next day.

If the designers of Lèger Nuage had actually considered moving long, narrow objects into the warehouses from the loading bay, their plans completely eluded us. What should have been a twenty minute task turned into two hours of a complex series of twists, lifts and slides.

I awoke the next morning to the smell of coffee. When I opened my eyes, I saw Tabby sitting on the bed, staring at me. I pulled up onto my elbows and accepted the cup from her.

"What's up?" I asked.

"We're ready to sail. Want to join us?" Tabby asked, handing me my earwig. "I let you sleep in, but it's 1300 and your cargo's loaded in the bay."

I leaned forward and kissed her. "That's awesome."

"Ada wants to take us in," Tabby said. "She wants more time flying in the heavy gravity."

"Fine by me," I said. "I'll catch a shower, but tell Ada to take off whenever she wants."

Tabby hopped up and jogged out of the room. First priority was a shower. After that, I'd reach out to my contact for the load we were delivering.

It was obvious when we dropped into the cloud bank, the inertial damper struggled to keep up with the quick drops and sudden changes in atmospheric pressure. Rain hammered against the hull and I hoped Ada wouldn't have too hard of a ride. My contact replied that they'd have porters waiting once we landed.

"How's it going, Ada?" I asked flopping onto the couch of the bridge.

"What a pain in the ass! I love it," Ada said. "I might avoid the lightning vines, though."

Twenty minutes later, Ada spun *Hotspur* around and dropped us lightly onto the landing strip. Unlike the last time we landed, this time there was a small atmospheric ship pushed to the side.

Marny and I had dressed for the cargo load in our armored vac-suits and once we were on the strip, we dropped the loading ramp.

"No more stowaways," Marny said.

"Copy that," I agreed.

We unloaded the cargo in only a few minutes. The dripping wet porters picked up the loosely packed packages and stacked them next to the ship, along the vegetation wall. At 1400 exactly, Ambassador Turnigy approached the loading ramp.

"Permission to board, Captain," he called out.

"Permission granted, Ambassador," I said. "Are you ready to get going?"

"There's been a small change of plans. Probably best to discuss it with your business partners," he said.

I nodded. "This way," I said.

"Nick, the Ambassador is on board, but he said there's a change in plan. Can you bring everyone down to the galley so we can talk about it?" I asked over the comm.

"Yup," he said.

We waited for the ramp to close and then showed the Ambassador to the galley where Nick, Tabby and Ada waited for us.

"Ambassador, meet Ada Chen," I said, remembering that he hadn't met her yet.

"My pleasure," he said, kissing the back of her hand.

"What kind of change?" I asked. "I was under the impression King Kostov wanted to meet with us."

"I assure you, he does," Turnigy said. "The change is that the Captain of the Guard is not willing to allow your ship into our sovereign air-space. Apparently, the tale of how you all destroyed an Oberrhein cruiser has become something of a legend."

"I was under the impression that Oberrhein has an overwhelming anti-aircraft capability," Nick said.

"We do. But, we'd be allowing a warship into our capital. If something were to happen, the King would appear weak and it is a sensitive time," he said.

"How do you propose we get there?" I asked.

"I've requisitioned an airship. I'm afraid it's only large enough for four of us, though," he said.

"Forget it," Tabby said. "We don't need this crap. We'll take care of Petar on our own."

"Aye, Cap. We have no assurance of safety. Without our ship, we'd be completely defenseless," Marny said.

"King Kostov has specifically requested Ms. Masters, Mr. James and Mr. Hoffen. I understand your reluctance, but I also believe he would see it as a sign of weakness if you turned him down. And Ms. Bertrand, I will give you my assurance, as a representative of Oberrhein, of their safety."

"Why Tabby?" I asked.

"To be truthful, I believe it is because of a vid that is being circulated of when she broke the wrist of one of Lord Kiirilov's crew. Otherwise, I am not sure," he said.

"I don't like how this feels, Nicholas," Marny said.

"I know, but we've talked about it. We need an ally. If we can enlist the help of the King, perhaps we can just end this," he said.

"What do you want to do, Liam?" Ada asked.

"I think we should go with the Ambassador," I said.

"On one condition," Ada said.

This got everyone's attention.

"What's that, my dear?" Ambassador Turnigy asked.

"Turn over complete control of your ship to *Loose Nuts*. When you bring them back in one piece they can turn it back over to you. If you attempt to deceive them in any way, or bring harm to them, the ship remains our property," she said.

"I can't do that, it's the property of Oberrhein, not my own," he said.

"But, you're the Ambassador. It will give them the security net they need," she said. "If something goes badly, at least they have some chance of getting out of there."

"I assure you, you're worrying about nothing," he said.

"So, it's an easy call," she said.

I looked at her, surprised. What had happened to our doe eyed Ada?

Turnigy looked to me, then to Nick. When he didn't getting a response, he sighed. "Very well. We'll do as you say. Now, may we go?"

"Tabby, Nicholas, put on armored vac-suits. Oberrhein has a tradition of respecting strength," Marny said.

"On this, Ms. Bertrand, we agree," Turnigy said.

Marny insisted that we bring our heavy blaster pistols, as well as nano-blades and several grenade marbles. She even insisted that I hide my junior-sized nano-blade in my prosthetic foot. It wouldn't be difficult to find if I was thoroughly searched, but a casual inspection would miss it.

"Ada, you'll take *Hotspur* back to Lèger. You'll both have to use your best judgement if you think things are going south," I said.

"Give us at least forty-eight hours, though."

We disembarked and made our way to the waiting ship. As far as airships go, it was beautiful. Unlike *Hotspur* with her stubby wings, this small ship's wings were long and swept back in a deep v-shape. I ran my hands along the shiny, medium-blue painted hull, finding it smooth to the touch. A single, small gun port on the bottom appeared to have an extremely small range of motion. The pilot would have to be directly lined up before it would be usable.

Turnigy palmed a panel on the side. A narrow stairway slid out just in front of the wing, locking in place above the surface of the landing strip.

The interior was surprisingly comfortable looking with glossy wood-paneling and synth-leather upholstery. To the aft of the entry, the cabin had three seats on each side arranged to best allow conversation with the forward seats pointing back. A single pilot's chair was forward of the entry hatch.

"Captain Hoffen, I believe you'll be flying, given Ms. Chen's proposal," Turnigy said as he dropped into a chair.

I turned forward, sat in the chair and attempted to interface with the ship. My HUD displayed a disconnected message. I waited for Nick and Tabby to get settled and then pointed out the obvious.

"I'll need you to hand over the controls and security lockout," I said.

He pulled up a virtual console and my HUD displayed the transfer of pilot's access to the ship. It was a clumsy attempt. I wasn't sure why he was playing games, but I could imagine it would be embarrassing if the Ambassador had to explain why he'd given us control of his ship, even if it was only for the duration of the trip.

"I'm not seeing the security administrative functions," I said, choosing to act like it was simple oversight on his part.

"Ah, yes," he answered.

A new set of functions popped up and I ran a quick audit. I had almost complete control of the ship, but Oberrhein security still had the ability to lock us out, if necessary.

"Almost there," I said. "I still see lockout capacity for your security forces."

"I'm afraid that's the best I can do," he said.

Nick got up from his chair and palmed the panel to re-extend the entry stairs.

"Mr. James, what are you doing?" Turnigy asked.

"We have a busy schedule and it doesn't seem like you are serious about this meeting. We'll have to reschedule in a neutral location," he said.

I stood up. I wasn't sure if Nick was serious, but I'd back his play.

"Come now," Turnigy said. "You can't expect us to give you a ship on your word that you'll give it back."

"I'm not negotiating," Nick said and continued down the stairs. Tabby was right behind him.

"Very well. I'll concede your point," he said.

I sat back down and looked. The final security block had been lifted. I added *Loose Nuts* to the security profile and notified Nick, who turned around and walked back up the stairs. I could see that even as he was walking, his AI was running an audit on the ship's systems. Several stealthed security programs were exposed and deactivated by the time he'd returned to his seat.

"We need to be able to trust each other, Ambassador," Nick said. "We're putting a lot of faith in your word."

"Trust me," Turnigy said. He had a strong, charismatic charm and I didn't have a difficult time understanding why he was a top level political operator within Oberrhein.

A destination popped up in a message from Turnigy. I hadn't seen him make a gesture to send it to me, but I was trying to familiarize myself with the new cockpit. My AI had done a very good job of rearranging all of the virtual controls. The ship's interface was more like the ore sled I was used to flying than that of *Hotspur*.

"All hands prepare for departure," I said.

My AI pulled up a modified checklist and I verified our fuel, small amount of O2, inertial systems and energy stores. I noticed that the gun-port powered a light blaster. I pulled a virtual stick from the left arm of my chair and extended the blaster. It had sixty degrees of freedom. It was more than I'd expected but we wouldn't be winning many dog-fights with this shuttle.

"Ready," Nick said.

"Good to go," Tabby agreed.

"Ada. We're set over here. We'll see you back on Lèger sometime tomorrow."

"Copy that, Liam. Stay safe," she said.

I pulled on my flight stick and the shuttle popped from the deck of the landing strip. I nudged us forward and we glided gracefully. My AI indicated that our minimum speed for unassisted flight was twenty-five meters per second. Under that speed the modified arc-jet system would be required to keep us aloft. I pushed gently and the shuttle accelerated, slicing through the atmosphere, the large wing surface responding to the heavy atmosphere.

The sensor package showed Ada in *Hotspur* following us and I pushed the stick harder, putting distance between us. I tipped the stick over, pulled it back so that we doubled back toward her and then dropped the hammer, executing a close fly by while waggling our wings.

"Ambassador, do you need to let them know we're coming?" I asked.

"I don't think you're headed in the right direction," he said. "We'll make contact when we're within three hundred kilometers."

"True enough," I agreed.

I pulled back on the stick and flipped around. I loved how responsive the small ship was in the atmosphere.

An hour later, as we continued our pass around Grünholz, we received a hail from Oberrhein control. Turnigy informed them of our mission and his diplomatic status and we were given a wide approach vector to their flight deck. I slowed to the speed requested and looked with anticipation in the direction of the city of Solnste. In the distance, a shiny, gray steel dome came up out of the sea, its top open as if cut off some fifty meters from sea-level.

"*Sensors indicate four turret weapons tracking our approach,*" the ship's AI informed me. I forwarded it to the ship's speakers for everyone to hear.

"Ambassador?"

"Standard welcome. I suggest you don't do anything too provocative," he said.

CHAMPION

The navigation path directed me to fly in through the opening at the top of the city's protective outer shell. For a nation without good access to steel, they'd somehow constructed a shell that was ten kilometers in diameter. The opening at the top was a full kilometer wide. We passed over a fleet of ships, which from the air, looked like they were not in the best repair, but certainly boasted some of the largest projectile turrets I'd ever seen. I wasn't sure who they were defending the city from, but I couldn't imagine they'd be unsuccessful.

We slowed and landed on an airstrip protected by the curve of the dome. Eight other airships were currently parked and the strip looked like it would be good for possibly twice that number. A cadre of soldiers, dressed in spartan, dark-blue uniforms approached upon our landing.

"I've got to say, I'm not sure what there was to worry about with *Hotspur*. It looks like this city is well defended," I said.

"All about appearances, my boy. King Kostov would be embarrassed if a ship were allowed in and was able to cause trouble," he said.

I nodded and palmed open the hatch, allowing the stairs to descend. I walked out and looked across and down into the city that had been built beneath the giant dome. It extended downward for what my AI informed me was two kilometers. Not unlike a space station, there were habitation complexes neatly arranged in tall buildings. There were also a few green areas where short trees and grasses had been given a foothold. All along the interior wall of the dome were level platforms like where we'd landed.

"How many people live here?" I asked.

"There are twenty-five thousand free men," he said.

"Free men?" Tabby asked. "What's that mean?"

"It is a self-explanatory term," he said.

I stepped up next to Tabby and held her hand.

"Are women not free?" she asked.

"Oberrhein families are different than you might expect. As an outsider, it will be easy for you to judge us. I suggest that you keep these judgments to yourself. King Kostov and other members of the court have little patience for impertinence. As our guest, though you are a woman, you are certainly free," he said.

Tabby stiffened but didn't respond.

"For our benefit, how can we recognize the different castes?" Nick asked.

"A wise question, Mr. James. Anyone with metal bracers on their forearms are in a lower caste and won't speak to you without their owner's permission and only then if you recognize them," he said.

"Slavery?" Tabby asked.

"No, not strictly speaking. We provide an environment where people's needs are provided. If one desires to leave, they simply need ask and they will be released at the end of their contract. But, we're not here to discuss Oberrhein's social structure and we shouldn't keep King Kostov waiting," he said.

He approached the uniformed guards that had been standing at attention during our conversation. They all wore bronze bracers.

"Where are we headed?" I asked.

"Kostovgorod Castle is just there," He pointed out across the open area under the dome.

My eyes followed his gesture and I saw what I'd missed before. A fortress, complete with pointed towers and tall walls, stood separated from the rest of Solnste. A green band of grass and trees completely encircled it. Kostovgorod wasn't the tallest structure within the dome, but it certainly was the most unique architecturally. It looked like it belonged to an age long ago and that at any moment we might see men on horses riding forth, holding tall lances with banners atop them to quell a peasant uprising.

"This just keeps getting better," Tabby muttered.

"Inspiring, don't you think?" Turnigy asked.

We followed our guard to an awaiting gravity-assisted transport. It was just large enough to fit us and our guard.

"It doesn't seem that Solnste suffers from the same technological problems as Nannandry," I said.

"It's the dome. The founders of the city knew very well about the electromagnetic pulses and built this dome to shield the occupants. It was quite the undertaking," Turnigy said.

"Are there more domes like this?" Tabby asked.

"Perhaps we should save our questions," he responded.

The grav-shuttle dropped from the high perch we'd arrived on and fell into the light traffic of other similar shuttles. As we descended, my understanding of the size of the city changed. Solnste had to be twenty times the size of Nannandry. I wondered what kind of trade they had outside of their walls - certainly, not much with Nuage, as far as I could tell.

The buildings we passed looked ancient. The steel at ground level was deeply pitted and rust stained the exterior of everything. The dome might be keeping back the EM waves, but Grünholz appeared to be winning a much longer-term war of attrition and destruction.

The people we saw running around, doing their business, all appeared to have bracers on and I started to wonder just what the ratio of free to enslaved might actually be.

The shuttle we were in finally pulled to a stop on the edge of the green band of semi-forested gardens that separated Kostovgorod from the rest of the city. Unlike the dilapidated structures of the city, the scene in front of us was like a storybook. The green grass was neatly cut, trees were well-groomed and flower beds were blooming. Even as we approached, we could see at least a dozen workers maintaining the grounds.

The castle towered fifty meters above us as we approached. Embrasures lined the top of the wall and it didn't take a lot to imagine men leaning out, raining arrows down on us as we rushed the besieged castle. It seemed excessive, but caused me to wonder if the heavily fortified structure had ever been attacked.

I wasn't disappointed in the décor of the interior, as it continued the theme of an ancient castle. Tapestries hung from the walls and shiny suits of armor stood at key locations. We followed our guard up an expansive central staircase to a grand hallway. The ornate doors at the end left no doubt in my mind as to where the king's court might be held.

Before we reached the doors, however, we were led into a side room where a buffet of food was set out along one wall.

"We're early, but the King's staff thoughtfully provided refreshments. Please eat, it could well be a long afternoon," Turnigy said.

And he was right. After standing around for twenty minutes, we finally moved over to the buffet and filled our plates. That, also, became old as minutes turned into hours.

"He is planning on meeting with us today, right?" Tabby asked.

"Yes, Ms. Masters. King Kostov and his council are busy managing an entire kingdom. You'll excuse him if his timing is inconvenient for you," Turnigy said.

"There's no need for condescension, Ambassador," I said.

Turnigy closed his eyes and nodded. "You're right, of course, Mr. Hoffen. Ms. Masters, my apologies."

Twenty minutes later one of our guards approached the Ambassador.

"The king will see us now," he said. "Remember, only speak when spoken to. Be courteous. Disrespecting the king or his court of Oberrhein is dealt with most harshly."

We entered the throne room from a side door. In the center of the grand room sat a thickset, dark-haired man, with plush dark blue robes trimmed in gold. He was sitting on an honest to goodness throne. I don't know what I was expecting, but I can say that wasn't it.

To his left, a row of ostentatious chairs were lined up and a council of old men sat atop them. None of the men were as outrageously dressed as the king, but wore clothing of a similar ilk. Banded servants scurried about on missions not immediately obvious.

Tabby grabbed my arm and I followed her eyes across the room to a knot of people I hadn't seen yet. It was Petar Kiirilov, Mihael Ivov and the captain of the *Kordun* – Milos Benesch.

"I don't like this, Liam," she said under her breath.

I didn't either, but we were in it now and there was no turning back.

"Ambassador Turnigy, you may approach," a man announced, standing just in front of where the king sat.

"Stay here," he said. "You'll be called up in turn."

King Kostov looked bored and drank from an ornate cup one of his attendants had provided.

"My liege," Ambassador Turnigy bowed as he approached the throne.

"Ambassador, why have you brought these criminals into my court?" he asked.

"My apologies, your eminence. To which criminals are you referring?"

"Don't play dumb with me, Turnigy, or I'll have your head," he said.

"Ah, yes. Again, my apologies. Today, I'm accompanied by the owners of the corporation, *Loose Nuts*," he said. "They've presented information that has been audited by an independent intelligence organization, which I forwarded to Colonel Yakovich. It was he who requested that we present this information to you."

"Colonel Yakovich, is this true?"

"Yes, my liege." A heavily muscled man stepped forward.

"Tell me, Yelisey, how does this relate to Lord Kiirilov's claim that this same group has attacked him?" The king asked in a familiar tone.

"If the video source is to be believed, the earlier testimony by Lord Kiirilov is an optimistic statement of the events."

"And this is an issue for my court, for what reason? Should not Lord Kiirilov deal with his own problems?"

"I find the circumstances to be compelling, but would not dare to speak for your majesty," Yakovich simpered. "My concern is much more for how these events might be interpreted by the Belirand Corporation."

"Belirand!" Kostov said, "Tell me what in a whore's naval I would care for what they think."

"Again. If the Ambassador's video is to be believed. Belirand could very well determine that we took part in the destruction of one of their ships," he said.

"I see. I will judge this video for myself," he said and turned back to Turnigy. "Ambassador, you may proceed."

"Your Majesty, I demand the right of challenge," Petar Kiirilov said.

This got King Kostov's attention. I caught the glimmer of a smile cross his face, which he quickly stowed. "Is that so? Ambassador. Lord Kiirilov has invoked his right of challenge. Do you accept?"

"I accept, your majesty," Turnigy replied.

A bead of sweat formed over his lip. The Ambassador had to have anticipated Petar's maneuver and his quick response told me he'd gotten just what he wanted. Turnigy had committed himself, but seemed unsure of the end result. There was more in play here and I needed to figure it out quickly.

"Lord Kiirilov, will you choose a champion?" King Kostov asked. His bored expression had disappeared and he'd slid to the edge of his throne.

"I do. Mihael Ivov will represent me in combat," he said.

"Ambassador Turnigy, do you have a champion?" Kostov asked. He actually clapped his hands together and rubbed them excitedly.

"I have no land, nor do I have vassals. Is there anyone in the court who would champion an old man?" he asked looking at the galley, where the King's council sat.

The room remained quiet as he looked at each of them in turn.

"Colonel?" he asked.

"Ambassador Turnigy. A challenge has been issued and

accepted. Without a champion, you must either concede your right to show the information or fight Lord Kiirilov's champion. What will it be?" Kostov asked.

"I'll do it," Tabby said, stepping forward before I could stop her.

"Unacceptable," Kiirilov said. "A woman has no right to speak in the King's presence."

"Be quiet, you fool," Turnigy said growling at Tabby.

"Step forward, woman," Kostov said. "Why do I recognize your face?"

Tabby stepped forward and looked up at King Kostov. I wanted to scream. We shouldn't have come. I felt a thump on my ring. Tabby was attempting to reassure me.

"I'm not sure how to address you, King Kostov. I'm not from around here," Tabby said. I was glad that she was being respectful.

"A woman who knows her place is to be treasured. You may address me just as you have – King Kostov. Now tell me, little one, why do I recognize your face?" he asked.

"I am not certain, King Kostov. I have had limited interaction with the people of Oberrhein, my first being an altercation with Mr. Ivov," Tabby said, lowering her eyes.

"That's it!" Kostov clapped his hand excitedly. "Lord Kiirilov, is your man Ivov turning down a chance to redeem himself?"

"It would not be fair, my liege," Kiirilov said. "The court would not accept a victory over a woman."

"Ambassador Turnigy, do you accept this girl as your champion?" Kostov asked incredulously.

"Yes," Turnigy responded. His upper lip was no longer sweating.

"Lord Kiirilov, there is no dishonor in defeating a champion, whether that be a woman or a pig. Do you withdraw your challenge?"

Kiirilov looked at Turnigy, his rage barely contained. "I should have killed you when I had the chance. No, my liege, the champion is acceptable."

Ivov wasted no time and rushed at Tabby, catching her off guard and taking her to the floor. I lunged forward protectively, but Turnigy intercepted me.

"No, Captain, you mustn't. To interfere would doom us all," he said.

"You're to blame for this," I said.

"It was the only way," he said, pushing me back.

Mihael rolled off from on top of Tabby and came up holding a short knife. Its blade was covered in blood.

"How's it feel?" he taunted as Tabby gained her feet.

She reached for her side and pulled back a bloody hand. The armored vac-suit hadn't stopped the blade. I could see pain in her face as she squared off and shook her head as if confused.

"Coward," she said.

Mihael lunged but danced away when he got close. His speed was remarkable and I had to remind myself that he was a Double-A pod-ball player. With her wound, she needed to hurry. Tabby would grow weaker as time marched forward.

She dropped her arms to her side and motioned to him. He couldn't resist the invitation and they lunged at each other. His anticipation of her grapple was excellent and he rolled backward, planting his foot into her abdomen and launching her into the galley of the King's Council. They pushed her off to the floor and scattered at Mihael's approach.

He jumped the velvet railing separating the council from the main floor at about the time Tabby rose up again. This time she raised her forearms defensively, as we'd trained in boxing. Mihael shook his head from side to side, as if limbering up, and raised his fists.

"Martial skills it is," he said.

He punched and kicked, all the while backing Tabby up. His speed was faster than I could imagine. Tabby's efforts were expended fending him off. She seemed to have no capacity to strike back.

"You're faster than I expected, but not fast enough, I think," he said.

"At least I didn't cheat and use a weapon," Tabby said defensively.

"Who said that was cheating? There are no rules."

He flurried after his explanation. Tabby, barely able to defend against his blows, took several to her mid-section, no doubt compounding the wound she'd received at the start of the fight.

"So, tell me something," Tabby grunted out as she pushed back in, this time keeping her guard up.

"Let's call it your last wish. What do you want to know?"

"How will they remember you once I've killed you with my bare hands?" Tabby asked.

"Give up and I'll let you live," Mihael said. "As my servant."

Tabby swung wide with a left-right combination, missing on both. Mihael, who had been capitalizing on poor technique all night, stepped in and landed a series of blows, once again to her abdomen. She screamed in pain and mashed her forehead into the bridge of his nose.

Mihael faltered, stepping back. He hadn't seen it coming. Tabby jumped at him, landing her foot on the inside of his knee and vaulting up his body, her other leg clearing his shoulder. As he fell backward, she wrapped her ankles together and rode him down to the floor. A sickening snap was heard as they both landed.

For a moment they lay there, not moving. I started to run over, but Turnigy held me back.

"Not yet," he said.

Finally, Tabby rolled off and rose to one knee.

"Liam," she said.

Something was wrong and I shrugged off Turnigy's hands and rushed over to her.

"What's wrong, Tabbs?"

"The blade. It was poisoned."

"She needs help," I said, looking up at King Kostov.

"Is he dead?" Kostov asked.

I shook my head, "She's been poisoned."

"Very likely. It was a magnificent challenge, though," Kostov answered. His glee drove me to the edge, if Tabby didn't need me, I'd have killed him right there.

Turnigy had approached and placed his fingers on Mihael Ivov's twisted neck. "Yes, my liege, he is dead. My challenge was successful."

"Well done, Ambassador. It's getting late, though. We'll have to postpone watching your video until tomorrow. I can only hope it will be as entertaining as today," Kostov said.

He stood up and waited for his attendants to straighten his robes.

"Call a physician. I believe she's earned it," he said casually.

A DEAL IS A DEAL

"She is strong and should survive," the physician said.

The physician had treated Tabby on the floor of the throne room. Once she'd been stabilized, we'd been moved to an opulent suite of rooms.

"What was it?" I asked.

"Giant coral venom, most likely, given how quickly it acted," he said.

"I thought it killed within a few minutes."

"That is its reputation, but it varies widely depending on the person. She is lucky. Ordinarily, the venom almost instantaneously blinds its victim. I understand she fought for several minutes after being poisoned," he said.

I shook my head. It all made sense. Tabby hadn't been able to see Mihael. Her taunting had been to get him to talk so she could locate him. She'd allowed him to hit her so she could fix his location.

"When will she wake?" I asked.

"I gave her a sedative. It will wear off in a few hours. The med-patch will repair as much of the damage as possible, but I'd check into a medical treatment center on Lèger when you return," he said. "The damage to her tissue was extensive and will take time to rebuild."

"Thank you," I said.

"You should thank King Kostov. He believes that wounds received in a challenge should be left untreated, at least for a few days - something about the honor of battle," he said.

"I'll try to remember to do that," I said. I think my sarcasm was lost on the man.

Turnigy entered the room after the doctor left. "How is she?"

"She'll make it, no thanks to you," I said.

"This was hardly my doing," he responded.

"Don't lie, Turnigy. This was all your doing," I said. "You knew Kiirilov would challenge the video and you also knew that Tabby wouldn't be able to resist it."

"You're giving me entirely too much credit," he said. "It did turn out well, however."

I glared at him.

"We have first audience with his eminence in the morning," Turnigy said. "I believe you made quite an impression. His good mood is a boon for us."

"Get out," I said.

"1000 tomorrow," he said as he left.

"Can you believe that guy?" I asked Nick.

"I'm sorry I got us into this, Liam," Nick said.

"She kicked his ass, blind," I said. I wasn't willing to wallow in what-ifs.

"Marny would have been proud," he agreed.

"What do you think this is all about?" I asked. "Why would Petar be here?"

"Turnigy's doing, I'd bet," Nick said.

"But he tried to kill Turnigy," I said.

"Turnigy is playing a dangerous game."

Our conversation was cut short by a knock on the door. Nick crossed into the outer chamber and opened the door. Two young women entered, carrying platters with food on them. With Tabby sleeping comfortably, I joined him to see what was going on.

"My Lords, we have a meal for you, please." The first through the door said.

They were dressed in filmy robes that left little to the imagination. Their wrists were adorned by narrow, bronze bracers. I caught an alluring scent as they entered the room and placed the platters on a sideboard. A boy, no older than twelve, entered behind them carrying a stringed instrument. He stopped just inside the door and started playing. With the platters down, the two women started dancing slowly.

"What are you doing?" I asked.

It was hard to deny the beauty of their dance, but it made me feel dirty.

"Do you not find us attractive, my Lord? We're yours for the night," the woman who'd spoken first said.

"What are your names?" Nick took over the conversation, probably after he saw my mouth hanging open in shock.

"I am Minah and this is Suhaad. The musician is Suhaad's brother, Tijah," she said. She and Suhaad continued to dance, suggestively.

"I'm Nick and this is my partner, Liam. Could you stop dancing?" he asked.

The two girls stopped their gyrating, which I found both disappointing and relieving. I could just imagine Tabby waking up and walking in on the scene. If that happened, I wasn't sure any amount of Chimera Beetle venom would save me.

"Yes, m'Lord," she said.

"First, we're not lords. Second, if we send you away, will you get in trouble?" Nick asked.

"It is our duty to entertain you. If you are displeased, we will be punished," she said.

"Can we ask you to leave without that occurring?"

"No, m'Lord," she said.

"I'm not sure how to explain this," Nick said.

"Let me give it a go," I said. "The woman in the next room is a warrior and my betrothed. She killed the man who poisoned her while she was blinded from the venom of a King Coral. Imagine what she would do to me if she discovered I'd been unfaithful."

"In Oberrhein, to lie with a slave does not break a man's vow. The king has decreed it," she said, looking at the floor.

"I'm afraid that's not how our women would see it," Nick said. "You are welcome to stay the night and share in our food, but Liam and I are off limits. You may leave when it is safe for you."

"Yes, my Lord," she said.

The rest of the night was uneventful. The trio stayed to themselves and Nick and I weren't overly interested in engaging them in conversation. At 0600, Tabby awoke.

"Liam?"

"Heya, kid, how are you feeling?" I asked.

"My head is pounding and my side hurts. Where are we? What happened?" she asked.

The doctor had already warned me that Tabby might not remember much from the fight, so I recounted it to her.

"That sounds about right," she said.

"Can you see okay?" I asked.

"Hurts to open my eyes. But, yeah, I can see fine," she said.

I handed her a cup of hot tea and helped her sit up.

"They don't seem to believe in med-patches, either," I said.

"Lovely."

A knock at the exterior door was answered by Nick. After some conversation, he entered the room. "We're going early to see the King. Petar took off in the middle of the night and Kostov wants to review our data streams right away," he said.

"When?"

"Right now," he said.

"Okay, give us a minute."

Tabby wasn't in her armored vac-suit and I wasn't about to bring her into the King's throne room without protection. I closed the door for privacy.

"You ready to get dressed," I asked.

"Help me to the restroom," she said.

Ten minutes later, we emerged, with me holding Tabby up on one side.

"Looking good, Tabby," Nick said.

"Shut up."

Nick just shook his head and smiled. It was a funny, dysfunctional world I lived in.

Much of the pageantry of the previous day had been dropped. Only a handful of the King's Council were in attendance and even fewer of the servants. I hadn't expected to see Milos Benesch, the captain of the *Kordun* present, given Petar Kiirilov's midnight departure.

"Ambassador Turnigy, you may present your video," the King's representative announced.

A two meter in diameter, round table rose from the floor and locked into place just in front of the King's throne. While it fit the over-the-top, Knights of the Round Table décor, it was also clearly a modern holo-projection device.

"Mr. James?" Turnigy asked.

Starting with the destruction of *Cape of Good Hope* and ending with the destruction of the *Stenka*, Nick patiently walked the captive audience through the series of aggressive actions of the Oberrhein fleet.

"What have you to say about this, Captain Benesch?" King Kostov asked.

"I cannot speak for what occurred before Lord Kiirilov arrived in Tipperary," he said. "As for the sequence where the *Kordun* was present, the video does not appear to have been altered."

"Ambassador Turnigy, what is your claim?"

"We have broken our treaty with Nuage by forming a space fleet and harrying free trade within the Descartes belt. Our attack on the *Loose Nuts Corporation* in open space is a direct violation of this treaty, as they carry the Nuage flag. Further, the coordination required to launch such an assault shows a disturbing link back to what I can only assume is a rogue element within the Belirand Corporation.

"I see. I'm not following the issue with Belirand," King Kostov said. "How is this our problem?"

"If Mr. James and Mr. Hoffen's assertion is correct - that Lord Kiirilov was involved in the events that led up to the destruction of *Cape of Good Hope* - Kiirilov will have single-handedly opened the nation of Oberrhein to hostilities from Nuage and Belirand. And for what? Has he delivered a single dram of ore? Has he done anything other than deplete our fuel reserves and carelessly get the *Stenka* destroyed?"

"Captain Benesch. Would you defend Lord Kiirilov's actions? It appears that he is unavailable this morning," King Kostov said.

"No, your Majesty. I have faithfully served Lord Kiirilov as I was ordered to do, but I have no insight as to his actions."

"How did you locate the *Loose Nuts* fleet in open space?" Kostov asked.

"We chased them from the Descartes belt to Belirand's Terminal Seven. Once they departed, we received a data stream," he said.

"From whom?" Kostov pressed.

"J.T. Emre, the station commander," he said.

"Why would he provide this?"

"So that we could run their fleet down and destroy it," Benesch said simply.

"Thank you, Captain, you are dismissed," he said.

Benesch nodded curtly, spun on his boot and walked out of the room.

"Council, I thank you for your participation this early morning. We will meet next week to discuss these events," King Kostov said, standing up.

"Ambassador Turnigy, I would see you and your guests in my chambers," he said.

As we followed Turnigy out of the throne room, we were flanked by a half a dozen guardsmen.

Kostov's chambers were less showy than the throne room and more functional. With the aid of a servant, he pulled off the heavy robes so he was down to a tunic and belt.

"Please, sit," he said as he plopped down behind a beautiful wooden desk. "Khalil, your intuition on Kiirilov was right. What would you have me do?"

"We get ahead of it. There is plenty of time to turn this to our favor," Turnigy said.

"Hang Kiirilov out to dry?"

"Yes. We take back his ship, persuade him to confess and then trade this information with Belirand for favorable status and better rates through the gates," Turnigy said.

"And, you can do this?" Kostov asked.

"Yes, Your Majesty, but I'll need some things," he said.

"I suspected that might be the case. What is it that you desire, Khalil?"

"I want command of the *Kordun*, so that we might use it to take the *Karelia*." he said.

"No. It is our last ship and it is critical for trade," Kostov said.

I cleared my throat which got me the attention of both men.

"Mr. Hoffen, you have something to add?" Kostov asked.

"We will capture the *Karelia* and turn Kiirilov over to you," I said.

"As generous as that sounds, you destroyed one of my ships. I had intended to take yours when you arrived, but for some reason, you showed up in a shuttle," Kostov said looking pointedly over at Turnigy.

"We'll give you the *Karelia*," Nick said.

"In return for what?" Turnigy asked.

"Leave us alone at Descartes. Better yet, trade with us. The miners can't produce ore if they're terrified of being attacked all the time, but they'll work themselves into the ground if they have someone to buy their ore," Nick said.

"Isn't your contract with Belirand?" Turnigy asked.

"It isn't exclusive," Nick said.

"What do you need from me?" Kostov asked.

"A squad," I said. "Men who can take orders and breach a ship."

"Done. It will be as you say. You will deliver the *Karelia* to me in working order. I will supply my Captain of the Guard, Colonel Yakovich, and a squad of hand-picked men. If you are successful, I will grant jurisdiction of your section of the Descartes belt to *Loose Nuts* in return for a trade agreement to be worked out later.

He turned to Turnigy, "Khalil, if you are successful at this, I will grant you Nannandry as your fief. We will take the city and I will make you its lord."

"Thank you, Your Majesty," Turnigy said, standing up and bowing.

I exchanged a knowing look with Nick as we stood. We'd spent much of the night trying to figure out what Turnigy would get out of this deal. Never in our dreams had we thought it might be the rundown city of Nannandry.

"When will you require Colonel Yakovich's services?" Turnigy asked as we walked out the entrance of the castle.

At the end of the path, a transport waited for us.

"It depends. Can you get us a location on Kiirilov?" I asked as we climbed aboard and lifted from the grounds of the castle.

I looked out over the dilapidated city as we flew up to the landing pad. It was a depressing sight.

"Reports are that he is headed to his fief in the Descartes belt," he said.

Tabby, who was walking better now, slid in next to me, wrapping her arm around my waist. I appreciated how she just knew that I was focusing on the gloom around me and needed her touch.

"We'll leave from Nannandry in twenty-four hours. Have him and his squad ready with armor and blaster rifles," I said.

We landed at the strip and transferred to the shuttle. Sitting down, I noticed the fuel had been topped off, although we'd only burned through a third of the tank.

"Nick, did you authorize a fuel transfer?" I asked.

"Yup. Request came through this morning," he said.

Negotiate departure with City of Solnste.

"Cleared for departure," the shuttle's AI replied.

Reminiscent of a simple ore-sled, the controls were all virtual and projected by my AI. Relying on comfortable routine, I pushed up on the flight stick, forward on the thruster and eased the stick back, lifting the ship toward the dome. The shuttle had been designed to be sleek, stylish and easy to maneuver. Most passengers would simply instruct the AI to fly it, making the need for actual flight hardware unnecessary. But piloting was in my blood and I needed something to focus on.

As soon as the nose of the shuttle lined up with the opening in the dome, I dropped the thrust down hard and we rocketed ahead. The loud boom we made as we passed through the sonic barrier was worse than it should have been, but, I felt, truly expressed my opinion of our visit. Infantile, maybe, but it felt really good. I'd had enough of Oberrhein and I couldn't get away fast enough.

"Nannandry work for you, Ambassador?" I asked.

"Yes," he said.

"You wouldn't happen to know if Oberrhein has any use for ten tonnes of nano-steel I-beams. We're selling them at a nice discount," I said.

"Ever the trader, Captain? I could ask our quartermaster or city planner. Do you have specifications?"

I gestured to move the specifications to him. "I'm looking for thirty-five thousand credits, and we'll only transfer them in Nannandry."

"Why Nannandry? That is hardly convenient," he said.

"Something to do with how your King was willing to take our ship by force, had we landed in Solnste," I said.

"It was fortunate you were instructed not to bring it along, don't you think," Turnigy said. "You do plan on returning my shuttle to me, don't you?"

"I believe our terms were very specific. No harm was to befall any of my crew and you were not to deceive us on the purpose of the visit," I said.

"Ms. Masters volunteered to be my champion," he said. "I can't be held accountable for that."

"And, if she hadn't and you'd been killed by Mihael Ivov? What would have happened to us then?" Nick asked.

"Hard to know. And, I just received word back. Yes, we're interested in the I-beams for thirty-five thousand credits."

"I'll make you a new deal, Turnigy," I said. "If we aren't successful in taking the *Karelia* from Kiirilov within the next two months, I'll give you your ship back. If we are, then we'll give you the *Karelia*."

"But that was already our deal. You'd already agreed to hand over the *Karelia*," he said.

"And you agreed not to put us in harm's way or you'd forfeit your shuttle."

"Toads and snakes. I hate traders," he said, mostly to himself.

FOOL ME ONCE

"You should have seen the look on Ambassador Turnigy's face as we lifted off from the landing strip. I really don't believe he thought Liam would take his ship," Tabby guffawed. We were all sitting together in Jake's lounge recounting the events of the last few days.

"He'd never have respected me in a negotiation again if I hadn't. To you, Ada Chen," I said, lifting my cup. "Your quick thinking gave us a ship."

"Hear, hear," Tabby said. She was feeling a lot better after seeing a medical technician in Lèger and generously spreading med patches up and down her ribs where she'd been stabbed.

"You know we can't let an armed squad of Marines onto our ship," Marny said.

"What if we require them to hand over their guns before boarding?" I asked.

"That could work. We'll install a temporary head and cots in the hold. As a Marine, I certainly lived like that often enough."

"It'd only be for the ride out, anyway," I said. "They can ride back in the *Karelia*."

"Copy that. What are you thinking? Basic run 'em down, breach 'em type tactic?" Marny asked.

"No. More insidious."

"Do tell," Ada said sliding forward.

"I'm thinking we give Kiirilov something he can't resist," I said looking around at the group.

"What?" Ada asked. She was always my best straight man.

"*Sterra's Gift*."

"No!" Ada was affronted.

"And by 'give,' I mean use it as a distraction," I said, mollifying

322

her a bit. "We make a big deal about diffusing the charges on Mom and Dad's claim, but we act like they were killed in the process. In the chaos, *Sterra's Gift* is left sitting on the asteroid - open - because, of course, Mom and Dad were planning on taking off while the bots worked, but got blown up."

"Kiirilov would have to inspect the area. He couldn't leave a ship like that alone. And while he's launching his away party, we breach," I said.

"How do you know Kiirilov's going to be at Descartes?" Ada asked.

"Turnigy already told me he's headed that way," I said.

"How'd Turnigy know that?"

"Just does. I didn't ask," I said.

"It's as good a plan as any," Marny said. "Who leads the boarding party?"

"I was hoping you'd tell me."

"I'll work it out with the Oberrhein Colonel," Marny said. "When do we pick him up?"

"0600 tomorrow," I said.

With the departure the next morning, we'd decided to make an early night of it. When we were walking out, Jake pulled me aside.

"Talk to you for a minute?" he asked.

"You okay?" Tabby asked, seeing that I'd stopped.

"I've got this, you go ahead."

I turned to Jake, "What's up?"

"I've got some news you might be interested in," he said.

"Really? I'm nearly broke at this point."

"On the house," he said and whispered his secret to me.

"Well... shite," I said. "Thank you, Jake."

"Just looking out for my best customer," he said.

I nodded and hurried to catch up to Tabby and the rest of the crew. I had some hard thinking to do and calls to make.

"What was that all about?" Tabby asked.

She needed help getting out of her clothes. She didn't like to let on, but the effects of the poison were still hindering her.

"Let's get some sleep and we'll talk about it tomorrow," I said.

"Sure," she agreed.

I lay awake for an hour worrying about the information I'd received. At some point, I drifted off to sleep only to wake a few hours later to my alarm.

"Jake passed along information I want to share with everyone," I said at breakfast the next morning. It was 0500 and since we'd been out the night before, no one was too chipper.

"Do tell," Ada said.

I shared what Jake had told me the night before.

"That changes everything," Tabby said. "I can't believe you didn't tell me last night."

"I don't think it changes anything," Nick said. "We can't run our business on rumors. We just need to adapt our plan."

"What do you have in mind?" I asked.

Fifteen minutes later we were flying through the atmosphere, getting ready to punch into the heavy cloud cover of Grünholz.

"You think Ada minded staying behind?" I asked Tabby.

"No. I think she understands we have to keep everyone safe," Tabby said.

I nodded. I didn't like singling Ada out like that, but we had to be sure.

"Here we go, folks," I said.

I set our course so we'd come in closer to the city instead of taking the scenic route over the ocean. We'd heard reports of a huge storm over Nannandry, but it wasn't anything we couldn't handle. And it begged the question - when hadn't there been a huge storm over Nannandry?

Once we dropped into the clouds, the severity of the storm hit us right away. We were buffeted back and forth and the rain pummeled the hull.

"Okay, this is new," Tabby said, her voice raised so I could hear her.

"We better strap in," I said. "It's probably going to get worse."

Lightning flashed through the clouds and I was momentarily blinded. The auto darkening armor glass was having a difficult time reacting fast enough to the random, brilliant pyrotechnics.

I pulled on my combat harness and helped Tabby with hers. It was hard for me to see her struggling.

"We should break free of the clouds at two thousand meters," Tabby shouted.

When we dropped below the clouds, the atmosphere became more stable, but the rain increased in intensity.

"Nick, what happens if we're struck by lightning?" I asked.

"We've been hit three times. It's not a big deal," he said.

I was kind of impressed.

Tabby pointed ahead. "There's the landing strip."

The storm had let up and she wasn't having to shout so much. I suspected it had something to do with being closer to the towering vegetation that the city sat upon giving us a break from the weather.

I swung *Hotspur* around and landed on the now familiar strip.

"You got this?" I asked Tabby.

"Of course. Just don't ask me to be your champion today, okay?"

I gave her a quick peck on the cheek and joined Marny on the lift. We were wearing our armored vac-suits and carrying blaster rifles. The show of force shouldn't be necessary, however, as we'd communicated our requirements to Colonel Yakovich. Their weapons should be neatly stowed in a crate that we would lock away in the armory until we arrived at our destination.

From inside the ship, it was impossible to see what was going on outside in the storm. Just in case, I chose to descend the stairs instead of dropping the cargo ramp. A rain-swept Turnigy met me at the bottom. Standing next to him was the Colonel.

"Ready to get going?" I asked.

"You should drop the ramp. We have lots of gear," Yakovich said over the storm.

"We'll come around," I said. "We need to check the weapons first."

"As you wish," Turnigy said.

When we rounded the back of the ship, the rain let up enough for me to make out at least two squads of marines, all holding blaster rifles pointed at us.

"Frak, it's a trap, Tabbs," I said.

"Tell your crew to open the ramp and no one gets hurt," Turnigy said.

"It's you, isn't it? You've been behind all of it," I said.

"Not all of it, but the good parts, certainly," Turnigy said.

"How could you kill all of those innocents on the *Cape*?" I asked.

"That was all Kiirilov. Now, drop your weapons and lower the ramp," he said.

From the side of the landing strip a burst of blaster fire erupted and traced across the front line of Oberrhein Marines. The sleek blue shape of the Oberrhein shuttle rocketed past.

"Go!" I yelled. Marny didn't need convincing and raced back to the stairway on the starboard side, which led to the exterior hatch.

"Liam, you've got company," Ada's voice said.

I dove through the hatch just behind Marny as Nick fired the bottom turret, trying to pick off the dodging Marines.

"Tabby, we're in. You need to take off," I said. Missiles launched from the tubes and blaster fire erupted from *Hotspur's* turrets as Tabby lifted us up, not at all gently, from the landing strip.

Marny and I stumbled through the bridge, trying to keep our feet as blaster fire rocked *Hotspur*. We were being struck by something heavy.

I clawed my way into my chair and pulled on the combat harness. I heard a great pfhawhump as our rear turret fired and drained the batteries by nearly fifty percent. Our sensors showed we were being pursued by both Oberrhein cruisers.

"Frak. Jake didn't say anything about both cruisers," I said.

Hotspur's lights flickered as a fresh round of blaster fire rocked us.

"Tabbs, I have an idea. Give me the helm," I said. "Marny, stay sharp. This is going to be close."

Tabby had been trying to gain altitude and the relative safety of the clouds. The thing was, we weren't going to make it. The cruisers were tearing us apart.

I pushed the stick over hard and accelerated. In a pure lift, we had just about as much thrust, kilogram for kilogram, as the cruisers. But with our wings, we could afford to drop more quickly, as we'd be able to use them to help us pull up when we needed altitude.

"Crap, Liam! Fifteen hundred meters, twelve-hundred, a thousand, eight hundred, five hundred ...," Tabby was counting down our elevation.

I pulled back on the stick and leveled off at a hundred meters. For the moment, I'd put some distance between us and the cruisers. Lightning and blaster fire flashed all around us and I pulled back on the throttle, slowing slightly.

"Are you crazy?" Tabby asked.

"Marny, you got this?"

"Fool me once, Cap."

The vegetation in this area was thick and I was forced to weave back and forth. I wasn't finding what we needed, but I knew it would be coming up shortly, so I bided my time. For now, this little game of hide and seek was giving us the break we needed from the action.

"*Incoming hail, Karelia,*" the ship's AI announced.

Accept. "Little busy just now for conversation, Petar," I said.

"Did you really think Kostov would keep any deals he made with you?" he asked.

"I certainly had my doubts," I replied.

"Give it up, Hoffen, or we're going to bury you here," he said.

"Like you did to *Cape of Good Hope*?"

"You really think you're going to trick me into admitting something?" he asked.

"Worth a shot, don't you think?"

Close comm.

The change in the vegetation was just what I was looking for and I pulled back on the stick. We lifted a couple of hundred meters into the thrashing chaos of the Lightning Vines.

"Now, Marny!" I said.

Another pfhawhump from our rear turret.

Quiet running, Engage!

I watched from our passive rear sensor as the energy from our aft heavy blaster contacted the *Kordun*. It was a nice, solid hit, but they would survive the blast just fine. Already, the energy was dissipating across their hull. If I could get three or four more of those, I'd rip right through the ship.

"Port," Tabby said. "Starboard."

I dodged and weaved and I think even rolled, trying to avoid the activity of the vines spurred by the sudden release of energy. The hungry tendrils weren't seeking out *Hotspur* as much as they were not caring we were in their path.

The *Kordun* shrugged off the first strike heroically, only slowing a moment. Recognizing his peril, Captain Benesch tried to nose over to the relative safety of lower elevation, but he was too late. Vine after vine ripped at his ship, bludgeoning it in a frantic search for the energy they desired. The last view I had of the *Kordun* was of it being torn into two pieces in the chaotic feeding frenzy.

I dropped back down to a hundred meters and continued at that elevation until we were out of the lightning vine's territory.

"That wasn't very nice," Petar Kiirilov said, contacting us once again.

I'd dropped out of stealth mode so we could gain altitude.

"You might want to send someone to see if there are any survivors," I said.

"You'll never leave this planet alive!" Kiirilov shouted.

"You need new material," I said. "We're out of here."

"I know. I'm right below you," he said.

Alarms started going off as we took a direct hit to our belly.

"Bottom turret is out," Nick reported.

I rolled to the side and narrowly avoided a second shot from the rising *Karelia*. I couldn't fathom how he'd picked us up so easily.

"They've got a ship on the surface," Marny said.

"Of course they do," I sighed. Nothing was ever easy.

I dropped the throttle into overload and prayed the engines would hold together long enough to get us out of here.

The *Karelia* was falling back, but very slowly.

Pfhawhump.

The rear blaster fire was enough to deter Petar long enough for us to make it into the cloud bank. After twenty seconds, I pulled back on the throttle. I could just imagine the bill we'd be getting from Meerkat shipyard after this encounter. That is, if we survived.

"Keep dodging. You don't want to be sitting still if they've got anti-aircraft," Marny said.

"You think they're tracking us?"

"Anything's possible," she said.

I checked my heading and altitude. We'd break free of the clouds any minute.

It's hard to describe the feeling you have when you emerge from clouds into bright, sunlit sky. Usually, nothing can top the rush. Today, however, we had the added excitement of emerging right in the middle of what looked to be a Nuage Air Defense training exercise.

"Incoming hail, Nuage Air Defense."

Accept.

"Captain Hoffen. It's Squad Commander Luc Gray. It looks like your ship has sustained damage. May we render aid?" He asked.

"Ada called him?" Tabby asked.

"And he came," I confirmed.

"Roger that, Squad Commander. We've been attacked by the Oberrhein Cruiser, *Karelia* and we're requesting assistance," I answered.

Just then, the *Karelia* emerged from the cloud cover and started firing on *Hotspur*. I'd been expecting the assault and rolled out of the way easily.

"Look at that," Tabby said, in awe.

The four squadrons of Nuage airships converged on the *Karelia* almost immediately. In the end, no additional shots were fired. The *Karelia* was more than a match for one or two of the small

Nuage craft, but three squadrons of five ships each was more than even Petar cared to deal with.

We followed the *Karelia* and the Nuage ships back to Nuage Gros.

"Meerkat has agreed to let us land for an eval," Nick said as we closed in on the city.

"How are we going to pay for it?" I asked.

"One thing at a time, Love," Tabby said.

Upon learning of our plight, Meerkat shipyard had cleared their deck. Apparently, with long range optics, they could see we were missing some of the requisite parts and pieces that would allow us to set down cleanly. Fortunately, it wasn't the first time they'd been tasked with this issue and a calm engineer talked me in.

Meerkat was right after all. For when we came to rest, the port-side wing was leaning against the deck. I couldn't imagine how much material had to have been removed for this to be the case. Then it hit me. My gorgeous, spotless, immaculate bilge had been destroyed. I wasn't usually an overly superstitious person, but I was starting to believe my bilges were cursed.

On the deck, Bing, the engineer I'd just seen not more than a two weeks ago, met me with his hand outstretched.

"What happened, Captain?" he asked.

"You'll have to tell me. Either an anti-aircraft gun or a heavy ship blaster, I would assume," I said.

"Give us a few hours to work up an estimate. I'd say you're going to be down for a few days, though," he said.

"Feels that way, doesn't it?" I said wryly.

"Don't worry, we'll get you all fixed up," he said. "Looks like you have a visitor, though."

I saw a uniformed officer from Nuage's Air Defense walking purposefully toward me. Another officer stood at the elevator with Nick, Marny and Tabby in tow.

"Captain Hoffen, would you accompany me?" he asked.

"Can do," I said.

The elevator dropped us at the, now familiar, Nuage Air

Defense Command Center. The officers turned us over to the man I recognized as Admiral Marsh's aide.

"Roger Carsen," he re-introduced himself. "I trust your crew sustained no injuries?" he directed the question to me.

"I believe that's correct," I said.

"It will be a few minutes," he said as he deposited us in a functional looking meeting room. It wasn't anywhere near as nice as Kostovgorod Castle, but that suited me just fine.

Roger's ability to estimate time turned out to be terrible. We were starting to wonder if we'd been forgotten when Admiral Marsh, Colonel Festove and Ambassador Stephano entered the room. Out of respect, I stood. My opinion regarding democratic, albeit bureaucratic, rulers had recently increased, significantly.

"You've quite a lot of explaining to do, Mr. Hoffen," Marsh started.

"Yes, Ma'am. Where should we start?" I asked.

"I dare say, you should start when you last departed this room," she said.

So I did...

A SMOKING GUN

"You are saying that Ambassador Turnigy set you up?" Colonel Festove had taken over the questioning.

"It looks that way, but we didn't have a chance to talk with him. Between the squads of Marines and two Oberrhein cruisers, we had to make some very hasty decisions," I said.

"By your own admission, you knew you were going to be double-crossed," Festove pushed.

"There are things you hear and things you know," I said with a shrug. "We have a crisis occurring on the Descartes mining colony and couldn't very well turn down help from King Kostov."

"But, you suspected betrayal strongly enough that you alerted Captain Gray and used the Nuage Air Defense to further your own objectives," he said. "If it were up to me, I'd lock you in irons and throw your whole crew in the brig. As it is, I'll have to discipline an entire wing of my best and brightest," he said.

"Colonel Festove, that is quite enough," Admiral Marsh said. "It is the duty of the Nuage Air Defense to defend *all* ships flying the Nuage flag. Captain Gray and his fellow team members will be commended for their brave actions. It is Oberrhein who is the aggressor here."

"But by his own admission, Hoffen knowingly set up a situation that would, at the very least, encourage Oberrhein to break the treaty - with the Nuage Air Defense as his backup plan! All without my knowledge. Furthermore ..."

"Enough. Ambassador Stephano, do you have any thoughts on this matter?"

"I agree it is a delicate situation, although I hardly find fault with our young privateers. To the contrary, we owe them a deep debt of gratitude..."

Festove harrumphed and interrupted. "Gratitude? For escalating tensions between us and Oberrhein?"

"No Colonel. For removing three warships from Oberrhein's control. Were you aware that Lord Kiirilov has requested asylum? He fears King Kostov will deal most severely with him for his failure," Stephano said.

Festove didn't answer, but shook his head sourly.

"Gentlemen, let's put a pin in that conversation. Our guests have, no doubt, learned more about our internal dialog than is necessary. Mr. Hoffen, do you or your crew have anything else?"

"We are officially filing a prize claim on the *Karelia*," Nick said.

"Of all the ridiculous ..." Festove sputtered.

Marsh held up her hand, cutting Festove's tirade short.

"Please, explain yourself. I'm inclined to agree with Colonel Festove on this," she said.

"Oberrhein is going to demand both Kiirilov and the *Karelia* be returned. By awarding the ship to *Loose Nuts*, you remove it from the conversation. In that we destroyed the other two cruisers, it's not unrealistic to think we captured the third," Nick said.

Marsh steepled her fingers, thinking for a moment, then answered with a coy grin. "Mr. James, if you ever decide to leave private enterprise, I believe Ambassador Stephano would have a position for you. Your proposition, as tempting as it is, does not solve our real problem; we have a neighbor who cares little for the treaty they have signed. You may certainly file your claim, but I must tell you, in my opinion, you have not met the criteria for a prize."

Nick tipped his head to the side slightly and nodded in acknowledgement. "Would you allow us a single request in that case?"

"Nuage owes you nothing. How dare you," Festove said.

Marsh continued, ignoring Festove's bluster, "What is your request?"

"Jake Berandor, a colleague of ours and a business owner on Lèger Nuage, has extensive knowledge of ship propulsion systems, having earned graduate degrees from the Mars College in Puskar Stellar. He's also assisted Mars Protectorate with digital forensic analysis with great success. He believes, with access to the data-stream from the *Karelia*, he could prove or disprove once and for all Oberrhein's involvement in the destruction of *Cape of Good Hope*. As you know, forty-five souls were lost in that accident," Nick said.

"You believe this Jake Berandor is better trained than our intelligence services?" Ambassador Stephano asked.

"Perhaps more specialized. It's not meant as an insult. Please, consider it," I said and flicked Jake's portfolio toward Stephano.

He received the file and I watched his eyes scan the information on his HUD.

"His credentials are most impressive. It begs the question; what is your Mr. Berandor doing on Lèger Nuage operating a bar?" he said.

"You'll have to ask him yourself."

"Indeed. Madame Marsh, I would like to grant their petition to have Mr. Berandor join our forensic team. In the event evidence is discovered related to *Cape of Good Hope*, we will be compelled by good conscience to share this information with Belirand through diplomatic channels," Stephano said.

"It is within your purview to do so," she agreed. "A good relationship with Belirand is certainly desirable."

"Are you even thinking about how Oberrhein will look at our involvement in accusing them of foul play?" Festove asked.

"We will not accuse anyone of anything, Colonel. We will gather data and if we deem the information to shed new light on Belirand's investigation, we will share it with them," Stephano answered. "We would expect nothing less from any of our allies and business partners."

"Don't be naïve," Festove said. "We have to live with Oberrhein."

"Mr. James, Mr. Hoffen, Mademoiselles Bertrand, Masters and Chen, we thank you for your help in this matter," Admiral Marsh said while standing up. "If you'll excuse us, we appear to have a busy day ahead."

As soon as Marsh, Festove and Stephano left, Roger Carsen entered the room to escort us back to the public area of the city.

"Now what?" Tabby asked, holding up her hand to pause the conversation. "And ... I want to be the first to say that Festove is an asshat."

We all laughed.

"I don't know about anyone else, but I could use a beer," Marny said.

"Lead on," I agreed.

We ended up back at the bar, *de Laroche*. It was early for drinks, but not a one of us felt like bowing to convention at that point.

"Ada's on her way over from Lèger in the shuttle with Jake," Nick said.

"That was a nice try on the prize-claim on the *Karelia*," I said. "We sure could have used the funds from selling it. What do you suppose the bill is going to be on *Hotspur*?"

"Four hundred fifty thousand," Nick said.

"Is that a guess, or do you know?" I asked.

"Just got it."

"We have four missiles left on board. We could sell them," I said.

"Maybe," Nick said. "But there's no market for missiles on Nuage."

"There's always a market. Let me see if Jake might have some ideas," I said.

Open comm, Jake Berandor.

"Go ahead, Liam," Jake said.

"Where are you?" I asked.

"Three hours out. Did Nuage really capture the *Karelia*?"

"Sure did. Say, I've a proposition for you. We're trying to raise four hundred fifty thousand. You think you could find a buyer for some of those missiles we brought along?"

"Not a lot of buyers out here, you're not going to get full value. Plus, I'll take thirty percent off the top," he said.

"Ten percent. It's not like you're delivering them."

"I could live with twenty percent. Let me make some calls.

We'll need five of 'em to raise that many credits."

"We've four here on Nuage Gros."

"Tell you what, throw in the shuttle as my commission and I'll get you an even half a million," he said.

"You're kidding? You couldn't possibly have sold them already."

"While you've been flitting around saving the universe, I've been expanding my network. I'll send you a release and we'll get 'em offloaded this afternoon. I assume you need the funds right away."

"Roger that," I said, and closed the comm.

"You sure you want to do this, Cap?" Marny asked.

"We've four in storage back at the Co-Op. All we need to do is stay out of trouble until we get home," I said.

"Aye, that's my concern," she said.

"I can't believe you gave away that shuttle," Tabby said.

"What good is a shuttle to us?" I asked. "It can't carry anything but people."

"Yeah, but it sure was sexy."

I nodded. It *had* been fun to fly.

I sat back and composed a quick comm to Mom and Dad. I let them know we'd be heading back once our ship had been repaired and that Petar Kiirilov was out of action for at least the near future.

Forty-five minutes later, a woman showed up and presented a reading pad to me. On it was a contract to trade our four missiles and the Ambassador's shuttle to Jake for the sum total of five hundred thousand credits. It was sixty percent of what I could have gotten in the Sol system, but we weren't in any position to negotiate.

"Let's hope Meerkat doesn't find anything else wrong with *Hotspur*," Tabby said, looking over my shoulder. "Or are you going to give her away too?"

"We still have *Sterra's Gift* back at Descartes. We really don't need two ships," I said.

"I go with *Hotspur*," Tabby said.

I knew she was joking, but I leaned over to kiss her anyway. She pretended to be offended and I had to work for it. We were bored and tired. Drinking and keeping it light was as good a way to pass the time as I could come up with.

A couple of hours later, Ada, with Captain Gray in tow, found us in the bar. For someone who wasn't serious, I found it interesting that she'd found him before she'd found us.

"Anything new shaking?" I asked.

"Petar Kiirilov and his entire crew are in custody," Gray said.

"Does that mean Nuage denied them asylum?" I asked sliding my chair over to make room at the table.

"Above my pay grade, but they'll be sleeping on cots tonight. Not exactly the red carpet," he said.

"Just hope you guys don't give that ship back to Oberrhein," I said.

"You should have shot it down when you had the chance," Gray said.

"We weren't in any position to do that. If we'd been in the deep dark, it would have been more of a fair fight. In the atmosphere, we were having a tough time doing anything but running for our lives," I said.

"Rumor is, you're two for three with these cruisers. Those are hardly bad odds," he said.

"Luck of the circumstance," I said. "You get Jake dropped off, Ada?"

"That's how I ran into Luc. They were waiting for us when we landed. Did you really give Jake my new shuttle?" Ada asked.

"He didn't even negotiate, just rolled over like a kitten," Tabby said, glaring at me.

I shook my head from side to side. I had no defense other than cold logic and I could see that was going nowhere.

"We're going to have to replace that tug if we want to haul ore. I wonder if Belirand would work with us on a loaner," Ada said.

"What would you think about a segmented container type freighter?" Tabby asked. "Mars Corporate preferred those to barges - must have had a good reason for that."

A segmented, container freighter was composed of a nearly infinite extendable series of common steel containers. Mars Colony Corporation, or M-Cor, had giant segments, each of which were twelve by twelve by six containers, packed in a neat, rectangular box. Between each segment of eight hundred sixty-four containers, was a coupling unit which had its own fuel storage and booster engines.

"It's not a bad idea. We could start with a smaller segment configuration, say an eight by four. Four segments would give us a hundred-twenty-eight containers," I said. "We could probably even push it with *Hotspur*."

"You wouldn't dare," Tabby said and hit me on the shoulder hard enough to hurt.

I raised my eyebrow and looked to an equally offended Ada.

Tabby pulled a reading pad from a nearby table and started furiously swiping and typing out commands. I had to laugh as Ada sat on the arm of Tabby's chair and they searched for freighter tractor options.

"The segmented design would be a good choice for us. We could manufacture containers on the station and then sell them at the destination if there's enough market demand," Nick said.

"I'm not sure we're in any position to buy anything," I said.

"I know it's hard to imagine, but we really could use *Hotspur* as the engine for a segmented hauler. Her design, with the engines on the wings, would work," Nick said.

He handed me a reading tablet showing *Hotspur* with four segments of containers strung out behind it. Between each segment of thirty-two containers, were small directional engines and fuel storage.

"You really know how to hurt a guy," I said.

"Thing is, *Hotspur* has plenty of power, so we could get by with linkage motors that aren't as powerful," Nick said.

"Where would we find the segment links?" I asked.

Nick gave me the look I had come to understand was him being patient with me. "We need six motors, gimbals, fuel storage, and frames. The only thing we can't manufacture are the motors."

"I can't believe this is what you are talking about." Luc Gray had a bewildered look on his face. We all looked back at him and he felt compelled to explain as the table grew quiet. "You just got out of combat, were threatened by the commander of Nuage Air Defense with imprisonment and have no doubt annoyed the king of one of the only two nations within a hundred million kilometers."

"Well, since you're not telling us anything, what are we supposed to do?" Ada asked.

"I can't," he answered. "I took an oath."

"So, this is what we have," Ada said matter-of-factly. "Speaking of, have we figured out when they'll be done with repairs and where we're staying tonight?"

Nick had us set up at the same resort we'd stayed in on our last visit. It was expensive, but with the stress of recent events, we agreed it was worth it. For the next few hours we sat around and talked about whatever came to mind. Reliving the combat for Ada and Luc and hearing about the events from their side as well.

We'd hoped to see Jake later in the evening, but he never did show up, although a number of Commander Gray's squad mates did. We bought several rounds and well into the wee hours of the morning we stumbled back to the hotel.

With little to do for the next few days, we exercised, ate, swam at the resort's beautiful pools and made plans for the future. Nick had a line on the engines we needed for the segmented transport and arranged to have them delivered and loaded into *Hotspur*.

On the morning of the fourth day, Nick said, "Jake's on his way up."

We were in the hotel suite's main room. I'd been looking for ore, ingot and sheet purchasers and discovered that there was a considerably better market if we sailed to the other side of the Descartes belt and to the mostly desert planet, Curie. The prices for the iron and steel weren't as good as Belirand offered, but we couldn't afford to lose another ship.

After a few minutes, we heard a knock on the door and let Jake in. He looked haggard and gratefully accepted a cup of coffee.

JAMIE McFARLANE

"I haven't been to sleep yet, but I wanted to talk to you all first," he said.

"You're welcome to crash here," I said. "Ada hasn't been using her room."

This got a raised eyebrow from him, but he didn't otherwise comment. "Thanks, but Nuage is putting me up."

"Tell me you found something," I said.

"We did and it might as well be a smoking gun with Kiirilov's DNA all over it," Jake said. "He tried to delete it, but Nuage finally found fragments of the backups in the septic processor and the refer units."

"We have data-streams backed up in the septic?" I asked. I didn't really know a lot about how data was stored, it was always just available.

"Every piece of smart fabric or AI system - which is just about everything we come in contact with - gets replicated. Ship systems are pretty good about not extending outside of the confines of the ship, but yes, in short, data is spread, replicated and duplicated hundreds of thousands of times. That's great for accessing it, but not great if you want to remove it. Kiirilov released a worm to delete the data, but it didn't get it all," Jake said.

"What did you find?" Marny asked.

"Kiirilov launched a veritable fusillade of magnetic particles into the *Cape's* engine. The composition of the particles set off a chain reaction when it entered fold-space. He did it, there's no doubt. Nuage also found communications with Atin Emre implicating him in the attack," he said.

I breathed out a sigh of relief.

"Was this communicated to Belirand?" I asked.

"That's what I've been doing for the last day. We've been sharing our discoveries with Belirand engineers back in Sol."

"Any of that going to splash back on Oberrhein?" I asked.

"We didn't talk about repercussions, it was just fact finding. I can say, though, that we had several of Belirand's top brass on the comm at different times and they want blood. I don't think anything is off the table for them," he said. "As an aside, I also

340

received word that the Emre brothers are on the run."

"How'd you hear that?" Tabby asked.

Jake looked at her with a smirk. "Let's just say, I heard they were looking for transport and I decided to pass on the opportunity."

BACK IN BUSINESS

Meerkat's repairs, while expensive, were thorough. The bilge and turret were repaired and spotless. It was an expensive area to get hit, as many of our life support systems were housed there.

Six large crates of motors filled most of the cargo hold and we packed in as much additional fuel and as many supplies as we could afford. The colonists at Descartes were nervous, but our first delivery of supplies and setting up purchasing agreements with them had done much to stave off panic. At this point, we had to start delivering the material we'd purchased or we were going to completely run out of operating capital and cash.

"Schedule-D, Ada," I answered in response to her query. She'd taken the responsibility of laying out our navigation plans and wanted to plug in how much fuel we were going to use.

"Roger that, Captain," she responded.

We hadn't seen much of her while we were on Gros, but Tabby had informed me that Luc and Ada were 'just friends.' I wasn't sure what that meant and suspected it was much like the relationship I'd had with Tabby before we finally figured it out.

Even on a Schedule-D, we arrived at Descartes six days later. We had been enjoying a period of time where the mining belt was well aligned with Grünholz. Now their orbits around Tipperary's star were starting to separate. Within eight months they'd be so far apart that the trip would take us more like twelve days on a Schedule-D and, at its very worse, eighteen. It was the life of a freighter pilot to worry about such things.

On the sixth day, we dropped from hard burn, closer to our destination than we would ever have considered when the small cruisers had been in system. My heart leapt when the warning klaxons went off as soon as our sensors were able to resolve the system around us.

Silent running, I said instinctively. I had no doubt that whatever had spooked the AI had also seen us drop out of hard burn and I wasn't going to present an easy target.

"Cap, we're being hailed by the heavy cruiser, *Fist of Justice,*" she said.

Crap.

"What is the ship's registration," I asked.

"It's Belirand," she said.

My mind whirled with the possibilities. If the Emre brothers had somehow managed to make off with a cruiser, they might be looking to exact their revenge on us.

Accept hail.

Tabby pulled up the forward holo display and it showed two heavy cruisers accompanied by two cutters.

"Captain, I need to lock down those turrets."

A request showed up on my forward vid screen. I hated the idea of giving over control of our only weapons, but we'd done it to ourselves, sailing almost directly into the middle of a fleet that could easily take us out.

I accepted the lockdown.

"Lorraine Tullas, Rear Admiral, Belirand Security Services," she said, introducing herself.

"Liam Hoffen, *Loose Nuts,*" I responded. For whatever reason, I was struck with how little punch my introduction had in comparison.

"Greetings, Captain Hoffen. We've been expecting you," she said.

"How's that?" I asked. I couldn't imagine the technology required to track us through space.

"According to a Mr. Big Pete, and I quote; 'you're not on the approved list, you'll have to wait until my son arrives and talk to him,'" she said. There was a flicker of a smile in those words.

"My apologies, Admiral, but we've not had the best working relationship with Belirand recently."

"Your father seemed most unimpressed when I informed him

that we could take out his defensive cannons, if necessary," she said.

"Do you mind if I ask what you're doing out here?"

"My mission is to secure the Descartes Mining colony," she said.

"From?"

"Anything that impedes the colony's primary mission. Would you be amenable to a face-to-face?"

"Certainly. I'd appreciate a chance to check in with the Co-Op and unload supplies," I said. "I'll add your fleet to our list of friendlies."

"We'll need turret control codes," she said.

"I'm sorry, Ma'am. That isn't possible. You've got to understand, Belirand has been party to nearly killing my crew several times and most of the colonists have been threatened directly by same. I don't believe you'd send the message you desire. Perhaps you'd be willing to leave your fleet on the outside of the security perimeter and sail in on one of the cutters?" I proposed.

Her lips pursed as she thought it through. She muted her end but didn't cut the feed and spoke to someone we were unable to see.

"I understand that we have to earn your trust," she said, returning to the conversation. "I'm risking my career by not taking control of your turrets, but I believe it is in line with the mission. If you'll promise not to fire on our ships, we'll concede the requirement to have positive control over the cannons."

"As long as your ships take no provocative actions against Co-Op property or personnel, we are in agreement," I said.

She sighed. "Aye, Captain, we'll agree to that. We'll be back at 1600, which gives you two hours. Is that sufficient time?" she asked.

"Yes, ma'am. Looking forward to meeting with you," I said and closed the comm.

As we sailed past the underside of the Co-Op asteroid, we saw that the number of habitation domes had grown considerably since we'd last been here. It made me wonder if there were any miners still out working their claims.

The piles of ore had also grown as well. It was impossible to tell if the ore had been mined from within the Co-Op station or if it had been dropped off from other claims. The AI reported that the Co-Op currently owned enough ore that, upon delivery, we would recover our losses and then some.

"Looks like Big Pete and Muir have the refinery up and going," Nick said.

"How can you tell?" I asked.

At Nick's request, my HUD highlighted an area I hadn't seen. A brand new platform had been constructed with the refinery set upon it. A small pile of pig-iron ingots were neatly stacked next to it.

"Look at that," I whistled.

Refined ingots netted ten percent more than raw ore and were a lot easier to ship. Once we were able to manufacture steel ingots we'd add another ten percent.

"What do you bet he's trying to get sheets rolled out?" I asked.

Nick just laughed. Neither of us were about to bet against Big Pete. We'd even cut him in for a share of the profits on any of the work the Co-Op churned out. That had been all the catalyst he'd needed to get off to the races.

When we pulled up to the docking bays, I was amazed at the amount of material that had been cleared. Long corridors led back from the bays and mining operations were in full swing as we approached.

"We'll meet you outside the warehouse." Dad's voice cut in on my comm.

"Roger that," I said.

We met up and before we were allowed to do much else, he took us on a tour of the Co-Op.

"We're about twenty percent cleared on Nicholas's plan," he said. "Once we start rolling out some sheet, we'll be able to close in the rock. We need an armor glass kiln unless we want to be buying glass all the time."

We passed more than ten different families, all mining material out of the co-op.

"How'd you figure to pay everyone?" I asked.

"They'll get a cut of the proceeds for the ore they mine. We're covering food, O2, tool breakage and all that. Most people get it though, they know we're building a safe haven and they want to be part of it," he explained.

"Now that it's safe, won't most of 'em go back to their own claims?" I asked.

"Aye. Most will. We've only three groups that will stay behind. Fact is, we got a heck of a jump on this station. Even with the reduced help, we'll be clear within a year. I expect to have pressurized sections within two months, that is if I can get some armor-glass," he said.

"We'll put an order together," Nick said. "I like the idea of a kiln, we're just a little short of capital."

"Understood. You all did the right thing, putting your company on the line to make sure everyone had what they needed. You can bet the corporations don't think that way," he said.

He led us through the central corridor to a vertical shaft that led deep down into the asteroid. When I looked down, I was shocked to see starlight.

"Does this lead to the bottom side?" I asked.

"Sure does," he said and jumped into the shaft head first. I followed close behind and we arc-jetted eighty meters, finally ending up on the bottom of the Co-Op, which was where all of the ore was stored.

It took a moment to get my bearings, but once I did, I jetted over to where I'd seen the refinery. Once I got close, gravity generators pulled me to the surface. The refinery wasn't currently operating, but it looked much like the refineries on Colony 40.

"This is up and running?" I asked.

"Sure is," Dad replied. "We were going to talk to you and Nick about how much ore we want to run through."

"According to Nick, it's all about labor," I said. "But, I'll let him work it out with you. You've done a lot in a few weeks."

"For a time, we didn't know how long we might be stuck here. Best if you keep busy at times like that," he said.

"We've another project." Nick explained about the motors he'd bought and the pattern he had in mind for the segmented freighter.

When we arrived back at the warehouse we found that all the lights were off.

"That's weird," I said. I was the last through the airlock.

The lights turned on and I was shocked to see the entire warehouse filled with people.

"Welcome home!" they mostly all said in unison.

Once things quieted down, the crowd looked at us expectantly. I felt Nick's hand in the middle of my back as he pushed me forward.

"Uh …. thank you," I said. "What's this all about?"

"Our last swap meet got shut down by Oberrhein. We all agreed we'd have a party when you got back. We've been planning it for days," Mom said.

"Let's start the festivities then," I said, looking over at Ian and Sylvia Folkson who took the cue and started playing their stringed instruments cheerily, Ian with his guitar and Sylvia with her fiddle.

An hour into the party, I'd completely forgotten about Belirand's imminent arrival.

"*Incoming comm*," my AI informed me. I accepted.

"Captain Hoffen? Admiral Tullas. Would you be willing to meet now?"

She was being polite, but I knew better than to make an Admiral wait.

"Yes ma'am. Would you be open to a suggestion?" I asked.

"Certainly, Mr. Hoffen," she replied.

"Better than three quarters of the colonists are in our warehouse attending a swap meet, which to the uninitiated looks a lot like a party. To the extent that you'd like to restore the colony's confidence in Belirand, your presence would mean a lot."

"You want me to come to your party?" she asked. Her voice was a mix of shock and amusement.

"At least send a delegation. People have questions. It's a perfect time to apologize and reassure them," I said.

"Apologize?" she asked.

"According to Belirand, Oberrhein was in charge of security. Kiirilov preyed on these people in the name of Belirand. In short, you let us down. We're hardy people and we'll get over it, but you may want to get in front of this thing, own your mistakes. It won't cost you a dime," I said.

"You're a lot older than you look, Mr. Hoffen," she said. "We'll arrange a delegation and be over in short order."

In person, Rear Admiral Lorraine Tullas was taller than I'd expected. Something about Commander Sterra's diminutive size had me believing all female officers were small.

"Welcome to the Descartes Co-Op, Admiral," I said.

She'd arrived with three other officers and a single Marine that stayed by her side.

"Mr. Hoffen, it is good to meet you in person," she said, shaking my hand and then introducing herself to each of the *Loose Nuts* crew. She had a little something personal to say to each of us, just to let us know she had done her research. I wasn't sure if I should be concerned or flattered.

As expected, her presence was well received and she worked the crowd like a professional. You probably didn't get to her level without having a strong basic charisma. After a couple of hours, she finally broke free and found where Tabby, Nick, Marny and I were resting. We hadn't seen Ada for a while and I supposed she had found Selig.

I stood up to greet her. "Thank you for doing that, Admiral. You've no doubt made quite an impression here today," I said.

"As is always the case, I'm richer for the experience," she said. "Would you be available to meet with me onboard my ship?"

"*Fist of Justice?*" I asked.

"That's right," she said.

"Kind of an intense moniker," I said.

"We're the enforcement arm of Belirand Security. Most of the time, you don't want to see the *Fist* showing up," she said.

I looked at her, stopping before entering the airlock. "Do we have a problem?"

She laughed. "Oh heavens no," she said and continued out of the airlock.

A shuttle was waiting for us just outside of the warehouse to take us to her cruiser. Like everything Belirand, the ship was spotless and beautifully appointed.

"Captain, the reason I invited you and your crew to meet with us was to formally communicate Belirand's deep-felt appreciation for your part in uncovering the corruption that was at the heart of Tipperary's Terminal Seven project," she said.

"First, these fine people are my partners, not my crew. Second, you're welcome, but you didn't need to call us over to your ship for that," I said. "Would you mind telling us what happened to the Emre brothers?"

"We haven't found them yet, but rest assured, we will. I've posted a ten million credit bounty on each of them. We'll find them within the month," she said.

"How about Oberrhein and Kiirilov?" Nick asked.

"That's a little harder," she said. "Kiirilov is in Nuage custody, so we'll have to go through an extradition process. As for Oberrhein, there's not much we can do, other than to disallow their ships through the gates. We're not about to start a war with a nation that doesn't have any remaining warships."

"What about the *Karelia*?" Tabby asked.

"Admiral Marsh has generously agreed to turn the *Karelia* over to Belirand, so that we might investigate further," she said.

"That sounds fair," Nick said. "How about Terminal Seven. Is it safe to deliver ore and are you honoring the original terms of the contract?

"We've deployed one of our three fleets to Terminal Seven. It is probably the second safest location in Tipperary," she said.

"Descartes being the first?" Tabby asked with a grin.

"As perceptive as I was led to believe, Ms. Masters," she said.

"There are two other matters I'd like to discuss with you. From the data-streams we received from Nuage, we understand that the *Loose Nuts Corporation* was substantially damaged financially. We always pay our debts and I'd like to know what you would feel is fair."

"The freighter we lost was worth seven hundred fifty thousand credits," Nick said. "We're not looking for recompense. The fact that you've set things right for that crew on *Cape of Good Hope* is the payment we've been hoping for."

I nodded my head in agreement. It was a sacrifice to leave the credits on the table, but it felt like it would sully the dead crew's memory if we took money at this point.

"Are you certain there's not something we can do?" Admiral Tullas asked.

"You could waive our fees when *Loose Nuts* uses the gates," Tabby said.

"Done," Tullas agreed.

"You said there was a second thing?" I asked.

"One of our scientists, a resident of Curie, has requested a chance to speak with you and your partners. He has a proposition he'd like to discuss with you," she said.

"Who?"

"You wouldn't believe me if I told you," she said.

"Tell us about it."

But of course, that's another story entirely.

ABOUT THE AUTHOR

Jamie McFarlane is happily married, the father of three and lives in Lincoln, Nebraska. He spends his days engaged in a hi-tech career and his nights and weekends writing works of fiction. He's also the author of:

Privateer Tales
1. Rookie Privateer
2. Fool Me Once
3. Parley
4. Big Pete
5. Smuggler's Dilemma
6. Cutpurse
7. Out of the Tank
8. Buccaneers

Guardians of Gaeland
1. Lesser Prince

Word-of-mouth is crucial for any author to succeed. If you enjoyed this book, please consider leaving a review at Amazon, even if it's only a line or two; it would make all the difference and would be very much appreciated.

If you want to get an automatic email when Jamie's next book is available, sign up on his website at fickledragon.com. Your email address will never be shared and you can unsubscribe at any time.

CONTACT JAMIE

Blog and Website: fickledragon.com
Facebook: facebook.com/jamiemcfarlaneauthor
Twitter: twitter.com/mcfarlaneauthor

87972337R00200

Made in the USA
Lexington, KY
04 May 2018